FAT
WHITE
VAMPIRE
BLUES

FAT WHITE VAMPIRE BLUES

ANDREW **FOX**

BALLANTINE BOOKS • NEW YORK

A Ballantine Book
Published by The Random House Ballantine Publishing Group
Copyright © 2003 by Andrew Fox

www.ballantinebooks.com

Library of Congress Control Number: 2003091481

ISBN 0-345-46333-1

Book design by Julie Schroeder

Cover design by David Stevenson
Cover photograph © Michael Wilson/Getty Images

Manufactured in the United States of America

First Edition: July 2003

10 9 8 7 6 5 4 3 2 1

For my mother, who bought me TOMB OF DRACULA comics; my father, who took me to a double feature of THE RETURN OF COUNT YORGA and SCREAM, BLACULA, SCREAM! at the drive-in movie; and my stepdad, who took down the poster of Bela Lugosi from my bedroom wall after it gave me nightmares.

This was New Orleans, a magical and magnificent place to live. In which a vampire, richly dressed and gracefully walking through the pools of light of one gas lamp after another might attract no more notice in the evening than hundreds of other exotic creatures—if he attracted any at all . . .

—Anne Rice, INTERVIEW WITH THE VAMPIRE

"Oh, you're truly fantastic," the young man said gleefully. "And although I didn't think it would be possible, you've gained weight. Where will you ever end? There's something so unbelievably tacky about your obesity."

Ignatius rose to his feet and stabbed the young man in the chest with his plastic cutlass.

—John Kennedy Toole, A CONFEDERACY OF DUNCES

FAT
WHITE
VAMPIRE
BLUES

ONE

Jules Duchon was a real New Orleans vampire. Born and bred in the working-class Ninth Ward, bitten in and smitten with the Big Easy. Driving through the French Quarter, stuck in a row of bumper-to-bumper cars that crept along Decatur Street like a caravan of bone-weary camels, Jules Duchon barely fit behind the steering wheel of his very big Cadillac taxicab. Even with the bench seat pushed all the way back.

Damn, he was hungry. His fat fingers quivered as they clutched the worn steering wheel more tightly. It was only nine P.M.; early yet. He didn't used to get this hungry, back in the old days. Could he be coming down with diabetes? Jules thought about this. Could somebody like him *get* diabetes? Half the population of New Orleans over the age of forty had it, and Jules was well past forty. He had half a mind to drive over to Charity Hospital and get himself checked out. *Yeah, right*, he thought to himself. He rubbed the side of his nose and tilted down his sun visor, forcing himself to look at the clipping from last week's *Times-Picayune* he'd pinned there. NEW ORLEANS FATTEST CITY IN NATION, STUDY SHOWS. Front-page news. *Talk about restating the goddamn obvious. Them scientists actually get paid to tell us this stuff?* He glanced quickly at the visor's lit vanity mirror, where his reflection would be, if he could still cast one. What the hell; he knew what he looked like. He still had the delicate, whitish complexion that women had made such a fuss about during his younger days. Back then, they'd said he looked like Rudy Valentino in *The Sheik*. Now he looked more like the Pillsbury Doughboy.

"Diabetes or no diabetes, if I don't get something down my gullet, I'm gonna keel over." Waiting at a stoplight, Jules considered his options. The streets and sidewalks of the French Quarter, glistening with a recent rain, were bustling with tourists. But that was the problem. Too much of a good thing—there were people and eyes everywhere. The light turned green, and Jules crossed Canal Street, heading for less popular parts of town. He would have to dig into his wallet for tonight's meal.

A few minutes later he was trolling past the New Orleans Mission, a soup kitchen and homeless shelter. It squatted in the shadow of the Pontchartrain Expressway, an elevated highway that separated the business district from a vast slum called Central City. Jules chewed his lower lip as he scanned the long line of human refuse that waited on the broken sidewalk outside the mission's door. Then he spotted her, standing near the end of the line. He'd seen her around town before, sitting on bus shelter benches or panhandling in front of fried chicken joints. A big-boned woman, as his mother used to say. Her thick, chocolate-brown neck was nearly hidden by a motley heap of metallic beads left over from last winter's Carnival parades, and her upper body oozed out the armholes of a tank top several sizes too small for her. Yeah, she fit the bill.

Jules stopped his cab, a Caddy Fleetwood of mid-1970s vintage, pressed the wobbly rocker switch that jerked his electric windows reluctantly to life, and stuck his head into the humid night air. "Hey, baby. You interested in some dinner?"

The woman swung her head around, her sparse eyebrows raised in surprise. "You talkin' to *me*?"

"Yeah, baby. I asked if you were hungry. You look hungry."

The woman took half a step toward the cab, giving its vast white bulk the once-over, then eyeing the equally imposing white bulk of its driver. "What you selling, mister? You a dealer? I ain't got no money to be buying no drugs, now."

Jules sighed heavily. His hunger was growing exponentially. "You hear me say anything about crack? I want some company, is all. I wanna buy you dinner."

The woman crossed her big arms in front of her ample chest. "I got me dinner right here, thank you. An' it's *free*."

"C'mon, you don't want to be eating the slop they got here. I'll get you some *real* food. An oyster po' boy and all the fixin's. We'll have us some fun, maybe take in some music afterward. Give a lonely guy a break, huh? How about it?"

The look of resistance on the woman's face softened as she contemplated a belly full of fried seafood. Wavering, she turned to her friend standing in line ahead of her, an older woman missing most of her front teeth. "Miss Gloria, whatchu think?"

The old woman appraised the Cadillac for a few seconds, then gave her friend a shove toward the street. "Go on now, Bessie darlin'. Dat's the best offer you be gettin' all week."

Her beads jangled loudly as Bessie made her way slowly around to the passenger's side. Jules leaned over and opened the door for her. Before getting in, she said, "Now, if I go with you, I get me a comfortable place to sleep for the night, right? That's the deal."

Jules licked his lips as he drank in her large figure, silhouetted in the weak glare of a streetlight. "Sure, baby. You'll be sleepin' real comfortable tonight. Deal. Now slide on in."

They drove back through the deserted central business district to a sleazy stretch of St. Charles Avenue. Jules parked in front of the Hummingbird Grill and Hotel, a brick-faced, 150-year-old building that had once been part of a row of luxury town houses. Its once pristine bricks were now coated with decades' worth of grime. Rattling air-conditioning units dotted the building's facade like mechanical zits. Jules liked the Hummingbird. It was cheap, it never closed, and it was a century past its prime. The place had character.

Jules popped open the Caddy's electric door locks. "Here we are, baby."

Bessie was unimpressed by their destination. "Shee-yit," she said, a petulant frown pulling down the corners of her mouth. "I thoughts we was gonna eat someplace *nice.*"

Jules was already halfway onto the sidewalk. "The Hummingbird *is* nice. Food's real good here. 'Specially the seafood. You'll see. C'mon."

Jules tried hard to remember his manners. He held the restaurant door open for his guest. She walked infuriatingly slowly, waddling through the foyer like an obese seal. It took every bit of his fading willpower not to nibble her neck as she paused to peek up the dim, narrow stairway that led upstairs to the hotel; but he reminded himself that good things come to those who wait.

Jules selected a table close to the kitchen, as far from the windows as they could get. He wanted nothing to distract her from her meal. While waiting for the waitress to bring menus and silverware, he amused himself by rereading for the hundredth time a handwritten sign posted near the pay phone by the cash register: NO TALKING TO IMAGINARY PERSONS. Jules got a kick out of that, being kind of an imaginary person himself. He wondered whether the waitress would be breaking house rules when she came over and asked him for their order.

After a couple of minutes of waiting for a server to come and furtively admiring his companion/dinner, Jules lost his patience. He half stood and snapped his fingers loudly, finally managing to catch the eye of one of the two waitresses on the floor. "Sweetheart. We need dinner here, not breakfast."

The waitress favored him with a half wave. "Hold your horses, dawlin'. I got ten other customers to take care of. Be right with you."

By the time she brought over the menus, Jules had made their selections off the chalkboard posted by the kitchen door. "The lady here'll have an oyster po' boy with a helping of red beans and smoked sausage and a side of corn bread, thanks."

Bessie thumped the table in protest. "Hey, what's wit' you? Don't I get to order what I wants?"

Jules quickly patted her arm. "Baby, it's more classy when the man orders for his lady. You want that po' boy dressed?"

Slightly mollified, Bessie turned to the waitress and said, "Dress it with tartar sauce and my-nezz and tomatoes and pickles, and don't skimp on them ersters!"

The waitress scribbled a few abbreviations onto her pad. "Got it, dawlin'." She turned back to Jules. "And what can I get for you?"

Jules frowned slightly. "Umm. Just good, hot coffee for me, sweetheart. And keep it coming."

"Sure thing."

Bessie's eyes widened. "What? You mean you just gonna sit there and watch *me* eat?"

"I'm not hungry, baby," Jules lied through his sharp teeth. "But it does my soul good to watch a pretty lady enjoy a big meal."

"Whatever floats yo' boat." Bessie took a long sip of water, staring at Jules over the rim of the glass. "Say. Y'know, you jus' about the *whitest* white man I ever seen."

Jules smiled, careful not to expose his teeth too much. "Yeah. I get told that a lot. Got a history of skin cancer in my family. So I tend to stay outta the sun."

The waitress brought a heaping basket of corn bread and placed it in front of Bessie. Jules grimaced when he glanced at the dish of spreads she set down. "Miss! Hey!"

The waitress turned back toward their table. "Anything the matter, dawlin'?"

"Yeah. Dump this low-cal margarine crap. Bring us some real butter, huh?"

"Ho-*kay*." She raised an eyebrow as she scooped the dish up from the table. "*Some* people worry 'bout their calories, nowadays. Rest of the food'll be out in a second."

Jules decided to ignore the insult. He gulped down his first cup of coffee as he watched Bessie slather great hunks of corn bread with butter. The po' boy sandwich, when it arrived a few minutes later, was more than a foot long—thick slices of French bread embracing dozens of deep-fried oysters, the whole concoction dripping with gobs of mayonnaise and creamy tartar sauce. The generous portion of syrupy red beans was replete with fat logs of sausage that overhung the bowl. Jules watched the light of the green neon sign outside the window glisten off the pools of grease that floated atop the red beans. His date appeared to have an appetite as fierce as his own. Already the po' boy was half gone. Jules's eyes half closed with pleasure as he imagined his repast to come. Somewhere in the back of his mind, a small shrill voice repeated the headline of the newspaper article he'd pinned up in his cab. Really, he shouldn't be doing this to himself anymore. But he buried the annoying voice with an avalanche of delicious anticipation. Hell, he could start dieting anytime. Why tonight?

By the time Jules was halfway through his third cup of coffee, Bessie had finished her meal. She wiped a few crumbs from the corner of her mouth, more crumbs than remained on her plate. Jules pushed aside his coffee cup and patted her plump hand. "Man alive, I love seein' a woman eat. You all filled up? Want some dessert?"

Bessie patted her round stomach and grinned. "No thanks, baby. I be stuffed solid."

"Good." He grabbed the check off the table. "Let's go, then."

She paused in front of the stairs by the cash register after he paid the bill. "Ain't we goin' upstairs? I could use a little lie-down after that meal."

"No, baby. We're goin' for a little drive. I've got me a nice cozy camp out by Pass Manchac, on Lake Maurepas. We'll have our lie-down out there."

Jules sighed with contentment as he headed up the on-ramp onto Interstate 10. The big Caddy was in its element on the highway, its air-pillow suspension letting Jules imagine he was piloting a yacht through gentle seas. As soon as they passed the western suburbs of Metairie and Kenner, they left the artificial glow of civilization behind, and the sky quickly filled with stars. It was a night for music. Jules reached for the pull knob on the radio.

"You like oldies music?"

Bessie grinned. "Sure! I likes any kind of music."

The radio was preset to the only station Jules listened to—WWOZ, a community radio station that specialized in old-time New Orleans music. Soon he was drumming his fingers on the steering wheel in time with the Dixie Cups, Clarence "Frogman" Henry, and Fats Domino.

He glanced over at his passenger. Bessie was staring intently out the window, watching the distant lights of fishing boats and oil platforms on Lake Pontchartrain as the Caddy sped along the Bonnet Carré Spillway. He figured she must not get out of the city much. "Enjoying the ride, baby?"

"Oh yeah." She turned around toward him. "What's it like, drivin' a cab for a livin'? You like it?"

Jules turned the music down a smidgin. He regretted having started a conversation. It never seemed right, somehow, getting too friendly with his meals. "It's all right, I guess. It's a living."

"You always done this?"

"Naw. I used to work in the coroner's office. Did it for years. Now there was a sweet job. *Lots* of on-the-job bennies. But then my boss couldn't get himself elected no more, and the new guy wanted to bring in his own people. So after twenty-seven years, I was out on my ass."

Jules went quiet. The bitterness of that memory seeped out of his head and into the car, turning the air-conditioned atmosphere somber. His boss at the city coroner's office had been maybe the best friend he'd ever had. Doc Landrieu had known almost from the start exactly what Jules was, and for decades he'd looked the other way while Jules discreetly satisfied his appetites with the blood of the recently deceased. Life was so sweet then. He'd had his meal ticket, in every sense of the word. But the city was constantly changing; longtime residents moved out to the 'burbs, and the new people didn't vote the same. Nothing ever stayed the same, he'd found. At least nothing good.

B.B. King came on the radio, singing "The Blues Is All Right." It was a song about being sad, but the way B.B. sang it, so enthusiastic and joyful and glad about being alive, Jules felt his sour mood evaporate. He began drumming his fingers on the steering wheel again. The Caddy passed beneath the sign for Interstate 55, and Jules took the turnoff that would lead him north to Lake Maurepas.

At that late hour, the elevated highway was deserted. The Caddy was an isolated blob of light gliding swiftly above a slumbering landscape of cypress tree stumps and wooden fishing shacks. Alligators silently stalked nutria, plump water rats, through a maze of swamp grass. Jules carefully watched for his favorite exit, a fishermen's route to a narrow dirt road by the water, half a mile from the closest camp. He spotted it, then gingerly braked the Caddy to a near crawl and aimed its big white hood down the off-ramp.

Jules felt Bessie's hand squeeze his thigh. "We near your place, huh?"

"Yeah," he replied. "But you're gonna kill me. I just remembered that I left the keys to my camp back at my house in town."

Her hand immediately left his thigh. "You did *what*? What'n hell we gonna do now?"

Damp gravel crunched beneath the Caddy's whitewall tires as Jules parked close to the turbid water's edge. "Don't sweat it, baby. Cab's got a backseat as big as Alaska. Nobody's gonna bother us out here. It'll be just like we're inside the cabin. I promise."

"Shee-yit. I does all my lovin' in the backseat of a damn car."

Jules cut the ignition. "Hey, at least dinner was A-One, huh?"

"Yeah, you right," she reluctantly admitted. "Dinner was plenty good."

Jules turned the key just enough to keep the radio and power accessories running, then opened his door and lowered himself slowly to the gravel. The air was surprisingly cool; Jules figured it must be their proximity to all the water. "You're gonna have to get out for a bit. Takes me a minute to move the seat all the way forward."

Bessie didn't budge. "Ain't no snakes around here, is there?"

Jules sighed heavily. By now, he was shaking with hunger, and all the coffee he'd drunk felt like acid at the bottom of his stomach. "No, baby.

And if there *were* any around, the car would've scared 'em all off. C'mon now."

Bessie slowly swung her door open and tiptoed down to the ground. Jules pressed a switch on the door sill, and the electric seat groaned into life, moving forward at the pace of continental drift. Two minutes later it had gone as far as it could, the seat cushion mashing into the dashboard.

"Can I get back in now?"

Jules walked around to the back of the car. "Just another minute, okay?" He opened the trunk and removed a folded plastic tarp and a sheet-cake-sized foil baking pan. Then he opened the driver-side rear door and awkwardly spread the plastic tarp over the seat. The baking pan he placed on the floor.

Jules walked around to the other side and opened the back door for Bessie. "What's that plastic wrap doin' there?" she asked, her voice more than a little petulant.

"Them's genuine cowhide leather seating surfaces. Gotta take good care of them, or they won't look worth a shit. Didn't your mama used to put slipcovers on her good couch? Same principle here. Big folks like you and me, we're liable to make quite a mess when we're doin' our business. Gotta take care of the seats."

Bessie turned up her nose, but she obligingly crawled onto the tarp-covered seat, dumping her Mardi Gras beads on the floor. Even with the front bench kissing the steering wheel, it was still a snug fit. While she was squirming to make herself more comfortable, her hand brushed against the baking pan. "And what's *this* here thing doin' here for?"

Jules peered into the dark space. "What's that? Well, I'll be damned. Some dumb-ass customer must've left that there earlier this evening. Well, guess it won't do us no harm."

Jules waited until Bessie stopped squirming, then he commenced the arduous task of climbing in on top of her. Trying to slide forward, grasping for handholds, was like struggling to scale a woman-shaped mountain of Jell-O.

"Hey! Watch with the knee, buster!"

"Sorry, baby."

Finally, his overtaxed heart pounding from exertion, Jules reached what he figured was his optimal position. His cold nose nuzzled Bessie's warm, fragrant neck. Jules tried to sort out the different elements that made up her scent. Cinnamon, for sure. A hint of chocolate, or maybe cocoa butter. And unmistakably, the smoked tang of the sausage she'd eaten an hour before. He kissed her neck, his salivary glands working double time. *Ah, bless you, New Orleans . . . greatest food in the whole god-damn world . . .*

"Oohh baby," Bessie cooed, "you be shakin' all over—"

"Yeah, baby, it's been too long, it's been *way* too long—"

Aretha Franklin's voice boomed from six speakers, declaring to all Manchac swamp, *"What you want, baby I got it!"* Jules surrendered to his appetite, a desperate, living hunger that knew it would soon be sated. He nibbled her now moist neck, searching out her jugular vein. He couldn't find it. He nibbled harder, frantic, but all he could sense was flesh and more flesh, a nigh-impregnable collar of blubber.

"Oohh baby, the way you bitin', you my *lover*-man, baby."

"Yeah, baby, sure," Jules stuttered, his voice laced with real terror.

Bessie shifted beneath him. "But how we gonna get all these clothes off now? The way you got us jammed in here, we's like pig's feet in a full-up jar. I can't move hardly nothin'—"

"Uh, you let *me* worry about that, huh?" *Shit!* He had to think of something. He honestly didn't think he had the strength left to make it back to the city and start all over again. His armpits were soaked with sweat, despite the cool breeze that blew up the back of his shirt through the open door. He kissed her neck mechanically, his mind racing. She moaned again, louder this time, and the flesh of her neck shimmied beneath his parched lips. Then he had an idea. A desperate ploy, but it might just work. He reached his hand under her dress, praying that he remembered where everything was. Her legs parted slightly, but there was still a formidable obstacle course for his thick fingers to overcome. It was like playing blindman's bluff in quicksand. Okay, there were her panties; he was moving in the right direction. Please, *please* let him remember—

Bingo! He must've hit the magic spot, because her moaning took on a new, deeper timbre, and her back and neck arched with pleasure. Suddenly, her neck had contours—her thick jugular appeared through the flab like Atlantis rising from the deep. Instantly, before it could submerge again, Jules bit deep.

"Oh *baby*, you the *greatest!*"

Okay, not as deep as he would've hoped. *Jeezus, it's like bitin' through elephant hide.* But the first tiny trickle of blood was heaven. Jules gathered the dregs of his strength and worked his jaws like a punch press, plunging his sharp canines deeper.

"Ouch-aaohww baby! Cut it out! You hurtin'—*ekkk!*"

Suddenly blood surged into his mouth with the force of a fire hose. Jules gulped it down as quickly as he could, but even his most ravenous efforts couldn't prevent waves of overflow from splashing into the pan on the floor below. Her blood was manna, caviar, ambrosia. *Oh, the incredible amazing richness*—*!* He gulped and swallowed so prodigiously that his body forgot to breathe, but he didn't care. The fresh triglycerides her blood teemed with hit his system like the purest heroin ever mainlined. The Cadillac spun around him; his ears filled with heavenly music (could that be his dear, long-departed mother's angelic voice leading the choir?); the warm, spasming body beneath his seemed to liquefy, simultaneously caressing every molecule of his vast form with omnipresent pleasure.

He had no idea how long he remained on top of her. By the time a series of annoying sounds pulled him back to full awareness (sounds, he soon realized, that were coming from himself, as he alternated between belching and sucking the last few rapturous drops from her neck), Bessie's body had gone cold. He wanted nothing more than to lay his head back down upon her soft, cool neck and doze for a week, but he glanced at his watch and realized that sleep would be suicide. Groaning at the injustice of the earth's unpausing rotation *(why can't there be more hours in a night?)*, he forced his somnolent muscles into action, ignoring their protests as he pushed himself, massive posterior first, out of the Caddy's scarlet-soaked backseat. He was careful not to upset the baking pan, which was filled to the brim with precious, New Orleans–prime crimson nectar.

He made his way slowly to the trunk, still fuzzy-headed from his enormous meal. Inside were a half-inflated spare tire, assorted pieces of a tire jack, a pile of old newspapers that he'd been meaning to take to a recycling bin, two badly wrinkled spare shirts, a pistol, a potato, and a crate filled with empty glass pickle jars.

Wishing ruefully that he had some slack in his pants pockets, Jules balanced the potato and the pistol atop the empty jars and lifted the crate from the trunk. He rested the crate on the great bulge his stomach made as it sagged over his belt, then turned halfway around before realizing that his weak knees couldn't support both him and his cargo. Muttering with irritation and impatience, he set the crate down on the damp gravel and pushed it along with his foot as he maneuvered back around to the open door.

Twice, the potato rolled off the top of the jars and bounced into the water. Twice, Jules cursed a blue streak as he fished it out, until he decided it would be better to leave the pistol and the potato by the water's edge anyway.

Back at the car, he pushed Bessie's stiffening legs out of the way and sat uncomfortably on the doorjamb. He took a bottle of sodium citrate solution from the crate and poured some into the pan of blood, in order to prevent clotting and extend freshness, a trick he'd learned from Doc Landrieu. Then he began plucking jars out of the crate, unscrewing their tops and dipping them carefully into the blood. After five minutes of cautious labor, he had filled eight jars. The ninth jar he hugged between his thighs as he gingerly tilted the pan above it, securing the last few precious red droplets. He held this last jar in his left hand and its top in his right, hesitating. He stared at the jar's viscous contents, glistening almost black in the dim moonlight, and shrugged his shoulders.

"Oh, what the hell. I'll need all the strength I got for what I gotta do next. A little lagniappe won't kill me."

He lifted the jar to his gore-stained lips. Already the blood had lost some of its freshness, tasting only like vintage Chardonnay instead of nectar of the gods; he floated in the clouds a few minutes, rather than being shot to Mars in a rocket. Returning to terra firma, he felt embarrassed and guilty at his lack of willpower. *Hell—that jar could've gotten me through a couple of dry nights.* Disgusted with himself, he threw the empty jar as far out into the swamp as he could (it was a pathetic throw, but he tried not to notice). Then he forced himself to stand.

"Night's not gettin' any darker. Time to get to work, son."

After ten minutes of sweaty, joint-grinding exertion, he had managed to drag Bessie's body out of the Cadillac and down to the water's edge. Grunting, he sat heavily on the alga-stained gravel. He picked up the pistol, a cheap Saturday night special he'd bought in a pawnshop, and the wet potato, his poor-man's silencer. He stared at Bessie's face, gone a milky chocolate instead of its normal dark chocolate, still frozen in an expression of pained surprise. Suddenly, sitting next to a dead woman in an empty swamp, ghostly silent except for the rumble of a distant car on the highway, Jules felt unbearably lonely. The space behind his eyes was pounding, and he was feeling a little sick. Who would fix him his chamomile tea, to settle his stomach? In all the long decades since his mother had passed, there had been no one to fix him tea and bring it to him in bed. No one except Maureen, his one great love, the woman whose bite had forever transformed him. And she hadn't spoken to him in ten years.

He briefly considered loading Bessie back in the car, taking her back to his house, and letting nature take its course. She'd been an okay companion. Not a scintillating conversationalist, but at least she'd appreciated his music. And she'd be lively in the sack, for sure. He set the pistol down and gave her another look.

He frowned. "Naww. What the hell was I thinking? Look at her. She's got an appetite bigger than mine, even. No willpower. No self-control. Too softhearted and softheaded. Let her become a vampire and before you know it this town'll be up to its ass in homeless little-old-lady vampires, bringing the heat down on the rest of us. And then the gig'll be up. Naww. Just get it over and done with."

In all his years of undead life, Jules had only made another vampire once. Maureen had lectured him long and hard about predator–prey ratios and how important it was to keep the number of vampires in New Orleans strictly limited. He'd only done it once, when he'd been dying for a sidekick, a pal. And he hadn't been all that happy with the way things had turned out.

"In this business, you've gotta be ruthless. Pity's good for nothing but a stake through the heart."

His lower back spasmed with sharp stabs of pain as he rolled Bessie over onto her stomach. He squashed the potato onto the .38's stubby barrel, then rested the potato at the base of Bessie's skull, where her brain stem would be. *Wipe out the brain stem, and a corpse stays a corpse.* Just like Maureen had taught him so long ago, back when pistols had been more elegant things. Jules pulled the trigger.

Plufff.

Knees aching, he rolled her body into the swamp and gave it a good push. It floated into an island of tall grass and partially disappeared. With any luck, it would sink into the mire before the sun got too high. And if somebody ended up spotting it, it wouldn't be any big deal. The cops would call the killing a drug hit, or conjecture that the victim had been some whore dumb enough to double-cross her pimp. That was a great thing about New Orleans. Dead bodies were nothing extraordinary.

Jules pulled the plastic tarp from the Caddy's backseat and rinsed it off in the water. Then he folded it up, stuck it under his armpit, and dragged the crate of blood-filled jars back to the trunk. Damn, his crummy knees really hurt tonight. He opened the trunk, peeled off his red-stained shirt, threw it on top of the spare tire, and pulled on a relatively fresh one. A glint of silver at the bottom of the trunk caught his eye. It was the head of his cane, poking out from beneath the tire. Jules pulled it out. It was a good old cane. He'd bought it back in his salad days, when a sharp-looking silver-headed cane had seemed exactly the fashion accessory for a young vampire-on-the-make. It was more than a fashion statement now. On nights like tonight, he needed it.

The *D* word flashed through his brain. *Diet.* As much as he hated to think it, it wouldn't go away. His damn knees kept reminding him. For the sake of his health, he had to lose some weight.

Jules cut off the radio on the forty-five-minute drive back to the city. He was in one foul, low-down mood. Why couldn't pleasurable things just be pleasurable and that was that? Why did the world have to be so complicated and twisted, so that the things you loved best were the very things that were worst for you? Even from behind the closed sun visor, hidden from his sight, the newspaper clipping taunted him. NEW ORLEANS. FATTEST. CITY. IN. NATION. He wanted to crumple it up. He wanted to tear it into a hundred tiny pieces, toss them out the Caddy's window, and watch them sink into Lake Pontchartrain. But he couldn't make himself do it. The damn clipping would just stay in his head, anyway.

Back in the city, driving along Tulane Avenue on his way back to the French Quarter, Jules approached the imposing edifice of St. Joseph's, the largest church in New Orleans. His mother had taken him there for Mass every Easter when he was a boy. Compared with their neighborhood parish church in the Ninth Ward, St. Joseph's had been immense, easily the biggest building little Jules had ever set foot in. The stained-glass windows looked a thousand feet high, and he'd imagined that every Catholic in the state of Louisiana could fit inside, with room to spare for folks from Mississippi.

Tired and dejected, wanting to rest a minute, Jules pulled over to the curb in front of the church. The area had been gorgeous when he'd been young, a neighborhood of mansions to rival those on St. Charles Avenue. Now the church's closest neighbors were a check-cashing joint, a cheap-jack furniture store, and a twenty-four-hour greasy spoon patronized mainly by housekeeping staff from the nearby LSU Medical Center. Jules hadn't looked this long at a church in years. Back in the late 1960s, after Vatican II,

Jules had satisfied his curiosity about the controversial changes by attending evening Mass at this very church. His mother had raised him right, after all; even half a century as a vampire hadn't eradicated his upbringing, and he'd been nostalgic for his old churchgoing days. Sure enough, the switch from Latin Mass to English had made a difference for Jules. The priest's intonations had merely caused him to be violently sick to his stomach, instead of making his skin smoke and his hair catch fire.

So why had he stopped in front of St. Joseph's tonight? Jules listened to the hum of traffic from the nearby elevated highway as he tried to figure himself out. Was he feeling guilty about what he'd done ? He rolled down his window and hocked a gob of phlegm into the street. That was *ridiculous*, too ridiculous a notion for him even to consider. "Everybody has to eat, don't they?" he told himself. "Do steak lovers feel guilty about the cows? Do vegetarians get all weepy when they're dicing carrots? *Hell no!* So why should *I* be different?"

Jules shifted the Caddy's Hydramatic transmission back into drive. It had been a tiresome night; it was time to head home. He passed by Charity Hospital and the tall, modern hotels that lined both sides of Canal Street, choosing a route that would take him back through the Quarter. Almost as soon as he turned onto shadowy Decatur Street, however, he had reason to regret his choice. This hour of the night, the street was teeming with vampires. Not *real* vampires, mind you. Just skinny kids with an attitude.

"Damn punk kids. Wanna-bes! The whole goddamn Quarter's crawling with them!" he muttered darkly to himself as he steered slowly around an obstacle course of deep, jagged potholes, the ever-present legacy of the city's having been built on swampland. Jules scowled at the black-clothed teenagers crowding the narrow, neon-lit sidewalks. Their sun-starved pallor was heightened by layers of pressed powder and liberal applications of dark eyeliner and tar-black hair dye. When local horror author Agatha Longrain had gotten hot and the vampire books and movies had begun pouring out of New Orleans, drawing hordes of vampire-crazed adolescents to the city, Jules had been able to laugh it all off. Not anymore. False vampires were everywhere—on the streets, on the television. There was even a New Orleans–based Goth-punk-Cajun band—led by popular singer Courane L'Enfant—whose vampire shtick revolved around such dubious spectacles as hovering above the concert stage suspended from a bat-wing harness and drinking the blood of a live rat.

He slowed to a crawl and watched a bone-thin boy, maybe all of seventeen, disappear into Kaldi's, a coffee bar popular with the Goth-bohemian crowd. Jules had been able to affect that wraithlike look back in his prime. *Yeah, Goth-boy, enjoy the look while you can. Spend a couple more years in the Big Easy and you ain't gonna be wearing those size twenty-eight black jeans no more.*

A loud banging noise from the front of his car startled Jules out of his musings. He immediately mashed his brakes, filling the air with asbestos dust and a loud screech even though he hadn't been going any faster than eight miles an hour. A young, chalk-white couple were standing by the hood of his Caddy. The boy was bashing the hood with his fist.

"Hey lard-ass! Watch where you're fuckin' driving! You almost fuckin' hit us!"

Jules felt his face fill with purloined blood. He rolled down his window as fast as it would go. "The street's for cars, asshole! Move over to the goddamn sidewalk!"

The boy kicked at the Caddy's grille. Jules heard the sickening crunch of boot against plastic. "Fuck you!" the boy shouted. "What are you gonna do, huh? Get out of your boat and sit on me, lard-ass?"

Jules stabbed his horn with a fleshy fist. "Damn gutter punks! Goth puke-heads!" he screamed out his window. "Go home to your mamas in Baton Rouge!"

He gunned his engine and jammed his brakes simultaneously, making the Caddy jerk forward like a mechanical tyrannosaurus. The boy must've decided that discretion was the better part of valor, because he dragged his chalky girlfriend over to the far sidewalk, where they vanished into Kaldi's, but not before shooting Jules a parting bird.

The car behind Jules honked annoyingly. Jules found himself without even enough strength to lean out the window and tell the offending driver to screw himself. He felt awful. His stomach had gone all acidy and his hands were shaking again. He felt as crummy as he had early in the evening, before he'd eaten anything at all. And his lousy knees were back to their throbbing.

Lard-ass. That was it. The final straw. He was going on a diet, no question about it.

♠

Ahh . . . home at last.

Jules felt his stomach quiet as he turned onto good old Montegut Street. Even his knees stopped throbbing, or throbbed a little less. In his more than one hundred years on earth, this was the only neighborhood he'd ever lived in. He'd been born here, not more than half a block from the Mississippi River. The river was in his blood. Midwestern mud, fertilizer runoff, toxic discharges from chemical plants—yeah, he supposed they were in his blood, too.

Sure, the neighborhood had seen some changes. In the old days this stretch of Montegut Street between St. Claude Avenue and the river had been crowded with closely bunched houses, bustling family homes separated by alleys the width of a garbage can. Now Jules's house was the only occupied structure left on his block. All the other homes had been abandoned, one by one, as the neighborhood had gone down over the last thirty years. Some had decayed into crack dens. Others, like the rambling three-story Victorian that once fronted the levee, had burned to the ground, victims of fires lit by vagrants on chill winter nights. None of this disturbed Jules overly much, especially since his mother hadn't lived to see it. He liked his privacy. The old Victorian had blocked his view of the ships on the river. And besides, sometimes the crack houses furnished him with a passable meal.

Montegut Street seemed unusually quiet tonight. The stoops of the boarded-up houses he passed were empty; none of the usual winos or junkies were sitting out, talking about their next score. No badass kids stood on his corner, playing Master P or the Ninth Ward Devil Dawgs on boom boxes bigger than a Yugo. It was almost eerie. Had the cops pulled a raid while he was out?

A stretch Cadillac limousine was parked on the bare dirt lot across from his house. Jules had never seen it before. In fact, he'd never seen one like it before anywhere, and he considered himself an expert on Cadillacs. He pulled into his narrow driveway, then walked over to take a closer look. It was a brand-new Seville with gold wheels and trim, windows tinted midnight black, a custom stretch job that probably cost close to seventy grand. Jules eyed the stripped cars that lined his block, rusting, doorless heaps that sat forlornly on their bare axles. *Whoever owns that limo,* Jules thought, *must not worry much about money if he parks his ride on this street.*

He turned to walk back to his house. He paused in the middle of the street to admire the sagging two-and-a-half-story camelback, silhouetted by the moon, leaning steeply toward the river with a lusty death wish. His castle. Each hurricane that had butted heads with New Orleans had made his house lean a little farther south, until now Jules estimated its riverward tilt to be at least ten degrees. But the house had persevered. It was a survivor, just like he was.

Something was different about it tonight. Hadn't he left his porch light on? The front of his house was just as dark as the surrounding blocks, which hadn't known working street lamps in nearly a decade.

Maybe the bulb had burned out.

Jules climbed the cinder block steps carefully; at his weight, a tumble could do him real damage. Despite his elaborate caution, he nearly tripped over something at the edge of the porch. Something hard and metallic that screeched against the worn wooden floor when he kicked it.

It was his iron-barred security door. It had been torn off its hinges. And its thick bars were twisted like pipe cleaners.

TWO

"What the hell—?" Jules muttered. His sense of comfort at being back home evaporated like spit from an August sidewalk.

The inner door to his house was partially open, swaying slightly with the river breeze. Its knob was crushed.

No ordinary burglar had done this. Run-of-the-mill thieves would've pried the bars off one of his back windows.

Jules knelt down to examine the twisted wreckage of his security door. The dried mud and dead leaves that had caked his porch for months were undisturbed, except for footprints. No signs heavy equipment had been used. But no one, not even a champion weight lifter, was strong enough to mangle that security door with his bare hands. Maybe back in his vampiric prime, Jules could've given those bars the kind of pretzel-job they'd suffered tonight. Maybe. Or maybe not.

Jules placed the twisted metal back on his porch and shook his head. Another vampire? It was unthinkable. Vampires didn't screw with each other. Ever since Europe's vampire population had nearly annihilated itself through internecine warfare during the years of the Black Plague, the notion of sovereign and separate territories had remained a sacred creed among vampires. One vampire might invite another to share his or her territory. But unwelcome incursions simply didn't happen.

Whatever. He pushed what remained of his front door open and strode into his living room. Whoever or whatever the burglar was, and however he'd managed to bend inch-thick iron, he'd picked the wrong homeowner to fuck with.

Jules headed straight for his music listening room, steeling himself for the worst. Outside Tulane University's music archives, he owned what was probably the most extensive collection of early New Orleans jazz on original pressings in the entire city. If sold to a knowledgeable dealer or collector, his vintage sounds could fetch close to ten thousand dollars. Yet not a single album was out of place.

His battered old Philips television set sat undisturbed on its stand, the half-watched Alan Ladd video from last week still loaded in the VCR. His Depression-era pulp collection? Untouched. His mother's antique flatware? In the drawer where she'd left it. Even the computer his buddy Erato had talked him into buying was still on Jules's kitchen table, half buried in dusty floppy diskettes.

So what had the thief stolen? Upstairs was nothing but a set of bedroom furniture and Jules's clothes, which he couldn't imagine anybody wanting. His mother's things were so moth-eaten that even the lowliest of Magazine Street antiques hustlers wouldn't touch them. The basement held nothing but Jules's coffin and seven decades' worth of accumulated junk. Surely, someone hadn't torn open his most securely locked door just to tour his home.

A clatter of falling cans made Jules jump. The sound had come from downstairs. Could the thief still be here? What would he want down in the basement? Jules's spirits perked up again. If the burglar *was* down in the basement, that meant he was trapped; the only exit was the narrow stairway Jules began to descend. And if the burglar was trapped, that meant an easy meal. Home-delivered and piping hot, more convenient than Domino's!

Jules pulled a cord that switched on a dim twenty-five-watt bulb. "Anybody down there?" He couldn't see anyone, and no one answered. From the top of the stairs, it looked like nothing had been touched at all.

Wait. That wasn't true. Something *was* different. His coffin.

He descended the stairs as quickly as his knees would allow. Someone had spray-painted his coffin in big red letters.

NO POACHING WHITE BOY

The words made no sense. Jules read them three times, figuring either he must be reading them wrong, or else the vandal was a product of New Orleans's dreadful public schools. He read them aloud, hoping maybe the sound of them would help him solve this puzzle.

"No. Poaching. White. Boy." *Maybe white boy's a kind of fish, like redfish?*

The shadows that draped the spare lumber in the corner of the basement sprang to life. A man stepped from the darkness to the center of the room. He was tall and broad-shouldered, dressed in a sharply tailored black suit, starched white shirt, and crimson bow tie. He couldn't be older than twenty-four or twenty-five. His skin was ash gray, a color Jules remembered from nights in the morgue. When he stepped into the light, a slight reddish brown tone underlay the gray of his face. He stared unflinchingly into Jules's eyes. The intruder looked confident enough to lead the Saints to a Super Bowl win.

"So you're Jules Duchon. Big-time New Orleans vampire. Huh. Pretty much what I expected. 'Specially after I seen this dump you live in."

"Who the fuck are you?"

The intruder smiled. His voice was velvety smooth, but higher and reedier than Jules would've expected. "Me? I'm your new landlord, Jules. I'm the man. I come to set down the *law*. You an' me hafta have a serious talk. You been steppin' outside the lines *way* too long."

Questions buzzed through Jules's mind like angry gnats. How did this interloper know he was a vampire? Why the strange skin?

"Buddy, I am gonna make you *seriously* sorry that you busted in here and messed with my property."

This infuriating young punk was undoubtedly faster than Jules was. He'd have to immobilize him somehow. Jules hadn't tried out his vampiric hypnotism in years. He had a nagging fear that he couldn't get it working again. But he was so pissed off, he figured his righteous fury was hot enough to boil away any rust.

Jules concentrated hard. He arched his eyebrows and opened his eye sockets as wide as they would go. Boy, would this prowler be sorry! He'd freeze him with terror. He'd turn his blood to freon. He'd make him shit icicles.

Nothing happened.

The intruder smiled expectantly. Then he laughed. It was one of the most unpleasant sounds Jules had ever heard.

"What was that supposed to do, huh? Scare the crap outta me? Make me think I was a worm or somethin'?" He laughed again, so hard this time that he leaned on Jules's coffin for balance. "Man, that vampire shit don't work on another *vampire!*"

Jules couldn't believe what he was hearing. His worst, most inconceivable fears were coming true. But he still struggled desperately to push them away. "You're bullshittin' me."

"Oh I *am*, huh? Take a look at these." He smiled an exaggerated smile. His canine teeth were sharp and elongated.

"Big deal. Half the young punks in the Quarter got their teeth filed and sharpened. That don't prove a thing."

"Man, you are one stubborn sonofabitch, ain'tchu? You seen what I did to your security door? Now who could do that 'cept somebody with the strength of ten men, huh?"

Jules was silent. The intruder shrugged his broad shoulders. "Oh well," he said. "They say seein' is believin'." He reached into the lumber pile and pulled out three of the thickest planks. Then he put his left foot on top of Jules's coffin and effortlessly snapped the three planks all at once over his knee.

He tossed the broken lumber onto the coffin. "Believe me now? Or do I have to reach up and pull your plumbing outta the ceilin'?"

"Skip it. I believe you," Jules admitted glumly. "So where are you down from? Chicago? Cleveland? Detroit? Couldn't take the cold anymore, huh? Well, there're rules against musclin' in on another vampire's territory. You can't just waltz into New Orleans and start puttin' the bite on people. I've got a good mind to report you to the National Council."

The intruder scowled. "*Fuck* the National Council. Them old-men vampires ain't got no jurisdiction over this. Ain't you been listenin' to the way I been talkin' to you? I ain't from outta town. I'm a *homeboy* vampire, Jules. I'm a Grade-A, crawfish-head-suckin', second-linin', Mardi-Gras-bead-catchin', *New Orleans* bloodsuckah!"

Could it be true? Jules certainly hadn't made him. He'd never seen this guy before. And Maureen wouldn't have made him, either. Jules had had to sit through lecture after lecture from her about the absolute necessity of keeping strict limits on the vampire population of a given territory. More to the point, Maureen had always been adamant about never, *ever* creating a colored vampire. The only vampire Jules had ever made was Doodlebug, his onetime kid sidekick, and Doodlebug had been living out in California for nearly twenty-five years. There were other, older vampires in New Orleans who kept to themselves in a walled compound near the parish line. But those old-timers were supposed to be even more prejudiced against blacks, Jews, and Italians than Maureen was.

"I don't believe you," Jules said. "You ain't from around here."

The other vampire straightened his bright red bow tie. "You don't hafta believe me if you don't want. All you gotta do is *listen*." He lifted the lid of the coffin so that Jules could read the spray-painted message again. "NO POACHING means your nights as Great White Hunter is *finished*. As of tonight, Jules, you is *out* of *Africa*. No more big fat black mamas for you. Capeesh?"

"What the hell are you talkin' about?"

"Thick as a brick, huh? Okay. Lemme say this in words you'll understand. Ready? If niggas gonna get fanged, then *niggas* is gonna do the *fangin'*. You stick to your kind—that's white folks, now, not black folks—and me an' my brothers stick to our kind. *That*, my friend, is the way it's gonna *be*."

Jules was stunned. Who was this Johnny-come-lately to tell *him* whom he could and couldn't victimize? "Pal, I been a vampire since before your daddy was knee-high to a nutria. I know tricks you ain't heard of or even thought of. Nobody but *nobody* tells me whose blood I can suck on my own home turf."

The other vampire nonchalantly scratched his pointed chin. "I guess you can call me 'Nobody' then. 'Cause I be the one tellin' you."

Jules waddled forward, trying his best to look menacing. "You and what goddamn army, punk?"

The intruder grinned. "Heh. You don't wanna know *nothin'* 'bout my army, Jules. I got eyes all over this town. Eyes in *every* neighborhood. I know ev'rythin' there is to know about Jules Duchon. Like that little hot chocolate snack you picked up from New Orleans Mission earlier tonight. Hope she was good and tasty for you, 'cause that there tamale stand is off-limits as of, oh, 'bout ten minutes ago."

Jules felt a small bayou of sweat begin to trickle down his back. This was awful. Never in his worst nightmares had he ever imagined anything like this. All he could muster was a feeble stab at humor. "I thought that affirmative action jazz was out of style."

Again the smile. Jules was coming to hate that smile. "Me, I'm a self-made man. Only kinda affirmative action I believe in is this—I tell you what to do, you reply in the affirmative, or I take action. Do we have an understanding here?"

Jules tried to figure an out, but his brain seemed stuck in neutral. "But—but more than three-quarters of the people who live here are blacks. Almost every poor person, every down-and-outer in town is, y'know, black. White people don't leave their homes after dark. They're afraid of crime. And the tourist trade is too hard to live on steady. You're cuttin' me out of my livelihood."

The black vampire clapped him on the shoulder. It hurt. "Well now, that's *your* problem, Mr. Jules. Not mine. You white folks are supposed to be smart. You'll figure somethin' out, I'm sure."

Quicksand pulled at Jules's ankles. He felt dizzy. His stomach called off its tenuous truce with the rest of him. If he wanted to avoid sinking above his nose, he had to grasp at any branch in reach. He needed time to think. He needed information. "I'll ask you one more time. Who the hell are you?"

"Still got a little fight left in you, huh? Good. I like that. You wanna know who I am? I'll tell you, 'cause I think we done come to an understanding. I had a lotta names in my years. *Jules Duchon*—that's the name you was born with, huh? How long you been around, Jules? A hundred years? No imagination—you white folks ain't got no imagination at all. Seventy years a big badass vampire, and you ain't got no more sense than to live in the shithole you was born in and keep the name your mama hung on you?"

He walked over to the coffin, dusted a spot with a handkerchief from his jacket pocket, and sat down. "Sit a spell, Jules. This might be a while. I usta run with a kid gang, see, back when I was alive. Picked the name Eldo Rado to be my tag. Eldo Rado. Something a kid would come up with, huh? Named myself after a car made by some white French guy come to America, who called his car some weird-ass Spanish word. When I became a vampire, that shit didn't cut it no more. So one night I went to the video joint. Checked out every tape on vampires they had. Figured I'd pick a new name after I watched all the tapes.

"You white vampires are lucky, you know that? You got tons of *bad*, I mean *bad* mothafuckin' bloodsuckahs to watch on the tube. You know? Christopher Lee. That dude is *bad*, man! And what do *I* have to watch? Fuckin' *Blacula*, man. You ever want to *piss* me the *hell* off, just try pinnin' that Blacula shit on me. So the tapes wasn't no help at all. Then I got to thinkin'. Maybe I didn't need a totally new name. Back in grade school, the teachers used to call me Malice, 'cause it sounded close to my real name and I was a bad little dude. Malice. I liked the sound of that. And I didn't need no Christian name anymore, 'cause as a vampire I sure wasn't no Christian. So nowadays you can call me Malice X. Any more questions?"

Jules had remained standing, uncomfortably, throughout Malice X's monologue. His knees were aching again. "Yeah. One more. Why the warning? If you got so many goons to watch where I go, how come you haven't just rubbed me out?"

The black vampire stood and straightened the crease in his pants. "I owed somebody a favor. I just paid it by givin' you a heads-up. Actually, I didn't lose nothin'. See, I figure you're too stupid to listen. A week, maybe a month from now, you'll gimme some excuse to come down on you. Hard. You know them big, fat white toadstools that grow on neutral grounds after a heavy rain? I always loved kickin' the shit outta them things. Stompin' 'em to pieces. Just like I'm gonna love stompin' you."

Jules's repertoire of wiseass comebacks was dry as a drought-stricken riverbed. The bayou of sweat dripping down his back had swelled to a Mississippi.

"Hey, Jules? You said before you can do some neat tricks, right?" Malice X removed his jacket, folded it, and placed it over the back of a rusty chair. Then he removed his shoes, unbuttoned his shirt, and loosened his alligator-skin belt and the clasp on his pants. "Well, here's a trick I just learned."

The black vampire's form shimmered and wavered like a reflection in a twisting fun house mirror. His limbs contracted, his face elongated, and his gray skin sprouted a dense, smooth coat of coal-black fur. Seconds later, a sleek, heavily fanged panther gracefully shook off Malice X's clothes. The bloodred bow tie remained tied around its neck. The great cat loped lazily to Jules's side of the room, moving like ball bearings on smooth ice. It rubbed its face, its neck, and its side against Jules's thick legs, purring hypnotically. Jules didn't dare breathe.

Then it trotted to the coffin and, before climbing the stairs, showered it with a steaming spray of pungent urine.

THREE

It had been ten long, sometimes lonely years since Jules had seen Maureen last. He'd stayed away a decade out of deference to her feelings, irrational though they might've been. Now he was about to step onto her turf again. He had no choice. Only she could tell him how to reach the High Krewe of Vlad Tepes. She'd just have to understand.

Jules rubbed his eyes and yawned. He'd had a lousy day's sleep. No amount of scrubbing and bleach had been able to completely remove the stench of urine from his coffin.

He paused on the sidewalk in front of Jezebel's Joy Room to stare at the photographs of the dancers. He wanted to be sure that Maureen still worked there before he committed himself to climbing the stairs. Jezebel's was on Iberville between Royal and Chartres, a stretch of the upper Quarter that had managed to avoid the rampant gentrification that had pasteurized most of the rest of New Orleans's central tourist zone. The club's surroundings had changed very little since the early 1960s, when the last few legitimate burlesque houses had died off and been replaced by bump-and-grind joints. This was a block respectable tourists rushed by on their way to the House of Blues or Café du Monde, averting their eyes from the yellowing photographs of naked female torsos.

Jules quickly scanned the contents of Jezebel's come-on display. It didn't take long to find her. *Yup; that's Maureen, all right.* None of the photos inside the roach-eaten display case showed any of the women's faces. The picture of Maureen, however, was unmistakable. Unlike all the others, it was a charcoal sketch, almost Fauvist in its primitive vitality. The caption beneath the sketch announced in bold lettering, ROUND ROBIN—BIGGEST EROTIC ATTRACTION IN THE QUARTER—YOU WON'T BE-LIEVE YOUR EYES! Staring at her picture brought a flood of memories crashing down on his head. Some good, some not so good. The picture was wrinkled from the oppressive humidity, and its edges had begun peeling away from the cork backing of the display case. If the sketch were true to life at all, then Maureen's torso had grown even more monumental than it'd been ten years ago.

Generic disco music blared from cheap speakers in the second-story room high above, making the heavy air throb around Jules's blunt head. He gathered his courage and pulled open the front door. Jezebel's was at a competitive disadvantage compared with the clubs located right at street level. It lacked the free and effective advertising of a front entrance, which displayed flashes of the goods inside to curious passersby every time the door swung open. Jules waddled into the landing. The stairs were steep and narrow, lit by a single naked lightbulb. His fleshy nostrils twitched. The aroma inside the foyer was a barroom classic—stale beer mingled with cigarette haze and a hint of drying urine. Lately, it seemed he couldn't escape the scent of piss.

Three minutes later, a veritable eternity of agony for his joints, Jules reached the second-story landing. The pounding in his ears obliterated the soulless, mechanical music howling from the speakers above the gaudily lit stage. His knees felt like huge, swollen beefsteak tomatoes, bruised, squeezed, and pinched by hundreds of manic shoppers at some pre-Easter sale at Schwegmann's Giant Super-Market. But when he caught sight of who was on stage, Jules immediately forgot all about his knees.

Beneath a glittering, revolving disco ball, Maureen danced like some fantastic vision from an antediluvian, pre–Weight Watchers world, a fertility goddess who'd be worshiped by a tribe of blue-eyed albinos. As she danced about the stage with almost supernatural grace, every part of her—her hips, thighs, belly, double-dimpled arms, buttocks, jowls, neck rolls—shimmied and gyrated in time with the music, an unceasing undulation of fleshy movement. It was hypnotic. Jules estimated that she had packed on at least two hundred additional pounds since he had last seen her.

He made his way, as quietly and unobtrusively as he could manage, to a table near the back of the club. He wasn't as invisible as he'd hoped to be. When he was just halfway to his destination, Maureen's eyes snapped open, as if from a trance. Her placid face dissolved into a mask of horror and abject humiliation, as Jules was treated, along with every other patron in the club, to the astounding spectacle of Maureen's immense, chalk-white body turning scarlet red.

She stumbled out of her dance routine like a punch-drunk boxer, then ran as quickly as her doughy legs would carry her to the side of the stage and the EMPLOYEES ONLY exit, covering her face with her hands. Jules frowned. He hadn't anticipated his presence having such a dramatic effect on her. What was it with women, anyway? Jules had figured she'd be surprised, maybe even shocked, by his sudden reappearance. But shouldn't she be happy to see an old friend again?

Another dancer hurried onstage as someone fumbled with the tape player and two employees stripped the black curtains from the mirrors surrounding three sides of the dancing platform. Compared with Maureen, the new girl was decidedly ordinary, apart from silicone-enhanced breasts. Jules overheard a few of the other patrons mumble with disappointment; several got up to leave.

Jules fidgeted for a few minutes while he tried to watch the new dancer. She wasn't much good. Half the audience had cleared out since Maureen had made her abrupt exit.

The floorboards to the right of his table creaked. He heard a bemused, exasperated sigh, one he remembered all too well. "Hello, Jules."

"Hey, Mo. Pull up a chair?"

"Sure. Long as I can find one that won't bust when I sit down."

She had dressed herself in a custom-made kimono, yards of black silk embroidered with green, purple, and gold dragons. Her long, frizzy blond hair was pulled back from her face by three glittery purple clips. Despite the forlorn, heavy sag of her alabaster jowls, Jules thought she was as beautiful as he'd ever seen her. As beautiful, even, as she'd looked the first night he'd met her, the last and only time he'd gazed at her with human eyes.

She settled herself uncomfortably on an armless chair, which protested but did not give way. "So what've you been doing with yourself?"

"Oh, y'know, the usual. Livin' the life."

"The afterlife, you mean."

"Yeah, you're right."

Her hard, cold stare unnerved him. He looked away, forcing himself to watch the clumsy, plastic-boobed dancer still trying to make a go of it. When he glanced back, Maureen was still staring at him. "I felt you come in, you know," she said. "When I first started dancing, I felt a little tingle behind my eyes, in my sinuses, like the start of a headache. So I knew you were downstairs, pacing back and forth in front of that sketch of me, trying to decide whether or not to come up. That damn tingle got worse with each step you climbed. I kept hoping I was wrong. But I wasn't. I can always sense when the ones I made are around. I'm like a bitch with her goddamn puppies."

Jules tried to think of something to say. He stared at his fingers, splayed on the table like white cigars. He'd always hated the way Maureen could nail him with a look, making thirty seconds feel like a century of deafening silence.

"Goddamn it to hell, Jules," Maureen whispered fiercely after a few seconds of deadly quiet. "Didn't I tell you never to come see me again? Didn't I?"

Jules finally found his voice. He wished he could still drink whiskey; his throat could use it. "Mo, that was ten years ago. I thought, y'know, maybe you'd changed your mind by now. Lord almighty, I'm practically the only relation you got in the whole world. Why're you holding this heavy grudge against me, baby? What's so awful about seeing me once every ten years?"

Maureen remained quiet for a few long seconds, smiling ruefully. "You just don't get it, do you? Naww. Of course you don't. You're a goddamn *man*." She sighed heavily. "I'll try to explain. Look at that stage, Jules. What do you see? Aside from a drug-addled bimbo with thousand-dollar tits, I mean."

Jules considered all possible answers before replying. He really didn't want to make her any more angry than she already was, not if he could possibly avoid it. "Uh, I dunno. Mirrors?"

Maureen smiled and slowly nodded her head, like she was trying to teach a retarded child the alphabet. "That's right, Jules. Mirrors. But when I'm dancing on that stage, do you see the mirrors?"

"No. They cover them up with velvet."

"And why do they do that?"

" 'Cause it's part of your act. You insist on it."

Maureen waved her pudgy hand in a brisk, circular motion. "And *why* do I insist on that?"

"Uh, 'cause it'd freak out the clientele to not see you reflected in any of those mirrors, right?"

"Yes, Jules. Very good. And guess what? If none of the clientele can see my reflection, neither can I. I haven't been able to look at myself in a mirror or a photograph for more than a hundred years. But you know what? That's been a good thing. A very good thing. Especially during the last five decades or so. I feel *blessed* that I can't look at myself in the mirror. I am the luckiest fat woman on earth, Jules. But you come waltzing in here, after ten years, and you know what you are to me? You know what you are?"

Jules had figured it out. But he didn't want to say it.

Maureen sighed again. No exasperation this time. Just sadness, a sadness weightier than the two of them put together. "A *mirror*, Jules. You're my goddamn mirror."

She took a deep breath, and her eyes moistened and seemed to soften. She reached across the table and took his fleshy paw between her hands. "Oh, sweetheart," she said in a hoarse whisper. "You were a *beautiful* man. Such a beautiful man. You know that? When I saw you that night, standing in front of the French Opera House on Canal Street, I knew immediately that you were the one. The one I wanted to give eternal unlife to. So I could spend the rest of eternity looking at beautiful, gorgeous you."

Whoa! Maureen had never talked to him this way before. Not even back in the days when they were first together. What in hell could he say to that? "You were beautiful, too, Mo," Jules said, a little haltingly. "Baby, you're *still* beautiful."

Maureen let his hand drop to the table. "Don't bullshit me, Jules. I know exactly what I look like. I look at you, add some frizzy blond hair, make the tits and hips a little bigger, and there I am." Her scowl melted into a melancholy frown, and she touched his hand again. "Jesus. It breaks my heart, honey, to see what you've done to yourself. It really does. If I had known, eighty years ago, what would become of you, I wouldn't have bitten you. I would've just let you be."

Jules felt his stomach do a double somersault with a half twist. If

Maureen pissed off was bad, then Maureen on the verge of tears was a million times worse. "Mo. It's gonna be different. You'll see. I'm going on a diet. That's, uh, that's one a the things I came here to tell you."

Silence. Deafening silence. Maureen stared at him as if he had just sung a Chinese opera. "This is a *joke*, right? You tried, in your pathetic little way, to cheer me up. A joke. Right?"

"No, baby. I'm dead serious. I made up my mind last night. I'm gonna come back here six months from now, and you won't recognize me. I'll be *half* the man I am now."

"Oh. You *are* being serious. You crazy, predictable, baboon's *ass*. How many times have I heard this shit from you, Jules? Do you have any *idea* how many times I've listened to your identical bullshit?"

"Aww, Maureen—"

"*Don't* you 'Aww Maureen' *me*. I'm *wise* to you, Jules Duchon. Why do you think I put you out on your ear ten years ago? You never change. *This* is the reason you came up here tonight? *This* is the reason you've trashed my routine, got me docked a night's pay, and probably loused up my whole week? To repeat your sorry old 'I'm-going-on-a-diet' bullshit?"

Jules took a deep breath, then exhaled slowly through his nose. "Well, actually, I came to ask you, uh, a little favor, see . . . but it's not bullshit, what I just said. I'm at the end of my rope, baby. I think I might be getting diabetes, or maybe something worse."

Maureen tried pushing herself away from the table, but instead her chair remained firmly planted and she shoved the table into Jules's gut. She rose awkwardly from her chair and smoothed the wrinkles from her kimono. "I think you'd better leave now. I can't continue this conversation any more. It's hazardous to my mental well-being."

A waitress in a spangled bikini hovered expectantly over Jules's shoulder. "Set's almost over, dearie," she said to him. A gold tooth in the middle of her false smile reflected the glare of the stage lights. "You gotta buy at least one drink. House rules."

Maureen glowered at her coworker. "Samantha, can't you see we're in the middle of a conversation here?"

The waitress placed her tiny fists on her not-so-tiny hips. "Well, it looked to me like you was leavin', Maureen. Ex-*cuse* a girl trying to make a living. You make your rent by wiggling around onstage an hour a night. Me, I don't move the drinks, I'm out on my ass faster than you'd sunburn on Panama City Beach."

Maureen jammed her bosom into the waitress's tray, spilling a shot of bourbon onto a pile of cocktail napkins. "Get the hell out of my face, Samantha. I'll pay for his drink later. *Okay?*"

Samantha cast an appalled look at the spilled drink and backed away. "Ohh-*kay*, Maureen. Whatever you say. You're the big-ass *star* around here. But you don't have to be such a *bitch* about it." She stalked back to the bar.

Jules eyed the empty space on the table, next to his right hand, which would ordinarily be occupied by a cup of thick, steaming coffee. "Hey. Maybe I wanted to order a joe."

Maureen redirected her withering glare on him. "I don't give a flying *shit* about your caffeine addiction—" Her tirade stopped in midsentence, like a wildfire suddenly deprived of oxygen. She sank back into her chair and wearily rested her forehead on her palms. "You said there was something else, didn't you? Something you had to ask me. A favor."

"Uh, yeah. A *little* favor."

She sighed. "You're like a crotch itch, you know? You show up at the worst times, and you won't go away until you're thoroughly scratched. Spill it. You've got two minutes, max."

"I need some information, okay? That's all. I need to get in touch with those vampires you used to live with before you went solo. The ones with the big compound somewhere near the parish line."

Maureen's thick makeup crinkled with surprise. "The High Krewe of Vlad Tepes? What the hell do you need to see those highfalutin assholes for?"

Now it was Jules's turn to sigh. "To get a rogue off my back."

"A rogue?"

The story began spilling out of him like a flash flood. "He was waitin' for me at my house last night. Busted up my door somethin' awful. He threatened me. Threatened *me*, in my own house! Wants to push me outta town. He pissed all over my coffin, and now I can't get the damn stink out—"

"Slow down. Who is this you're talking about? You're not making much sense."

Jules took a few seconds to gather his thoughts. "There's a rogue vampire in town. A colored guy. Young. A real badass. He says he's got a whole army of other vampires backing him up, and they've been watching everything I been up to. He told me I better stop fangin' black folks, or else he's gonna have his goons lean on me. Can you believe this shit?"

Maureen was silent for several seconds. Her cheek twitched. "What's—what's his name? This rogue?"

"What the hell does that matter? His name? It sounded like that crazy preacher guy from the sixties. Like a girl's name . . . Alice. Malice X."

Maureen turned her head away suddenly and glanced at the empty stage. "A *colored* vampire, you say?" Her fingers tightened on the edge of the table. "Where do you think he's in from?"

"He says he's from here. New Orleans born and bred."

"That's impossible. No one here would've made him."

"*You* argue with him. I'll send him over to your place the next time he drops by for a chat."

Maureen looked back at her companion. Jules noticed anxiousness in her eyes. Maybe even fear. "Do you think he's on the level? About having an army of vampires, I mean?"

Jules considered this. "An army? Well, I dunno. But it makes sense that he's got others with him. He knew too much about me and where I been to be working on his own."

Maureen's face brightened, as though she'd experienced a sudden revelation. Her voice returned to the motherly, half-cajoling, half-commanding tone he knew so well. "Have you thought about maybe doing what he said? Laying off the colored victims?"

"*What?* Whose side are you on?"

"Yours, you big dummy. Weren't you just bragging to me five minutes ago about how you plan on going on a diet?"

"Well, yeah, sure, but—"

"Well, how do you think you got so damn fat in the first place? Me, I've been a vampire twice as long as you have, so I've had a lot more time to earn my blubber. But you, you've always preferred the colored victims. Always said they were tastier. Do you know what those people *eat?* Fatback. Pigs' knuckles. They fry their *vegetables*, for Varney's sake! You want to slim down? If you do—if you really, *honestly* do—then this is the best thing that could've happened to you."

Jules mulled this over. Could Maureen be right? Maybe this whole awful experience was really a blessing in disguise? "Well . . . well, maybe . . ."

But then he thought about his coffin again. His coffin, streaked with drying urine. All the helpless indignation he'd experienced in the past fifteen hours came boiling to the surface. "*No.* No way! I can't let that little asshole get away with that shit. You weren't *there*, Mo. It wasn't *your* coffin he pissed on. My own house! This whippersnapper has the nerve to bust into my own house and try and muscle me around! Well, Jules Duchon don't knuckle under to nobody. The High Krewe'll tell that little snot-nose where to get off. You gonna give me that address or not?"

Maureen's voice dropped fifty degrees. Celsius. "If you're so bound and determined to make an ass of yourself, heaven forbid I should stand in the way. Just don't come crying to me after those buzzards give you the bum's rush."

She gave Jules the address he was looking for. He wrote it down on a ragged little pad of paper. She volunteered some additional information, the lines of a poem that would act as a code to get him through the gate.

She grabbed the pad away from him once he was done writing and checked it for accuracy. "All right." She flung it back at him. "Now get the hell out."

Jules felt a great, big lump grow in his throat. He didn't want it to end like this. Until he'd actually been sitting across from her, he'd barely realized just how much he'd been looking forward to seeing her again. "Look, Mo, about what you said before—y'know, layin' off the colored victims . . . I'll think about it, okay? One way or another, I'm gonna slim down. For you and me both. Have a little faith in me. Just a *little*. Huh?"

Her voice was flat as a bottle of Big Shot soda left open for a week. "Sure, Jules. You'll come back in a year. Or five years, or ten. And you'll be bigger than a house. We'll both be. The people around here eat the most fattening crap in the world. And we eat *them*. That's the way it is. That's the way it'll stay. Good night."

He could tell from her voice that there was nothing more he could say. He scooted back from the table, which was poking painfully into his liver. He pantomimed a tip of his hat to Maureen, but she had already turned away and started walking back to the stage door.

Jules tried shrugging his shoulders. The gesture felt false, somehow. He started shuffling toward the exit. At least those damn stairs would be easier to get down than they'd been to get up.

He was halfway to the door when he heard her voice behind him. "Jules. It's a different world out there than it used to be. Watch your ass, honey. Okay?"

Leaning on his cane, he swiveled back around and smiled a winning smile. "As big as my ass is, baby, it's impossible *not* to watch it!"

He was pleased with himself. That had been a good line to exit by. But as he made his way cautiously down the steep steps, her parting words of warning made him uneasy. And unlike a crotch itch, the uneasiness wouldn't go away, no matter how much he scratched it.

◆

Next stop, Bamboo Road, Jules thought to himself.

In all his years as a cabdriver, he'd never had the opportunity to drop a fare off on Bamboo Road. Not too surprising—the folks who could afford to live there either drove their own imported luxury cars or hired chauffeurs to drive them.

As he neared the address, he drove past acres and acres of above-ground marble crypts. Metairie Cemetery was the largest, most elaborate "city of the dead" in all New Orleans. Its crypts and miniature cathedrals housed the earthly remains of Confederate heroes, several mayors and governors, and much of the royalty of the Krewes of Rex, Comus, and Proteus. Jules estimated that even the smallest crypt in Metairie Cemetery was worth more than all the houses on his block of Montegut Street added together. Here and on neighboring Bamboo Road, the dead did well for themselves.

Jules turned off Metairie Road onto the loose gravel path, shadowed by ancient oak trees, that led to his destination. He parked his Caddy a dozen yards from where the path ended at an iron gate. Perhaps it was due to the abundance of trees and shrubs that lined the drive, but the air became tangibly cooler as Jules approached the lordly stone wall that surrounded the mansion and its outlying buildings and gardens.

When he reached the gate, Jules pressed what he assumed was a doorbell on the stone gatepost. To his surprise, a small door at face height slid open, revealing a glowing picture tube. A second later, a man's face filled the screen. He appeared to be in his late sixties and was dressed in a butler's livery.

"Yes? What can we do for you?"

The face didn't look entirely natural; it was too smooth and regular. Jules wondered whether it was a computer-generated image. In any case, the man's (or image's) patronizing tone made Jules's ears burn. He looked for the camera that he assumed was pointing at him. He couldn't see any lens, but he figured the butler could see as well as be seen, so he squared his shoulders before replying. "I need to talk with Krauss, Katz, and Besthoff."

"Are the masters expecting your arrival?"

"No. But it's important. I've got news they'll want to know about."

The butler's expression didn't change. "May I inquire as to the nature of your business?"

"Just tell them it's important." When the other man said nothing, Jules added, "I can't talk specifics with the help."

"Then I'm afraid I can't let you in. The masters see no one without a prior invitation."

Jules felt his face redden. "Look, Jeeves. I'm practically a member of the family. I *know* they'll want to see me. You gotta know I'm a vampire, don't you? I mean, take a good look through that camera of yours. Do you see my face? Or do I look like a bunch of empty clothes held up by wires?"

The face on the screen didn't twitch a muscle. "Of *course* I realize you are a member of the undead. But that makes no difference. Since you are incapable of enlightening me as to the nature of your business, I must return to my other duties and pray that you will have a pleasant evening." He turned away from the screen. The concealed door began to slide back into place.

"Hey! Wait!" Jules grabbed Maureen's poem from his coat pocket, hurriedly unfolded it, and started reciting as quickly as he could, before the screen was entirely closed.

"At end of day
In deepest night
We feel the thirst
Spread wings, take flight
No power on earth
Deters our bite
Some think us cursed
But blessed we are—
With eternal life."

Almost reluctantly, the metal panel covering the screen slid open again. For the first time, the butler's too-smooth face betrayed an emotion: exasperation. "Oh, very well," he spat. "I'll let you in, and at least one of the masters will see you. Do try not to step on any of the roses in the garden as you come through."

An electric motor whirred to life, and the thick doors of the front gate pivoted inward. The air that drifted out to greet him was scented with orchids, lilies, and exotic strains of roses. Jules stepped into the compound somewhat cautiously, half expecting a pack of guard dogs (guard wolves?) to descend on him. But the only movement within the front courtyard was the rising and falling of spurts of crimson-tinted water within a series of fountains leading to the main house's marble front steps. Jules glanced at the colorful tile mosaic on the bottom of one fountain as he walked past. It was a medieval-looking portrait of a severe, wiry, bearded king on horseback, driving a long lance through a Turkish enemy's chest. Jules recognized the portrait. It was Vlad Tepes of Transylvania.

He climbed the steps to the mansion's grand front door. The butler opened it before Jules could lay a finger on the brightly polished wolf's-head knocker.

"Please step inside," the butler said, his face once more an expressionless mask. At least his kisser looked real in person, though. "Master Krauss is out of town, and Master Katz is otherwise engaged at the moment, but Master Besthoff will see you. Please follow me." The butler shut the door, a massive fabrication of oak nearly ten feet high and a foot thick, with an effortless press of his fingers. The door shut with a resounding *boom*. Jules followed behind him and stared at his guide's stiffly erect back. So it *had* been a computer-generated image on the screen. Krauss, Katz, and Besthoff must be pretty high muckety-mucks in the undead community to have a butler who was a vampire, too.

The servant silently led Jules through gilded, marble-floored hallways lined with Italian Renaissance statuary and tapestries. Turning a corner, Jules half hoped to see twin rows of human arms jutting from each side of the hall, holding lit flambeaus in their ghastly white fingers. He was disappointed; there were only more tapestries of knights beheading swarthy Turks.

"Here we are," the butler said, stopping in front of a gold-rimmed door. "The library. Master Besthoff is expecting you."

Jules walked into the fanciest reading room he'd ever seen. No moldering paperbacks or pulp magazines here; the gleaming oak shelves were lined with thick leather-bound volumes, many of them in languages Jules didn't even recognize. But even more impressive was the man who rose from a plush red leather reading chair in the center of the room. Well over six feet tall, with steel-gray eyes and carefully coiffed black hair tinged with flashes of silver, Besthoff didn't look any older than his early forties, although Jules guessed he was probably centuries older than that. And he couldn't help but notice that, in polar opposition to his own physique, beneath his host's expensive Italian suit were the sleek shape and well-defined musculature of an Olympic swimming champion.

Besthoff flashed Jules a cold but correct smile and held out his hand. "Mr. Duchon? I am Georges Besthoff. I understand that you have news you wish to share with me?"

Jules shook the proffered hand. Besthoff's grip was viselike. "Yeah. Uh, nice to meet you. Heard a lot about you. I've got me a problem, see, and I think it's the kinda problem that maybe could affect both of us. So I was hopin' you and yours could give me some help. Especially since y'all are the senior vampires in the community."

"I see." He gestured to a Queen Anne–period couch facing the leather chair. Jules sat down as delicately as he could, afraid of damaging the fragile antique. Besthoff returned to his seat. "Shall I have Straussman make you a cup of coffee? Or would you prefer a brandy?"

So these vampires still had the stomach for alcohol? Jules wondered why his host didn't offer a goblet of blood. Oh, well. "Uh, yeah, a cuppa coffee'd be great."

Besthoff pressed a small stud set into the marble top of the end table next to his chair. "Straussman? Please bring a cup of coffee for our guest." He turned his attention back to Jules. "I understand you recited part of 'Night of Blood' for Straussman. Only a small handful of persons have ever been exposed to that particular poem. My own composition, by the way. A product of my romantic younger days in Romania. Where did you find it? Not on the Internet, I hope?" He smiled briefly, his eyes never leaving Jules's.

"Maureen Remoulade gave it to me. She's a friend. She wanted to make sure I could get in to see you."

Besthoff's eyes ignited with sudden interest. "Ah, Maureen! The breakaway. I am surprised she still retains any memory of that poem, as I assumed she never intended to use it to return to us here. Tell me, is she still employed as a dancer at that so-called gentlemen's club in the Vieux Carré?"

"Yeah, she's still packin' 'em in."

Besthoff smiled. "What a spirited girl she was. I am almost sorry to see her reduced to her present state. But I could've predicted that she would fall to this. Indeed, I did, although she paid me no mind." His host's eyes drifted to a small portrait set between two towering bookshelves. Jules realized, with a start, that the willowy limbs and delicate cheekbones of the girl in the portrait belonged to a much younger Maureen; after so many decades of gradual expansion on both their parts, he'd forgotten she'd ever looked that way. Besthoff tapped his long fingernails on the end table. "But enough of nostalgia. What is this news you have to share with me, Mr. Duchon?"

Jules cleared his throat. He chose his words carefully, for maximum impact. "There's a new vampire tryin' to muscle in on our territory. A *black* vampire."

Besthoff slowly interlaced his long, slender fingers. "A 'black' vampire? Come, come, Mr. Duchon. There is no need to hide behind such euphemisms here. Please speak plainly."

"All right. A colored vampire. Anyway, this wiseass little snot-nose says he's got a whole army of other vampires behind him. You've gotta figure they're all colored, too. This asshole—Malice X, he calls himself— he's trying to scare me outta town. He barged into my house, messed up my coffin, and told me I couldn't be puttin' the bite on any more black, uh, colored victims anymore. How's that for nerve, huh?"

Jules leaned forward in his chair, eager to catch every iota of indignant outrage that he expected would soon darken his host's face.

But Besthoff's expression did not change. "And exactly how," he asked calmly, "do you anticipate this could affect me and mine?"

Jules's jaw dropped, but no words came out. He couldn't believe what he had just heard. Maybe his host's advanced years had left Besthoff with a hearing problem? "Er, Mr. Besthoff, maybe you didn't, y'know, understand what I'm saying. This is some pretty heavy-duty shit I'm talkin' here. I mean, somewhere out there in the darker parts of town, there's Lord-knows-how-many colored vampires who mean to push you an' me out—"

Besthoff stopped Jules's rant with a regal gesture of his hand. "No, Mr. Duchon. They mean to push *you* out."

Jules's mind swirled like the spin cycle on a crapped-out washing machine. Straussman entered the library and set a silver tray holding a carafe of coffee, a sugar bowl, a small pitcher of cream, and a white china cup on the table near Jules's elbow. For want of anything coherent to say, Jules snatched the cup from the butler's fingers, poured himself an overflowing helping of steaming black coffee, and gulped three deep swallows.

The combination of anger and caffeine focused his mind somewhat. "Whadda ya mean," he sputtered, "*me*? You an' me an' everybody else in this fancy palace of yours, we're all in this thing *together*! How much simpler do I hafta make this? We're all *white, Caucasian, pale-skinned* vampires—"

Besthoff stood. "Obviously, Mr. Duchon, there is much you do not understand." He walked toward the door and gestured for Jules to follow. "Come. Let me show you something. Please, bring your coffee with you, if you would like."

Straussman refilled Jules's cup and handed him the saucer to take with him. Cup and saucer clattered noisily in Jules's hands as he followed Besthoff. The butler opened a pair of leaded-glass doors, which sparkled with reflected gaslight, and Besthoff and Jules walked through a topiary garden to a second house. This other structure was much less elaborately embellished than the main house and only a single story, although still quite large.

Besthoff unlocked the front door with a massive iron key. Jules was surprised to enter a long, wide, open ward, lined with four rows of narrow cast-iron beds, which were covered with simple white starched sheets. Nearly all the beds were occupied. Soft grunts, moans, and wordless intonations filled the air as a crew of uniformed aides fed and tended to the prone figures.

"Welcome to our pantry, Mr. Duchon."

Jules downed his last mouthful of coffee. "Your 'pantry'? This place looks like one of Charity Hospital's wards from eighty years ago." He took a closer look at the people lying in the beds closest to him. Their eyes seemed too small and too widely spaced. Their arms and fingers were stunted, and their expressions were unfocused and oddly cowlike. "Who are all these people?"

"The assistants you see are all members of our household. With the exception of a few founding fathers, all who live here take their turns tending to the livestock."

"Livestock? What? You mean the retards?"

Besthoff smiled. "The 'retards,' as you so charmingly put it, are the descendants of the inmates of an imbeciles' hospital run by an obscure, impoverished order of French nuns. In 1873 the order was disbanded by Rome, and the sisters were faced with the morally devastating situation of having to turn their helpless charges out into the streets. Fortunately, Mr. Krauss, Mr. Katz, and I took heed of their plight. Never ones to turn our backs on opportunity, we offered to take over the care and housing of the imbeciles, at no charge to the Church or state. The imbeciles have been marvelously docile and tractable creatures. We've bred six generations of them since we took over their care."

It took a few seconds for the full implications to sink in for Jules. As his eyes adjusted to the dim lighting, he recognized the blood extraction equipment standing by several of the beds on the far side of the room. "You mean to tell me . . . you breed them for their *blood*?"

"Of course. Why else would we house and feed more than two hundred imbeciles? We carefully control their diets, feeding them the proper nutrients to ensure that their blood is well balanced and healthful. Thus, the blood that we consume is considerably superior to that obtained from random victims. Especially those from the New Orleans area." He glanced condescendingly at Jules's more-than-ample gut and wryly smiled.

Jules was too occupied with conflicting emotions of revulsion, jealousy, and grudging admiration to realize that he'd just been slighted. Two hundred imbeciles—how many gallons of blood did that equate to in a year? He tried to do the math in his head, but the numbers overwhelmed him. "Sweet Lord almighty—what a setup you've got here!"

Besthoff smiled again. "I thought you might think so. Perhaps now you understand why we need not bother ourselves with the affairs of free-range vampires such as yourself. We of the High Krewe of Vlad Tepes evolved beyond the hunting-and-gathering stage well over a century ago."

Straussman appeared at Jules's elbow to retrieve the cup and saucer, and the rotund vampire was quickly and efficiently shown to the front gate.

FOUR

The bum's rush. They gave me the bum's rush, just like Maureen said they would.

Jules forced himself to open his eyes. He'd stewed and fumed in his coffin long enough. Long enough to develop a painful crick in his neck. Much as he hated to admit it, his coffin was getting too small for him again. He'd been putting off that inevitable trip to the lumberyard as long as he possibly could, but it was as plain as the belly overhanging his belt that he couldn't procrastinate any longer. Hell. One more reason to go on a damn diet.

Jules pushed open the hinged lid on his coffin and sat up. He grabbed hold of the wrought-iron clasps he'd bolted onto the adjacent wall and pulled himself out of the box, which was almost as wide as it was long. He brushed the clumpy earth off his flannel pajamas, trying to make sure most of it landed back in the coffin. Sweeping dirt up off his basement floor was a task he disliked almost as much as building new coffins.

He glanced at his watch. Nine thirty-nine P.M. He'd wasted almost an hour of darkness with his stewing. But he just couldn't get over it. Those stuck-up *bastards*! In their own way, they were just as bad as Malice X was. Looking out for nobody but themselves, not giving a shit what happened to the rest of the bloodsucking fraternity. They'd landed their fancy house and their hundreds of retarded blood-cows, so they felt perfectly at ease letting their less well-off inner-city cousin twist in the wind.

So he was on his own. If he couldn't get the High Krewe to lower the hammer on Malice X, then he'd just have to do his best to round up some white victims, inconvenient as that might be. Maybe it was for the best. The upside of this regrettable turn of events was that the average white kill in New Orleans was way lower in fat than the average black kill. And if Jules played his cards right, maybe he could accelerate his weight loss by harvesting some *extremely* low-fat white victims.

It'd be a few hours yet before his friend Erato would make his nightly appearance at the Trolley Stop Café; Jules planned to hit him up for information on health-related conventions coming to town. That left Jules time to do some work on the Caddy, maybe even listen to a little music, before heading out.

He walked past his woodworking machinery to the back of his base-ment, which was actually the windowless ground floor of his house, then laboriously climbed the stairs to the main story. He walked across his checkerboard-tile kitchen and descended a separate set of stairs to his garage. He'd had the garage added on to the house in the early 1960s, after his mother had passed on to her heavenly reward. He yanked the frayed bit of rope that clicked on the ceiling bulb. A quarter of the garage was filled to overflowing with five decades' worth of tools, auto supplies, and broken hi-fi sets that he'd never gotten around to fixing, plus bits and pieces of old coffins. The rest of the garage was filled with the Cadillac.

He hadn't messed around with his jury-rigged gas injection system in four years, not since he'd yanked the components out of the Caddy following his initial debacle. *Well, if George Washington had stopped tryin' after Valley Forge, we'd all be livin' in the United States of Canada.*

He opened the Caddy's passenger-side rear door as far as it would go. Then he slid down from its place on a shelf a long, thick piece of Plexi-glas, specially fitted to divide the cab's interior into separate passenger and driver compartments. Jules had purchased the divider five years ago, after a spate of cabdriver murders had prompted the city's Taxi Bureau to offer the protective shields to drivers at an enticing discount.

His original conception had been good, Jules reminded himself as he crawled into the Caddy's backseat and pulled the Plexiglas divider in behind him. What had ruined his plan had been his failure to pay attention to the little details. He reached through the open window and grabbed a socket wrench and a Ziploc bag full of bolts. Then, grunting with exertion, he lifted the shield into place and partially screwed in the first two retaining bolts. Five minutes later, the shield was secure. But not snug. Not quite.

Jules inserted the tip of his index finger between the top edge of the Plexiglas and his cab's head liner. That quarter-inch gap had been enough to royally screw his plans the last time. Enough to almost make him total the Caddy. The memory made him shiver. He wouldn't make the same fuckup again; he'd be sure to putty the gap this time.

Jules clambered out and opened his trunk. He leaned inside with a flashlight and carefully examined the rubber gas-feed lines that snaked from the rear right corner of the trunk through holes drilled into the passenger compartment, connecting with spray nozzles hidden inside the rear speaker housings. The hoses looked to be in good shape, with no visible cracks or kinks. But Jules would be certain to test them before he took his knockout system back out into the field. He glanced over at the dusty red canisters of laughing gas, purchased from Tiny Idaho, a local hippy anarchist, that were lying in a corner of the garage. Maybe he could get another use out of them? How long did laughing gas stay good? Jules had no idea. He'd just have to test the stuff before heading out on the hunt.

Jules glanced at his watch again. Ten twenty-three. He had another hour to kill before heading over to the Trolley Stop. Good. His visit to Bamboo Road the night before had left him off-kilter, so a little cultural relaxation would do him a world of good.

First, he'd treat himself to a little snack. All that exertion with the car had perked his appetite. He climbed up the stairs to the kitchen, opened the refrigerator (one of his mother's last purchases before she'd been loosened from her earthly shackles), and took out one of the jars of blood from two nights ago. He unscrewed the cap and sniffed the contents. *Hrmmm.* Already, the blood had lost much of its freshness. He'd have three days, maybe four, before it'd be undrinkable and he'd have to pitch whatever was left. Erato'd better have a juicy tip to give him tonight. He took a swig of blood, then rescrewed the top and put the jar back in the fridge. Jules swished it around the back of his mouth before swallowing it; actually, it wasn't all that bad. His biggest problem was that he'd let his standards get too high.

In the living room, Jules perused his collection of classic, original jazz pressings, most purchased during his first two decades as a vampire. Following a few minutes of delicious indecision, he selected a thick, heavy, seventy-eight-rpm record and arranged it carefully on his Victrola. As soon as the worn stylus touched the venerable platter, the warm, rich tones of Bix Beiderbecke's Jazz Wolverines emerged from the gramophone's lacquered horn. Jules didn't play his original records much anymore; he usually listened to reel-to-reel or cassette tapes he'd made, rather than subjecting his irreplaceable collector's items to more wear. But sometimes only the first-generation recording, playing on the equipment it'd been made for, would do.

Now for some appropriate reading material. In his mother's old sewing room, long ago converted into his library, Jules breathed in the rich, glorious odor of decaying pulp, a bouquet he'd always associated with immeasurable pleasure. Three walls were lined entirely with hundreds of adventure, mystery, and horror pulp magazines dating back to the Great Depression, and thick stacks of comic books from the war years. As a young vampire, Jules had thrilled to the nocturnal adventures of the Shadow, Chandu the Magician, and the Spider. Once comic books began displacing the pulps, Jules quickly discovered a strong affinity for Bob Kane's Batman. Better still were Captain America Comics, which usually featured great gobs of vampires, even if they were invariably portrayed as evil Japs or Nazis. Jules had actually written a long letter to the editors at Timely Publications concerning that subject. He suggested that, since the Axis seemed to have an unlimited supply of vampires to fight on their side, surely the United States should have its own vampires, too. Wasn't it unrealistically one-sided to portray all the vampires in the world as evil Fascists? Shouldn't Captain America occasionally team with a heroic American, Canadian, or British vampire, one eager to sink his fangs deep into Hitler's repulsive neck? Jules never received a reply to his letter, and he'd been bitterly disappointed when the editors neglected to print it on the "Captain America's Fan Mail" page.

The whole notion of a boy sidekick had come to him from the comics. Captain America and Bucky. Batman and Robin. The Sandman and Sandy. The Hooded Terror and . . . Doodlebug.

Doodlebug. Rory "Doodlebug" Richelieu. Hard as Jules tried to forget him, the memory of his ex-sidekick wouldn't fade.

When Pearl Harbor was bombed and Jules heard President Roosevelt's stirring declaration of war on the radio, the young vampire had felt a powerful urge to serve his country. Only the thought of having to submit to an army physical had kept him away from the local recruiting office; what the army physicians would have made of his room-temperature thermometer reading and his fatal vulnerability to sunlight could only be conjectured.

He nursed his frustration at his inability to serve with a renewed plunge into the escapism of comic books. Happily, he discovered that most of the costumed adventure heroes had also stayed off the troopships, opting to remain behind and fight fifth-column saboteurs on the home front. Striking terror in the hearts of Ratzi spies seeking to blow up the landing craft factory on Bayou St. John—now *there* was a job Jules could sink his teeth into. And of course, every masked mystery man worth his salt needed a teen sidekick. So Jules Duchon, the Hooded Terror, hadn't been without one for long.

How many weeks had he haunted Bywater's movie houses, ball fields, and drugstore soda counters, searching for exactly the right kid? And out of hundreds of possible candidates, what had made him pick Rory "Doodlebug" Richelieu?

Maybe it'd been because the kid had always been by himself, hanging out at the soda counter next to the neighborhood newsstand. A kid without any friends would have fewer people missing him and looking for him. Maybe it was because Rory had seemed to like the same things Jules liked. The kid'd always had his nose in a mystery pulp or comic book; either that or he was sketching outlandishly costumed adventure characters in the margins of his Holy Cross School writing pad. Heck, maybe Jules picked him because Rory hadn't instinctively shied away from the vampire the way so many of the other kids did.

So Jules had followed Rory outside one November night in 1942, when the evening air was still unseasonably warm and smelled of the river, and Press Street echoed with the Klaxons of freighters entering the Industrial Canal. And there, in front of the darkened newsstand, he'd asked the boy:

"Hey kid, do you wanna be stronger than ten grown men put together?

"You wanna be able to change into a bat whenever you damn well feel like it?

"You wanna send all the Ratzis you can get your hands on to hell?"

He'd saved the best for last—

"You wanna be around forever?"

And the kid had said yes. Yes to all of it, without a second's hesitation.

Doodlebug had made a good little vampire. He'd hardly missed sunlight at all, or his foster parents, or the nuns at Holy Cross School. He'd been a damn good sidekick, too—at least for a while. Always good company, quick with a funny quip, a helpful suggestion, or a belly-warming cup of coffee. Having him around had made the long nights of patrolling the waterfront factories fun.

The costume and secret identity thing had been icing on the cake. Doodlebug had loved dressing up. Loved it way, *way* too much, as it turned out. And that had been, ultimately, what blew their partnership apart. Blew it apart far more decisively than any Nazi grenade ever could.

The sound of the gramophone's needle scraping against the record's hub interrupted Jules's remembrances. The grandfather clock by the Victrola indicated it was a quarter past eleven. Time to get a move on.

Before getting into his car, he paused a few seconds, as he usually did, to admire his house, his street, and the levee, all glowing peacefully in the moonlight. Despite all its changes over the years, the neighborhood couldn't be better suited for him if he'd designed it himself. Jules smiled. He couldn't imagine ever living anywhere else.

◆

The tiny front and back parking lots of the Trolley Stop Café were packed with taxis and police cruisers—mammoth Crown Victorias, Caprices, and Roadmasters that sprawled across the universally ignored yellow divider lines onto the sidewalks. Jules circled the block, then found an open spot on St. Charles Avenue and pulled in. The all-night breakfast joint was on a stretch of the avenue that had seen its ups and downs. Swank when first developed, the neighborhood had managed to stay upscale through the Depression and two World Wars, but then had gone precipitously downhill in the 1970s. Now, however, it looked to be coming back up. *Stick around long enough,* Jules thought to himself, *and you see everything come back round again.*

The Trolley Stop itself was a converted gas station, made to vaguely resemble a St. Charles streetcar by an application of kelly-green paint and the addition of wooden cutouts of a Victorian streetcar conductor and riders, dressed in their Sunday going-to-church finery. Jules preferred the less touristy atmosphere at the St. Charles Tavern, another twenty-four-hour dive down the street. But when the overwhelming majority of cops and taxi drivers had transferred their allegiance to the Trolley Stop right after the new place had opened, Jules, grumbling, had felt he'd no other choice but to go along with his pals. Besides, he had to admit that the coffee *was* fresher at the Trolley Stop.

Before stepping inside, Jules checked the parking lot for Erato's cab. Sure enough, there it was—a Lincoln Town Car painted the unmistakable green, gold, and purple livery of the Napoleon Taxi Co. Erato hadn't been his best pal for that long—only the past fifteen years or so—but Jules felt closer to him than any human friend he'd ever had. It was kind of weird, given Jules's recent circumstances, that his best human pal ever, and the man he was now seeking out for advice, happened to be a black man. The more he thought about it, the more the injustice of Malice X's threats rankled. Of all the white vampires out there, why pick on *him*, Jules Duchon? Jules had always been decent to black folks, even back during the old Jim Crow days. Heck, nearly all the musicians on his most-admired list were black guys from New Orleans.

He pushed his musings aside and entered the restaurant. The cab-drivers had staked out their usual territory: they were lined up on the closely spaced stools fronting a long wooden bar adjacent to the cash register and the men's room, sipping from cups of dark, aromatic coffee. Some of them scraped the last few sticky granules of grits off the bottoms of greasy plates, while others snatched quick glances at the counter lady's heart-shaped ass in the full-length mirror behind the liquor bottles. That was one thing Jules *really* disliked about the Trolley Stop—having to deal with that damn mirror. Luckily for him, at each end of the bar was a stool that faced oak paneling instead of silvered glass. Unluckily for him, both stools were currently occupied. However, one of the corner occupants was Erato himself.

John Xavier Erato was a head shorter than Jules, but just as wide across the shoulders. Thirty years ago he'd been a star varsity wrestler at Alcee Fortier High School. He'd won a record number of matches, despite a lazy eye that would concentrate more on the girls in the bleachers than the task at hand. But twenty-five years of sitting in a cab ten hours a night had grafted a generous middle-aged spread onto his once taut abdomen. The one-eighth Natchez Indian ancestry he always boasted of was evident in his skin's reddish brown tint and the slightly Asiatic cast of his eyes. His shiny scalp was crowned by a still-credible thicket of dyed and processed curls.

Jules sidled up behind him. Then, in his best George Raft whisper, he hissed into Erato's ear, "Hey, pal, I hope the only reason your ass is on that seat is to warm it up for *me*."

Erato half choked on a mouthful of red beans, then recovered enough to glance over his right shoulder, wiping bean flecks from his chin with his napkin. The anger in his eyes faded when he saw who it was.

"Hey, hey, look what just crawled in! Jules Duch-bag, king of the gypsy cabdrivers hisself!" Erato tossed his napkin onto his plate and turned to the man sitting next to him, a wispy-haired, jowly driver dressed in a shapeless plaid jacket. "Hey, Conrad, push on over, will you? My man Duch-bag needs an end seat, or else he stands around and makes your skin crawl 'til you get your ass off his fuckin' stool."

The other driver's face puckered into a scowl, but he pushed his plate and coffee cup to his left and moved over. Erato then slid gracefully from the end stool onto the stool Conrad had vacated. He glanced to his right as Jules maneuvered into the space between the end stool and the bar and awkwardly settled his rump onto the round, red vinyl cushion.

"Man, you hurtin' my eyes again!" Erato pulled a pair of sunglasses out of his shirt pocket with a flourish. "You get any whiter, you gonna make me go blind, man!"

Jules smoothed the edges of his place mat and straightened the utensils the counter lady set down in front of him. "Yeah, and if you get any blacker, Community Coffee's gonna grind your ass up and stick it in one a their cans."

"Ouch! So where you been hiding yourself these past few weeks? I was beginning to think you'd up and left town."

Jules signaled the counter lady for a cup of java. "Been busy. Trying to get my life in order, y'know?"

"Oh, I hear what you sayin'. You live and work around these parts, things is *bound* to get messy now and then."

"Buddy, *messy* is too piddly a word for the fix I'm findin' myself in. To cut to the chase, I'm hopin' you can maybe drop me a good lead. You're always connected to what's goin' on around town."

Erato nodded sagely. "Pal, you can count on it. Whatever you need. In our line a work, you gotta *give* good tips to *get* good tips. What kinda info you need?"

Jules took a sip of coffee. "Business has been shit lately. All I'm getting is these little bumfuck fares that barely pay my gas money. I need an angle."

"How 'bout airport fares? That's a dime clear each way, at least."

Jules frowned. "You know how hard it is for an independent to land any airport gigs. To grease all the palms I'd have to grease, I'd have to mortgage my goddamn house."

"Man, haven't I been tellin' you for *years* to leave that gypsy shit behind? Join Napoleon Cab already! Management's decent. They been treatin' me all right goin' on ten years now."

Jules pushed his empty coffee cup in the counter lady's general direction. "We been through this already. A hundred times now. I can't be workin' for no boss but myself. I got special needs."

"Yeah—like keepin' that lazy ass a yours in bed all day. So, Mr. Special Needs, what kinda angle you lookin' for?"

Jules tried to catch the counter lady's eye, but his curt little wave overshot the mark. A woman sitting by herself at a table across the dining room caught Jules's wave and met his eyes with her own. A *spectacular* woman. How could he have failed to notice her when he'd first walked in? She was like a pre-Marilyn Norma Jean, only fifteen dress sizes bigger. Even from the far end of the dining room Jules could see she was perfectly proportioned, every supervoluptuous curve precisely sculpted to awaken the long-dormant beast that slumbered within his loins.

"Hey, Jules? Mission Control to Spaceman Jules. I was askin', what kinda angle you lookin' for, anyway?"

Jules forced himself to refocus on the conversation. "Uh. Yeah. Here's what I'm lookin' for, see. Health nuts. You know the kind. Joggers. Bike riders. Those wackos that swim the Gulf of Mexico and then box fifteen rounds dripping wet. I wanna be the official driver for all the health nuts that come to New Orleans."

Erato waited for Jules to continue, hanging expectantly for a punch line of some kind. But his large companion looked perfectly serious. "Uh, I don't get it."

"Think, Erato! Think! You're some runner in for a marathon runners' convention in the Big Easy. You're booked in one of those swanky hotels downtown. You got a big race comin' up next week, after your convention, so you want to stay in shape. You can't be scarfin' down all that greasy andouille shit they serve up in the Quarter. You gotta find some healthy chow. But the few healthy restaurants this town's got are miles from your hotel, in neighborhoods you never heard of. What are you gonna do? Save a few bucks by eatin' local and pack on ten pounds?

You're screwed. You got no choice but to open up the wallet and let your friendly, know-it-all cabdriver take you to wherever the alfalfa sprout joints are tucked away."

Erato stared at Jules with new respect. "Y'know, you ain't half as dumb as you walk in here lookin'."

Jules grinned. "Good thing, huh? So, you heard of any health-nut-type conventions around town?"

Erato rested his stubbly chin on a large, callused fist. His eyes narrowed to dark slits as he accessed his formidable data bank of hearsay, newspaper stories, and talk-radio rumors. Then, just as Jules was wondering if he'd fallen asleep, Erato's orbits popped open to their full size. "Yeah. I think I got one for you. There's a convention of river kayakers staying at the Hotel La Boheme, one of them new places on Convention Center Boulevard. If it's nuts you lookin' for, these fellas fit the bill. They's planning to paddle up the Mississippi all the ways to Natchez or thereabouts."

Jules leaned against the bar for support as he backed his rump off the stool. The waitress refused to meet his eye; a second cup of coffee was clearly a lost cause tonight. "Yeah, that's good, that fits the bill. Thanks, Erato. I owe you one. Next bowl of red beans is on me."

Erato leaned closer and grabbed Jules's thick arm. "You in the mood to do me a favor, huh? How about gettin' into a *real* car? When you gonna dump that Caddy a yours for a *Lincoln*? My brother-in-law's in sales at Lamarque Lincoln-Mercury over across the river, in Harvey. He'll set you up in a Town Car—cherry, nice an' pretty—and he'll give you good trade for that hunk a junk a yours, too."

Jules pulled a dollar from his billfold and tossed it onto the bar, figuring that'd leave the waitress a seven-cent tip. "You know when I'll drive a Lincoln? When the Streets Department shells out for a fleet of snow-plows, that's when. Thanks for the tip, Erato. Your taste in transportation stinks, as always. Don't go playing any three-card monte on Bourbon Street, okay?"

"You neither, okay?" Erato's yellow-toothed grin was quickly obscured by the *Times-Picayune* comics section. "Take care, man. And good luck with your angle."

"Thanks, pal."

Jules smiled. His step had a bit of extra spring to it as he turned to leave the diner. Now he had a plan. *Plan your work and work your plan, that's what Mother always said.* Without even thinking about it, he chose a path that led him within a French bread's span of the table occupied by the spectacular woman he'd locked gazes with earlier. He couldn't help but notice what she was eating. She stabbed a stack of chocolate-chip pancakes as tall as her fork, dipping her fire-engine-red fingernails into fluffy protrusions of whipped cream and blueberry syrup each time she buried her utensil in the mountain of fried batter.

Jules had never seen anyone like her. Not in the flesh, anyhow. She conjured up memories of the Turkish harem girls in the old French paintings at the New Orleans Museum of Art, where Jules's mother had taken her young son for cultural outings. Her blond hair was like a movie star's, seductively framing her round, beautiful face. As she carefully raised a wedge of pancake, syrup, and cream to her full lips, touching the white cream with the tip of her tongue before plunging the sweet mass into her mouth, the ceiling lights glinted off the yellow down on her expansive arm; it looked as if she were wearing a sheer golden negligee.

Midchew, she raised her eyes slowly to Jules's. And winked.

Jules blushed as vividly as Maureen had the night before. During the ride home and for hours afterward, his pants felt even more uncomfortably tight than normal.

♠

The next evening, Jules pulled his Caddy into the taxi line in front of the Hotel La Boheme barely half an hour after the sun had set. He hadn't wanted to miss the dinner hour—either the conventioneers' or his own. His hunger had returned with a vengeance. The last few bottles of his reserve blood had gone stale, two days earlier than their estimated expiration date. *Damn refrigerator's on the rag again. One more goddamn thing I got to spend money on.* He was hungry and nauseated and a little weak, and he was in a testy mood.

Jules's disposition improved greatly when he saw who exited the lobby and walked over to his cab. The man sliding into the Caddy's rear compartment was a little gray at the temples, but his thin T-shirt revealed a rippling set of upper-body muscles. This guy was definitely an athlete. Jules salivated gratefully, anticipating his most healthful meal in years.

He slid open the small window in the plastic shield between the front and rear seats. "You lookin' for dinner, pal? I know where all the healthy spots are. A guy like you wants to eat right, right?"

The fare jutted his sharp-nosed face close to the little window. "You know a good place for grilled fish? Someplace the locals go. I'm sick and tired of tourist traps. Get me the hell away from the French Quarter."

Jules steered onto the Uptown-bound lanes. "Sure! Bucktown's where all the locals go. It's a bit of a haul from here, but the food's worth it."

"Yeah. Whatever; as long as it won't cost me more than fifteen bucks. But don't take the 'scenic route,' okay? Let's just get there. I get any hungrier, the acid's gonna eat a hole through the bottom of my stomach."

Jules stepped on the gas. "I know what you mean, pal. Believe you me, I *know* what you mean."

Jules was accelerating up the Calliope Street I-10 on-ramp when his passenger rapped angrily on the plastic screen. "Hey! It's hotter than hell back here! Doesn't this hack have a/c?"

Uh-oh. Jules hadn't thought of that. The Caddy's only a/c vents were in the dashboard. Closed off behind the plastic shield, the backseat must've felt like a windowless attic. Jules slid the little sliding window open again. "Sorry about that, buddy. Last few years it's been open season on cabbies, so the Taxi Cab Bureau made us install these damn plastic gizmos. Let me crack those back windows for you. The air outside's nice an' natural and all."

Where should he do it? Maybe the levee alongside Bayou St. John? The levee was dark, heavily shadowed by long-limbed oak trees, and the fact that it was a popular lovers' lane meant that cops normally didn't molest people who parked by the murky, slow-flowing waterway. On the other hand, choosing a lovers' lane meant that there would be lovers about. The boat launch at West End? *Nix that; too many fishermen snooping around.* Jules finally decided upon a small playground he knew of behind a boarded-up refreshments stand along a closed-off section of Lakeshore Drive. It was a more open area than he would've preferred, but it should be deserted enough for his purposes.

Jules exited the interstate and headed north toward Lake Pontchartrain. As he turned onto Robert E. Lee Boulevard, he pressed the buttons to close the rear windows. His passenger angrily tapped the plastic shield, but this time Jules kept the window tightly shut.

"Hey! What'd you shut the windows for? You want me to broil back here?"

Jules's only answer was to press a small jury-rigged stud near the Caddy's left wheel well with the toe of his shoe. His sharper-than-human hearing detected the low hiss of gas being released into the rear compartment. Stomping the accelerator to race through a yellow light, Jules glanced in his rearview mirror to see how his fare was reacting.

"Jesus! Something *stinks* back here!" The rapping on the plastic divider escalated to a frenzied pounding. "What the fuck's going on? I'll report you to the city—aha, aha, *a-ha-ha-ha-ha*!"

The crazed laughter was music to Jules's ears. So the laughing gas hadn't been too old after all. Seconds later his passenger slumped unconscious on the backseat, an angelic grin on his previously furious face. Jules depressed the stud on the floor a second time, shutting off the flow. Then he opened the rear windows wide, letting the accumulated gas escape into the humid night. He'd done a very thorough job plugging the open spaces around the shield's edges, but there was no sense in taking chances. There'd be no fucking up tonight, not like the last time.

Jules turned right and headed through an upscale neighborhood adjacent to Lake Pontchartrain and Lakefront Park. He slowed down to five miles per hour below the speed limit, eager not to attract attention. The portion of Lakeshore Drive at the end of Canal Boulevard was a jumble of broken concrete and dried mud, the result of a project meant to repair the roadway from the ravages of erosion but that seemed to only be making matters worse. Jules cut his headlights, relying on the illumination of a half-melted moon and its shimmering reflections off the lake to slowly maneuver around parked backhoes and haphazardly placed barricades.

The short trip along Lakeshore Drive did the Caddy's suspension no good. Jules figured at least one strut had given up the ghost by the time he reached his destination. At least his passenger wasn't awake to complain. He pulled onto the grass and parked between a shuttered refreshment stand and the kiddie play lot behind it, out of sight of the road. His thick fingers fumbled with the key as he shut the ignition. Tonight's meal couldn't come too soon. Jules climbed out of the car. The balmy breeze that caressed the fleshy gap between his shirt and distended trousers did little to calm his nerves. He stared at the Lake Pontchartrain wavelets that stretched to the black horizon. Lately he'd been having all his meals near water. Did that mean anything?

The turmoil at the base of his stomach nearly knocked him off his feet, so he wasted no more time in opening the rear door and crawling inside. Too late, he realized that he'd forgotten to move the front seat forward. His shoulders and arms had fit inside the rear compartment without a problem, but now his belly was wedged tightly between the rear seat back and the plastic shield. Only carnivorous desperation gave him the strength to wiggle forward the last few inches to his sleeping fare's waiting neck. He swore fiercely to himself that this was the last humiliating jam he'd let himself get stuck in. Very soon, he'd parade his body beautiful in front of an appreciative Maureen. Tonight was the first night of the rest of his unlife.

He bit deep, and his mouth quickly filled with warm gore. But the blood didn't taste right, somehow. It wasn't just that it was thin and watery, reminding him of tomato soup from a cheap buffet. The flavor was definitely off, like overchlorinated tap water. Drinking it made his nose tickle. His rear molars felt like they were sprouting flowers. Jules paused in wonder as he sensed soft petals wriggling against his tongue. Delicate roots pushed their way through the roof of his mouth and into his sinuses, like spiders made of water vapor. Strange laughter filled his ears, manic and loopy and off-kilter. Jules didn't like the sound of it. Whoever was laughing seemed to be right in the car with him. *I don't get it,* he wondered. *What the hell is so damn* funny . . .

♦

Jules awoke to the sound of voices.

"You think it's a couple of faggots, maybe?"

"I dunno. Hard to tell. I can't see if the one on the bottom's a man or a woman. Can you?"

"Jesus Christ! Look at that ass! You ever see anything so fat in all your life?"

Jules forced his eyes open. Flashlight beams probed the Caddy's interior. He removed his mouth from his passenger's neck. The man was still breathing, which was a minor miracle, considering the dead weight that had been resting on his chest. Jules tried to back out of the car. He was stuck tight.

Something blunt and hard prodded his posterior. "Okay, buddy, fun time's over. Come on out of there."

The poke of the nightstick really woke Jules up. *Shit!* It was either cops or Levee Board police. In any case, they'd be sure to ask him why he was drinking a drugged tourist's blood in a playground in the middle of a no-trespassing zone. He had to get away. But he was trapped! Like a rat!

This last thought gave Jules an idea. He had to make himself smaller.

He hadn't transformed himself in a very, very long time. But desperate times called for desperate measures. Which form would be best? His wolf-shape would scare the bejesus out of the dicks, but there was an equally good possibility that his canine form would find itself no less wedged in than he was now.

Another poke on his helpless rear region. "Come on, pal. We haven't got all night. Get moving, or we'll pull you out of there."

Maybe mist? He'd ooze out of the Caddy in seconds and quickly lose himself in the grass. But his mind flooded with stark terror as he recalled the last time he'd tried turning himself to mist. He'd become such a dense, heavy fog that he'd instantly settled over a field like dew, and he'd barely been able to reincorporate himself and escape back to his coffin before being evaporated by the rising sun.

"Okay, pal. Time's up." Hands roughly grasped his foot. "Grab the right leg, Chuck. Fatso's decided to be cute."

Just one more choice remained. It was now or never. Jules took a deep breath. He clenched his eyes tightly. He tried to blot out the outside world and concentrate on black, leathery wings, flight, long furry ears—

"What the *hell*—?"

"Some kinda cloud—"

"Hey! Where'd his foot go?"

Jules sensed his body twist and melt. It felt like a cross between a whole-body orgasm and a wisdom tooth extraction—with emphasis on the wisdom tooth extraction. He couldn't let himself get distracted now, or there was no telling *what* he'd end up as. *Wings! Wings! Wings! Wings!*

He was trapped in his own clothing. It was like being smothered by a collapsed tent. He beat his wings furiously—*yes! yes! I've got wings!*—expressing a small mammal's instinctive horror of confinement.

"These pants are empty, Chuck!"

"I can't believe it! I simply can't believe it!"

"Hey! There's something crawling around inside the shirt—"

Flapping blindly, Jules managed to poke his snout through the waist of his shirt. His weak eyes were dazzled by the strobing glare of the flashlights. But he saw an avenue of escape—the Caddy's door was wide open, and between the patrolmen's shocked faces and the car's ceiling were several feet of clear airspace. Jules spread his wings wide, tensed his tiny leg muscles, and sprang off the seat.

He fell in a flapping tangle onto the Caddy's transmission hump, landing on his ears and rolling heavily across the floor and onto the damp grass outside. Dazed and bruised, he scrambled to avoid the patrolmen's dancing feet, dragging his rotund body across the grass with clawed wings.

"Holy Jesus! It's some kinda bat!"

"Bat, hell! It's a nutria with wings!"

How had everything gone so wrong? He had to get away—one solid kick could put him in Charity Hospital for months. Frantically beating his wings against the ground, he scurried in a zigzag toward the trees that shaded the tot lot, barely avoiding a fusillade of blows from steel-toed boots and nightsticks. He reached the gnarled roots of one of the live oaks and dug his claws into the tough bark, pulling himself up the trunk as fast as his wings would take him. His tiny heart beat like a trip-hammer. *What a time for a heart attack! It'd be just my shitty luck!*

"It's crawling up the tree! You want we should go after it?"

"Naw. Don't bother. Just let the goddamn thing go. I'm beginning to think this was some kind of gag."

Jules reached a thick branch about ten feet above the ground and was finally able to rest. He felt nauseated and dizzy. He flopped forward into a hollow in the branch, his flaccid wings drooping over the sides. But his keen ears continued eavesdropping on the conversation below.

"A gag?" the first patrolman said. He was dressed in a gray uniform and wore a gray cap that said CAJUNCOP NEIGHBORHOOD SECURITY. "What do you mean, a gag?"

"You know—a prank. I'll bet it's those damn SAMMYs from Tulane. Those frat brats are always up to no good."

"What, you mean the fat guy was some kind of balloon or something?"

"Could be. I've heard of crazier stuff."

"So who's that guy with the bloody neck who's sleeping in the backseat? He don't look like no frat boy."

"Maybe he's an alumnus. Who knows? I say we call the real cops and let them sort it out."

The first patrolman grunted. "Okay, Chuck. You radio it in. I'll keep an eye on things here. And if that damn bat-thing comes down out of the tree, I'll kick the shit out of it. Maybe it's the frat mascot, huh?"

Jules could do nothing but gather his feeble strength and wait for them to go away. The wait was interminable. His painfully sensitive ears were assaulted by the incessant buzzing of thousands of insects, which gave him a pounding headache. Chuck took the security car, a puke-green Chevy Cavalier, and returned half an hour later with two cups of coffee. The aroma of stale gas station java made Jules's headache even worse. Then an NOPD squad car showed up. The cops managed to re-vive Jules's passenger, who mumbled a few incoherent phrases about rude cabbies and nasty smells before being gently led away to the squad car. One officer gathered the empty clothes from the backseat and removed Jules's wallet from a pant pocket. He also took the Taxi Bureau certificate from its holder on the dashboard.

The bitter coup de grâce came with the arrival of a city tow truck. Jules watched helplessly as his beloved Cadillac was dragged off to the NOPD impoundment lot.

An angry squeak grabbed Jules's attention away from his captive Caddy. A rat, large but barely half Jules's size, glared at him from where the branch met the trunk. Apparently Jules was occupying its nest. In no mood to take shit from anyone anymore, Jules hissed vociferously at the rodent, until it finally realized it was outmatched and ran away.

♦

With a stolen DON'T GIVE UP THE SHIP! flag draped around his ample midsection (he'd pulled it down from a flagpost at the New Orleans Yacht Club), an exhausted, human-shaped Jules dragged himself through the front door of Russell's Marina Grill. A well-coifed young man inter-cepted him before he could cross the foyer.

"Sir! I'm very sorry, sir. We can't serve you inside unless you're wear-ing shoes and a shirt. Would you like to place a take-out order and wait for it on our patio?"

Jules considered asking the greeter if *he'd* like to place an order for a knuckle sandwich, express delivery, but he stopped himself. Instead, he took a deep breath and rearranged the flag around his middle. "Look. I'm not here to eat. I'm a cabby, and I just been robbed. That's why I'm wear-ing this flag instead of a fuckin' Brooks Brothers suit, okay? If you'll be so kind as to spot me thirty-five cents so I can make a call, I'll gladly herd my fares to your fine establishment here for the next year. Deal?"

The young man considered this for a second or two, then dug into his pocket and handed Jules a quarter and a dime. "The pay phone's by the men's room in the back."

"Thanks."

Jules avoided meeting the stares of the paying customers as he made his way to the phone. He clutched the two ends of the flag with his right hand as he lifted the receiver and hugged it awkwardly between his shoulder and chin. One phone call—he had to make it count. He dialed Erato's cell phone number. He was tremendously relieved when his friend's familiar baritone voice answered.

"Yeah? Hello? Who is this?"

"It's Jules. I'm at Russell's by the lakefront. I've gotta ask you to come pick me up."

"Jules? Whassa matter? Your Caddy break down?"

"Caddy got stolen. Everything's gone. Damn robber even took my clothes. I'm standing here talking to you wearing a goddamn flag, if you can picture it."

"A *flag*? I'll be right over. This I gotta see."

Once outside, Jules didn't have to wait long before a familiar tricolor Town Car rounded the corner and pulled into an empty handicapped parking space. Erato put his window down and leaned out, his wandering lazy eye eagerly taking in the spectacle.

"Hey! Who's your tailor, my man? I gotta get *me* a outfit like that!"

"Fuck you, Erato. Thanks for coming so quick."

"You was lucky. I was droppin' a fare only five minutes from here when I got your call. Get your ass in the car, already."

Jules clambered in. He reluctantly admitted to himself that the Lincoln had a nice, spacious rear seat. "Take me straight home," he said in an exhausted, defeated voice. "You know the way."

Erato backed out and headed for West End Boulevard. "What? Don't you want me to take you by the police station first? You've gotta report what happened, man. Give them cops a chance to catch those motherfuckers."

"No. Straight home. I seen enough of cops tonight to last me a lifetime."

They took the interstate until they reached Esplanade Avenue. They drove along the grand, crumbling old Creole boulevard, following the edge of the French Quarter until they reached Elysian Fields. Jules's depressed musings were interrupted by a sudden exclamation from Erato. "Hey!" His friend dug through a pile of cassettes in an open shoe box on his front seat. "I got somethin' here that'll cheer you right up. This tape's by a new blues guy named Mem Shannon. He's a cabby, just like us. It's called *A Cab Driver's Blues*. Is that perfect, or what? Take it. It'll do your sufferin' soul some good, believe me."

Jules examined the cassette. Its cover pictured a handsome, somewhat heavyset young black man, dressed in a cabby's uniform, leaning against a dark gold taxi. "Aww, Erato, I can't take this offa your hands. It's brand new. Musta cost you fifteen bucks or so." He tried handing it back.

Erato wouldn't take it. "No, you keep it, man. Right now, you need it lots more than I do. I'll just pick myself up another copy."

A few minutes later they turned onto Montegut Street. The street, with its weed-strewn lots and graffiti-covered, termite-eaten shotgun houses, looked even more desolate than usual. On a normal night Jules would feel happy and secure driving through his old, familiar neighborhood. But tonight he felt scared, vulnerable, and alone.

They pulled up the narrow concrete driveway in front of Jules's garage. Erato put his transmission in park and leaned back over his seat. His face was creased with concern. "You gonna be okay? You want me to come in for a few minutes?"

Jules mustered a smile. "Naww. I'll be fine. Thanks, Erato. Thanks for everything." He patted his friend on the shoulder, then opened the door to get out.

"Well, you need anything, you just call me on my cell phone, okay? Day or night. Hey! How are you set for cash? The Caddy insured? I could, y'know, ask some of the guys down at the Trolley Stop to pitch in. We could get some kinda benefit going. Maybe Mem Shannon would play!"

Jules carefully, respectfully shut the Town Car's rear door. "Don't you worry about me none. I'm flush. Me, I always land on my feet. I'll be in touch, pal." He remembered Maureen's final words from two nights earlier. "Hey, you watch your ass, okay? Don't let no shitheads take *your* cab. 'Cause I won't be able to come rescue you, least not for a while."

Erato smiled. "Sho 'nuf! God bless, Jules. You be good, you hear? And let me know what you think of that tape."

Jules stood and waved as Erato backed out of his driveway. He walked to the curb and watched the massive Lincoln disappear down Montegut Street. Only when the cab was out of sight did he open his front door, still not repaired from Malice X's invasion, and go inside.

His living room was hot, musty, and silent. He turned on a lamp. Its weak bulb cast long, ominous shadows over the room. As if on cue, his stomach emitted a tremulous moan. He stumbled to the couch and collapsed.

What to do now? He stared at his alabaster belly, which rose from the couch like a mountain of refined flour. Its lower extremities pulsed and jiggled as his gut sent out distress signals. Maybe the solution to his weight problem was to crawl into his coffin and stay there until he either wasted away to nothing or his gut, in desperation, devoured the rest of him.

His eyes fell upon his mother's portrait on the mantelpiece. He tried looking away, but her stern, Victorian gaze held him fast. *Son, I didn't carry you in my belly for nine months, nourish you from my breast for another thirty-six, and watch over you until the day I died so that you could be a* quitter.

For the second time in as many nights, Jules felt himself blush from head to toe. He forced himself to sit up. Then he picked up the nautical flag from where he'd dropped it on the floor. He read the embroidered inscription again. DON'T GIVE UP THE SHIP!

Jules climbed the stairs to his bedroom, pulled on a pair of briefs, and selected his best trousers, shirt, and jacket from his closet. Then he tied a bright yellow-and-green polka-dot necktie around his collar. He was many things, a lot of them no good. But he was no quitter.

Out on Montegut Street, he began singing French-Irish drinking songs in a slurred tenor. He affected an inebriated, stumbling gait; given his many infirmities, this wasn't hard at all. After a few minutes of weaving along the middle of the empty street, he detected hurried footsteps coming toward him from a side alleyway. He stopped singing.

An unpleasant voice broke the stillness. "Hey, Slick! Shoney's Big Boy! Wait up! I got to talk wit' you!"

Ah, music to his ears. He turned and zigzagged unsteadily toward the dark alley. The black man approaching him carried a switchblade in one hand, and what looked to be a bag of fried pork rinds in the other. He was shirtless, his ebony skin glistening with sweat. Multiple rolls of fat hung over his faded jeans. Jules's saliva glands went into overdrive.

Come to Papa, Jules thought. *Fuck the goddamn diet. And while I'm at it, fuck Malice X, too.*

Laissez les bons temps rouler!

Let the good times roll!

At last, the night was kind to him. But for Jules Duchon, the good times would not roll for long.

FIVE

The Third District police station on Moss Avenue didn't look like a government building at all. From the outside, the spacious complex, with its horse stables and neatly parked rows of large white sedans, looked like an upscale jockey club. Several horses whinnied nervously from inside the dark stables as Jules crunched across the gravel parking lot.

He rubbed his aching posterior as he ruefully remembered his public bus ride from his neighborhood to the station, along Esplanade Avenue. He hadn't been on a public bus in more than thirty years, and this ride had reminded him why; aside from being way too cramped for a person of his magnitude, the stale air inside had smelled of rancid chicken grease and the bodily odors of dozens of people who'd been standing in ninety-degree heat waiting all day for buses. *Erato's cab would've been* way *more comfortable,* Jules thought as he approached the front entrance. *But some things you just can't drag your buddies into. And stealing my stuff back from the New Orleans Police Department is definitely one of those things.*

Jules wondered what his mother would think of him now—her only son, sneaking into a police station to commit a felony. Sure, he'd killed plenty of folks, but he never thought of that as a *crime*—that had been *eating*. Even his mother had accepted this; or she'd seemed to, anyway. It had been one of those things they'd never gotten around to talking about. During his early years as a vampire, whenever Jules had tried to relate to her the guilt his feedings were causing him, she would quickly turn on the radio, and instead of talking they'd listen to the New York Philharmonic or *Fibber McGee and Molly*.

Inside, the station looked like most other city government buildings, except maybe a little cleaner. There were the downscale bureaucratic accents Jules remembered well from his nearly thirty years in the coroner's office—faded, ugly wallpaper; framed photos of the mayor; and fluorescent lights that hummed annoyingly and made everyone look ghoulish (not just Jules, who looked that way in any kind of light).

Jules approached the front desk and coughed. The phlegmy sound made the petite desk clerk look up from the New Orleans Fairgrounds racing form she was studying. Jules was surprised; not that a city employee would be studying a racing form during work hours, but horse-racing season had been over since the spring. He watched her eyes widen for an instant as she took him in. But only an instant; her expression quickly reverted to studied boredom. "Yes? Can I help you?"

"Yeah. I got a call from somebody in your, oh, what's it called, uh— y'know, where the cops store the stuff they grab from criminals?"

"Evidence and Recovered Items?"

"Yeah. That's it. They asked me to come in and pick up some stuff of mine that got stolen."

"Okay. You'll need to sign in on this list here. And you'll need to wear this visitor's badge. Also, you're gonna need to show some ID before Marvis will release your stuff to you."

"Yeah, but what if what I'm here to pick up happens to *be* my ID? Those thieves left me naked as the day I came into the world. I got a friend who'll vouch for me. His cell phone number's here in my pocket."

The clerk looked infinitely disinterested. "Whatever. Work it out with Marvis." She slid a clipboard across the desk.

Jules signed his illegible scrawl at the top of the paper, trying to ignore the coffee-induced rumblings in the pit of his stomach. He clipped the bright pink badge to his shirt pocket. "Thanks. So where do I need to go?"

"Down that hallway there. Fifth door on your left. Just past the ladies' room." Before Jules could even manage to maneuver himself through the gateway by her desk, the clerk had returned to studying her racing form.

Jules followed her directions, hoping he wouldn't accidentally walk into the ladies' room. The room he entered, marked EVIDENCE, was much larger than he'd expected. The air inside smelled of dust, machine oil, sweat-stained leather, and dried herbs. Except for a desk and a narrow walkway by the door, nearly all of the space was taken up by row after row of metal utility shelves. The floor and shelves were packed with bicycles, chrome-plated pistols, purses of all shapes and colors, cemetery statuary, wrought-iron gateposts, sawed-off shotguns, car stereos, television sets, computers, Mac-10 machine pistols, a grenade launcher, and the cleanly severed marble head of Jefferson Davis. It looked like an unlikely hybrid of a Royal Street antiques boutique and a St. Claude Avenue pawnshop.

Jules loudly cleared his throat and waited for the officer in charge to appear. A minute later he heard a loud rustling from the back of the room, and Sergeant Marvis Mancuso, a short, stocky, balding man who looked to be on the cusp of retirement, carefully picked his way through the tangle. " 'Evening! What can I do for you?"

Jules was disappointed. He'd halfway been hoping that Mancuso would be familiar to him, one of the cops who used to drop bodies off at the morgue. It would've made things easier. But he'd never seen Mancuso before. Now he'd have to rely entirely on his wits and on his long-untried powers of vampiric hypnosis. The thought made Jules's stomach turn over like the contents of a cement mixer.

Jules leaned across the desk, putting his face as close to Mancuso's as possible. "Me? I'm here to pick up my things. Wallet, shoes, shirt, belt, pants. The works."

The officer stepped back from the desk to avoid Jules's coffee breath. "Do you have your Form 108-B?"

"Form 108-B?"

"You would've received it in the mail. It lists what we recovered of yours. I'll need to see that and a photo ID, please."

How could he bullshit his way through this? Jules tried desperately to think, but his mind was blank as tapioca. This was the moment he'd been dreading all night. It was now or never. He took a deep breath, then stared piercingly into Mancuso's watery gray eyes.

"My name is Jules Duchon. Your will is my will. You will get my clothes, my wallet, and my taxi certificate and bring them to me. Then you will forget you ever saw me."

Mancuso looked confused. His cheeks and eyebrows twitched, like he was lost in the middle of a bad first-day-of-school dream where everyone else was dressed in freshly ironed uniforms and he was naked. Then his eyes refocused on Jules. "Honey," he stammered. "Honey, look, I'm sorry, okay? I'll paint the garage next weekend. The Saints are playing the Raiders today. One more win and they could win their division."

Jules sighed. He was obviously rusty. He redoubled his concentration and spoke even more slowly, sounding like a seventy-eight record playing at thirty-three rpm. "My name is Jules Duchon. You will turn around and bring me my clothes and all my things. After I leave, you will forget I was ever here."

Mancuso was as glassy-eyed as Christine Gordon in *I Walked with a Zombie*. "Bring you—your things . . ."

"Yeah. That's right. Bring me my things."

A cloud lifted from Mancuso's face. He smiled broadly at Jules, a kindly twinkle lighting up his eyes. He turned and walked into one of the narrow, cluttered aisles. Jules waited expectantly. *Hey*, he thought, *that wasn't so hard after all. I've still got the touch.*

Mancuso returned with a small pink bicycle, training wheels still attached. He held it by its banana seat and tasseled handlebars and rolled it through the gate. "Here you go, sweetheart," the officer said, his voice dripping with honey. "We caught the bad man who took this away from you. He's in a place where he won't be scaring any pretty little girls anymore, okay?"

Jules turned red. *Okay, the hypnosis definitely needs work.* "Aww, fuck this already," he muttered half under his breath. "Mancuso, you stay here. Don't move a muscle. I'll get my shit myself."

The sight of Jules wiggling through the gate roused Mancuso from his trance. "Hey!" he shouted, rubbing his eyes groggily. "You can't go back there! Only authorized personnel are allowed behind the desk!"

Shit! This was exactly the kind of scene Jules had hoped to avoid. Panic-induced spasms surged through his gut. What to do? Mancuso shook off the last of his grogginess and grabbed Jules's arm. The vampire's stomach rumbled like a freight train. Jules locked eyes with Mancuso. One last desperate shot at hypnosis—

The sergeant clutched his belly, a stunned, pained look on his face. "Oh, Jesus—!" His protruding stomach emitted a gurgling rumble, an exact duplicate of the angry noises Jules's gut had been making. He let go of Jules's arm and stumbled backward toward the door. "Jesus Christ! Oh Mama—!" Holding his stomach like it was about to explode, Mancuso bolted out the door. Jules listened to his frantic footsteps echo down the hallway. Then a door slammed. Jules presumed it was the door to the men's room.

That would keep Mancuso plenty busy for the next few minutes, at least. The notion of pushing his way through the tangled thicket of stolen possessions and actually finding his stuff was a daunting one, but Jules had no other choice. He sucked in his stomach and dived in.

Most of the recovered clothing was stored in clear plastic trash bags in the back of the room. Jules examined the endless mounds in disbelief. Then Fortune graced him with a bucktoothed smile. His checkered pants were pinned to a corkboard on the rear wall, spread out like a tablecloth on a clothesline. Someone had attached a sign to the pants. It read, in blue magic marker, HEY MANCUSO, EAT ANY MORE DOUGHNUTS AND YOU'LL END UP WEARING THESE. Sitting on the floor beneath the pants, in an open plastic sack, were the rest of Jules's clothes, his wallet, and, most important, his taxi certificate.

Jules grabbed the sack, yanked his pants off the clipboard, and stuffed pants-sans-sign into the bag. Tucking the bundle under his arm like a football, he hustled his way back to the desk, knocking a few car stereos to the floor and stubbing his toe on Jefferson Davis's chin.

The door burst open just as Jules was wiggling past the desk. Two officers rushed in, a man and a woman, and drew their guns.

"Freeze!" the man ordered, pointing his revolver at Jules's stomach, an irresistible target.

"What the hell's going on here?" his partner said, her eyes flaring as she saw the catastrophe behind Jules. "Mancuso runs past like his ass is on fire, and now Tub-O-Lard thinks he can rip us off like we're some Circle K?"

Jules's intestines turned to squishy ice. There was only one thing to do. The new trick he'd pulled on Mancuso still vibrating in his synapses, Jules stared piercingly at the male cop and summoned the hideous memory of the last time he'd attempted to eat a po' boy. The man belched like a hippo, dropped his gun, doubled over, and rolled on the floor, groaning in agony. Then Jules turned his gaze on the woman, who still pointed her gun at him, although much less confidently than before. He forced himself to mentally relive the obscene torments that final taste of fried shrimp had cost him. The woman ran screaming from the room.

Jules waddled into the hallway as quickly as his bulk would allow. Back at the front desk, the clerk tried to block his exit through the gate.

"Hey! Stop! You can't leave here with that visitor's badge! I've gotta sign you out!" A quick dose of his Diarrhea Stare shut her up fast. If only Maureen could see him in action now!

Outside, Jules sucked in a deep, proud breath. The damp night air smelled like victory. Actually, it smelled like horseshit and a Dumpster stuffed with rotting cardboard boxes, but that was all right. Jules felt good. Fuck that—he felt *great*! He hadn't felt this alive and on top of the world since his war days, when he'd stalked the docks as the Hooded Terror. *Damn! I wish I had my mask and cape on me! I'm a young buck again! Jules Duchon is back! Good as I ever was—ready to take on the whole fuckin' world!*

The wind on his face as he ran along the bayou toward Esplanade felt like soft kisses from every woman who'd ever turned her nose up at him during the past thirty fat years. Jules didn't feel sick at all. His legs were coiled springs. The weakness, the shortness of breath he'd suffered for decades, had fallen away like a pair of soiled underwear he'd kicked off and tossed in the garbage. Even his inconsolable stomach had settled down.

When he reached Esplanade, he tried flagging down a taxi. Two empty cabs passed him by, despite his energetic waving. The third didn't get the chance—Jules ran into the road and blocked both narrow lanes, confident he could turn to mist in time if the driver couldn't (or wouldn't) stop short. After a dramatic, screeching skid on bald tires, the cab halted three feet short of Jules's stomach. The driver, an Arab or maybe an Iranian, screamed a long litany of Arabic or Persian curses at Jules, undoubtedly involving various bodily parts of a camel. Jules flung a rear door open and pressed his way into the backseat.

"You stupid fat *ee-di-oot*! You almost make me hit you!"

"Shut up and drive, Ayatollah. I'm a fellow cabby. Show me some respect. I'm not some asshole tourist."

"Where you go, huh?"

"Gimme a second. Just drive toward the French Quarter, okay? I'll tell ya in a minute."

The driver screeched his tires as he accelerated down Esplanade, eager to get Jules to wherever it was Jules was going and get him out of the cab. Jules pondered his options. He was on a roll. Should he go straight to the auto impoundment lot and steal back his Cadillac? Only problem was, the lot was sure to be padlocked, and Jules couldn't be certain of smart-talking his way inside. His newfound skill wouldn't get the watchman to unlock the gate. He'd better spend a few days practicing the hypnosis. His Caddy wouldn't be going anywhere.

"Head for Montegut Street," Jules said.

They were turning off Esplanade onto North Rampart Street when a pair of speeding fire trucks ran the light, scattering a group of tourists and forcing the driver to pull halfway onto the sidewalk to avoid getting clipped. "Whoa! Son-of-bitch! Must be some mighty big fire they chasing after, you think?"

Jules watched the fire trucks disappear down North Rampart, turning onto St. Claude Avenue with sirens blaring. "Naww. It's probably the mayor's fuckin' cat stuck up a tree."

The sense of triumph he'd felt so strongly only ten minutes ago was already beginning to fade. Sure, he'd gotten his pants and taxi certificate back from the cops. But now what? His weight-loss plans had crashed and burned like the bloated carcass of the *Hindenburg*. Fanging white victims was as hard as it ever was. His damn laughing-gas setup was better at getting Jules caught than it was at catching him a meal. And there was still that fucking Malice X to consider.

Malice X. Just thinking the hated name was enough to make the last droplets of Jules's good mood evaporate. Him and his army. Shit. Who's to say the bastard even *had* an army? It could be all bluff. A pile of bullshit. He said he'd been having Jules followed, right? He'd bragged about knowing of Bessie, Jules's "little hot chocolate snack" from last week. Well, learning about that certainly didn't take a private army. Malice X could've hired some low-rent shamus to follow Jules around for a few days, just to make it seem like he had eyes everywhere.

This line of thinking began raising Jules's spirits from the mire. New Orleans was a big city. No matter how many rent-a-snoops Malice X hired (and how much money could the shit-nosed little punk have, anyway?), there was no way in hell they could keep Jules under observation all the time. The city was full of tasty black potential victims, more than enough to go around. If Jules wanted to enjoy his share, all he needed to do was be careful and cover his tracks. That's all.

Tasty black victims. The thought was enough to get his mouth watering. Last night's mugger had been scrumptious, almost as delicious as Bessie had been. Blood so rich, so loaded with cholesterol and fatty lipids . . . draining that malevolent lardo, especially after so many days without a fresh kill, had shot Jules to the moon. He chuckled to himself; he'd been like a Bourbon Street drunk after his meal. He couldn't remember walking home again and climbing into his coffin. He couldn't even remember how he'd disposed of the body. The end of last night was a smudged blur, but a damn delicious one.

Jules spotted the entrance to the alleyway where he'd enjoyed last night's meal. The sight made his fuzzy memories come more into focus. What *had* he done with that corpse? Plenty of victims to go around . . . all he needed to do was be careful . . . cover his tracks— *Oh. No.*

He started to sweat. Jules remembered now—he remembered draining his lured-in assailant of blood, then plunging the mugger's own switchblade into the base of his skull (at least he'd been with it enough to do *that*). But the memories got worse. He'd been too satiated, too inebriated to roll the body several blocks into the river. And dragging it to the railroad tracks, waiting for a train to pause, and loading the bloodless corpse into a freight car hadn't even occurred to his foggy brain.

He'd been lazy. Sloppy and lazy. He'd left the body in a corner of the alleyway, covered it with a mildewed awning torn off an abandoned shotgun house, then covered the awning with trash he'd found lying in the gutters. He'd planned to return the next night and properly dispose of the corpse. But by the time he'd woken up earlier tonight, he'd completely forgotten the need to finish cleaning up after himself.

The cabby weaved around a pair of dogs chasing each other across St. Claude Avenue. Jules watched them sniff each other. Dogs. The neighborhood was full of stray dogs. They would've found the body by now. And if dogs had discovered the body, then people wouldn't be far behind. People who might call cops. Cops meant crime reporters. Crime reporters meant newspaper stories, which meant the whole damn city would know. Including Malice X.

They were next to the alleyway now. Maybe he still had a chance to fix his boneheaded mistake. "Hey. Let me off here."

The cabby's dark eyes questioned him from the rearview mirror. "This not Montegut Street."

"I changed my fuckin' mind, okay?"

The cabby jammed on his brakes, screeching the cab to a ragged halt. "This a bad neighborhood, mister. But it your ass, huh?"

Jules threw the man a five-dollar bill from his newly retrieved wallet and stumbled out onto the curb. The cab roared away in a shower of gravel and flattened malt liquor cans. Another fire truck raced past, sirens echoing off clapboard buildings. The sound made Jules's spine quiver.

Heart pounding, Jules entered the alleyway. He didn't have to walk far to confirm his dreaded suspicions.

Shit.

The far end of the alley was roped off with yellow plastic police barriers. The body was gone. Its place on the filthy asphalt was marked with a chalk outline that looked ludicrously like a plump kindergarten child's self-portrait.

Shit, shit, shit!

He had to get home. He had to figure this thing out, figure all the angles. His shirt clung to his fleshy sides like damp toilet paper. Looking down, he saw that his jacket had two huge crescent-shaped maroon stains under its sleeves. He had to have time to think. Was that so much to ask, time to think?

He walked quickly out of the alleyway. Off to the south, in the direction of the river, low clouds reflected a dull orange glow. *(The fire?)* He had to get home. *(Please don't let it be my house.)* Mother would tell him what to do. He'd stand in his living room and stare at her portrait and after a couple of minutes the answers to everything would pop into his head. Mother knew all the angles. She was smart, even smarter than Maureen.

Oh please oh please don't let it be my house.

Sirens pierced the air, growing louder the closer Jules came to the levee. He found himself running. His great belly sloshed up and down like a water bed in an earthquake. The gray sky ahead of him flashed with drifting sparks. Faster. He'd fix it. He'd fix everything. His heart beat like a crazed metronome. Like Gene Krupa's right hand. Like a jackhammer made of scared meat.

He turned the corner onto Montegut Street, wheezing, praying to Varney and Jesus and Moses and Mary and any other deity he could think of that some crackhead had torched the abandoned Wilson place. Or the old Giusseppe house. Or that little shithole of a bar that the cops had closed down four times since last Christmas.

He should've saved the energy. His house and everything in it, including Jules's graffiti- and urine-stained coffin, were engulfed in lurid orange flames.

SIX

"My record collection! My pulps! Aaahhhhhhh!!!"

"Sir, you can't cross the line— Sir! *Hey!* Somebody stop that big lunatic!"

Jules bludgeoned aside a cop and a pair of sooty-faced firemen on his mad charge across the lawn to his front steps. Like a maddened rhino, he was almost impossible to stop once he got up to speed. Belying his bulk, Jules sprang up his front steps in two bounds. He struggled through the wreckage of his front door, smashed in by firemen's axes. He was suddenly caught in the streams of two high-pressure hoses, but the force of the twin torrents only added to his momentum, shoving him through the smoke-blackened doorway like an immense plaid beach ball pummeled by a giant wave.

His sport coat and pants reduced to dripping rags, Jules didn't feel the heat surging through his living room at first. The flames, the smoke, his tearing eyes—none of it seemed real. His sagging couch ignited, and a gust of superheated air slammed the reality of the conflagration in his face. The greedy flames leapt across mildew-stained cushions to the pile of musty afghans his mother had knit over a span of ten thousand radio-filled nights. The old blankets lit up like drought-parched saw grass.

"Jesus *fuckin'* Christ!" Sparks landed on Jules's eyebrows. His nostrils were filled with the stench of his own burning hair. He slapped his fore-head wildly, looking like a clumsy comedian trying out for the role of a fourth Stooge. What to save? What *could* he save? The library was a lost cause. He stumbled across the burning sofa and reached for his gramo-phone, a priceless antique. But as soon as he managed to get a firm grip on its walnut base, the gramophone's horn, made of highly flammable lacquer, lit up like a Roman candle.

"Fuck!" He dropped the gramophone and shoved his burned fingers into his mouth. His records! Maybe he still had a chance to save some of them. Maybe just the most valuable ones—? *Maybe whatever the hell you can get your singed paws on, you stupid fucker. Go!* He dropped to his knees and crawled furiously in the direction of the oak cabinet where he stored his most valuable and rare platters. Armstrong. Teagarden. King Oliver. The black smoke above his head had gotten as thick as blood left out of the refrigerator overnight, and it dropped lower with each passing second. Could vampires asphyxiate? Jules didn't know. He didn't want to find out the hard way.

He was crawling blind, navigating his cluttered living room by a hundred-plus years of memory. His head smashed into something hard but hollow. The cabinet. He pulled the oak doors open and reached in-side. His throbbing fingers flipped sightlessly through endless dozens of LPs. *Not the vinyl! The old stuff! The old stuff!* Which shelf were his oldest platters on? Which side of the cabinet?

His feet and calves felt as if they were in an oven. But at last his fin-gers brushed against the stiff cloth and cardboard casings of his oldest records. As fast as he could manage, he pulled out as many of the thick platters as he could grasp, piling them on the floor near his knees.

"There he is! I see him!"

"Where?"

"Over there, in the corner!"

Firemen! They'd come in after him! Jules began scooping platters into his bearlike paws, but in his mad hurry sent many sliding across the hot floor.

Rubber boots and padded knees shattered eighty-year-old shellac discs as the firemen crawled toward Jules. "What the hell are you up to, buddy?" the lead fireman shouted. "You've got to get the hell outta here!"

"Hey! Look out! Don't step on those platters!" Jules furiously tried gathering up his records. Some were ominously hot to the touch. "Give me a minute, will ya? Can you guys help me grab these things, maybe?"

"We've got a fuckin' nutcase here!" the closest fireman yelled back to his partners. "Grab his arms! We're gonna have to pull him out!"

"No! Wait! I'll go! I'll go!" But already three pairs of strong hands had grabbed him by his arms and were pulling him toward the door, forcing him to spill much of the precious cargo. He stopped fighting the firemen, desperate to save what he still had in his hands. Risking smoke inhalation, he got to his feet and crouched down as low as he could while still moving forward, hugging the remaining platters to his still-damp breast. Tongues of flame licked at his elbows as he pushed his way through the burning velvet shreds of the curtains that had once separated his living room from the entrance foyer.

As his singed shoulders brushed the jagged front door frame, Jules succumbed to the same foolish impulse as Lot's wife and looked back. Illuminated by the garish flames was the portrait of Jules's mother, her stern gaze still fully intact and transfixing him from above the burning mantelpiece.

"Mother!" Despite the ruddiness caused by the fire, Jules's complexion instantly turned three shades whiter than normal. He lunged back into the house, toward the portrait surrounded by flames, but half a dozen powerful hands grabbed him and pulled him outside.

"Noooo! Muhh-thuurrrr!"

But it was too late. Flames blocked the entrance foyer. Part of the ceiling over the living room collapsed, blowing a cloud of plaster dust out the door and into Jules's tearstained face. He'd failed her again. The hot platters slipped from his hands onto the brown grass, but he didn't notice. Some son he was. All he'd been thinking about were his pulp magazines and his old records. He'd forgotten all about his most precious keepsake—of his mother—until it was too late. Too damn late.

A small hand tugged on Jules's damp sleeve. "Hey, mistah?" Jules looked down. A tyke from the neighborhood, maybe five years old, had removed one of Jules's records from its cardboard sleeve. Clasped in the boy's hand, the shellac disc drooped like a charbroiled flapjack. "Hey, mistah? What dis 'posed to be?"

Jules clenched his eyes tightly shut. Maybe a vampire's powers included traveling back in time? He concentrated as hard as he could, imagining his street as a row of newly built, white-painted, gingerbread-trimmed cottages. But as hard as he tried, the stench of burned velvet lingered in his nostrils; a stench as nasty as a vampire left out in the sun.

Sunrise! Jules checked his watch. It was a quarter past eleven. His coffin was a pile of ashes and charred plywood. In barely seven hours, the first rays of daylight would boil the thickly padded flesh from his bones.

Who could help him? A crowd had gathered on the sidewalk. Small cliques of men drank malt liquor from tall, skinny cans and watched the firemen battle the remaining flames, some boisterously pointing out when fresh shoots of flame crackled forth from previously pacified corners of Jules's house. Women hugged babies to their ample breasts and watched their children play with warped records on the dead grass. Some of the faces Jules recognized from the neighborhood. Many were strange to him. Every few seconds another face would turn in his direction. Some eyes regarded him with sympathy. Most were unreadable, contemptuous, or even hostile.

A chill quivered Jules's spine. How many of those onlooking faces belonged to Malice X's spies? Who's to say the black vampire would stop with burning down Jules's house? How many of these "neighborhood folks" were actually enemy vampires, eagerly waiting for the firemen and police to disperse before plunging sharpened stakes into Jules's chest, or severing his head and stuffing his screaming mouth with garlic?

He had to get out. Out of the neighborhood. Out of New Orleans. His whole world had been turned on its head, transformed into an evil, brutal, twisted mirror image of itself. Just days ago, he'd had everything he'd ever wanted. Now he had nothing. Once the proud, skillful hunter, now he found himself the hunted.

Jules pushed his way through the crowd. If he didn't make a break for it now, he'd end up a three-dollar pile of powdered chemicals at dawn for sure. He turned a corner, leaned heavily against a graffitied wall, and checked his wallet. Thirty-seven dollars. That wouldn't take him far. His Hibernia Bank ATM debit card would take him maybe twelve hundred dollars farther. He rifled through the dog-eared business cards stuffed into the pouch behind his dollar bills until he found the one he was looking for: BILLY MAC'S GARAGE AND PRE-OWNED AUTOMOTIVE EMPORIUM— WE STAY OPEN LATE! Billy Mac had been his mechanic for more than twenty years. For almost as long, he'd been haranguing Jules to buy one of his used cars, but Jules had always purchased his chariots from other, more upmarket lots. Tonight, however, Billy Mac was Jules's only possible ticket out of town.

Eleven. I think he stays open 'til eleven. Which means maybe I can catch him before he goes home. The St. Claude Avenue garage was only a few blocks away. Jules picked up his pace. At the corner of Montegut and

North Rampart, a lively crowd loitered on the buckled sidewalk in front of the Beer 'N' Cigs Grocery. Jules picked up snatches of conversation, mostly concerning the big fire. A young woman wearing a pink shower cap talked excitedly into a dilapidated pay phone. "I saw the whole thing, yeah! This long-ass limo pulled up on Montegut Street, and then four *fine*-lookin' brothers got out, all with big cans in dey hands. Five minutes later, the limo pulls off, see, burnin' rubber, and this fat ofay's house goes up like a bonfire. Yeah! That creepy-lookin' fat-ass white guy livin' on Montegut—"

Jules scowled at the woman on the phone, stopping her conversation dead. Then he hurried past, ignoring the stares of the crowd. Billy Mac's was just another block away. As he rounded the corner, Jules was enormously relieved to see a light on in the tiny office next to the cinder block garage with its sagging aluminum roof. Billy Mac must still be going over the day's receipts.

Jules knocked loudly, maybe too loudly, on the office door. He heard something break inside the room, followed by a stream of muttered curses.

"We're *closed*!" a deep voice shouted from the office. "Closed for the night! Come back in the morning!"

Jules knocked again, more urgently. "Billy Mac! It's Jules Duchon! I've gotta talk to you!"

"Jules *who*?"

"Jules Duchon. Cadillac Jules. Nineteen seventy-five Fleetwood. All white. Cream leather interior."

"*Cadillac* Jules? The big, big guy?"

"Yeah!"

"I'm sorry. The garage is *closed*, man. If that damn serpentine belt a yours done busted again—"

Jules cut him off. "Billy Mac, this isn't about my Fleetwood. The Fleetwood is gone. I need to buy another car from you. Tonight."

"*Tonight?* Hey, I'd love to oblige you, but I'm bone-ass tired, y'know? Just got done workin' a fourteen-hour day. I 'preciate the patronage, believe me, but it's gonna hafta wait 'til tomorrow."

Heart pounding, eyes wide, Jules lost the last shreds of his composure. "It *can't* wait 'til tomorrow! If it waits 'til tomorrow, I'm a dead man!" Forced to the brink, he uttered the words he knew he'd regret later. "I'll pay you top dollar!"

In the ensuing silence Jules could almost hear the mental tinkling of the cash register in Billy Mac's head. "You just said the magic words, Cadillac Jules."

The door opened and the diminutive proprietor emerged, all smiles. He shook Jules's hand vigorously. "The sales manager of Billy Mac's Pre-Owned Automotive Emporium is on duty and at your service. Follow me out to the display floor. If you don't mind my saying, you look like shit."

"You just worry about getting me a car," said Jules.

The "display floor" was an L-shaped dirt lot that fronted on St. Claude Avenue and wound behind the garage. Jules's heart sank as he gave the sparse selection of dusty vehicles a quick once-over. Most cheapo lots could at least be counted on to have a decent selection of older American full-sized gas guzzlers, but Billy Mac seemed to specialize in the worst aberrations ever produced in the field of compact cars. Side by side sat a virtual freak show of small cars—an egg-shaped Renault Fuego, a Chevy Vega with two flat tires, and a lavender AMC Gremlin, a misshapen, hunch-backed monstrosity that truly resembled its namesake. The least objectionable choice on the lot was an early-1980s Subaru GL, but its body appeared to be made up more of Bondo than sheet metal. And besides, there was no way Jules could ever fit behind its steering wheel.

Billy Mac turned toward his customer to gauge his reaction. The mechanic's smile emanated a surprisingly childlike innocence, a quality it'd had ever since a dissatisfied customer had knocked out Billy Mac's four front teeth fifteen years earlier. Often mistaken by his customers for an American Indian, Billy Mac was actually from Java; he had come to New Orleans as a small boy from Dutch Indonesia just after World War II, and he had quickly "gone native" in the Crescent City. He had become an exceptionally skilled mechanic, even though, at four feet nine inches tall, he had to stand atop a specially built stepladder to see into the innards of the bigger cars.

The plain look of dismay on Jules's face did not diminish Billy Mac's smile one iota. "See anything you like?" he asked, beaming.

"Jesus Christ, Billy Mac! Is this all you've got?"

Billy Mac grinned even wider as he caressed the lumpy hood of the Gremlin. "Whas the matter with the selection, Jules? People gotta protect the environment, man. Small cars are *in*. Damn Arabs gonna jack up the price of gas to five dollars a gallon any day now, you'll see."

Jules scowled. "That's a crock! Gas has been under a buck fifty a gallon for the last ten years."

"So? It'll go up again. Besides, I thought this was a life-or-death situation, right?"

Jules found himself backing down slightly. "Sure it is. But you can't expect me to fit inside any of these kiddie carts. Don't you have anything bigger on the lot? Some old Fleetwood or Sedan DeVille? I need the biggest trunk you got."

Billy Mac crossed his arms belligerently, looking a bit like Chief Crazy Horse just before Little Big Horn. "Sure! Sure I've got other cars on the lot! But you didn't gimme a chance to show them to you, did you? No—you wasted three minutes of my precious sleepin' time bitchin' about the stock I got out front here!"

"Okay, look, I'm sorry. So where're you hidin' these other cars?"

The mechanic's angry frown turned back to a smile. "Behind the garage. Follow me!" Despite Billy Mac's short legs, Jules found it hard to keep up with the little man. "I'm gonna show you the peach of the lot, Jules! You always been a Cadillac man, right? Well, this beauty I got back here, you take a drive in it and you'll see why Cadillac's called 'The Standard of the World'! Just to sit in it, man—leather seats like butter, I mean, you sit down and you never want to get up again. It's like pussy on wheels! Electric windows! Electric door locks! Electronic speed control! This baby's got it *all*!"

The longer Billy Mac's monologue rambled on, the higher Jules's spirits rose. Sure, his house had burned down. Yeah, he was being chased out of his beloved hometown by a gang of homicidal vampires. And Billy Mac was certain to drive a hard bargain. But at least Jules was going to get his hands on a sweet chariot again.

Billy Mac abruptly stopped walking and spread his short arms as wide as they would go. *"Taa-daah!"*

Jules looked around confusedly. "Yeah? So where is it?"

"You're standing right in front of it."

Jules stared, dumbfounded, at the small gold-metallic sedan in front of him, barely wider than he was. "What're you talkin' about? That's a Chevy Cavalier."

"Nope. That's a Cadillac. A Cimmaron! Gets the best gas mileage of any Caddy ever made. A collector's-item classic! They only made these for two or three years, y'know."

Jules's recently inflated spirit withered like a slug buried in salt. He wanted to scream. The only Cadillac on the lot, and it had to be the dinkiest, crummiest rip-off-mobile to ever wear the wreath and crest, a

Chevy economy car with a Cadillac grille bolted on front. "No, no, *no*! Full sized! I need a full-sized car, with a big trunk! I'll take a Buick, an Oldsmobile. I'll even take a Pontiac. But it's got to be *full sized*."

Billy Mac looked thoughtful. "Oh. You mean you want a *big* car."

"Yes. Big. That's right."

"But that Cimmaron's awful nice."

"*Fuck* the Cimmaron! I couldn't fit my *dick* in the goddamn Cimmaron!"

"Hey! No need to go postal on me, man. I think I got just the right car for you. I picked it up at auction late last week, so I haven't had time to clean it up yet. But it's cherry, man. Vintage cherry. Honestly, I didn't show you this one yet 'cause I was thinkin' about makin' it my own personal car. But since you ain't findin' anything else to your likin', I'm willing to make a sacrifice. 'Cause that's just the kinda guy I am."

Jules sucked in a big breath. "Okay. Okay. Just show it to me."

Jules followed Billy Mac to the corner of the mechanic's property farthest away from the street. "There she is," Billy Mac said, his eyes brimming with emotion. "A real beaut, ain't she? It's gonna smash my heart in little pieces to see you drive her off the lot."

"A Lincoln," Jules whispered, his voice etched with despair. "It *hadda* be a *Lincoln* . . ."

♠

Three hours and eighteen hundred cash dollars later (Jules started negotiations at four hundred, but his bargaining position was weak), Jules climbed into his newly purchased 1974 Continental Mark IV. The car had once been silver. But a quarter century beneath the Louisiana sun had oxidized the paint nearly to the metal underneath, leaving the car a multitoned dull gray, mottled with dimples of brown rust. Its black vinyl roof had cracked and flaked so badly it appeared the car was suffering from terminal psoriasis. Jules walked slowly around the car's massive hood. Its driver-side disappearing headlight assembly was permanently stuck in a half-open position. The battered coupe seemed to be winking at Jules, like the pathetic come-on of an elderly whore. The odometer read 37,256 miles. That could mean 137,256 miles, 237,256 miles, or maybe even 337,256 miles. Jules winced at the sight of the torn zebra-print upholstery, perfectly complemented by the sun-faded pair of red fuzzy dice that hung limply from the rearview mirror.

Billy Mac enthusiastically patted the car's dull gray hood. "That inside trunk-release latch you had me install carries a seven-day warranty, so keep your receipts. You'll love her, man! This li'l honey runs like a fuckin' Swiss watch!"

Reminded of the late hour, Jules checked his own watch. It was already three-thirty. Barely three hours to sunrise. He grabbed the keys from Billy Mac's hand, mumbled his thanks, and shoved the Lincoln's bench seat as far back as it would go.

♦

Jules had read Jack Kerouac's *On the Road* when it first came out. The book hadn't tempted him to leave New Orleans one tiny bit. Now, after thirty minutes of westerly highway travel, Jules had formulated an unshakable opinion of life on the road. It sucked. The Lincoln's tranny was missing its third gear. Jules couldn't go any faster than forty-five miles per hour without pitching his pistons through the hood. Other cars raced around him in a nonstop blur of red taillights, their angry horn blasts distorted into twisted bleats by a severe Doppler effect. Jules tried hard not to think about the royal screwing he'd just been subjected to, but he couldn't help it. For a guy with no front teeth, that Billy Mac was the worst bloodsucker he'd ever crossed paths with. Jules had cleaned out his savings account to put money down on the car, and then financed the remaining six-hundred-dollar balance, three hundred dollars for the trunk release, and fifty dollars for a crummy, broken-down shovel, all at a usurious rate of twenty-four percent. As soon as Billy Mac had finished installing the trunk release, Jules had debated whether or not to fang him and save twenty-eight hundred dollars. He'd almost done it, too. But a good mechanic was just too hard to come by.

He'd used the fifty-dollar shovel to scoop soggy earth from the front yard of his destroyed house into the bottom of the Lincoln's trunk, coating it with about six inches of mud. Jules wondered how accurate that old legend was about vampires needing to rest in soil from their birthplace. Would any dirt from anywhere work just as well? He'd never had to wonder about it before. If the legend was, in fact, factual, how strictly or loosely was the term *birthplace* defined? Would dirt from Uptown New Orleans, City Park, or Baton Rouge (to go even farther afield) work just as well as earth from his own yard? Maybe he hadn't needed to take the risk of returning to his neighborhood so soon after the fire? Well, that was a moot point now. Considering the way his luck had been running, he'd been smart sticking with the tried and true.

As soon as the word *luck* entered his head, it started raining. The falling moisture was an angry, living thing, an avenging fury that beat on the oxidized metal of his hood and roof like a gigantic millipede with a thousand claw hammers. Jules wondered whether the storm might be a manifestation of his mother's earthbound spirit, furious at her only son for losing their home. The Lincoln's bald tires quickly began hydroplaning on the rutted, waterlogged asphalt. The big car weaved from lane to lane as Jules struggled with the unfamiliar steering wheel and jerky brake pedal. He didn't dare slow down, however. Not with sunrise barely an hour away. He had to at least make Baton Rouge before first light. No closer place outside New Orleans had the enclosed parking garages that might give him shelter.

The sun-rotted wiper blades only served to spread the rain evenly over his field of vision. The metal tips bit into the windshield glass, etching the car a pair of eyebrows. Jules turned the wipers off. He rolled down his window and tried clearing the glass with his hand. No good; the outside world remained a watery blur.

Faded outlet-mall billboards and the gnarled trunks of dead cypress trees drifted past at forty-five miles per hour, signposts of his grim exile. Jules felt a mysterious lump in his coat pocket. Aside from the shabby clothes on his back, that lump could well be the last connection he had to his beloved former life.

He reached into his right pocket. The lump was the plastic case of a cassette tape. Jules lifted it quickly in front of his eyes. He could catch only a flash of yellow and the outline of a man standing by a car, but it was enough to spur his memory. Of course! It was Erato's tape! The gift Erato had given him! He'd taken it along with him at the beginning of the evening, which seemed like a century ago, hoping he'd have a chance to listen to it once he'd retrieved his Cadillac. Then he'd forgotten all about it.

This little cassette was the last survivor of what had been a mighty, incomparable music collection. *A Cab Driver's Blues.* How fitting. Jules glanced quickly at the Lincoln's dim dashboard. Yes, the car had a tape player of some kind. Maybe fate was beginning to smile on him once more. His best, most loyal friend had provided him with a gift that would now serve to buoy his spirits when they were at their lowest ebb. Jules thought about his friend Erato, safe in his bed in New Orleans with his family, and his eyes misted over.

He carefully removed the cassette from its case and inserted it into

the tape player's mouth. He glanced at the dash. The PLAY button was illuminated. Maybe Lincolns weren't so crummy, after all. He pressed the
button, anticipating the sweet blues music that would help soothe his
ravaged and insulted soul.

Nothing happened. Jules glanced at the dash again.

"Of all the . . . Hell. It just damn well figures."

Aside from a desultory whirring of gears, the Lincoln's eight-track
tape player remained stubbornly silent.

◆

The deluge subsided to a thick drizzle by the time Jules reached the out-
skirts of Baton Rouge. The interstate was surrounded by an endless, mo-
notonous vista of strip malls, fast-food emporiums, beige motels, and
gambling casino billboards. *So this is what the whole damn country turned
into when I wasn't payin' attention,* Jules thought. He'd heard it from
people who'd seen it firsthand, but he hadn't dared believe it until now.

The eastern sky was beginning to turn a grayish pink in his rearview
mirror. He had maybe ten minutes—fifteen, tops—to find himself a
covered garage and check himself in for the day. He scanned the myriad
featureless buildings lined up alongside the highway. Land must've been
cheap in Baton Rouge, because all the businesses, even the office com-
plexes, made do with exposed surface parking lots. Jules frowned. He
couldn't be positive the Lincoln's trunk was completely daylight-proof,
and besides, he didn't relish the thought of broiling in a steel box twelve
hours beneath the South Louisiana sun. He imagined himself slowly
roasting in his own fat, not an appealing picture at all.

Sweating profusely from a surefire combination of stress and one
hundred percent humidity, Jules figured his best shot at locating a public
garage would be to head downtown, where the old state government
buildings were. An overhead sign announced a Government Street exit
two miles away. That sounded right. Behind him, the pinkish sky was
beginning to turn ominously orange.

The Government Street exit appeared just after the interstate forked
and Jules turned north. From the top of the exit ramp, Jules saw what he
first took to be a heart-stopping premonition of his own eternal damna-
tion. The western horizon was shackled in a steel corset of glowing pipes
and effluent tubing. Sulfur-yellow smokestacks belched clouds of smoke
and steam in unearthly oil-slick colors. It wasn't hell, Jules reminded himself. It was merely the terminus of the chemical and oil refinery complex

lining the Mississippi River's banks along the seventy miles between Baton Rouge and his lost home; the origin of the toxic soup that gave New Orleans's tap water its distinctive flavor and aroma.

St. Louis Street looked promising. Signs pointed the way to a Centroplex Convention Center, and besides, there was a St. Louis Street in the French Quarter in New Orleans. Jules's eyes grew watery with the memory. But before he could become totally rheumy, he spotted a parking garage. And just in the nick of time, too—something was beginning to smell like cinnamon toast left in the toaster one cycle too long, and Jules was pretty sure it was none other than his own vagabond self.

The wide-bodied Lincoln scraped both sides as Jules piloted the car through the garage's entranceway. He grabbed his ticket from the dispenser. At least the daily rates were relatively cheap; less than half the typical garage rate in downtown New Orleans. Good. He might end up staying here a long time, and the more days his remaining twenty-nine dollars would stretch, the better.

He pulled into the most shadowy, isolated spot he could find. The garage wasn't underground. Louvered metal walls let in stray photons of the first rays of the morning. Jules cut his engine and got out of the car. The scattered bits of sunlight hit him like tiny incendiary missiles. Yet he found himself hardly caring. He was so sore all over that he could barely tell new pains from old. The floor where he had parked was filled with noxious blue smoke. Jules couldn't tell whether the smoke had come from the Lincoln's tailpipe or his own skin.

He popped open his trunk. The earth from his front yard had remained mud; it shimmered in the early-morning light like black molasses syrup. Jules didn't bother taking off his jacket. What was the use? He flopped into the soupy trunk like a plaid sack of cement. The cool mud soothed his burning skin a little. He reached for the lid and pulled it closed, then squirmed a bit in a futile effort to get more comfortable.

The exiled, homeless vampire couldn't remember a time when he'd ever welcomed the darkness more.

♦

"—nuh-no! *No!* You won't get me! Keep *away*—"

Soft hands grasped his shoulders and shook him awake. "Jules! Jules, wake up! You're havin' yourself a nightmare!"

Jules opened his eyes. He blinked once. He blinked twice. But the pink walls and white lace curtains refused to fade away. He was lying in a downy-soft four-poster bed. The air was perfumed with essence of citrus. He turned his head to the side. Sitting next to him, resplendent in a gauzy white negligee, was Maureen.

She smoothed the wrinkles from his forehead with her soft fingertips. "Poor baby," she said, her eyes brimming with concern. "You were howlin' like the wolfman got hold of your throat. Real bad dream, huh?"

"I—I was stuck in Baton Rouge, baby. It was . . . it was *hell*. Everything I ever owned got taken away from me. Everybody hated me. The whole world was out to get me—"

"Hush. You just hush yourself now, baby." She smiled and stroked his hair, letting her fingers glide down his cheek and neck to play with the tufts of hair on his bare chest. "You just let little ol' Maureen make it all better now."

She slowly slid her big body over his. "*Mmmm*, I'll bet I know a way to get you to fall back asleep. . . ." Her creamy skin felt like satin against his legs and belly and chest. She let her full weight settle on him, and every cell in his body was engulfed with pleasure.

Her breath smelled of peppermint and fresh blood. "*Mmmm*, give Mama a big fat kiss. . . ." Her lips were a feast, an endless repast that both perfectly satisfied his hunger and made him ravenous for more. She plunged her tongue into his mouth, sucking his teeth in a deliciously erotic fashion. He felt himself stirring, stiffening, growing proudly immense beneath her skillful ministrations.

And then she unzipped the back of her head.

"Hiya, Jules! Didn't think I'd forgotten about ya, had ya?"

"*Aaahhhhhhh!*"

Malice X's hot, garlicky breath filled Jules's nostrils as he licked Jules's face. "Mm, mm, *good*! Me, I always did prefer white meat."

"Nn-nooo!" Jules tried to hurl the other vampire off him, but powerful black hands shackled his wrists and ankles. Jules's heart beat like a trip-hammer. "Wha—what do you want with me?" he spluttered. "Haven't you done enough to me already?"

Malice X smiled maliciously, letting his long fangs hang over his lower lip. "Why, Mistuh Jules, you an' me, we've barely *begun*." He shifted his right hand from behind his back, revealing a wooden stake shaped like a twisted ram's horn. Clutching it in both fists, he raised it high above his head. Then, snickering softly, he plunged it into Jules's spasming heart.

"*Nooooo!*"

Jules's eyes snapped open. He was engulfed in darkness. His hands flew to his chest, above where his heart beat painfully fast. There was no stake there, twisted or otherwise. All his fingers felt were the soggy lapels of his sport coat, his heaving chest, and granules of dirt. He smelled drying mud and his own sour, frightened sweat. He stretched his arms out, exploring his lightless environment. Before he could reach very far, his hands bumped against the familiar, faintly comforting contours of the inside of the Lincoln's trunk.

Shifting position so that he was leaning against the left rear tire hump, he pressed the glow button on the side of his watch. The blue digital numerals read 7:52 P.M. The sun had been down for a good twenty minutes. He was free to leave the cramped chamber of horrors that was the Lincoln's trunk.

He pulled on the wire that Billy Mac had rigged up. The trunk creaked slowly open, letting in the humid, petroleum-scented evening air. He glanced around the nearly empty garage. He had to make a plan. For the past nineteen hours, the only thing on his mind had been getting out of New Orleans. Now that he had escaped, he had to figure out what the heck to do with the rest of his undead existence.

Hrmmm . . . After his uncomfortable day's sleep in the trunk, the effort of so much thinking made his head pound. Using the Lincoln as a taxi was out of the question. It was a two-door, and besides, nobody in their right mind would pay a dime to be driven around in that heap. So he'd have to buy another car (preferably another Fleetwood . . . a late-1960s model in good condition, one of those beauties with the stacked quad headlights, some little old grandmother's car with ridiculously low mileage, would be ideal).

He'd have to find some entry-level night-shift job, at least until he'd stashed enough away to clean himself up. Somewhere downtown there had to be a twenty-four-hour diner or coffee shop. Those kinds of places were always looking for dishwashers. Washing dishes was beneath him, of course, but he'd only be stuck at the bottom for a little while, until he was able to afford some new clothes. Then, thanks to his first-rate talent for servicing the public, he'd be promoted to wait staff, or maybe night manager. And hey, the kinds of folks who patronized all-night diners usually made the easiest, most convenient victims, too.

Now that he had a plan, Jules felt one hundred percent better about his prospects. *Plan your work, then work your plan—that's what Mother always said. I'm like a crafty ol' tomcat,* he told himself, brushing some of the mud from the front of his pants. *Throw me off the roof a hundred times, I'll always land on my feet.*

He marched assertively down the parking ramp, his stiff neck stuck at a thirty-degree tilt, eager to see what downtown Baton Rouge had to offer him. The answer, he discovered after walking a few blocks, was "Not much." The boarded-up storefronts along Convention Street, North Boulevard, and Florida Street reminded Jules of old Dryades Street back in New Orleans; Dryades had withered to the point where the only commerce that took place there involved the trade of green paper for white rocks and black skin. If anything, these streets were even sadder and lonelier than Dryades was, because not even crack dealers and streetwalkers bothered pushing their wares here.

Finally, on Florida Street, Jules found the one business establishment that wasn't a windowless phantom. Richoeux's Café was closed, but at least it looked like it might be open sometime. The faded Coca-Cola sign over the restaurant's entrance mocked Jules with its invitation to PAUSE . . . REFRESH. He thought about the Trolley Stop Café back on St. Charles Avenue, the rough-and-tumble cabby fellowship he could always find there, the decent, if not outstanding, coffee. He stared through the dark front window, trying to see if the café's hours were posted somewhere inside.

Jules heard a rumbly clanking behind him, on the street. "You lookin' for sumptin' to eat?" a voice asked.

He turned around. The voice belonged to a tiny, white-haired black man who was pushing a rusty shopping cart half filled with crushed tin cans. "You lookin' for sumptin' to eat? Dat place don't open up 'til seven-thirty in the mornin'. It ain't cheap, neither."

"Yeah, I'd like to find me somewheres to eat," Jules said. "You know of any places around here that're open late?"

"No, suh." The old man shook his head sadly. "But dem holy rolluhs gonna be handin' out samwiches an' joe any minute now, over in the park."

"The park? Where's that?"

"Jes' up the street," the old man said, nodding his head toward the river. "I'm goin' over dat way now. Youse welcome to follow me."

Jules shrugged and silently followed the old man and his rickety shopping cart down Florida Street. Where there was one homeless person, there were likely to be others, he reasoned. They might not help him earn money for a new Caddy, but at least an enclave of street people would ensure that Jules wouldn't starve.

Lafayette Street Park was an acre of oak-shaded green space tucked between the Mississippi River levee and the old State Capitol Building. Jules noted with satisfaction that the park was home to a sizable community of derelicts, at least two dozen. Most of them were clustered around a large station wagon parked at the edge of the trees. Several people were setting up a coffee urn on the wagon's tailgate and beginning to pass out wrapped sandwiches to eager hands.

Jules's companion aimed his cart at the gathering and sped up his pace. "Dey make you sing," he said, smiling shyly. "But I don't mind none. Me, I kin sing dat gospel real good."

Jules let the old man hustle off toward the chow line and drifted into the park. From a distance he endured several ragged choruses of "What a Friend We Have in Jesus" and "Go Tell It on the Mountain." One of the women volunteers noticed Jules watching from beneath the oaks and waved at him to come over, but he ignored her. He'd never taken a handout in his life, and he sure as hell wasn't about to start now, especially not from some Bible-hugging Baptists who probably considered Spam on white bread manna from heaven.

He waited for the station wagon to drive off and then watched the various park dwellers carry their meals to their favorite benches. Many of the derelicts clustered together in small, wary groups. Jules thought they behaved like something he'd seen on the *Wild Kingdom* show, packs of hyenas nervously guarding a half-devoured carcass abandoned by a lion. One white woman looked promising, however. She appeared to be a bit better nourished than the others (iron-poor blood wasn't good for a vampire, Jules reminded himself), and she kept to herself, walking with small, quick steps to a bench near the levee, away from the others.

Jules approached her as casually as possible and sat down on the edge of her bench. She looked to be in her late thirties, and her clothes weren't nearly as disheveled as those worn by the other park dwellers. She glanced at Jules several times with startled, birdlike movements, looking quickly away whenever Jules attempted to make eye contact, but she kept eating her sandwich and made no effort to leave the bench.

Jules smiled his warmest, most homespun smile at her. "Hiya, gorgeous," he said, racking his brain for an appropriate opening line. "What's a fine-lookin' lady like you doin' in a low-rent situation like this?"

She placed her sandwich carefully on her lap and made eye contact with Jules for the first time. "You're from the guv'ner's office, aren't you?"

A little nonplussed, Jules responded, "Uh, no. Actually, I'm from New Orleans. Just got into town this morning."

"The guv'ner's got offices in New Orleans, doesn't he?" the woman shot back. "The guv'ner drives around in a big black limousine. It's got a TV in it. He watches the TV to see what's inside my mind."

"Uh . . . yeah. I see." Jules fidgeted with his fingernails, trying to figure a way to turn the woman's unfortunate mental state to his advantage. "Well, actually, I really *am* from the governor's office. The governor, uh, he sent me to find you, so I could give you a nice tour of that big nice house over there." Jules pointed toward the old State Capitol Building, which glowed in the evening mist like a white castle from a Cecil B. De-Mille knights-and-damsels epic.

"Really?" she said, edging closer to Jules.

"Really," Jules said warmly, taking advantage of the moment to slide closer to her. "We can go take that tour right now, if you'd like."

"I *knew* it! I was the guv'ner's mistress. He used to let me live there in that castle until I said I wouldn't vote for him no more."

"Yeah, well, he's changed his mind. You can go live there again, and you can vote for anybody you like."

He held out his hand to her. She stiffened, staring at Jules's hand like it was leprous. "You're trying to bribe me to vote for him, aren't you?"

"Huh?"

"Your hand—it's full of filthy bribe money."

Jules stared at his empty hand. He wished it *were* full of filthy money. "No, baby, it's nothin' like that. We're just gonna go on a little tour, is all."

Her eyes grew wide. "No!" She scooted away from Jules and wrapped her sandwich in the hem of her dress. "He's full of tricks! He'll do anything to get me to vote for him!"

"Now, baby, you just calm yourself down—"

"Don't come near me!" She abruptly stood and backed away from the bench. "He's trying to bribe me!" she shouted to the nearest group of park dwellers. "He's trying to seduce me with his video poker money! Then the feds will come get me and put me on trial! Briber! *Briber!*"

All eyes in the park focused on the two of them. Jules got up from the bench and stepped away from her, his hands spread in a futile gesture of conciliation. "All right, all right already! I'm leavin', see? I'm leavin'. We'll forget the tour, okay? Just settle down."

Every other park dweller now eyed him like he was a walking time bomb. His repast for the evening was spoiled. Unable to think of anything else, he climbed to the top of the levee and watched the colored smoke belch from the tops of the tall refinery stacks. He passed a few hours counting the eighteen-wheelers that occasionally crossed the Mississippi River bridge. As the echoes of their passing bounced off the levee's grassy slope, Jules felt the first cold fingers of real despair touch his soul.

♦

Three nights later Jules was running out of curses to mumble to himself. He'd revised his earlier opinion of his new home: Baton Rouge *was* hell. He'd tried shifting his hunting grounds to LSU, hoping to corner an unwary undergraduate behind a dormitory, but security guards had chased him off campus. Back downtown, he'd hoped to cut his growing hunger with a cup of free coffee, but the Baptist missionaries had refused him even a drop when he wouldn't sing hymns with them. And his fellow street people still shunned him like he was a dose of HIV.

Even among the outcasts, he was an outcast. The unbearable bitterness of that realization rubbed on his frayed soul as he aimlessly wandered the bleak, empty streets of downtown, blowing down the cracked sidewalks like a wadded-up page of yesterday's newspaper. He had no idea how long he'd been walking, or where he'd gotten himself to, when he heard the *tap-tap-tap-tap* of someone, or something, following behind him.

He wasn't afraid. He recognized his lack of fear with a dull, slow surprise. In fact, he half hoped it was Malice X following behind him, twisted stake in hand.

Jules turned around.

It wasn't a vampire, or the bogeyman. It was a dog. Just a mournful-eyed, matted-furred, droopy-eared mutt.

The dog stopped walking as soon as Jules turned to face her. She looked at him shyly and fearfully and eagerly, her tail wagging with a quick, nervous stutter.

Jules's heart began to defrost at the sight of the timid, hopeful animal. He'd never been a dog lover. But here was a fellow outcast, just as dirty and hungry and lonely as he was. A fellow outcast who was reaching out to him.

Jules knelt down, ignoring the painful protest of his knees, and held out his hand. "C'mere, girl," he whispered, terribly afraid she might spook and run away from him. "C'mere. I won't hurt you, darlin'. I swear. I just wanna be your friend."

Slowly, with short, hesitant steps, the dog approached him. He held his breath, not daring to move even a millimeter. Time seemed to stop as he waited for the cold touch of her nose against his fingertips.

Finally, she sniffed his hand. With the first whiff of his scent, she began wagging her tail more confidently. Jules waited for her to get more accustomed to him before he dared pat her on the head. Her nose moved swiftly from his fingers to his arm to his knee, then to his crotch, her tail wagging more enthusiastically with each passing second.

"Yeah, sweetheart. You like the way I smell, don't you?" He hesitantly patted the top of her head. When she responded by licking his hand, he threw caution to the winds and scratched behind her ears and vigorously rubbed her scabby back. "Yeah. Aren't you sweet? You aren't mean an' nasty like them others. You're just a sweetheart, ain'tchu?"

While he was picking burrs out of her matted fur, he noticed how her ribs pressed through her paper-thin sides. He stood up. "We've gotta find you somethin' to eat, sweetheart. You're lookin' even hungrier than I am. And that's pretty fuckin' hungry."

The two of them wandered the streets until they came upon a closed but still-in-business convenience mart. Jules stared through the window. There, on aisle three, sat half a dozen bags of dog food.

He looked down at his new friend. She stared up at him and wagged her tail hopefully. He looked back through the window. "Aww, what the fuck," he muttered to himself. "The worst they can do is toss me in the slammer, and that'd be a helluva lot more comfy than sleepin' in that damn trunk of mine, anyway."

He walked around to the back of the store. The rear window was barred, but the door, with its rotting wood and flimsy, loose knob, looked promising. Jules gathered what remained of his strength and threw his shoulder against the door. The old wood gave some, creaking in protest. He backed up five paces and got a running start. Faced with the impact of 450 pounds of newly invigorated vampire, the sagging door split into five pieces.

An off-key symphony of Klaxons, bleats, and hoots sounded as Jules picked himself up off the dirty floor, rubbed his sore shoulder, and headed for the dog food aisle. He grabbed as many of the ten-pound bags as he could squeeze into his arms, then ran out the way he'd come in. The shrill whistles of the store's alarm system chased him into the street like pursuing harpies. His canine companion barked excitedly at the noise and the tumult, despite Jules's out-of-breath pleas for her to be quiet. He lurched into a dark alleyway and dropped his five sacks of purloined dog food onto a torn, stained mattress. Then he fell back against the wall, slid to the ground, and waited for the sirens and flashing red lights of approaching patrol cars.

They never came. Once Jules's heart settled down a bit, he crawled over onto the mattress and tore open one of the bags of dog food. His companion had her head inside the bag before the first dried protein pellets hit the mattress's yellow-stained surface. She ate ferociously, as if she might never see food again.

Watching her, Jules felt happy for the first time in more than a week. *Look at her go!* he thought. His own stomach groaned piteously, adding its plaintive note to the alarms still echoing through the streets. He found himself wishing he could join his friend in her meal. *She sure is wolfing that stuff down,* he thought, half enviously; and his stray thought gave him the glimmer of an idea. A nasty, depressing idea, but an idea, nonetheless. Maybe he *could* join her in her meal.

He found himself remembering a time in his life he usually avoided thinking about, the last time he'd been in straits as dire as these. He'd just been laid off from his job in the coroner's office, cut off from the easy, simple existence he'd enjoyed for nearly thirty years. Suddenly on his own, he realized with horror that after three decades of living off the blood of the recently deceased, he'd totally lost his knack for hunting up a meal. Sitting alone in his house, he'd nearly starved, until one evening he noticed that his next-door neighbors had moved out, and in the pile of trash they'd left behind were several half-emptied sacks of dog food. Desperate, delirious with hunger, he shifted into his wolf-form and attacked the abandoned meal. It wasn't brunch at Brennan's, but that dog food kept him going for a couple of weeks, until he came up with the plan of driving a taxicab and having his meals pay to come to him.

That was years ago. It was an experience Jules had hoped he'd never have to repeat. The very notion was degrading. Resorting to eating as an animal was as low as a vampire could sink. Plus, he couldn't be sure that his wolf-form's digestive tract could still tolerate solid food; his human-form's certainly couldn't. But the longer his dog companion chomped away, the more Jules's agonized, shriveled stomach pleaded—no, *demanded*—that he try something, anything at all. Sighing, he dragged himself to a corner of the mattress, leaned against the wall, closed his eyes tightly, and concentrated on a mental picture of the full moon.

The dog paused from her voracious eating long enough to produce a fearful whimper at the unnatural spectacle of flesh rearranging itself in a flurry of swirling mists. Jules pounced on one of the other bags of dog food and tore it open with his fangs. He was surprised at how good it tasted; maybe those paid flacks on dog food commercials who claimed that their brand was super delicious weren't lying after all. He polished off the first bag before he even thought to wiggle free of his clothes. The second bag went down his gullet just as fast. The third bag was heavenly, and the fourth bag nearly as heavenly, even though by the time his long nose reached the bottom half of the sack, his wolf-gut was full to bursting. He had the unmitigated gall to stick his snout into his companion's bag of food, but a few angry nips on his nose and tail were enough to convince him that discretion was the better part of valor.

Sated, exhausted from the exertion of eating so much so quickly, he felt his four paws splay out from under him as the heft of his grotesquely stretched potbelly dragged him down to the mattress. Damn, he felt *good*! He hadn't felt this good since . . . since . . . since he couldn't remember when. Floating in a half-conscious fog of satisfied gluttony, no longer fixated on the need to consume, he began to notice the input of his heightened wolf-senses. Tiny insects buzzed in the storm gutters high above his head, the beating of their wings like distant applause. He sniffed the stains on the mattress and was able to differentiate the various urine stains, chicken grease stains, and semen stains by their unique scent signatures. And there was something else, another odor that overpowered all others, a potent muskiness that insinuated itself in his veins and sinews and bones and made him crazy, absolutely *crazy*—

He hadn't realized it before, with his limited human nose, but his friend the bitch was in heat.

I've gotta turn human again, Jules told himself as he avidly sniffed his companion's hindquarters, caught in the throes of a lust unlike any he had ever known. *I've gotta turn human again, right now, immediately, before I do somethin' really stupid—* But before he could even begin to muster the concentration necessary for a transformation, he had already mounted her.

The much smaller dog yelped with pain as Jules's comparatively tremendous weight landed on her back. She tried to scoot away, but his strong paws clamped onto her sides and held her fast. As he pumped faster than he thought possible, his body trapped in the iron hold of canine pheromones that screamed *"Make puppies! Make puppies!"* his still-human mind was filled with remorse. *I'm sorry, baby, I'm so sorry, I'll make it up to you, you'll never want for dog food again. . . .*

Nearly as quickly as when he was in human form, it was over. He slid off of her and collapsed in a furry heap on the mattress. He waited for her to reproach him, maybe bite him, and then run off. It was only what he deserved, after all.

But she surprised him. Rather than running away, she nuzzled him, then licked his face. Jules was astounded. Overcome with emotion, he licked her all over with his huge tongue until her fur was cleaner than it had ever been. They snuggled close together on the mattress, his bitch warming herself against Jules's great potbelly. Jules fell into the deepest, most blissful sleep he'd had in years.

When he awoke a few hours later, startled out of sleep by a news-paper delivery truck, he was alone. Seized with panic, he crisscrossed the streets within a five-block radius, searching vainly for her scent. But she was nowhere to be found.

Jules howled. And every street dweller in downtown Baton Rouge knew that some creature had just lost its only friend.

♦

Please deposit thirty-five cents, the mechanical voice said.

Jules fumbled through his coat pocket for a fistful of change, then pulled a frayed piece of paper from his wallet. He had to squint to see the faded writing in the yellow phosphorescent light of the parking garage. He punched in the number, almost forgetting to include the three-digit area code.

The number you have dialed requires a deposit of—two dollars and twenty cents—for an initial call of five minutes. Please deposit an additional—one dollar and eighty-five cents. Thank you for using Baton Rouge Telecom, your telecommunications specialists.

Jules shoved seven quarters and a dime through the slot. The coins fell into the bowels of the pay phone like desperate wishes tossed into a lucky fountain. The phone rang. She picked up on the fourth ring.

"Hello?"

"Mo, don't say anything. Just let me talk, okay? I know you probably hate me. You probably think I'm scum, like everyone else on this god-damn planet. But I've got nobody else to turn to, baby." His voice cracked. He quivered and leaned heavily against the booth, fighting to maintain some tiny shred of control and dignity. "I'm at the end of my rope. I've hit rock bottom. My life has been nothin' but hell these past two weeks. I lost everything I had, and then I kept losin' more and more. I don't know what to do. I just don't know what to do."

"Jules, hush yourself—"

"Don't hush me, Maureen! Let me finish before you rip into me! You know how hard it is for me to call you like this? You think I wanted to? But I'm on my knees, baby. You made me what I am. You're almost as much a mother to me as my own mother was. If you don't help me—"

"Jules, hush yourself, sweetheart, and come on home."

SEVEN

The next evening Jules stood hesitantly before the front door of Maureen's French Quarter town house, fidgeting as nervously as a boy about to pick up his prom date. For the first time in years, he found himself wishing he could see his reflection in a mirror. He spat in his palms and slicked down his unruly hair as best he could. Then he brushed the last few flecks of dirt from his threadbare sport coat. It would have to do. Finally, he lifted the big brass pineapple-shaped knocker and let it crash against the door's cracked red paint.

A few moments later, he heard a slow, heavy tread approaching the door. After a few seconds of queasy silence, three balky dead bolts clicked, and the door opened.

Maureen's nose twitched violently. She made no effort to disguise her revulsion. "Oh. My. Gawd."

"Hi, baby." Jules smiled weakly. "It's good to see you."

Maureen stepped back quickly from the doorway. She pointed curtly in the direction of the bathroom. "Shower. Now."

"Don't I even get a 'hello'?"

"Scrape that toxic waste off your hide and I'll consider it. Bathroom's through there. Drop all your things through the big chute in the hallway. And I mean *everything*."

Jules stepped inside. He briefly considered trying for a hug, but the fact that she was eyeing him as though he were a gigantic cockroach changed his mind. He walked down the hallway until he came to the chute and began peeling off his clothes. He dropped his coat on the polished cedar floor; a cloud of gray dust swirled around his ankles. His shirt clung to him like a massive strip of cellophane wrap. He opened the chute, which was big enough to stuff a body through, and peered inside before dropping in his wadded-up shirt, pants, and socks. A wave of heat hit his face from the darkness below.

"Hey, baby, where does this thing lead to? The laundry?"

"No. The incinerator." She picked up his coat with a pair of fireplace tongs. "Reach in and take out your wallet," she commanded. Jules obediently followed orders. Then she dropped the coat through the opening.

"Hey! That's my best sport coat!"

"Not anymore," she said, prodding him toward the bathroom with her tongs.

After half an hour of scrubbing himself beneath a scalding, high-pressure cascade, Jules began to feel vaguely human again. Every few minutes Maureen's pudgy hand would appear through the shower curtain, handing him a series of astringent soaps and shampoos to use. Finally, she reached in and turned off the hot water, signaling that he was allowed to come out.

After he toweled himself off, she handed him a fluffy pink robe through the door. He was surprised by how well it fit. He searched through her drawers until he found a razor (a lady's razor, but it would have to do), then felt his way through an uneven shave. Failing to find any aftershave, he wet down his hands with some of Maureen's perfume and patted it onto his semismooth, but burning, cheeks and neck.

He found Maureen waiting for him in the kitchen, pouring the contents of several plastic bowls into a tall blender. "Your friend the cabdriver was worried sick about you," she said, scraping what looked like raw eggs into the blender with a wooden spoon.

"Erato? He was worried about me?"

"Yeah, Erato, that's the one. He came looking for me at the club the night after your house burned down. He thought I might know where you'd disappeared to." She flicked on the blender for twenty seconds, then poured the contents into a large glass and handed it to him. "Here. Drink up. I'll bet you're hungry."

Jules eyed the reddish mixture uncertainly. "What's in this?"

"Egg whites, Italian stewed tomatoes, okra, mirlitons, V8 juice, and a little Tabasco sauce. Oh, and blood, of course."

Jules winced slightly and set the glass on a table. "Sounds to me like a surefire recipe for the runs. Uh, thanks for goin' to all that trouble for me, but can't I just have some blood by itself?"

Maureen sank her fists aggressively into her billowy hips and stared Jules down. "Jules Duchon, you're going to drink that mixture and you're going to like it."

"But, Mo, aside from coffee, I ain't been able to tolerate normal food in years—"

"Well, consider this a start, mister! You need to lose weight and get yourself healthy! *Especially* now! What, you think you can just waltz back into town and go back to all your old bad habits like nothing's happened? You might as well just waddle down the middle of Martin Luther King Boulevard with a great big target painted on your chest. A sign that says, KILL ME NOW—I'M TOO FAT AND *STUPID* TO TAKE CARE OF MYSELF. Sure! Let's go visit this Malice X of yours right now and save him the trouble of looking for you."

"Aww, Mo—"

She slapped his hands away, then knelt down and feigned breaking a leg off one of her kitchen chairs. "Better yet, I'll just sharpen up a wooden stake for you—right here, tonight—and you can plunge it through your heart yourself. Wouldn't that be faster and easier?" She yanked more strenuously, and the leg began to crack. "Huh? Wouldn't it?"

He leaned down and pulled her hands away from the chair, as gently as he could. "C'mon, stop it. Just calm down, huh? Look—I'll drink your concoction, okay? Here. Watch me." He lifted the glass to his lips and downed its contents in four mighty gulps, forcibly suppressing both his gag reflex and a series of shudders.

Maureen appeared at least partially mollified by his efforts. "Good," she said, taking the glass from him and rinsing it in the sink. "My house, my rules. The one hundred percent blood I keep in the fridge is *strictly* off-limits to you. Understand? If I come home some evening to find that you've been sneaking any, you'll be out on the street again before you've even had time to belch. You clear on that?"

"Like glass, baby."

"Yeah, you'd better be." She reached over and smoothed the wrinkles from the shoulders of his robe, then brushed a stray thread from his cheek with a surprisingly gentle flick of her fingertips. "Heh. You actually look pretty good in that robe of mine. But I guess we'd better get you some new clothes of your own."

Jules allowed himself to smile, even as he fought to ignore the small-scale tropical disturbance in the pit of his stomach. "Yeah, I guess we better, seein' as how you just burned up the last set of clothes I had to my name."

♦

They drove up Canal Street to Krauss's. The grand old department store at the corner of Canal and Basin, just outside the French Quarter, was in the final months of its "Going Out of Business" sale. Jules and Maureen had both shopped there often over the years, due to the store's tradition of late closing times and its well-stocked Big-and-Tall (Men's) and Youthful Stouts (Women's) Clothing Departments.

Jules parked his Lincoln behind the store, within spitting distance of the vaguely menacing apartment blocks of the Lafitte Housing Project. Slamming his creaking door shut, he couldn't help but notice how much at home his car looked against the backdrop of boarded-up windows and exposed, broken pipes. A gust of wind blew through the parking lot, and Jules pulled his reluctantly borrowed wig lower around his ears to keep it from blowing away. The edges of his muumuu were lifted up around his trunklike thighs so that for a second he looked like a Daliesque Marilyn Monroe standing over the subway grating in *The Seven Year Itch*.

Maureen noticed Jules's pained expression. "Oh, like I told you, there's no need to get all embarrassed. This dump's going out of business any day now, so it's not like you'll ever be seeing any of these salesclerks again, anyway." She grabbed his hand and hustled him toward the rear entrance. "And besides, 'Julia' my dear, with you in that getup, there's much less chance of some unfriendly bat-boy noticing that you've come back into town."

Jules grabbed back his hand. "Whoa whoa *whoa*! This is a one-time-only deal! You can't expect me to trick myself up like some goddamn Bourbon Street transvestite every time I leave your house—"

"Oh, I wouldn't *dream* of demanding that of you, Jules. There's too much danger that you might take to it and begin raiding my wardrobe.

No, we'll only take these more drastic precautions until I can drill it into that thick skull of yours that you need to call in some help. And you *know* who I mean."

Jules was about to demand some further explanation of Maureen's cryptic remark when they were swept into the human maelstrom waiting inside. The department store's shelves and racks looked like they'd been ransacked by looters. Or maybe locusts. Dozens of shoppers scanned price tags for red slashes and enticing markdowns. Jules stared at the elderly cashiers furiously pecking away at their equally elderly mechanical cash registers, all relics of the Swing Era, and remembered when his mother had brought him to shop and gawk here on Krauss's opening day, more than a hundred years ago. Looking around him, he was surprised by how little the store had changed. New Orleans had managed to hold on to its musty, familiar, comforting haunts much longer than most other towns, he told himself. Even so, this would soon all be gone: the horseshoe lunch counter on the second floor, next to the Shoe Department; the odd little fourth-floor section that juxtaposed candles, hand-dipped chocolates, and nautical knickknacks; and the clerks who knew their favorite customers better than they knew their own families.

Maureen gave his arm a powerful yank. "Come *on*, Jules! You lollygag much longer and they'll toss you out with the old mannequins. I'm due at the club in a little over an hour, and so long as I'm your meal ticket, you'd better not make me late for a shift!"

The Big-and-Tall section was tucked away in a corner of the Men's Clothing Department on the first floor. Jules noted with relief that its racks were a bit less depleted than racks elsewhere in the store.

A frazzled-looking salesman, his wrinkled tie drooping at half-mast, approached them. "Can I help you ladies with anything? Shopping for a husky husband or son? We're runnin' great closeout specials on safari suits."

Jules cleared his throat. "Actually," he said, "we're shoppin' for *me*."

The salesman, who'd obviously served a wide range of customers in his years on the floor, barely cocked an eyebrow.

Jules ended up walking to the cash register with three safari suits (two in mauve, one in lavender—the more popular colors were long gone), two pairs of drawstring pants, a black-and-gold checkered suit coat, a parcel of lime-green and melon-colored Oxford shirts, and a red velvet vest that even Maureen had to admit looked rather stylish on him.

But his best purchase by far was the wonderful trench coat that the clerk dug out of back stock for him. It was a near-exact copy of the famous garment worn by Humphrey Bogart in *Casablanca*. Even better, it had the intriguingly exotic pedigree of having been manufactured in the People's Republic of Poland.

While they were standing in line, Jules nudged Maureen with an over-stuffed shopping bag. "Say, what'd you mean earlier about me needin' to call in help?"

She glanced back at him, her eyes flashing with irritation. "I meant just that. It's pretty clear. You need help." She glanced nervously at the mostly black crowd, then pulled Jules out of line to an isolated corner. "The *staying alive* kind of help. You can't keep wandering around the city by yourself like some big goofy clown looking for the rest of the circus. You need someone who's good at figuring things out. You're not exactly a rocket scientist, you know."

Jules felt himself redden all over. Maureen, for reasons known only to her impenetrable female mind, had just launched a direct assault on his self-esteem. "What? Are you sayin' I'm not *smart* enough to solve my own problem? Hey, maybe I wasn't head of the class in arithmetic, but when it comes to good ol' common sense, I got *plenty*, sweetheart. Look, I got through World War Deuce, didn't I? The navy wouldn't have had *half* as many landing craft on D-Day if it weren't for me and Doodlebug puttin' the bite on them saboteurs—"

Maureen's eyes flashed with triumph. *"Exactly!"*

"Huh? 'Exactly' what?"

"You just said it yourself. You didn't fight those saboteurs all by your-self. It was you and Doodlebug."

"Well, yeah, sure. But he was my sidekick. He didn't really *count*. I kept him around for laughs. I mean, his biggest job was when he used to run to the corner while we were on stakeout and get me coffee."

"Don't you fool yourself. I was around back then, too. That 'kid' was the *real* brains behind the Hooded Terror. You would've tripped over your own cape without Doodlebug around. You need him now more than ever."

Jules wasn't smiling. "Yeah? Well, read my lips, Miss Know-It-All. *No Doodlebug*. No. Doodle. Bug. Ain't gonna happen."

Maureen's voice softened, and she batted her eyes at Jules in a way that might almost be construed as coquettish. "Oh, I don't see why you have to be so *stubborn*. After all, you and Doodlebug were such good partners during the war. And besides, I'm sure the two of you would work together even better now," she said, playfully running her fingertips along the seam of Jules's muumuu, "now that you have even *more* in common."

"*Why, you—!*"

◆

A few minutes later, after Maureen had paid for all of Jules's purchases with her platinum charge card, a thoroughly chastised Jules fumbled through his newly purchased pockets for his keys and opened the passenger-side door for her. "Look, Mo, I'm sorry, okay? I didn't mean to blow up in front of all them cashier ladies. I really, *really* appreciate all you're doin' for me." He waited patiently for her to latch up her seat belt, then carefully closed her door and hurried back to his own side. "Say, you wanna maybe go over to the Trolley Stop for some coffee before your shift? I'd get to show off my new duds, and I could introduce you around to some of the guys."

Maureen sighed with exasperation; her long, heavy breath left a circle of vapor on the passenger window. "This is a perfect example of what I was talking about before. You crow about all this 'common sense' you supposedly have, and then your first decision is to go straight to the one place where people know to find you. The one place in the whole city Malice X is *certain* to have a lookout watching for you. Do I need to spell it out any more clearly?"

"Nope." Jules felt himself redden again as he backed out of Krauss's parking lot onto Basin Street. Much as he hated to admit it, Maureen had a point. He couldn't just fall back into his old life as if nothing had happened.

"Just drop me at the club," she said. "As is, makeup'll have to be a rush job tonight."

Jules crossed the seedy boundary of North Rampart Street and entered the Quarter. On Iberville, two preteen boys savagely kicked a third and peeled off his expensive basketball shoes while a pair of tourists holding half-drained Hurricanes watched.

"You want my best advice, Jules? You just stay put at my place tonight. Stay put and *think*; come up with a plan before you run out somewhere and get yourself killed."

Jules was silent until he pulled up to the curb in front of Jezebel's Joy Room. "Just one question before you go. Where am I sleepin' at the end of the night? You got a 'guest coffin' or somethin'?"

Maureen hesitated before replying. "Look, you can sleep with me for a couple of nights—just until you get a new coffin built."

Jules smiled. *"Really?"*

Maureen, pointedly, did not return the smile. "Now don't you go reading anything into this! You have *exactly* two nights to get yourself a new coffin built. In the meantime, as you may remember, my bed is very large—it takes up a full room, in fact—so you and I will *not* be sleeping in close quarters. Think the Petries, from the old *Dick Van Dyke Show.* One foot on the floor, buster."

"That's okay with me, babe. Just as long as I got somewhere to sleep."

"It *better* be okay. Because that's the way it is." She gathered her things and opened the door, which scraped loudly on the sidewalk. And then she surprised him by leaning over and awkwardly pecking him on the cheek.

Jules waved out his window as he drove off in the direction of her Bienville Street home. But instead of putting his car in the garage, he turned onto Canal Street and headed west. Maureen was right about a lot of things. He would need to be at the top of his game to make it through even a week back in New Orleans. That meant getting as healthy as he could. No more aching knees. No more shortness of breath or incipient diabetes (or whatever the hell he was beginning to suffer from).

There was only one man who could possibly help him. Only one man who both understood Jules and maybe had the medical smarts to figure out a cure for what ailed him. The man who'd signed his paychecks and fed him the blood of the recently deceased for nearly thirty years. Jules wasn't sure that Dr. Amos Landrieu, onetime city coroner, was still among the living; after all, he'd been near retirement age when he'd been voted out of office twenty-three years ago.

But so long as the Lincoln didn't throw a piston on the way, Jules was determined to make this a night of reunions. ♦

The name on the mailbox in front of the big old Greek Revival–style house on Cleveland Avenue, near the Jewish cemetery, still read AMOS LANDRIEU, M.D. The doctor's car, an aged but well-maintained Mercedes sedan, was parked in the driveway. Jules saw a light on in an upstairs bedroom.

He hadn't spoken with his old boss in more than fifteen years. After Dr. Landrieu's comeback election campaign sputtered before it could even get off the ground, there hadn't seemed much point to staying in touch. Jules regretted this now. The events of the past few weeks had taught him that you couldn't have too many friends.

The emaciated branches of the spindly trees in the nearby Jewish cemetery rustled with a sudden gust of wind as Jules gathered his courage to ring the doctor's doorbell. Even after nearly three decades of working side by side, Jules had never been totally sure what his boss had really thought of him. Their interactions had always been short, direct, and work-related; clinical, in both senses of the word. Dr. Landrieu was the only human being in New Orleans who knew what Jules was. He knew about the victims whose blood Jules had drained. In fact, suppressing Jules's appetite with the blood of the dead had been the main reason the doctor had kept him on as his assistant for so many years. How would the doctor react now, seeing Jules again after so long? Would he call the police? Or toss a basin of holy water in Jules's face?

Jules rang the doorbell. Half a minute later he heard footsteps descend the stairs inside the house. A light illuminated the foyer, and a second light flickered into dusty brilliance above Jules's head. He sensed himself being observed through the peephole set in the middle of the oaken door.

A moment later the door slowly opened. Dr. Landrieu was in a robe, standing a little more stooped than Jules remembered, the lines and folds shadowing his eyes a bit deeper, his hair whiter and more scarce.

"Hiya, Doc," Jules said. "Remember me?"

"Jules Duchon. How could I forget you?" The doctor's voice was tired and weak and resigned, the sound of gravel bouncing down a rusted old tin roof. His eyes were very round and very small, like a startled sparrow's, and a large blue vein that crossed his left eyebrow pulsed strongly. His thin fingers traced the sign of a cross on his chest.

Jules flinched, but he quickly recovered his composure. "Uh, Doc, can I come in?"

"Then the game would be all over, wouldn't it?" Dr. Landrieu said, smiling faintly. "According to the old legends, you can't enter my home until I invite you in. Isn't that so? But if I remember correctly, you didn't play by a lot of those old rules. No, a lack of invitation on my part will not suffice to save me. I always expected, Jules, that when my time on this earth was done, the Angel of Death would wear your face when he came for me. Very well. You may come in. But do we have time for a final cup of coffee before you, eh, do your business?"

Jules nervously rubbed the bridge of his nose. "Gee, Doc, you've got me all wrong. I'm not here to, y'know, fang you or anything. I mean, you've never done anything but good by me, so you're probably the last person on earth I'd ever slake my thirst on. Well, one of the last, anyway."

The old physician's breathing became more regular. "Then what brings you to my door, Jules? It's not as though you've been in the habit of paying me impromptu social calls over the last two decades."

"I'll cut to the chase, Doc. I need your help. All these years of livin' the New Orleans lifestyle"—he patted his bulbous stomach for emphasis—"they've caught up with me. My knees, my hips—practically every joint in my damn body feels like an exploding firecracker when I put any weight on it. Just crossing a street can make me winded. And to top it off, I think maybe I'm comin' down with diabetes."

Dr. Landrieu's eyes brightened with sudden interest. "Diabetes? What makes you think that? What sort of symptoms have you been experiencing?"

"Well, I'm thirsty a lot more often then I used to be. Some nights, I'm thirsty all the time. And sometimes right after I, uh, feed, my heart goes all nutzo and my vision gets blurry. I been readin' articles about diabetes in *Modern Maturity*, so I figure I sorta know what I'm talkin' about."

"I see. This is very interesting. Most interesting, indeed." Dr. Landrieu opened his door wider and gestured for Jules to enter. "Please come in. I'd like to perform some tests. Perhaps I can help you."

Jules's face lit up like a sunrise. "Really? That's great, Doc! That's just great! Thanks!" He stepped into the foyer, then followed Dr. Landrieu into the living room, tastefully furnished with Victorian and Edwardian antiques. "Say, is that offer of a pot of coffee still good?"

"Of course. It'll just take a moment to prepare. But why don't you hold off on drinking any until after I've extracted some samples from you? We wouldn't want any caffeine or sugar to skew the results."

"Sounds right to me. What do we do first?"

"Come downstairs with me. I've maintained a modest private practice since my, *ahem,* retirement from public service, and my instruments are down there in my office."

Jules clung tightly to the banister as he descended the steep stairs to the doctor's office, wincing as each of his knees bore his full weight in turn. "Uh, Doc, not that I doubt you or anything, but will instruments that work on, y'know, *normal* people also work on me?"

"That's actually quite a good question, Jules," Dr. Landrieu replied as he reset the weights on his clinical scale to zero. "But rest assured, the entire time you were working for me, you were somewhat of a hobby of mine. I was probably the only physician in the country with an on-staff vampire available to study. Do you recall the blood samples I took from you over the years?"

"Sure. Every six months or so, you were stickin' me."

"And do you remember the reason I gave you for taking all those samples?"

"Uh, yeah . . . it was somethin' about wanting to see if drinkin' all that blood from dead people was havin' any effect on me over the long haul."

"Yes. That's exactly what I told you." He gestured for Jules to step onto the scale. "Come. Let's get a weight on you. I'll want to compare your present weight with the old charts I kept from thirty years ago."

Jules didn't move. "Uh, Doc, I don't wanna be a party pooper or nuthin', but that's a real nice scale you've got there, and I'll bet it cost you a bundle—"

The doctor smiled. "Oh, you really needn't worry. This being New Orleans, many of my patients are within fifty pounds of your weight. My scale is what you call 'industrial strength.' So hop onboard."

Jules reluctantly complied, gingerly stepping onto the scale one foot at a time to make sure its springs wouldn't bust. Once his patient was standing firmly on the scale, Dr. Landrieu began pushing the steel weights steadily to the right. Three hundred, 400, 450 pounds, and still the scale's nose remained glued in the stratosphere.

"There we are. Four hundred and sixty-three pounds," the doctor said. "That's quite a gain since the last time I weighed you."

Damn lying scale, Jules thought. *I must've lost weight during those hell-nights in Baton Rouge. 'Course, I did eat four or five sacks of dog chow . . .*

"One of the reasons I took regular blood samples from you," Dr. Landrieu continued, "was to determine whether your unusual diet was having any long-term effect on your health. But I had other reasons, as well." He handed Jules a small clear plastic cup. "Please expectorate in this."

"Huh?"

"Expectorate. *Spit.*"

"Oh. Okay."

After Jules swished and spat in the most polite way he could, his host continued. "I never mentioned this to you, because I wasn't sure how you'd react, but at first the primary goal of my researches was to find a cure for your vampirism."

"You're shittin' me, Doc—*really?*"

"Oh yes, really and truly. Unfortunately, I soon found that my reach exceeded my grasp, I'm afraid. The issues involved were well beyond my limited knowledge and resources. As you might well imagine, I was quite disappointed by my failure. However, I soon consoled myself by turning my researches in another direction. I was fascinated by your apparent resistance to many of the outward signs of aging, with the exception of your considerable weight gain. I wanted to determine whether your kind of person would be susceptible to the range of diseases medical science believes are brought on by advancing years or by various 'unhealthy lifestyle' factors. Diseases such as diabetes."

"So what exactly are you tellin' me, Doc?" Jules handed over his cupful of saliva.

"Oh, thank you. Just one more extraction left. I'll need a bit of your blood." Jules followed Dr. Landrieu over to a table covered with an assortment of sterile syringes, alcohol swabs, and other medical implements. "Roll up your left sleeve, would you? So many fascinating questions. Even after we were no longer working together, I continued with my research. How does insulin work within the body of a vampire? Does it serve any function at all? Will diseases of the pancreas progress in the same fashion as they do with normal human beings?"

Jules bit his lower lip as Dr. Landrieu poked the syringe through the white skin of his biceps and slowly drew back the plunger, collecting about an ounce of blood. It seemed so disturbingly unnatural for someone else to be drawing blood from *him*. "So give me the short version, huh, Doc? You able to help me or not?"

Dr. Landrieu carefully transferred the blood sample from the syringe to a test tube. "The 'short version,' Jules, is that if my tests indicate that you are indeed suffering from some form of adult-onset diabetes, I have on hand an experimental compound that may serve for you the same function that insulin injections do for a normal diabetes sufferer."

"You're sayin' you've got a cure for me? You're a miracle worker, Doc! I knew my shit luck was bound to turn around!"

"Now hold on a minute there. I didn't say anything about a cure. What I may have for you is a *treatment*. A drug that, if it's effective, you'll need to take every day for the rest of your, er, life. Just as many normal diabetes sufferers need to take their insulin injections every day in order to keep their blood sugar levels stable."

"Hey, that's good enough for me! So when will we know the results of your tests?"

"Oh, that shouldn't take very long. Go relax up in the living room. I'll be up in a few minutes. And then we'll have that pot of coffee."

Jules waited patiently upstairs, perusing the doctor's bookshelves, which, apart from the expected medical and anatomy tomes, also held a respectable collection of nineteenth-century Persian erotica. He felt a jagged twinge in his heart when he recalled his own lost collections. After a few moments, Dr. Landrieu appeared in the doorway.

"Everything is 'cooking,' as they say. We should have our results shortly. Why don't you come with me into the kitchen?"

Jules forced the memory of his recent losses from his mind. "Sure thing."

"I don't believe I ever told you this," Dr. Landrieu said while pouring bottled water into his coffeemaker, "but the most crushing disappointment of my professional life was losing those last two races I ran for city coroner. Not because I was out of a job—I stood to make far better money in private practice, particularly with my connections. No, I suffered the torments of the damned because I knew that, out of office, I no longer had the opportunity to lure you away from live victims. How many lives did I save during those nearly thirty years you were in my employ? A thousand? Fifteen hundred? I was a good and conscientious public servant—with the possible exception of a kickback or two, and that was rather small beer—but I always considered my greatest service to the people of this city to be keeping you off her streets at night. Here. Here's your coffee. I have some nondairy creamer, if you'd like."

"Uh, thanks. No creamer, though." Jules's first sip of coffee tasted especially bitter. "Gee, Doc, I never knew you felt that way. If I'd a known, I dunno, maybe we could've worked out some kinda arrangement or something, y'know, after you weren't in office no more . . ."

"I have a proposal for you." Dr. Landrieu sat across from Jules and lanced him with a penetrating stare. "What I suggest may sound somewhat unusual, or even outlandish, but you must believe that I am absolutely serious. I have been thinking about this for a long time. You can't know how many nights I turned on the evening news to see the police pulling a dead body from a swamp or a vacant lot, and always I wondered, *Is this the work of my old friend Jules?* And illogical though it might be, each time I asked myself that question, an arrow of guilt pierced my heart."

The doctor sighed, his gaze dropping to the steam rising from his mug of coffee. His moment of self-absorption did not last long, however. "But that is neither here nor there. This is my proposal—come to Argentina with me. Now that my Eudice is gone, there is no longer anything to hold me to New Orleans. Work as my assistant again, train with me, and you will never again need to hunt."

"What're you talkin' about, Doc? Argentina? What, you got a new job as a coroner lined up down there?"

The doctor allowed himself to smile. "No, not as a coroner. A much more lucrative job than that, both for me and for you. Down in Argentina, you see, there is a national craze for cosmetic surgery. All segments of society, both rich and poor, indulge in it. Among Argentine women, body sculpting is especially popular. A procedure you might know as liposuction. There is a tremendous shortage of cosmetic surgeons in Argentina. For anyone with a medical degree and a few years of experience in virtually any specialty, acquiring a license to practice cosmetic surgery in Argentina is child's play."

Jules took another sip of coffee while he tried to put the pieces together. "Uh-huh. I see as how that might be good news for you. But how do I fit into all this?"

"You obviously don't know much about the liposuction procedure."

"Nope."

"To put it simply, liposuction involves the insertion of a cannula, a sort of combination scalpel and vacuum cleaner, into areas of a patient's body that harbor intractable and unsightly fat reserves. The surgeon sweeps the cannula beneath the patient's dermis, snipping away and then suctioning out masses of fatty tissues."

"Yeech! I mean, dieting's bad enough, but this—"

"Don't be so quick to pass judgment, my friend. Liposuction, as it currently stands, is a very crude procedure. Along with every ounce of fat tissue extracted, two or more ounces of subcutaneous fluids are also removed. Including"—and here Dr. Landrieu paused for effect—"blood. The resulting slurry is an extremely rich organic mixture, typically composed of nearly two-thirds plasma components. Virtually all cosmetic surgeons dispose of this slurry as medical waste. I, however"—he raised his right eyebrow pointedly—"could very well imagine other uses it might be put to."

Jules felt his mouth begin to water, even though his mind hadn't yet struggled through all the implications. "You mean, uh, me, eh, like, drinkin' it?"

Dr. Landrieu brought his hands together in a thunderclap. "Yes, Jules! Imagine dining on milk shakes and caviar for the rest of your unlimited existence! For I have little doubt that eventually, with a judicious application of bribes, we could set you up in your own practice in the hinterlands. So that after I pass on to my inevitable reward, you would not want for anything." He reached across the table and grabbed hold of Jules's free hand. "Now tell me, am I making *sense?*"

Jules felt beads of sweat trickle down the interior seams of his new safari suit. He felt he had come to a decisive juncture in his undead existence. The bitter coffee roiled in his stomach like a boiling black gumbo. "Wait—I can't think about it all at once. Doc, I can't change my whole fuckin' life in just five minutes. You've gotta give me some time to think this through."

Dr. Landrieu released his hand. "Of course. I hope my enthusiasm didn't intimidate you. Let me go downstairs and check on your results. Then we'll have more to talk about."

Jules rested his forehead heavily on his hands. Argentina sounded like a paradise. But could he bear to leave New Orleans? Hadn't his miserable five-day exile proven to him that living outside the Big Easy was like trying to survive without air?

Dr. Landrieu reentered the kitchen and sat down across from Jules. "It's as I'd expected. You're suffering from the beginning stages of a condition analogous to adult-onset diabetes mellitus. Fortunately for you, since we've caught it early, and little permanent degeneration has occurred, my experimental compound should prove very effective in staving off further symptoms."

"Doc, I just thought of somethin'—if this diabetes has been caused by what I've been eatin' all these years, wouldn't going down with you to Argentina and livin' off those 'milk shakes' make it a whole lot worse?"

Dr. Landrieu smiled. "As your physician, I'm a step or two ahead of you. Should my compound be as efficacious as I have every right to expect it will be, your dietary worries will be at an end. You will be in the envious position of being able to eat whatever you damn well please. So tell me, what do you think of the notion of relocating down south?"

Jules paused before answering, slowly stirring his coffee with a teaspoon. "Well, Doc, I've gotta be honest with you . . . it'd be awfully hard for me to leave New Orleans."

The doctor leaned forward across the table. "Why?"

Jules shifted uncomfortably in his chair. "It's just . . . well, this old town's a part of me, like my fingernails or the calluses on the bottoms of my feet. I never have to wonder where my pals are or where I can get me a good cup of joe. I can drive through the French Quarter and roll down my windows and hear my kinda music floatin' through the air, for free. I can hardly imagine even *visitin'* some other place."

The doctor was silent. Jules avoided meeting his gaze, instead staring into the murky depths of his stone-cold coffee. "So, uh, do I still get to try out that medicine of yours?"

Dr. Landrieu slowly stood. "Of course, Jules. I'm a physician, not a blackmailer. I have a small supply in the refrigerator. Let me get it for you." He opened the refrigerator behind Jules and was hidden by the door as he fumbled with the contents inside. "Just give me a moment longer; I need to make sure there is enough to get you started on your regimen. . . . Yes. We are in good shape."

He closed the refrigerator and handed Jules a small white plastic bottle with a child-resistant cap. Sticky shreds of an old label still clung to the bottle's sides. "Please pardon the looks of that bottle. I try to recycle as much as I can. Well. You have enough tablets there for fifteen days. Take two each night, one upon rising and one before you retire."

"Thanks, Doc!" Jules placed the bottle in one of his trench coat's many pockets, then took out his wallet, which Maureen had generously restocked with forty dollars of walking-around money. "What do I owe you?"

Dr. Landrieu pushed the money aside. "Nothing. I can't ethically charge you a fee for an experimental drug. Come back in fifteen days and tell me how you feel, and then we'll discuss payment. In the meantime, the only favor I ask of you is that you not reject the idea of accompanying me to Argentina out of hand. Promise me you'll reconsider over the next two weeks?"

"Sure thing, Doc. It won't hurt me none to think about it some more. So anyway, what do I need to know about this here wonder drug of yours? Is it safe to take it with coffee?"

"Certainly. There should be no adverse caffeine interactions."

"Should I go ahead and take my first one now?"

"I don't see why not. The sooner you begin, the sooner you'll experience relief from your symptoms. Actually, you may experience a marked improvement in as little as a day or two."

"Really? Hey, that's terrific!" It took Jules a few seconds to get the bottle open; those child-resistant caps had always given him trouble. He tapped a small, round, white tablet into his palm. Jules was surprised to see that it had the letter *A* engraved on it. Perhaps the *A* stood for "Amos," Dr. Landrieu's first name? He popped the tablet in his mouth and downed it with the dregs of his coffee.

Dr. Landrieu picked up Jules's empty cup and saucer and deposited them in the sink. "Well. I'm glad we've had this little reunion, Jules. I'll see you again in fifteen days?"

"Sure thing. I hope these pills're as good as you say they are."

Dr. Landrieu led him through the living room to the entrance foyer. "Oh, I suspect you'll be very pleasantly surprised."

◆

Jules drove along the edge of the Jewish cemetery until he reached Canal Street. Then he made a right turn toward the French Quarter. No doubt about it, his luck was beginning to turn. By the time he reached the garage across from Maureen's house, he was already feeling the tinglings of a fresh surge of energy. Shuttling his packages from the Lincoln's trunk, down the garage's stairs, up Maureen's front steps, down her hallway, and up more stairs to the closet she'd assigned him, he could swear that his knees already hurt less than before. His stride had more zing in it. Maybe it was just his imagination, but he felt twenty years younger and two hundred pounds lighter.

He sat for a moment on Maureen's front stoop, pondering how he should spend the rest of his night. A Lucky Dog vendor wheeled his wiener cart along Bienville Street, and Jules waved and wished him a good evening.

"You want I should fix you a dog, pal?" the vendor asked. He looked to be in his late sixties, with a well-tanned, deeply furrowed but personable face.

"Wish I could, buddy," Jules answered mournfully, eyeing the bin of wieners and tray of condiments with an expression just short of lust.

"I understand," the vendor said in a consoling voice. He cocked an ear toward the tiny portable radio he carried on his cart and turned up the volume. His gentle smile faded into a grimace. "You been listening to this crap on the news? Those dopes on the North Shore want that asshole Nathan Knight to get back into politics again."

"What's this?"

"You've gotta remember Nathan Knight, right?"

"He ran for governor or somethin', didn't he?"

"Yeah, and the bum got his racist ass kicked. But now this committee of 'concerned citizens' over there across the lake are trying to convince him to make another run for office. They're holdin' a big rally a couple of nights from now." He shook his head sadly. "People like that give me the willies. I don't know what your politics are, pal. But me, my folks brought me over from Germany when I was five years old. Just before WW Two. So people like that . . . well, they give me the willies, is all."

Jules had never given Nathan Knight and his followers much thought. Or any politics, for that matter. He'd always been too concerned about where his next meal was coming from to pay any attention.

The Lucky Dog vendor switched off his radio. "Sorry I disturbed you. Have a good night." He hefted the handles of his cart and began moving off down the street. Too late, Jules realized that the man had probably interpreted his lost-in-thought silence as disagreement. He hated the notion that the vendor had pegged him as a Knight supporter. But the man was already halfway down the block.

The scent of boiled wieners lingered in the air. Jules thought some more about what he'd just heard. A huge rally of black-hating white people on the North Shore? *Hrrmmm* . . . now *that* smelled like an opportunity. A foul-smelling opportunity, for sure; Jules didn't relish the thought of associating with people who wouldn't be caught dead sharing a cup of joe with Erato. But Jules had watched enough trash haulers make a good profit from stuff that stank to know it could be done. He could wash his hands of the whole lot of them after it was all over and his life had returned to normal.

Jules smiled at the ingenuity and sheer audacity of his idea. Maureen had wanted him to come up with a plan of action. Well, he just did.

If Malice X could form his own vampire army, then by golly, so could Jules Duchon.

EIGHT

Action Plan Step One: He needed to find out more about this Nathan Knight rally—when and where it would be held, how many supporters were expected to show.

Action Plan Step Two: As a reward for formulating and accomplishing Action Plan Step One, he needed to do something really nice for himself. Maureen had given Jules some walking-around money. Although he couldn't even begin to replace his one-of-a-kind record collection, there was another vital personal collection he could begin replenishing. Nudie books. And the best thing about Jules buying new nudie books was that he could accomplish Action Plan Steps One and Two at the same time and in the same place, a valuable saving of effort.

With renewed determination fueled in part by Doc Landrieu's miracle tablets, Jules walked purposefully in the direction of Royal Tobacco and News, downtown's most discreet late-night source of newspapers, cigars, and pornography. The walk from Maureen's stoop to the newsstand was only four and a half blocks, but the streets were shadowed and desolate, mostly comprising warehouses and parking garages unused at night. Ordinarily, Jules wouldn't have given such surroundings a second thought; or, if he did, he'd be feeling happy twinges of anticipation as he searched for an isolated derelict to drain dry. But tonight, these abandoned blocks felt vaguely menacing. He couldn't walk more than three steps without glancing back over his shoulder.

Jules sighed with relief when he reached the one hundred block of Royal Street. This stretch of Royal, just off Canal Street, bustled with people. Sure, the people who hung out there tended to have lengthy police records and suffer from unusual venereal diseases, but Jules wasn't in any mood to be picky about company.

As he walked past the Funland Amusements Arcade, whose window was plastered with anti-loitering signs in seven different languages, a mustachioed black man wearing a fringed buckskin jacket stepped out of the entranceway and blocked the sidewalk.

"Hey, man, you need a prepaid calling card?"

"No," Jules answered.

"Turkish cigarettes?"

"No."

"Diet pills? I bought up a good stash of Flabovate just before the FDA banned it, man."

Jules frowned. "You need a fat lip to go with that big fat hat of yours?"

"Uh, no." The man faded back into the shadows. Just beyond the arcade's blinking lights, Jules paused to glance back, wanting to see what rap the huckster would lay on the next sucker to walk by. But the huckster was gone.

Royal Tobacco and News was a narrow, cluttered storefront with a pull-down corrugated metal shutter for a front wall, hardly bigger than a kiosk. It sat next to a bedraggled aid station for foreign sailors; the plastic-wrapped magazines in the back of the newsstand had supplied far more assistance to sailors than any employee of the aid station ever could. Apart from an ever-varying parade of newspapers and magazines, the newsstand had hardly changed in the last fifty years, which was one reason why Jules loved it. Even with its open front, the place smelled like an all-night poker game. It was a home away from home.

The newsstand's owner and only employee sat in a battered office chair behind a wood-paneled counter, smoking a cigar and reading an issue of *Alfred Hitchcock's Mystery Magazine*. The small man's outstanding feature was his nose, which, scarred by a profusion of ulcers and melanomas, bore a startling resemblance to a topographic map of Peru.

"Hey, Philip, how's it goin'?"

The white-haired owner looked up from his magazine. "Oh, hey,

Jules! I was just thinkin' about you earlier this week." His badly chapped lips formed a puzzled frown. "Although I'll be damned to hell if I can remember why."

"Don't rack your brain too hard. Say, you got any *Times-Picayune*s left?"

The salesman cocked a wry eyebrow. "You upgradin' your class of readin' material? Yeah, I got a few left. They're out in front."

"How about yesterday's edition?"

"I might have some stacked out back by the Dumpster. Why?"

"I'm lookin' for one story in particular, and I'm not sure what day it got written up. You mind diggin' me out one of them papers from yesterday?"

Philip scowled. "Goddamn customers with their goddamn special orders . . ."

Two minutes later, Jules was busily unsticking damp pages of newsprint from one another. He found the story he was looking for in the local section of a fragrant newspaper from the Dumpster. He smoothed down the page on Philip's worn wooden counter and began to read.

> Knight Supporters Hope to Spark Run with Rally
> by Vicki Hyman, St. Tammany Bureau
> Supporters of white supremacy advocate and perennial political candidate Nathan Knight plan to rally in Covington in the hope of luring their preferred candidate into the race to fill two open St. Tammany Parish Council slots. Knight, who in the last decade has mounted unsuccessful campaigns for the U.S. presidency, a U.S. Senate seat, the Louisiana governorship, and the position of Louisiana commissioner of agriculture, has in recent years limited his public activities to appearances on his weekly radio show, promoting his Web site, and conducting occasional real estate seminars. He currently resides in Covington. The organizer of the rally, who declined to be named, stated, "The St. Tammany Parish Council has suffered for years from a leadership vacuum. They need Knight. Only a leader of the caliber of Nathan Knight has a prayer of maintaining the high quality of life that sets St. Tammany apart and makes it a haven for decent, Christian families." The rally will take place at the American Veterans Union Hall in downtown Covington and is scheduled for 9:00 P.M. on Wednesday. Organizers expect a crowd of at least 200 supporters

and have extended an invitation for Knight to attend. Knight's plans regarding participation in the rally could not be verified.

Jules's mind raced. *Two hundred white supremacists? All gathered together like presents under a Christmas tree! It could work . . . sure it could work! Sure! Who could be better for me to recruit than nutcases who already hate black folks?*

He smiled at the obvious brilliance of his brainstorm. An army of two hundred white supremacist vampires would make Malice X shit his skintight leather pants; Jules would be in a position to demand any sort of deal he wanted. Nobody would ever dare fuck with him again. And Maureen would have to be impressed. Diet or no diet, she'd just *have* to be bowled over by his victory, eager to take him back as her coffin-mate again.

Now that Action Plan Step One had been dispensed with, Jules remembered Action Plan Step Two. "Hey, Philip, any good nudie stuff come in recently?"

"Ah-*ha*!" the salesman exclaimed. "*That's* what I was tryin' to remember! Funny you should ask about nudie books. I got somethin' really special fer you."

"Oh yeah?"

"Yeah. Hang on a sec. I gotta dig it out from under the counter." He disappeared beneath the counter for a few seconds, then reappeared with a folded-over brown paper bag. "This is the last one I got. Maybe the last one in the whole city. I swear, I never had a book fly off the shelves like this one. Y'know, with *Big Cheeks Pictorial*, I usually order four, maybe five copies a month. It's a pretty regular seller, but it's no *Hustler*. But this sucker I've had to reorder twice, and last week my distributor said the whole run's gone. I knew you'd love it, so I pulled the last one and stuck it under the counter, figurin' you'd be in sooner or later."

Jules opened the bag and took out the magazine. The enormously voluptuous blond woman on the cover lay on a leopard skin draped over a red leather couch. But the kitschy props surrounding her faded from Jules's attention like mist, leaving only a vision of luminosity. Her ivory white skin was flawless, glowing with an inner light. Her tremendous, gravity-defying breasts seemed shaped by a master craftsman, perfectly symmetrical, her nipples shining like pink jewels. Beneath them, three gorgeous tummy rolls descended like a stairway to paradise.

It was the same woman Jules had seen two weeks earlier in the Trolley

Stop Café. The woman who had enjoyed her whipped-cream-covered pancakes so provocatively.

"Y'know, usually fat women don't do nuthin' fer me," Philip continued, "but I gotta admit, I took one look at this one, and my fuckin' trousers were like a Boy Scout tent fer an hour."

Jules dug eight dollar bills out of his wallet and slapped them down on the counter. "Philip, you're good as gold."

"Yeah. Well, you enjoy it, my friend. That soggy newspaper you can have fer free. See you next month."

"Sure thing, pal. Take care."

Jules could hardly wait to get back to Maureen's house. Not only because of his new magazine, either—all those cups of coffee he'd downed at Doc Landrieu's had him needing to piss like a racehorse. Why oh *why* hadn't he used the bathroom before he left?

He still had that nagging sense of being watched. To be safe, he really should stick to the busiest, most populated streets. This would mean a zigzag course back to Maureen's house, maybe eight or nine blocks.

But Jules wasn't sure he could last that long. He didn't want to have to spend $4.50 in some dive bar on a beer he couldn't even drink just for the privilege of using the bathroom. The direct route to Maureen's was only four and a half blocks. Those four blocks were some of the most desolate in the Quarter. On the upside, if he just couldn't hold it anymore, he could pee in an alleyway without worrying that some cop would drag him down to the station for indecent exposure.

His bladder didn't let him debate too long. The direct route it was. Holding himself with one hand, his newspaper and precious magazine with the other, Jules headed west on Iberville Street as fast as his legs would carry him. Trying to distract himself from his most immediate problem, he thought about the woman on the cover of *Big Cheeks Pictorial*. What had she been doing in New Orleans a couple of weeks before? Maybe she lived here? What a weird coincidence, his seeing her in the Trolley Stop and then buying a copy of her whack-off mag barely two weeks later. Her and that stack of flapjacks . . . now *there* was a woman who knew how to enjoy a meal. What an incredible sight that had been, a woman of her size and classy grooming eating massive quantities of fattening food with such sensual gusto—in public, yet! Man, if only Maureen could learn to be so relaxed about her size . . . what a refreshing change *that* would be. . . .

Something in the window of a parking garage attendant's booth caught

Jules's eye. A flyer was taped to the inside of the window, with a picture of a woman on it. The caption beneath the image read, I'M MISSING—HAVE YOU SEEN ME? followed by a phone number to call. The photocopied snapshot was blurry, dark, and indistinct, but Jules was almost positive it was a photo of one of his most recent victims. Bessie. Hummingbird Bessie.

Naww, that can't be right, he told himself. *She was just some homeless lady. Nobody cared whether she lived or died. Nobody's lookin' for Bessie. It must be somebody else.*

But the thought that it might actually be Bessie on the leaflet wouldn't go away. The suspicion haunted him like a pesky mosquito, fluttering against his nose and ears no matter how fiercely he tried swatting it away. The tiny hairs on the back of his neck stood stiffly. He had the queasy, prickly sensation of being followed. He passed other windows and telephone poles that had similar flyers taped or stapled to them, but he didn't stop to look at any of these. Jules walked as fast as his chafing thighs would allow.

Three black men emerged from the shadows of an alleyway. One was dressed in a flashy sharkskin suit, with gold cuff links the size of golf balls. The second guy Jules recognized as the buckskin-jacketed huckster from the amusement arcade. The lead man, a couple of inches taller than Jules, wore a black cowboy hat with a silver medallion, snakeskin boots, black leather pants, and a Los Angeles Raiders starter jacket inlaid with gold thread.

What the hell is this? Jules thought as the three blocked his path. *That dumb-ass cowboy huckster couldn't sell me any shit on his own, so now he's hunted up a couple of buddies to help part me from my hard-earned cash? This some kinda Texas-based pyramid scheme for black guys?*

"Look," Jules said, "I don't want no diet pills, I don't want no Turkish cigarettes, and I don't want no prepaid calling card, okay?"

The lead man grinned. "Chump, you ain't gonna *need* no callin' card. Unless you plan on makin' calls from wherever it is dumb-ass bloodsuckahs go when they dead."

The other two men smiled broadly, revealing sharp fangs.

Jules's blood ran cold. *"Oh shit—!"* He tried dodging into the street, but the two henchmen were way too fast for him. They grabbed his arms and manhandled him into a nearby alleyway, nearly dislocating his shoulders in the process.

They slung him against a dirty brick wall like he was a rug that needed beating. The cowboy in leather pants took his sweet time walking into the alleyway after them. He was clearly enjoying this and wanted to make it last.

"Y'know, you is one *stoo-pid* white-ass muthahfuckah," the cowboy said with relish. "Malice, he be happy as a pig in shit when he gets word tonight that you's back in town. If it ain't for some deal he got tonight down at City Hall, he be here hisself to do ya. But instead, lucky li'l me . . . I gets the pleasure."

Sweat ran down Jules's sides like rivers of ice water. He struggled against his captors, but they were just too strong. Easily as strong as he'd been as a young vampire, and there were two of them. The cowboy walked to a corner of the alleyway and picked up an empty wooden fruit crate. With hardly more than a quick flick of his wrist, he smashed it against the wall. What remained in his hand was a long, sharp, jagged plank, rusty nails protruding from its splintered length like shark's teeth.

The cowboy tested the plank's uneven point with his fingertip. "Heh. Guess it'll hafta do."

He stood in front of Jules, blocking what little light spilled into the alleyway. "Don't know if ya still say yo' prayers, chump. If ya do, now's a good time."

Jules's coffee-stretched bladder felt as though it would burst. For the second time in as many weeks, the faces of his friends and loved ones flashed on the big movie screen of his mind. Staring extinction in its ugly mug was getting to be a bad habit.

"Hold him tight now, boys. I miss, it get messy. And you don't want no stains on them pretty outfits."

Lord, if only they'd let him piss before they killed him . . . his damn pants were so tight, they were squeezing the life out of him even without a stake through his heart. If he could loosen them just a *little*—

With a wicked flourish, the cowboy twisted the stake over his head and behind his back like a pair of nunchakus. Then he advanced toward Jules.

Bowel-shriveling panic gave Jules a desperate idea. Clenching his eyes shut, he forced himself to think of the moon, the fat white full moon rising over a muddy levee . . .

"Boss, somethin's happenin'!"

"He's changin'! The muthah's changin'!"

Jules's bones melted and reformed like hot wax. Sinews twisted themselves into new shapes. His skin sprouted thick gray fur, as though he'd been dipped in Ultra-Rogaine.

"Hold him, you idjits! He still gots a heart! I can still git him!"

His massive belly lost some of its heft as it shifted to a more oblong shape. His previously constricting pants and underwear fell down around his suddenly thin hind legs. Released from its imprisonment, his coffee-engorged organ obeyed the laws of hydrodynamics and burst forth like a fire hose. Right in the cowboy's leering face.

"Ugglbbuh! Fugghh!"

Stunned, the two henchmen loosened their grip on Jules's forepaws. Jules fell heavily onto his back, still spouting like a broken hydrant.

"Look out!"

"The *suit*—fuckin' suit cost five hunurd—!"

"Aww *shit*—!"

Jules rolled onto all four paws and ran. Dragging his safari jacket and trench coat, he bounded across the cowboy's prone body, stepping heavily on the fallen vampire's chest and treating him to a final squirt or two. Then he was out of the alleyway and into the street. His still-pendulous belly bounced along the ground, smacking asphalt and ancient cobblestones. Greased lightning he wasn't. But he was moving a hell of a lot faster on four legs than he would've on two.

Sure, he was moving faster—but where to run to? He couldn't head directly back to Maureen's house. Not only would that give away his hiding place, it would endanger her. He had to lead his pursuers in the wrong direction, then lose them somehow.

Behind him, multiple sets of running footsteps echoed off warehouse walls. Jules shook loose of his safari jacket and trench coat. Brand new. Maureen would kill him. He scampered around the corner, slipping and sliding in a puddle of spilled pineapple daiquiri, and fled toward Canal Street.

Even at this late hour, there were still people out—bums, doomsday preachers, taxi drivers, and the occasional lost or foolhardy tourist. The scents were overwhelming, almost maddening. A toxic mélange of sour sweat, bus exhaust, spilled beer, and beer piss assaulted his nostrils. Jules weaved in and out of the forest of legs, poles, and trash cans, trying to put as much distance between him and those pursuing footsteps as possible.

He didn't go unnoticed.

"A rabid dog!"

"Filthy beast!"

"A sure sign of the End Days—"

"It's *obese!*"

Closer. His hunters were drawing closer. No matter how fast he ran, their muttered curses grew nearer and louder, the pungent scent of his own urine on their clothing closer and stronger.

He bounded into Rampart Street without a glance at the stoplight. A late-model Oldsmobile Aurora swerved wildly to avoid him. Its neon running boards left glowing slashes in the night air as the heavy car plunged through the boarded-up display windows of the closed Woolworth's five-and-dime on the corner.

Did that stop them—?

No. They were too fast. Too agile. Their footsteps still beat the asphalt behind him, closer than ever.

Gulping down yelps of terror, Jules caught the scent of what might be salvation. Could it be—? *Yes!* The Goodfeller's Fried Catfish next to the Saenger Theater was still open! Three boys stood near the bus stop, their hands full of heaping platters of fish, the cardboard trays already soaked through with grease.

The black vampires were so close now. Jules leapt at the boys, knocking their platters from their hands. The trays of Goodfeller's Fried Catfish, the greasiest substance known to man, scattered across the sidewalk behind Jules, coating the walkway with a thick scrim of deep-fry oil and slippery flesh.

"Hey, my food—"

"Watch it! Watch it!"

"Shee-yit—!"

Jules listened with tremendous satisfaction as his pursuers lost their footing, smashed into garbage cans (all emblazoned with the mayor's smiling face), and tumbled into the gutter. He rounded the corner of the Saenger Theater, headed north on Basin Street for a block, then cut back toward the Quarter and Maureen's.

Panting heavily, he reached her home on Bienville Street. Home base! He was safe! He'd duck behind that thick door, crawl up into the attic, and they wouldn't find him in a thousand lifetimes.

Then he realized he had one small problem. His key was in the pocket of his trench coat. And Maureen wouldn't be home for at least another three hours.

Shivering from exertion, he squirmed through broken masonry and bent chicken wire into the wet, muddy crawl space beneath her house. He had no choice but to hide in the damp darkness until Maureen came home from her shift at Jezebel's Joy Room.

He crawled behind an ancient, rotting Jax Beer shipping crate and dug a shallow hole in the dirt for his belly so he could rest more comfortably. Those bastards! They'd cost him the last copy of *Big Cheeks Pictorial!* Maybe tomorrow night it'd still be lying in the alleyway where he'd dropped it? . . . Naw, that was too much to hope for; some bum would stumble on it and praise the Lord for his good fortune.

Voices—maybe two blocks away. His pursuers? Jules perked up his amazingly sensitive ears and listened.

"—think he came back this way."

"You sure?"

"Man, this place got more nooks an' crannies than my ol' lady's ass. He could be hidin' anywheres."

"I tell you what then. It take a wolf to catch a wolf. Take yo' clothes off an' change."

"Why *me*? I hate doin' that shit."

"Why you? 'Cause I's *tellin'* you, that's why. Now strip, suckah."

"Can't Leroy do it?"

"Did I tell *Leroy* to do it? Whatchu complainin' 'bout, anyhows? Yo' suit's drippin' with wolf piss. You oughtta be *happy* to get outta them rags, man."

"Aww, fuck, all right then. . . ."

Uh-oh. This meant big trouble. A fellow wolf would sniff him out in no time. What now? He was too tired to give them much of a chase again. And where could he run to, anyhow? To the Trolley Stop? No. They'd catch him before he got even three blocks uptown.

The only solution was to become something without a scent. Jules knew what *that* meant. And the thought gave him cold shivers. The last time he'd transformed into mist, he'd almost died. In mist form, he had virtually no control over his body at all. The wind could take him anywhere. In the very worst scenario, he could become so dispersed that he'd be unable to transmute back to human form before deadly sunrise.

Not far away, a human moan of pain slowly transmogrified into a wolf's guttural snarl. It was now or never. Possible death by dispersal versus certain death by a stake through his heart. No choice at all, really.

Jules concentrated on memories from ninety years ago, from before he'd become a vampire, when he could still go outside early on a Sunday morning and greet the sun. Memories of climbing the levee outside his house and watching the thick blanket of river mist swirl and coalesce over the Mississippi like a jealous and loving thing.

"Hey, Leroy, I think yo' bud's caught a scent already!"

"Yeah, lookit him go!"

Gray hairs melted into tiny floating water droplets. Bone and flesh liquefied, then recoalesced as cloud. Of all his possible transformations, this was the one most amazing to Jules, the most alien and the most terrifying. Was he even still alive in this form? He didn't breathe. He didn't have a pulse—nowhere in his expanding form was there a heart to pump, blood to be pumped, or veins to pump it through. But he could still think, even if his thoughts were scattered, diffused, difficult to focus. And even without ears, he could still "hear." Sound vibrations traveled across the water droplets of his "body" in an unceasing flow, an incredibly rich matrix that became easier for Jules to decipher with each passing second.

The first sounds Jules was able to recognize were canine whines of frustration.

"Damn! What happened?"

"He was headin' straight for that house—"

"Now he's lookin' around like some ghost slapped him upside the head—?"

"He lost the scent! Damn! We fucked, man! Fuck!"

A warm glow of satisfaction spread through Jules's vapory form. Age and guile would trump youthful strength and energy every time . . . so long as the punks gave the old guy even half a chance.

He "listened" to the three of them stomp away in angry frustration. *Heh.* If he had a mouth, he'd laugh. Maybe those punks would think twice before screwing with Jules Duchon again. There was more to being a good vampire than flashy clothes, a bad attitude, and an army of flunkies to back you up. Hell, he was more vampire than any of these wet-behind-the-ears pissants would *ever* be—

Huh? He was moving. He hadn't willed himself to move. He wanted to stay right where he was, under the house, until Maureen showed.

It was the wind. A strong wind was pushing him out from beneath the house. He struggled to stay in place, trying desperately to "grab" the Jax Beer crate and the house's pilings, but his misty form flowed right around these potential anchors.

Before he could begin thinking of a Plan B, he was spread across

Bienville Street, portions of him drifting under derelict cars or condensing on rusty fire hydrants. It was all he could do to keep himself together. His scattered thoughts ricocheted back to terrible memories, memories of him slowly dispersing across a tremendous field, being pulled into the obscene embrace of the tall grass, helpless, so terrifyingly *helpless*—

The wind shifted. He found himself blowing back the way he'd come. He collected himself off the various metal surfaces where he'd condensed, relying on the almost magical attraction of water molecules to other water molecules. He wasn't heading back to Maureen's house, however. He was being pushed into the cavernous old building next to her home, a coffee warehouse that had been converted to a parking garage.

He mentally breathed a sigh of relief. This was one of the safest places the wind could've deposited him. There was no vegetation to absorb him, and the walls of the garage would keep him compact enough that he could condense on the relatively cool concrete floor and gradually pull himself back together.

What a night! After this, he'd definitely take Maureen's advice and cool his heels in the safety of her house for a while. Give Doc Landrieu's pills a chance to work their magic to the fullest before he'd confront the cruel world again—

A wall of sound shattered the garage's early-morning quiet. The high-pitched mechanical whine reverberated off the brick walls, quaking Jules's entire form with brutal vibrations. What could it possibly be this time? Why couldn't he have even five minutes of peace? And then he was moving again.

Only now he wasn't being pushed. He was being pulled. Suctioned. He realized with a jolt of horror what was vibrating him so violently.

It was a vacuum cleaner. And not just your run-of-the-mill Hoovermatic. The mechanical beast sucking him toward its maw was a sidewalk sweeper, part of the fleet that cleaned the walkways of the Quarter in the hours just before dawn.

The whine was the whine of stainless-steel death. Obliteration dealt by an array of sharp fans rotating hundreds of times a second.

There was no escaping those blades. Jules desperately tried to change, but the ceaseless vibrations shattered his concentration and made any transformation hopeless. He was caught. Like a rat in a trap. No, *worse* than a rat in a trap.

Slowly, inexorably, the cruel steel blades sucked him in.

NINE

If Jules'd had a mouth, this is what he would've screamed:

"Whoa *whoa* WHOA *WHOA-HAAAAA!*"

Thankfully, he didn't have a mouth, or any other organs or limbs, because the whirling vacuum blades scrambled him up worse than a ride on the old Pontchartrain Beach Zephyr roller coaster. The suction pulled his gaseous form apart. The blades minced the separate clouds into stray atoms. Tiny fragments of Jules shot the rapids through the suction tube. Sudden compression knocked him into blissful unconsciousness; blissful because he didn't have to experience the forced mingling of his substance with the street filth already in the sweeper's canvas waste bag, a mingling that would later play havoc with his delicate complexion.

Half an hour later Jules regained a semblance of consciousness. The machine was silent. His atoms had coalesced in the bottom of the waste bag. He groggily wondered whether it was safe to attempt a transformation back to his habitual shape; after the scrambling he'd undergone, the change could leave him with fingers sticking out of his head and his nose where his asshole normally was.

He had no idea where the sweeper had stopped. He didn't even know whether the sun was up or down. But a quick reflection upon what *else* might come hurtling down the sweeper's tube to mingle with his atoms convinced him to make the effort. Any fate was better than intermixing with the disgusting slurry that collected in the gutters of Bourbon Street.

The horror of that thought popped him quickly back to human form. His head and one leg protruded through the sweeper's canvas bag. He quickly realized that the sweeper was still inside the parking garage; Jules figured the operator had left for a coffee break. A minor application of his strength allowed him to push his other leg and both arms through the bag, which—when torn away from the sweeping apparatus—became a rustic, but serviceable, coverall.

Jules crawled to the front entrance of the parking garage, doing his best to stay out of sight. The sun hadn't come up yet, thank goodness. The absence of light across the street at Maureen's house meant she hadn't come home from her shift yet. So it couldn't be any later than four A.M.

He cautiously peered up and down the street, looking for any sign of his pursuers. The street seemed deserted. He considered his options. The parking garage was too open to serve as an effective hiding place while he waited for Maureen to come home. The best thing for him to do, he decided, was to squeeze himself into the crawl space beneath Maureen's house and hide behind her front stoop.

He'd managed to shove about two-thirds of his body beneath her front steps when he heard a very familiar, very agitated voice behind him.

"Well, Jules, I hate to say I told you so. *But I told you so!*"

His already cool blood ran even colder. Facing Maureen's scornful fury was more ball-shriveling than being hunted by dozens of Malice X's thugs.

"You just *had* to go out, didn't you?" she continued. "You couldn't even stay inside for, what—six lousy hours? Why do I even bother trying with you?"

He tried turning around to face her, but the space beneath her steps was a tight fit. "Mo, honey, I can explain everything—"

"Oh, I'm *sure* you can! How about we start with the reason you're wearing a ripped-up sack instead of your clothes? Let's see . . . you donated your ensemble to some sweet old five-hundred-pound homeless man, right? Or you just landed a role as an extra in a caveman picture, and the producers were too cheap to provide you with a bearskin—"

"Can I maybe get a word in edgewise here?"

"No!"

"I'm glad you're being so reasonable, baby. You think maybe we could continue this inside?"

"Why? Am I embarrassing you? Is it *possible* for me to embarrass you worse than you've already embarrassed yourself?"

"Probably—*eh!*—not." Jules managed to back his way out of the crawl space. He dusted the mud off his hands and knees, then glanced nervously up and down the block. "Look, honey, I enjoy an open-air humiliation as much as the next guy, but it's just not safe for us to be out here right now. Can we *please* go inside?"

Maureen blocked the door with the formidable barricade of her body. "Not until you promise to tell me exactly what you've been up to tonight. And don't even try to bullshit me—when it comes to you, my bullshit detector's as sensitive as a just-circumcised pecker."

Jules peered fearfully up the deserted street. "All right! I promise! I promise!"

Maureen unlocked the door and stalked into her kitchen. She flung open her refrigerator door, grabbed a glass milk container filled with blood, and took a long, deep slug straight from the bottle. Pointedly, she didn't offer Jules a drink before slamming the refrigerator door shut again.

"Tell me," she said.

Jules cautiously sat himself opposite her, careful to keep the table between them. "Well, since you hafta know, I was out doin' some research."

"What kind of research?"

"Research on recruitin' an army."

"*What?*"

Jules told her about his brainstorm. Maureen's face remained strangely expressionless, almost dazed. Hoping to curry favor by reassuring her that he was taking good and prudent care of his health, he also mentioned his acquisition of the miracle antidiabetes pills.

Maureen sank heavily onto a kitchen chair. "The rest. Out with it. Considering how I found you dressed and where you were, that can't be *all* you were up to tonight."

"Uh, well, yeah . . ." Jules paused before mustering enough courage to continue. "I got jumped by a few of Malice X's thugs. But don't worry—I managed to give 'em the slip."

Maureen sighed and slowly shook her head. "From bad to worse."

She leaned her forehead against her hand, leaving her palmprints's impression in her thick makeup. "So now he knows you're back in town. It's amazing what you've been able to accomplish in a single unchaperoned evening."

She rose from the table and walked crisply from the room.

Jules had steeled himself for a screaming fit. But seeing her leave was even more alarming. "Where are you going?"

"I'm going to do something I should've done the instant you arrived on my doorstep," she shouted from the next room.

Jules overheard the distinct tones of a long-distance number being dialed on a push-button phone. He quickly followed her into her living room. "Who are you callin'?"

Maureen finished punching in the number from her red leather-covered phone directory. "It's obvious that you are too headstrong, unpredictable, and stupid to be left unsupervised. Unfortunately, my work makes it impossible for me to be your full-time nanny. So I'm calling someone who can hopefully keep you from getting yourself permanently extinguished."

"Who?"

"Do the initials *D.B.* mean anything to you?"

It took a few seconds to register, but when it did, Jules's face turned purple in a hurry. "Don't you dare. Don't you dare call him!"

Maureen smiled tightly. "Oh, but I just did. And it sounds like he's picking up. Yes, here he is now—"

"Put that phone down!"

Maureen tensed her free hand into a menacing claw and waved Jules away. "Hello, Doodlebug? You'll never guess who this is—yes, that's *right*! I'm amazed you still recognize my voice, honey. I *know* it's been ages! How the hell are you?"

Jules squared his shoulders and took two hulking steps forward. "Maureen, this is the last straw! Either you hang up that phone right now, or I'm outta here. Hear me? Keep talkin' to that little nutcase, and you'll force me to walk right out the door."

Maureen's smile remained stiffly frozen on her face. "Oh, that's *wonderful*, Doodlebug! Look, could you hold on just a minute? I've got a visitor here, another person from your past, and he's *unpardonably* impatient to speak with me."

She put her hand over the phone's speaking end. All traces of a smile immediately melted from her countenance. "You want to walk out the door, Jules? Be my guest. Better yet—*don't* be my guest! Just go. My watch says you've got about fifty minutes to sunrise. If you intend to sleep anywhere outside this house, I suggest you get busy. Oh, and while you're tending to your sleeping arrangements, please don't forget to give my best to your playmates from the projects."

Jules knew when he'd been nailed. And she'd just nailed his feet to the hardwood floor. His bluff twitched briefly, then stiffened into rigor mortis. Unable to think of a single word in reply, he stalked out of the room. Behind him, Maureen resumed her conversation. "Oh, I'm so sorry, thank you for being patient. Yes. He was suffering from a bit of stomach upset, the poor dear. . . ."

Scowling under his breath, Jules climbed the stairs to Maureen's bedroom, a windowless room set in the middle of the second floor. Apart from an impressively large flat-panel television, the only piece of furniture in the high-ceilinged room was a custom-built double-king-sized water bed. This monumental contrivance sat low to the ground in the midst of a neatly combed plot of earth, which was planted with a variety of night-blooming flowers. The orderliness of the indoor garden was marred somewhat by the uneven mounds of dirt Jules had taken earlier from his car's trunk and dumped around the bed.

The strangeness of this setup compared to the traditional coffins he'd occupied barely even registered on Jules's troubled mind. Still boiling with anger and humiliation, he grabbed the remote control from atop the flat-panel display and flopped onto the water bed, purposefully mashing a few blossoms on the way.

The slow-motion sloshing did nothing to better his mood. He braced himself against the bed frame and turned on the TV. For the next five minutes he clicked ceaselessly through dozens of satellite stations, searching for a glimpse of naked female bodies (or anything less repulsive than a miracle-diet show or an infomercial promoting adult incontinence products). He finally settled on a low-budget erotic retelling of the Snow White story, dubbed into Spanish. Everyone was a lesbian—Snow White, the wicked queen, all seven dwarfs, and even the prince(ss). Jules made a few feeble attempts to whack off, most energetically during the "Whistle While You Work" musical orgy scene. But his heart wasn't in it. By the time Maureen climbed the stairs half an hour later, he'd switched over to an episode of *The Rockford Files.*

"Are you done sulking yet?" Maureen asked, standing in the doorway. She'd removed her makeup and changed into a surprisingly modest and tasteful white nightgown.

"Men don't sulk," Jules answered, returning his attention to James Garner.

"Yeah. Right. And pigeons don't shit in Jackson Square, neither."

"So what kinda big plans did you and your little pervert pal hatch behind my back? Or am I too 'stupid' and 'unpredictable' for you to bother tellin' me?"

"Turn off *Rockford* and I'll fill you in, Mr. Pouty."

Jules clicked off the TV.

Maureen crossed the path leading through her garden and sat on the bed's padded frame. "First off, you should know, whether you're willing to admit it or not, that Doodlebug is a damn good friend of yours. I told him the whole story, and he's dropping everything to fly out and help you the night after tomorrow night. Now keep in mind, he's the head of a very important business—"

"A freaky cult, you mean!"

"A very important and profitable *business*—more than you've ever accomplished in *your* long unlife, I might add—and he's putting everything on hold to fly here from his compound in northern California. Now *that's* friendship for you! He's very devoted to you, Jules. I just don't understand why you shun him so."

Jules slapped the mattress, making himself bob atop a stormy sea. "Oh, you know damn well why! I'm *ashamed* to think I'm the one who made him a vampire! I mean, the only person I ever picked to do the change on, and look how he ended up!"

Maureen grabbed his shoulders. "Just get *over* it, Jules! He could've turned out way worse, and you know it! You never hear *me* complaining about how *you* turned out, do you?"

Quickly deciding that discretion was the better part of valor, Jules bit his tongue.

"Well," she continued, "he'll be here two nights from now, and it's out of your hands. So just get used to the idea. You'll thank me when this is all over. Believe me, you'll thank me." She clapped her hands twice to turn out the light, then settled into her side of the bed, leaving a foot and a half between herself and Jules. "All right, enough yacking already. I'm pooped. Good morning, Jules."

Jules clung tightly to the bed frame until the waves subsided. " 'Morning, Mo," he said. He knew it would take him a long time to fall asleep. There was too much to think about. He lay on his back and listened to the sounds of Maureen's breathing. It had been so long since they had been this quiet together. This close.

Just before she started snoring, he felt her shift onto her side. In the undulating darkness her arm fell across his shoulder and chest like a scented pillow.

♦

Jules was awakened the next evening by the deep tones of the front doorbell. He hurriedly rubbed the sleep from his eyes. Maureen's side of the bed was empty. While he was recovering from his disappointment and trying to decide whether the doorbell had maybe been a dream, it rang again. His sack lay crumpled at the foot of the bed. Rather than squeeze into the makeshift garment again, he went into the adjoining room and pulled one of Maureen's terry-cloth bathrobes out of her walk-in closet.

Downstairs, he went to the front door and peered through the peephole. A white man stood on the front stoop, an impatient look on his face. Jules recognized him as a bouncer from Jezebel's Joy Room. He was holding a large paper bag.

Jules opened the door a hand's width, so that a bare minimum of his robed body could be seen from the street.

"You Jules?" the man on the stoop asked.

"Yeah," Jules said cautiously.

The visitor handed over the bag. "Here you go, buddy. Maureen asked me to come over. She found these on the street. Had to pull the coat away from a bum who was using it as a blanket. Two words of advice for you—*dry clean.*"

He turned, loped down the steps in a vaguely simian fashion, and walked up Bienville Street in the direction of the club. Jules closed and bolted the door. He set the bag down in the hallway without opening it, not especially eager to see what was inside. But then he remembered that Doc Landrien's antidiabetes pills were in the trench coat's pocket. Relieved, he removed the pill bottles, telling himself to leave it somewhere more secure this time.

He walked into the kitchen, his empty stomach emitting watery, squishy noises, much like those made by the water bed mattress. He tried to remember how Maureen had fixed her blood-tomato-juice-vegetable concoction the night before.

A happy surprise awaited him. On the counter, a tall glass sat next to the blender, which was full of Maureen's patented mixture. He poured himself a glassful, then put the remainder in the refrigerator for later. He sat at the kitchen table, where Maureen had left a handwritten note. The note was short and to the point:

> *Jules,*
>
> *There's coffee grounds and water in the coffeemaker; all you have to do is press* ON. *I left your dinner on the counter to warm up for you, but don't leave it out of the fridge too long. I'll be back around 4:30* A.M. *Don't do anything stupid.*
> *M.*

Jules downed his initial glassful of Mo-8, then turned on the coffeemaker. As the blissful burbling and heavenly aroma delighted his senses, he mulled over his plan to recruit Nathan Knight's followers into a white vampire army. Wednesday night, when the rally would be held, was two nights from now. The night after Doodlebug was scheduled to fly in. *Hell.* Thanks to busybody Maureen, he was stuck with the little deviant for a while. At least pulling off a masterstroke like creating an army would demonstrate conclusively that Jules was still boss.

He couldn't afford to screw this one up. Too much was at stake. He'd have to plan very carefully. He poured himself a cup of coffee and paced the kitchen. The central question, the one he couldn't quite get his head around, was this: How could he turn dozens of people into vampires all at the same time?

Gas.

Of course! He could use laughing gas to knock the whole room unconscious at once. Then he could pick the best ones, the biggest, strongest, and meanest, and transform them into vampires at his leisure while they snoozed helplessly away. Oh, he knew the pitfalls, after his last experience with gas, but they'd be easy to avoid. Terrific!

Let's see . . . he'd need canisters of gas, of course. And a timer of some kind; that way he could set the canisters to release during the middle of the rally, when attendance would be the highest, and he wouldn't have to be in the room himself. If he was going to use a timer, then he'd have to set up the whole knockout apparatus ahead of time. A timer meant complications—batteries, wiring, and some sort of electric ON switch for the gas nozzles. But luckily, he could get free construction advice from the same man who'd happily sell him the parts.

That man was Tiny Idaho. Anarchist. Tree hugger. Bearded ex-hippie radical. The best gadget man Jules had ever run across. Tiny did most of his business over the Web nowadays, but he still maintained an inconspicuous, disguised storefront operation in a broken-down strip mall buried on a side street in suburban Kenner. Jules had used his services for years.

He checked the contents of his wallet. Thirty-two dollars and a dollop of change. Not a heck of a lot to offer Tiny Idaho for what Jules wanted rigged up. Maybe Tiny would consider it a down payment? Jules hated the idea of going into hock yet again, but he couldn't think of any alternative. Maybe he could cut a few corners. If the gas canisters in his old garage had survived the fire, then he wouldn't have to buy new ones.

There was just one more hurdle he had to jump before he could begin his night's work. What to do about Malice X's toughs, who might still be scouting the neighborhood for him? Once he was in his car, he could be out of the Quarter in hardly more than ninety seconds; but the short walk from Maureen's door to the garage was too risky. Even his wolf-form was too conspicuous.

Too conspicuous—maybe that was the answer. If he couldn't make himself small or stealthy, then hiding in plain sight was his best option. The Quarter was *full* of weird characters . . . mimes, human statues, and tuba players, to list only the most common. Dressed as a costumed street performer (the more outlandish, the better), he could fit right in.

He climbed the stairs and returned to Maureen's walk-in closet. Surely she'd have some old thing lying around that would fit the bill . . . a stage outfit she used in her stripper's act, or maybe even a Carnival costume. After digging through a tangle of outsized dresses and gowns, Jules found what he was looking for: a harlequin's outfit. The black-and-white checkered jumpsuit, with its garish frills on the collar, sleeves, and cuffs, certainly looked big enough for him. There was an easy enough way for him to find out.

The jumpsuit was a considerably tighter squeeze than Maureen's bathrobe had been. The fully elasticized waist was stretched to its limit. So long as he didn't inhale too deeply or try any fancy gymnastics, he'd be all right. He couldn't find the bell-trimmed cap that went with the outfit, so he went searching for something else to cover his head and face with. A broken pink lamp shade from the attic, with two eyeholes cut out, fit the bill nicely.

He slung his trench coat over his arm and headed fearlessly out the door. Malice X might scoff at him. Maureen might doubt him. Doodlebug might pity him. But starting tonight, he'd show them all.

♦

Jules circled his old block, scanning the street and weed-strewn lots for lurkers. Montegut Street was as deathly quiet as a Pacific atoll after a bomb test. He rolled down his windows. His nose twitched happily as it detected the familiar scents of diesel train exhaust and fermenting grain wafting in from river barges.

Jules parked. His garage appeared to be the least damaged portion of his house. If the neighborhood's scavengers hadn't been too thorough, he might still drive off with a couple of usable gas canisters. At least the looters had made it easy for him to get inside. A roughly five-foot-tall hole had been cut through the garage door's aluminum panels.

He peered through the darkness at what remained of nearly a century's worth of personal and family history. As he'd figured, every one of his power tools was long gone, along with his lawn mower and gardening implements. They'd even taken the poured-concrete lawn Madonna that Jules had wrapped in burlap and stored away after his mother died.

But over in the corner, half buried under the cinders of a pile of *Life* magazines fallen from an overhead shelf, were three of Jules's laughing-gas canisters. Obviously, the looters hadn't known what to make of them. Jules smiled. The winds of luck were finally blowing his way. He dragged the canisters over to the ruined door and shoved them through the jagged hole.

His foot hit something hard and sharp-edged. The object scraped loudly against the concrete floor. The sudden screeching nearly made Jules's heart burst through the top of his head. As soon as he regained his breath, he looked to see what lay at his feet. It was a box. A metal footlocker.

He bent down to open it. He hadn't seen one like it since the war years.

Then a vague but thrilling recollection tickled the ivories of his memory synapses. Could it be—?

The footlocker's rusty hinges gave way as Jules forced the box open. The distant moonlight revealed a bundle of carefully folded cloth, faded and musty but immeasurably vibrant. Jules's heart leapt as he lifted the bundle out of the locker. He was certain now that his luck had changed.

Once more, after a span of half a century, he held in his hands the hood, shirt, and cloak of that fabled nemesis of saboteurs, that mysterious defender of freedom and democracy . . . the Hooded Terror.

♦

Jules loathed Kenner with every fiber of his being. After dark, the suburb, penned in by swamps and airport runways, had the feel of a graveyard where even the ghosts were too bored to stir up trouble. The only exciting thing that ever happened out there was the occasional plane crash. But Kenner was where Tiny Idaho worked his magic, so Kenner was the place Jules had to be.

He pulled into the parking lot of a small, poorly lit two-story shopping strip. Its windows were boarded up and plastered with FOR LEASE signs, except for two occupied storefronts. One was an uninviting bar on the ground level called The Lounge Lizard—only it was really called The Longe Lizard, because *lounge* had been misspelled on the hand-painted sign next to the screen door. The other tenant, Readwood Forest Used Books and Comix, was on the second level.

Jules climbed the stairs to the second-story bookstore, barely visible as an operating business from the street. From downstairs, a jukebox voice warbled on about hunting dogs and guns, punctuated by a sharper, more distinct sound, possibly a pool stick being broken over a skull. Readwood Forest was dark, but Jules knew that Tiny Idaho lived in an apartment and workshop behind the store.

Jules rang the bell. He waited a long minute, listening to the scratchy country music from below. No footsteps. No lights turning on in the store. Jules rang again. This time, a distorted voice crackled from a weather-beaten intercom beneath the doorbell.

"The store's closed, man. The weekly comics shipment comes in tomorrow afternoon after three. Good night."

Jules spoke quickly into the intercom. "Hey, Mr. Idaho? It's Jules Duchon. We done business before. I'm a buyer of your 'special' merchandise."

The intercom was silent for a few seconds. "Oh yeah? Hang tight while I put on some pants. Be there in a sec, man."

A minute later the door creaked open. "This better be important, man. You yanked me away from an episode of *America's Most Wanted*. C'mon in before the skeeters eat you alive."

Under the dim illumination of a bug zapper, Jules took a look at his host. He'd only seen Tiny Idaho in this much light once before, about four years ago, when he'd picked up his first set of laughing-gas canisters. The man's most prominent feature was his long, thickly tangled beard, made up of curly clumps of gray and red hair that reached all the way to his outsized belt buckle. His small eyes, made even smaller by wire-rimmed bifocals, and two large, somewhat yellowed teeth were all that was visible through his abundance of hair. In overall stature, Tiny was neither small nor huge. Jules ached to ask this medium-sized man where his nickname had come from, but he thought it wisest to keep the question to himself.

"So what's with the clown suit?" Tiny Idaho asked. "You coming back from a kiddie party?"

"I'm *incognito*," Jules answered, straightening his collar. It was a good word, and he liked using it whenever he could.

"That's cool. So what can I do you for? You need exploding balloons, or a nitrous kit for your clown car?"

"Naww. A few years back I bought some laughing gas off you. And you sold me a set of plans for installing it in my trunk and releasing the gas into the passenger compartment."

"Oh yeah?" His host shut the door behind Jules and rubbed his hairy chin. "Yeah . . . I remember now. How'd it all work out, man?"

Jules decided not to go into the whole sad story. "Eh, all right. But now I got another project I need your help with."

Tiny Idaho raised an eyebrow and grinned. "It involve explosives? I just got in some great stuff from Taiwan. These little honeys'll peel the tread right off a battle tank."

"Uh, no. It's another laughing-gas deal. Only this time, I need an automatic-release nozzle that works off a timer. Think you can throw somethin' together for me?"

The bearded man laughed, his small eyes sparkling behind his spectacles. "That's all? Man, you come in here dressed like that—I figure you'd give me something *interesting*! Come on back to my workshop while I cobble something together. Unless you'd rather browse out front here?"

Jules quickly glanced around the bookshop. The closely bunched shelves were packed with books on ecology and the evils of industrialism. An entire wall was taken up by racks of comics. Jules recognized vintage copies of *Zap! Comics* and *Fabulous Furry Freak Brothers*; neither of them his favorites. He followed Tiny Idaho through the door at the rear of the bookshop, into the workshop beyond.

"Welcome to my humble abode," his host said. Jules inhaled the strong, metallic odors of machine oil and freshly tooled steel. Long wooden tables set along three of the walls were covered with a jumble of drill presses, plastic explosives, tangles of wire, and shiny green plastic motherboards. "You got one of them gas canisters with you," Tiny Idaho asked, "or you need me to rustle you up some new ones?"

"I got 'em downstairs in my trunk. You need me to bring one up?"

"Yeah. That'd be what we call in the biz Step One."

Jules went downstairs to his car and fetched the canister, then spent a few minutes describing the kind of setup he envisioned. As his host listened and asked questions, Tiny Idaho rifled through a series of tool chests and parts drawers, pulling out lengths of wire, a soldering iron, and a digital timer.

Jules leaned against a table and watched him work. The gadget man's fingers danced a ballet of miniaturized construction.

Jules noticed that his host had paused to give him the fuzzy eyeball. "Hey, man. This gas project of yours—is it political or personal?"

"Personal. Politics is a dirty business. You see this?" Jules put his hands around his own neck.

"Yeah?"

"This is what I'm tryin' to save."

"I got you, man. That's good." Tiny Idaho seemed to relax some. He grinned and picked up his soldering iron again. "These last few years, man, I've gotten so sick and tired of building antipersonnel bombs for every right-wing Fascist wacko who visits my site on the Web. . . . I mean, business is business—I got bills to pay just like everybody else— but this gig of mine ain't half the fun it used to be. Y'know, back in my salad days, I was doing stuff that *mattered*. Shit, I even got a gig from the Weathermen once, back in 'seventy-one—"

"Yeah, pal, the times, they are a-changin'."

"You can say that again. Hey, I'm runnin' a special this week on tree spikes. Can you use some?"

Jules raised an eyebrow. "If they're wood, I could use some."

"You can't pound wooden spikes into a tree, man."

"It's not trees I'm wantin' to pound 'em into. Hey, you ever make up a batch of silver bullets before?"

"*Silver* bullets? That's definitely a special-order item. What, you going hunting for werewolves?"

"Somethin' like that. Hey! How about a gun that shoots *wooden* bullets? Can you do that?"

Tiny Idaho frowned. "Naww. The ballistics would be all off. Besides, the bullets'd probably shatter before they left the barrel. How about some kinda souped-up crossbow?"

Jules flinched slightly. "Eh, maybe. But don't call it a *cross*bow—and it can't be shaped like no cross, neither."

Forty minutes later, Jules left Tiny Idaho's shop with everything necessary for the remote and precise release of laughing gas. Jules gave him thirty dollars as a down payment. After a lengthy discussion, the gadget man said he'd have a prototype "handheld wooden-projectile launcher" ready for Jules's inspection by the end of the week.

Jules carefully loaded the equipment in his trunk. He climbed into the Lincoln and started its rumbly engine. Before he yanked the transmission stalk into drive, the scream of a jetliner shook the night. For a brief second the plane was silhouetted against the yellow orb of the moon. Jules's right hand drifted across to the old metal footlocker resting on the seat beside him.

He opened the footlocker's lid. Tenderly, he smoothed a decades-old crease out of his cloak, rubbing the rough, dusty cloth between his forefinger and callused thumb. He smiled. In just another few nights jetliners wouldn't be the only great winged things darkening the moon.

♦

Three and a half hours later Jules piloted his Lincoln through the empty stall spaces outside the French Market and parked behind the Palm Court Jazz Café. It was relaxation time. And catching the second set of Theo "Porkchop" Chambonne's midnight jam session of traditional jazz fit the bill to a T.

Some R&R was definitely called for. The trip to Kenner had been unsettling, a frightening vision of the strip-mall horror that had sprung up outside New Orleans. Then there had been the trip across the Causeway . . . twenty-four nerve-racking miles with nothing but a slender guardrail between him and the black depths of Lake Pontchartrain. That old wives' tale about vampires and moving water might just be a myth, but even so, the idea of being surrounded by so much water gave him a case of the jitters.

Setting up his equipment inside the American Veterans Union Hall had gone surprisingly easily (once he'd found the place). The building was set a good way back from Highway 190, half hidden in a patch of piney woods, perfect for Jules's purposes. The thin plywood door had a puny lock, which busted easily in Jules's huge paw. The meeting hall was nothing more than an oblong room with a low ceiling, a plain podium, and stacks of folding metal chairs leaning against the walls. Jules quickly located a broom closet, which held his canisters of laughing gas very nicely.

But now it was definitely time for some R&R. A small group of black men, all dressed in sweat-rumpled suits, stood beneath the music club's rear overhang, talking and laughing, their faces lit by the orange glows of stubby cigarettes. Musicians, not vampires, Jules told himself; they were all right. He recognized the slight, elderly man at the center of the group, even though it had been months—years, maybe?—since he'd last heard him play in person. That beak-shaped nose, combined with the tufts of fuzzy white hair that peeked from the edges of his brown fedora, was a dead giveaway.

"Chop!" Jules called, waving vigorously. "Hey, Chop! You on break?"

"Yeah. Who's that?" Porkchop Chambonne turned to stare at the hulking figure approaching him from the street. He tipped back his fedora to get a better look, and his watery eyes widened. "Oh mah Gawd, boys, it's Mr. Bingle, come to pay us a visit!"

Being mistaken for the Maison Blanche department store's round-headed Christmas snowman wasn't exactly flattering; still, Jules was overjoyed to see his old friend. "No, Chop! It's Jules! Your old pal, Jules Duchon!"

The elderly trumpet player's willowy forearm vanished between Jules's huge hands as the vampire vigorously greeted his friend. The other musicians, all much younger than their bandleader, either backed away from the pair or were innocently elbowed into the gutter by Jules's sidewalk-hogging enthusiasm.

"Jules *Duchon*? Why ain't you out drivin' your cab?" Chop backed out of Jules's smothering half embrace and looked him up and down. "What's with the outfit? You got yo'self a new gig? Doin' kiddie parties or somethin'?"

"Naww. I'm just comin' back from a costume party. My cab's in the shop, so I'm on temporary vacation. How the hell've you been?"

"Oh, all right, all right. Doin' as well as an eighty-year-old trumpet player with fake chompers can hope for, I guess. But me, I ain't doin' *half* as well as *you*." He walked slowly around Jules, clucking appreciatively and shaking his head. "I swear, you never *change*, do you? Oh, maybe a little bigger here and there. But not a wrinkle. Not a gray hair on yo' head. And you's *kept* all yo' hair! When did we first meet? Lessee . . . I was just a kid startin' out on Bourbon Street, no older than Leroy there"—he pointed at the taller of the two school-aged sidemen—"why, that was back during the early days of WW Two—"

Jules smiled and shook his head. "No, Chop, that was my *dad*, Jules *Senior*. I'm Jules *Junior*, remember? We been through this before."

The jazzman scrunched his mouth into a frown. "You *sure?*"

Jules laughed, along with a couple of the sidemen. "Sure I'm sure!" He felt a twinge of guilt, like a rusty nail in his heel, upon deceiving his old friend yet again. But some things just couldn't be helped.

The old man sighed, then took a long, hard look at the blunt, hand-rolled cigarette held between his fingers. "Yeah, I guess you *is* sure. Maybe I'm gettin' too old to be messin' round with this stuff anymore." He held the joint out to Jules. "Want a puff?"

"No, thanks. I just stick to coffee."

"Yeah, you right. Jus' like yo' pop." He took a final drag before pinching it out. Then he placed the roach in a silver cigarette box he took from his jacket pocket. "Funny you should mention yo' pop. Just earlier this evenin', I was reminded of my own pop in the weirdest of ways."

"Oh yeah?"

"Yeah." He turned to his sidemen. "You boys go on back inside. I want to talk with Jules here a bit. I'll be along in a minute."

The old jazzman waited until the younger musicians had ambled around the corner before continuing. "I didn't mention this story to none of the youngsters. Didn't want 'em to think I was 'touched,' y'know? But somehow, I got the notion *you'll* believe me just fine."

Jules grinned and stepped closer to his friend. A pair of large cockroaches scurried out of his way. "You drive a cab in this town, there's not much you *don't* believe."

"I hear ya." The jazzman sat down on a window ledge and fanned himself with his hat. "Well, my pop, he growed up in the Quarters, back when it was piss-poor Italians livin' here instead of all these tourists. And man, did he used to tell me *stories!* One that always stuck in my head, it was about the rats that live in the Quarters. These rats, they live inside all these two-hundred-year-old buildings we got here. Inside the *walls*, see. They got it so good in there, they never need to come out. In fact, my pop, he told me there was whole generations of rats that lived and died without ever seein' the sun. Imagine that! Generation after generation, they got whiter and whiter, those rats, livin' in the dark like that, until their skins got so white that you could look right through it. Right *through* it, and see their hearts and lungs and stuff!"

"No shit?"

"No *shit*. I never forgot that story. Well, just earlier tonight I be walkin' over here from my apartment, takin' the same old route I always take, when I hear a noise from this alleyway. Sounds like trash cans bein' spilled over. I figure it's some dog or somethin'. Just outta curiosity, I take a look down the alleyway. There, sittin' on top of one of them cans, be a rat big as my trumpet. Bad enough, huh? But it's like no other rat I ever seen. I'm starin' at it, and *it's* starin' at *me*, and I can see its heart beatin', and blood flowin' through its veins. Like its skin is *glass*."

"It wasn't no trick of the light, you think?"

The musician shook his head vigorously. "No trick of no light, no sir. That rat was clear like a neon tube. And the whole while I was starin' at it, I had the sense my daddy's ghost was standin' there next to me, his hand restin' on my shoulder. That's the absolute truth." He stopped fanning himself and stared directly into Jules's eyes. "There's more strange stuff out there than you or me can imagine, my friend."

Jules grunted his agreement.

Porkchop Chambonne glanced down at his watch. "Shee-yit! Time slipped away on me. I gotta git. You comin' inside to hear the second set?"

"I brought my ears, didn't I? Lead the way, pal."

They rounded the corner onto Decatur Street. The bandleader hurried through the Palm Court's door and headed directly for the stage, where his sidemen were already playing an opening tune. Jules paused outside to slip on his trench coat; he didn't want to distract attention from the band.

The stage was lit with red and green spotlights. The rest of the club, divided evenly between a polished oak bar and a restaurant seating area, was dimly but charmingly lit with glass-enclosed candles. Jules couldn't make out faces among the audience; all he could see were silhouettes and hands clutching glasses of beer or wine. The place was about three-quarters full. The six-piece band wound down its rendition of "Chimes Blues," leaping immediately into a rousing "Basin Street Blues" as Jules wormed his way through the crowded room to an empty table near the back.

The kids were good—damn good—but even the most precocious among them couldn't touch the lyrical artistry flowing so effortlessly from their leader's trumpet. Sixty-plus years of experience counted for something, after all. Jules listened, enraptured, as his friend slid sinuously into the famous blues first popularized by King Oliver and Louis Armstrong. That was just after World War I, back in the days of Jules's youth. Maybe Chop didn't have Oliver's fiery aggressiveness on trumpet, and perhaps he couldn't match Satchmo's almost supernatural virtuosity, but he had a languid warmth all his own. As long as music like this endured, New Orleans would always be heaven for Jules Duchon.

At first he didn't feel the soft hand that settled lightly on his shoulder. "Mind if I join you? The other tables are all taken, and I hate listening to the blues alone."

It was a woman's voice. Unfamiliar, but as warm and smoky as Chop's tireless trumpet. Jules leaned back in his chair, and when he saw who it was, he nearly fell out of it. It was *her*—the woman from the Trolley Stop. The cover girl from *Big Cheeks Pictorial*!

She smiled at him, her teeth sparkling in the candlelight. "I'm so sorry to bother you," she said. "I could see how much you're enjoying the music. But seeing you again is such a wonderful coincidence. I simply couldn't live with myself if I didn't come over and introduce myself. May I sit down?"

Was this really happening? Or was it a hallucination brought on by accumulated stress, a bizarre waking wet dream? He pinched his upper arm with every last ounce of his vampiric strength. She didn't fade away. He could smell her musky perfume. He could feel the electric warmth of her body, so provocatively close to his own. *If this is a wet dream,* he told himself, *I'm gonna go all the way with it, all the way to the sticky finish line.*

"So may I sit down?" she asked again. So patiently, so unpetulantly (so unlike Maureen, who would've bitten his head off by now).

"Uh, you wanna sit with *me?*"

"Yes," she smiled.

"Buh-be my guest," he said, catapulting himself out of his seat in an effort to pull out a chair for her.

"That's very gallant." He noticed her voice had a sweet trace of a hill-country twang. Gracefully, she settled herself down, smoothing the folds of her emerald silk pantsuit to avoid wrinkling. Beneath her jacket she wore a daringly low-cut T-shirt, which showcased her mountainous cleavage. Jules's dream girl turned appreciatively toward the stage, closing her eyes and nodding gently in time with the music. No matter how sublime Chop's solos were, Jules might as well've been stone deaf. His complete attention was glued to the rise and fall of her magnificent chest.

When the band slid into the closing bars of "St. James Infirmary," she sighed with pleasure. "Isn't the music simply *wonderful*?"

"Some of the best in the city," said Jules, trying hard to sound authoritative. "That means some of the best in the whole world."

"You sound like someone who knows his music."

"Sure! I been around music and musicians my whole life."

Her eyes flashed with interest. "How fascinating!" She laughed and patted his arm affectionately. "I promised to introduce myself, didn't I? My name's Veronika, with a *k*. I'm visiting from New York. I know this'll sound *horribly* immodest, but I'm a model—a plus-sized model—and I'm in New Orleans working on a series of shoots for various magazines. Most of my photos are for women's clothing magazines, and the others— well, let's just say I doubt a gentleman such as yourself would've seen them."

"My loss," Jules said with a poker face.

"I think your city is simply *magical*. I've been hoping to meet someone who could help me see it with a native's eyes. When I saw you at that little trolley car diner, you seemed so friendly and *interesting*, and I wanted to meet you, or at least say hello, but at the last second I was too shy. Then you were gone. So seeing you again tonight, in this place, with this wonderful music, I just know that we were meant to be friends."

Jules felt suspended in a warm velvet fog. Every honey-coated word she spoke sizzled a path from his ears straight to his groin. He caught sight of his empty outfit in a mirrored post. Why did this woman have to meet him on a night when he was dressed in Maureen's harlequin costume?

"I, uh, I'm comin' back from some kids' party. Crippled kids, actually. All stuck in wheelchairs. Charity work, y'know. I do this sorta thing all the time."

"That's so *noble* of you." She grasped his paw tightly between her two soft hands and stared into his eyes. They listened to the remainder of the set in silence. When the band finished their final number the house lights came up like a sudden dawn. The forty or so patrons gathered their coats and purses and began shuffling toward the doors.

Veronika turned to Jules and smiled warmly. "Oh, that was simply *exquisite*. Thank you for sharing such a fabulous evening with me." She leaned across the table and lightly stroked his forearm with her fingertips. "Would you mind escorting me back to my hotel? I'd feel *so* much safer."

"I—" Maureen's face flashed on the mildewed movie screen of Jules's mind. Hadn't she put her arm over him the night before, just as she'd fallen asleep? What would *she* think? Oh, she'd be fine with it if he intended to fang the woman . . . but *fanging* was not the verb Jules had in mind. He thought hard and furiously about the nature of luck. Until today, his recent luck had been *shit* luck. What would happen if, now that his luck had turned amazingly, fabulously *good*, he ungratefully turned his back on it? Would it go and dry up into a desiccated turd again?

"I, uh—I'd be *honored* to walk you to your hotel."

♦

Veronika's hotel was a Spanish Colonial–style mansion on Barracks Street that had been converted into time-share condominiums. She opened the front door, recently renovated to show off its intricate moldings. The air in the foyer was chilled to a crisp sixty-five degrees, a nearly twenty-degree drop from the temperature outside.

Veronika removed a handkerchief from her purse and delicately dabbed her forehead and neck. "Please *excuse* me . . . I'm simply not used to this humidity anymore." She looked at her companion, who was arid as a white desert. "How do you manage to stay so dry in all this dampness? A big husky man like you?"

Jules leaned against the gilded back of a French Restoration side chair. "Oh, y'know, when you've been livin' in New Orleans as long as I have, you kinda get used to a bit a stickiness."

She took his hand and led him to a stairway at the rear of the foyer. "Come. I'm up on the third floor." She laughed, sounding more like a schoolgirl than a (very) grown woman. "The only fault I can find with this place is it doesn't have an elevator."

"That's okay. I can handle two flights easy enough." Heck, with her holding his hand, her perfume tantalizing him, he'd climb to the top of One Shell Square, fifty stories up.

To Doc Landrieu's credit, Jules made it to the third floor without even breathing hard. Veronika fumbled with her room key; her excitement buzzed his skin like static electricity. Jules was excited, too. But he was also nervous as hell. His nerves accomplished what the nighttime humidity hadn't; sweat poured out of the pinched glands beneath his arms. He half expected that when Veronika finally got the door open, Maureen would be standing on the other side, vengefully clutching a stake pointed at his (cheatin') heart.

After what felt like a sizable chunk of eternity, Veronika got the key to work. The door opened. No ten-foot-tall Maureen made a jealous grab for his testicles. He took a deep breath and followed Veronika inside. The room was sumptuous. It was dominated by a startlingly large whirlpool bath, which managed to overpower even the red-velvet-covered king-sized bed.

"Would you like a drink?" she asked him as she stepped quickly to the mini bar. "My employers are very generous. Anything I want, I just put it on their tab."

"I'll skip it, thanks," he stammered, fingering the velvet bedspread.

"Well, I'm going to make myself something. I'm *thirsty*!"

Jules watched her pour Sprite, cranapple juice, cherry concentrate, and vodka into a tumbler. She mixed it with her pinkie and gulped it down quickly, not even pausing to add ice cubes. She set the glass down on the dresser by the bed. Then, before he could brace himself, she was all over him.

Her lips engulfed his mouth. He tasted cherry on her tongue, and a hint of vodka. He felt himself losing his balance as their bodies collided. He tumbled backward onto the bed, and Veronika followed. Their stomachs, like air bags, cushioned their impact, but her top front teeth banged into his as their combined weight mashed the bedsprings to full compression. She rolled off him, laughing uproariously as he struggled to regain the air that had been squeezed out of his rib cage.

"*Ah-ha-ha-ha,*" she laughed, turning red as she tried catching her breath. "Oh, I think I busted a tooth! *Ouch!* Are you all right? Oh, that's not what I meant to do at all! Let's try that again, okay?"

"Just give—just give me—a second to catch my breath, baby—"

"Sure, sweetie. Ha-heh. Sure." They both lay there a minute, side by side, each half on and half off the bed. She reached over and tentatively, but amorously, caressed his arm. "Tell you what. I'm so hot and sticky from the walk back from that jazz club. How about we relax together in that big tub?"

"Sure—sure thing!" Jules groaned, rubbing his side where he'd slammed into the bed frame. *I'll have me a bruise worse than Mikhail Gorbachev's birthmark,* he told himself. *Good luck explaining* that *to Maureen.*

"I bet I know how to get you in the mood," she said, her eyes sparkling. She stood up from the bed and danced to the middle of the room, her hips gyrating to a mambo only she could hear. She slipped off her shoes, then sensuously slithered out of her jacket. The white flesh of her arms was toned and flawless, but that wasn't what stunned Jules. Her black silk T-shirt clung to her Amazonian form like a good coat of paint. Embroidered just above her left breast was the stylized slogan: I (HEART) VAMPIRES. The picture of the heart was pierced by a pair of cartoonish fangs and dripped droplets of Day-Glo blood.

Veronika noticed Jules's wide-eyed expression. "Isn't this shirt just *darling*? I picked it up a few days ago at Agatha Longrain's boutique in the Garden District. She had so much wonderful stuff there. I've been one of her biggest fans almost as far back as I can remember."

"Er, yeah, it's beautiful, baby. You got good taste."

"Thanks." She grinned slyly. "*I* think I've got good taste, too. Especially in *men*." She continued her striptease. The shirt came off next. Her bra was massive but exquisitely stylish. Expensive lace hid an underwire apparatus on a par with da Vinci's marvels of engineering.

She leaned against an antique bureau and gracefully removed her pants. Jules expected to see a girdle of Victorian severity heave into view. Surely her hourglass figure required one—no hips on earth could be so gargantuan and yet so classically and smoothly curved all on their own. But all she wore beneath her pants was a pair of lace panties, which were nearly hidden by the tummy rolls that cascaded down her upper thighs like ripples in a lake of pure cream.

The sight hit Jules like a thunderclap—those photos in *Big Cheeks Pictorial* hadn't been airbrushed one bit—!

She grinned salaciously at him, turned on the spigot, then pressed a button on the wall next to the Jacuzzi. The big tub's waters poured forth and bubbled into life. Veronika eased herself slowly and carefully into the hot froth, a Venus returning to her birthplace in the surf. "Oh God, this feels *heavenly*!" She settled herself onto a submerged seat molded into the tub's steps and leaned back, spreading her legs wide. Her painted toenails peeked above the bubbles. "Okay, handsome. I'm not the only one who gets wet here. Your turn."

"Uh, maybe you'll give me just a minute to, eh, get naked in private?"

Her full lips formed an exaggerated pout. "Oh, now what fun is *that*? Don't I get a striptease, too?"

Jules turned red all over. He couldn't remember the last woman (aside from Maureen) he'd stripped in front of. The notion of taking off his clothes in a well-lit room in front of a strange woman made him feel eight years old again, the little boy who didn't want to take a naked shower in the St. Ignatius locker room.

"Eh, this, well, this is gonna sound real *stupid* . . . but I'd be a helluva lot more comfortable takin' off these clothes in the bathroom. And you think, maybe, we could turn these lights down some?"

Her toes sank out of sight as she sat up straighter in the Jacuzzi. "Will that make you feel more in the mood?"

"Yeah. Actually, it would."

"Okay." She pointed to her dresser. "Look in that top left-hand drawer there. You'll find some scented candles and a box of matches. Light some of those and you can turn off the overhead light."

He did as she instructed. Then he hung his trench coat on the coat-rack by the door before slinking into the bathroom.

Good thing this was a luxury condominium—given the size of the typical hotel/motel bathroom, Jules expected to barely have room enough to turn around, but there was ample space here. He examined the harlequin suit after he managed to wiggle out of it. He'd definitely have to get it dry-cleaned; the sides beneath the sleeves were already yellowish with drying perspiration.

He leaned against the sink as he stepped out of his underwear. So he was actually going to do this. He was actually going to get laid. Jules stared down at his stomach. He couldn't see his privates, but his belly's white folds were sturdily propped up in the middle.

Maybe his pecker was happy, but for some reason his eyes were beginning to water like hell. What the devil could be causing *that*? He checked behind the shower curtain. He saw nothing but a bar of soap, a bottle of conditioning shampoo, and a Lady Bic razor. He examined the sink a little closer. The stinging in his eyes got worse. He knelt down and opened up the cabinet beneath the sink. *Whew!* What a stink! When his vision cleared, he saw a canvas duffel bag sitting beneath the drainpipe. He pulled it toward the edge of the cabinet and opened it. The contents nearly knocked him against the opposite wall.

What the fuck? Garlic cloves! Enough to cook a feast for the entire Mafia! And crucifixes? What was she doing with all this crap (and in the bathroom, yet)?

"Jules? What's taking you so long in there, handsome? I'm getting lonely."

He shut the cabinet and quickly dabbed his eyes with some toilet paper. When he left the bathroom, his fleshy tent was already beginning to sag. Should he ask her about the weird crap under the sink? Or should he just climb in the tub and pork her while it was still an option?

"*There* you are," she said brightly. "I was afraid I'd turn into a prune before you got here. Come on in! The water's *delicious*!"

His big head (the one atop his neck) told him to leave. His little head (the one below his stomach) told him to get the hell in the hot tub already. Little head overruled big head. Jules grabbed hold of the side of the tub and climbed in. It was a big Jacuzzi, true, maybe big enough for four or five normal-sized folks, but with Veronika already ensconced, he felt like the proverbial sardine squeezing into a sardine can.

The upside of this situation was that his naked flesh was jammed tightly against her naked flesh. "Mmmm, c'mere, lover," she whispered. "This time, you aren't going *anywhere*."

She kissed him more expertly this time. He felt lost in her glorious body. Lost, and he never wanted to be found again. And then she stopped kissing him.

"Huh?" He opened his eyes. "Whassa matter? You were doin' *great*, baby—"

"Hold your horses, handsome." She removed the cork from a small bottle of clear liquid. "This bath oil is my absolute *favorite*. It'll make us smell all flowery fresh for when we climb into bed."

She poured the contents of the bottle into the tub. The water's bubbling immediately tripled in intensity. Jules felt the stings of a thousand fire ants over every submerged inch of his body.

"*Aahhh!* Holy *fuck*! What'd you do?"

Agonized, Jules struggled to pull himself out of the cramped Jacuzzi. The water boiled fiercely, but Veronika was unaffected—far from being in pain, she tightened her legs' vise-grip around Jules's torso, forcing him back into the violent froth.

"Lover, what's the matter?" Her strong hands pressed down on his shoulders. "Stay in the tub with me, darling—"

"Leggo, you crazy broad! Let *go*!" He plunged his hands into the burning bubbles and dug his jagged fingernails into her imprisoning thighs. She yelped. Her grip on him loosened, just enough for him to propel his bulk onto the top step and scramble over the Jacuzzi's edge. Veronika screamed in dismay and made a last-ditch grab for his privates, but her fingers slid off the slippery, reddened folds of his belly as he flung himself over the side.

His foot whacked her head as he tumbled onto the floor below, hurling her back into the water. He landed on his left shoulder. A sudden sharp pain told him he might've dislocated it, but that hurt was nothing compared to the burning he felt from the neck down. He crawled across the floor to the bed, grabbed the bedpost, and pulled himself to his feet.

"Jules! Don't leave me!"

He didn't look back. He grabbed his trench coat from the rack, then winced as he flung it around his shoulders. He nearly tore the door off its hinges getting out of the room.

"Jules! Come back! *Jules!*"

Her plaintive screams followed him into the hall. His thighs rubbed against each other like poison-coated sandpaper as he stumbled toward the stairs. Every last quivering part of him burned with the fires of hell. Especially the part that had gotten him into this mess in the first place. It'd be a long, *long* time before his little head was in any shape to give the rest of him orders again.

Served the little bastard right, Jules imagined Maureen hissing as he limped into the darkness of Barracks Street. *Served the boiled little bastard right.*

TEN

Doodlebug's flight, the red-eye from San Francisco, was already two and a half hours late. The Delta terminal's coffee stands had all closed long ago. Glum, sleepy, and surly would-be greeters were sprinkled throughout the waiting area, which had been fitted with plastic seats that were reasonably comfortable if judged against the standard of medieval torture devices. Worst of all, Jules's body felt like a throbbing wad of gristle.

For the hundredth time in the last five minutes, Jules shifted position in a futile effort to achieve a modicum of comfort. Successfully concealing the rashlike physical evidence of his latest misadventure from Maureen had been a minor miracle. He wondered if that miracle would last another night.

At last, the lights of an approaching jetliner flashed through the terminal's windows. Like zombies crawling from their graves, the greeters bestirred themselves, rose from their seats, and shuffled toward the gate. Jules joined the bedraggled procession. He tried hard to convince himself that Doodlebug's visit would have its positive aspects, but the only one his flailing mind could grasp was that Maureen *might* harangue him slightly less while his ex-sidekick was in town.

The first passengers to exit the tunnel were three teenagers, all struggling under the weight of overstuffed duffel bags. One was a brown-haired boy about the same age as Doodlebug had been when Jules turned him. It'd been years since Jules had seen his onetime sidekick; could this be—? No; the boy was immediately scooped into the arms of a gaggle of relatives and dragged toward the luggage retrieval.

The jetliner continued vomiting out passengers—tourists in lewd T-shirts, ready for Bourbon Street; businessmen with their copies of the *Wall Street Journal*; purple-haired grandmas toting giant stuffed bears. Jules began to wonder if maybe Doodlebug had missed his flight. Wouldn't *that* be the kicker! But then one of the deplaning passengers hooked Jules's interest. This one was a real stunner. Skintight red mini dress; long auburn hair that looked good even under the ghastly fluorescent lights; big gorgeous blue-gray eyes; slender hips; and legs that would flatter a Parisian runway model. Way too skinny to be Jules's type, but he still could appreciate her from a purely aesthetic point of view.

Surely a classy, upscale babe like this would have some Cary Grant–type investment banker waiting to pick her up. She looked a little dazed coming off the plane. She blinked rapidly in the bright, evil light and searched the crowd for a familiar face. Then she turned his way. Her eyes brightened with recognition. She waved. She wasn't a she after all.

Oh shit.

"Jules! Sorry I ran so late! There was a hang-up at the Denver airport. I tried phoning from the plane, but no one answered at Maureen's."

Yeah, it was Doodlebug, all right. Despite the pricey dress, the high heels, and the perfectly applied makeup, Jules recognized the tiny cleft in the middle of his delicate chin. And his voice hadn't changed—it was still the same high-pitched, prepubescent voice the kid'd had the night Jules interfered with nature and permanently halted his growth and physical maturation.

"Hey, partner! It's so good to *see* you!" Doodlebug said as he enthusiastically embraced the much bigger man. Doodlebug's strength, ten times that of a normal man, belied his slight frame. Jules's ravaged skin didn't take the hug kindly.

"Gahh! Jeezus! Leggo, will ya?"

Doodlebug immediately backed off, his face marked with concern. "Are you okay? What's wrong?"

Jules unsuccessfully tried stifling a grimace of pain. "Nothin'. Let's go."

"Are you hurt? Maureen told me about the trouble you've been in—"

"It's *nothin'*, okay? Let's go pick up your luggage."

"I express-shipped it all ahead. Everything's waiting for me at the bed-and-breakfast. Clothes, coffin, everything."

"Then let's get the hell outta here. These fuckin' lights are makin' me sick to my stomach already."

♠

Jules muttered hardly a word on their walk to the Lincoln. He didn't speak on their drive out of the parking garage either, aside from demanding that his passenger pay the five-dollar parking fee. Seeming to sense Jules's volatile mood, Doodlebug wisely kept his end of the conversation to a bare minimum. He commented briefly on the humidity and on the improvements to the airport since his last visit.

Only after they turned onto Airline Highway did Jules begin to talk. His voice was flat. Harsh. "Let's get one thing straight before I drive another block. You're only here because Maureen insisted. I don't want you. I don't need you. No matter what Maureen says, *I'm* the one in charge. You help me, or if you can't do that, you stay outta my way. Got it?"

Doodlebug folded his perfectly manicured hands on his lap and responded in a calm, agreeable voice. "Perfectly."

"You *sure*? There ain't no room for negotiation on this."

"I wouldn't have it any other way. It's *your* life that's at stake . . . your *un*life, actually. Of *course* you're the one in charge. You're the responsible party here, partner."

Jules had steeled himself for an argument. Now he felt like a man who'd gotten a running start to knock down a door, only to have it flung open in his face at the last second. "Well, okay, then. Just so long as we got that straight."

They continued driving east along Airline Highway, a cratered four-lane road surrounded by rent-by-the-hour motels and bars barely hanging on to their liquor licenses. Jules was in no big hurry to get back to the Quarter, but Maureen had insisted that he bring Doodlebug to see her at the strip club as soon as he got in. He turned the air conditioner up a notch and unbuttoned the top four buttons of his shirt, hoping the cool air would soothe his burning chest. Doodlebug immediately noticed the inflamed color of Jules's skin. He reached up and switched on the overhead dome light to get a better look.

"Those look like pretty bad burns," Doodlebug said quietly. "How did you get them?"

"None of your damn business," Jules grumbled.

His passenger pointed to a brightly lit storefront across the street. "There's an open drugstore. Swing around and pull in there. I've seen burns like yours before. I think I can help."

Jules glanced over at the red-and-blue neon sign across the street. "No way. That's a Rite Aid. There ain't no fuckin' way I'm settin' foot in a Rite Aid."

"Why not?"

"I know you ain't been around in a while, but you remember K&B?"

"The local drugstore chain? Sure. K&B purple, who could forget? Everything they sold was purple."

"Well, there ain't no more K&B. Fuckin' Rite Aid bought 'em out. Those corporate bloodsuckers put a big hunka New Orleans history six feet under."

Doodlebug thought for a few seconds. "I really *can* help you, Jules. If you'll let me. Are there any *locally owned* drugstores or supermarkets near here open this late?"

"Yeah. There's a Schwegmann's up the road a mile or two."

"Um, not to pop your bubble or anything, but didn't I read somewhere that Schwegmann's was bought out by a New York grocery conglomerate?"

Jules growled.

Thirty seconds later, after a reluctant but resigned U-turn, he pulled into the Rite Aid's parking lot. He trailed behind his visitor as Doodlebug headed purposefully toward the Liniments and Ointments aisle.

"I don't expect I'll find any *luhk daht quan* here," Doodlebug said as he scanned the rows of plastic bottles. "It's a shame there aren't any late-night Asian markets around here like there are in San Francisco . . . oh, well, we'll just make do with what's at hand. Something with a good dollop of aloe in it should work reasonably well. *Here* we go." He selected the largest available bottle of Vaseline Intensive Care lotion and walked quickly to the only open checkout line.

Jules exited the store with a disgusted sneer on his face. "Well, ain't *you* the president of the genius-of-the-month club. Don't you think I *tried* smearin' myself with every damn ointment in Maureen's medicine cabinet last night? I even used half her jar of Oil of Olay. None of this shit does me any good. You just wasted six-fifty, pally."

Doodlebug sighed. "Oh ye of little faith . . ." He took firm hold of Jules's hand and squirted several ounces of lotion into his open palm.

"Hey!"

"Indulge me a second, please. Just hold your hand like that, and I'll show you a little trick I picked up from my teachers in Tibet."

"I ain't in no mood for this—"

"Hush! Be a *little* patient? I promise you, there is absolutely no way this will make you feel worse, and there is a very *good* chance it will make you feel better." Wielding the sharp, turquoise-painted fingernail of his right pinkie like a scalpel, Doodlebug cut an inch-long incision across his own left palm. He then squeezed the wound so that a thin trickle of blood fell into the lotion in Jules's hand. Doodlebug mixed the two fluids together for a few seconds with his forefinger, until Jules's palm was filled with a thick, pinkish paste.

"There. Now try spreading that over your burns."

Jules stared dubiously at the paste covering his palm. "I ain't never heard of nothin' like this—"

"Just *do* it, Jules. It can't hurt." Doodlebug squeezed his left hand into a fist to stanch the flow of blood and, at the same time, undid the rest of Jules's shirt buttons with his other hand. The big man's chest was rippled with oozing blisters.

Gingerly, Jules dabbed one of the biggest and ugliest with a few drops of the mixture. "Huh." He gave another blister the same treatment. "Not bad. Not bad." A little more daringly, he dipped two fingers into the paste and lightly rubbed it into his belly, where some of the worst blistering had taken place. "Y'know, I think you might have somethin' here. . . ." Throwing caution to the winds, he slathered his entire upper body with his handful of paste. "Hey, this stuff is fuckin' *great*! I feel like a new man! Doodlebug, pal, how the hell did ya ever figure this out?"

His auburn-haired companion smiled. "Well, maybe I *am* president of the genius-of-the-month club, after all." He graciously opened the driver's door for Jules. "Shall we?"

♠

Maureen was applying the finishing touches to her makeup when Jules and Doodlebug entered her dressing room. Maureen swiveled on her padded stool as the two men walked through the door.

"Doodlebug! Darling! I'm so *thrilled* you've come!"

The slight vampire was completely enveloped in the huge woman's hug. "Hello, Maureen! Oh, it's been too long, dear!"

Maureen released her visitor and ushered him over to a leather couch, leaving Jules standing in the doorway. "It *has* been too long. What— twenty, twenty-five years?" She directed a scathing glare at Jules. "Really, Doodle darling, you shouldn't have let *this* old grouch keep you away so long. But look at you! You're absolutely *lovely*! And so *thin*! I swear, honey, you haven't gained an *ounce* in the last forty years! Oh, that California lifestyle . . . I should've followed you out there, honey. Instead of staying put in this moldy, *unhealthy* dump of a town with ol' stuck-in-the-mud Jules here."

"Hi, Mo," Jules said from the doorway. "Nice to see you, too, darlin'."

Dinah, one of the club's other strippers, pushed her way past Jules into the dressing room. "Hey, Maureen, any chance I can borrow some baby powder?" She eyed Doodlebug with interest. "Who's this snazzy little guest of yours? This one looks like a better class of people than you usually hang with."

Maureen looked irritated at the interruption, but she opted to be gracious. "Dinah, this is Doodlebug; Doodlebug, Dinah. Doodle here is one of my very oldest friends on earth. Actually, her name's Debbie, which we shortened to D.B.—that's where *Doodlebug* comes from."

"Real pleased to meet you, Doodlebug." Dinah shook the visitor's hand. "Hey! That's a strong grip you've got there. Especially for a little gal."

"Thanks. I spend a lot of time in the gym. Sometimes I think my nickname should be *Nautilus*."

"Say . . ." Dinah ran a fish-eyed glance up and down the newcomer's svelte form. "This is awful rude of me to ask, but . . . you're a *guy*, ain'tchu? Or you used to be a guy?"

Jules chuckled. Maureen gasped in horror. But Doodlebug merely smiled Mona Lisa–like. "Actually, I follow a strict 'Don't ask, don't tell' policy."

Dinah snorted. "Uh-huh. I hear ya. Not that it's *obvious* or anything— only reason I picked up on it is that I'm a professional. Adam's apple's just a *bit* too big. And honestly, those legs of yours are just *too* good for any real woman to be walkin' around with."

"I'll take that as a compliment," Doodlebug said, smiling.

"Please do. And that's some *incredible* boob job you've had done. Real natural, honey. So how about that baby powder, Maureen?"

Maureen grabbed hold of Dinah's shoulders and pushed her toward the door. "I'm all out, okay? Go pester one of the other girls."

"But you got two great big containers right there—"

Maureen slammed the door shut as soon as she'd pushed Dinah into the hallway. "Oh, Doodlebug, I am so *sorry*! I simply can't believe how rude and obnoxious some people can be! I'm going to seriously reconsider the value of my friendship with that brazen hussy!"

Doodlebug took her hand. "Oh, never you mind. No harm was done. Actually, I like being 'made' now and then. Reminds me when I need to sharpen up my act." He closed his eyes a few seconds, and his brow furrowed with concentration. The petite vampire's throat wiggled as if he were gargling with Jell-O cubes, and the slight prominence of his Adam's apple shrank from sight. At the same time the contours of his thighs changed, becoming softer and less muscular.

"Whoa!" Jules said. "How'd you pull that off?"

Doodlebug opened his eyes and smiled. "Oh, it's no big accomplishment. It just takes a little practice, that's all. Give me an evening or two, and I'm sure I could teach you to do the same."

"No thanks! Seein' you do it is creepy enough!"

Maureen moved to shush him. "Jules, cut the crap. Doodlebug just flew in all the way from California. I'm sure his time is way too valuable to be taken up with your foolishness. Now, Doodle, I explained to you on the phone a couple of nights ago this whole big mess that Jules has gotten himself into. You've probably already figured out some brilliant plans for how we can keep this big doofus from getting his head handed to him. I'd *love* to hear them. I've got forty-five minutes before I have to go on."

Doodlebug walked to Jules's side. "Actually, I can't say that I have much of anything figured out yet. My first thought is simply to sit with Jules for a while over a hot pot of coffee and get his version of what's been happening."

Maureen clucked dismissively. "Oh, *he* can't tell you anything worthwhile! The only thing he's an expert on is how to get himself killed. Surely on your flight over here you contemplated *some* ways to keep him out of trouble? Maybe chaining him to the brick wall down in my basement would be a good start?"

Jules bristled. Doodlebug quickly stepped between them. "Maureen, Jules is a responsible adult. He's perfectly capable of shouldering most of the load of protecting himself. Just on the way here from the airport, he was telling me about a plan *he* has—"

Maureen laughed uproariously. She shook so hard that she had to steady herself against a makeup table. "*Ah-ha, ah-ha* . . . what a great little kidder you are! His *plan*! Recruiting a bunch of rednecks from the North Shore and turning them into vampires . . . *Ha ha ha ha!*"

Doodlebug didn't laugh or smile. "It may sound a little far-fetched. But Jules is the responsible party here. And if he has a plan, then it's my duty as his friend to help him make it work."

"Really?" Jules said, edging closer to the smaller vampire.

Maureen's good humor evaporated. She stared at her visitor as if he were an artichoke from outer space. "You—you're *serious*, aren't you?"

"Yes. Perfectly serious. I didn't fly here to take charge, Maureen. I came to offer my dear and *respected* friend any help within my power in meeting *his* goals."

Maureen's face seemed to crumble. "But—but you're the *smart* one, Doodlebug! How *could* you—? Oh, this is a nightmare! I can't believe what I'm hearing. . . ."

"Aww, get over it," Jules said. "This ain't no tragedy. I'm the boss of this dynamic duo, just like I always been. Everything's gonna work out great—"

"*Men!*" Maureen spat the word like the foulest curse she could muster. She whirled savagely on Doodlebug. "I thought you were different! I thought *you* at least had a woman's common sense! But no—you're just a jackass like all the rest! Stick together if you want to! Get each other killed! I don't care!"

"C'mon, Mo, calm down—"

She yanked her arm from Jules's grasp as though she were recoiling from poison ivy. "*Out!* Get out! I'm disgusted with both of you! *Both of you!*"

Jules tried mollifying her with words and caresses, but all he accomplished was to ignite a fusillade of furious slaps. Doodlebug grabbed Jules's arm and pulled him into the hallway, closing the door quickly behind him.

Jules dabbed his face with a handkerchief, then checked to see if the cloth had any blood on it. "Whew! She sure knows how to put a mad on."

"Definitely. I've always treasured Maureen as a role model of femininity."

Jules placed both his huge hands on his friend's slender shoulders. "Hey. Thanks for backin' me up in there. I really appreciate it, pal."

"What are friends for?" Doodlebug said as they passed the stage, heading for the exit. "Let's go have a meal, and you can tell me everything."

♠

"Swanky joint you picked out for yourself, D.B.," Jules said with genuine admiration. He steered his Lincoln off Bayou Road onto the gravel driveway leading to the columned portico of the Twelve Oaks Guest House. "I never woulda expected a place like *this* on a dumpy, run-down street like Bayou Road."

"I like the fact that it's off the beaten track, but not too far from the center of town," Doodlebug said. "And the owners are very discreet."

They parked in front of the main entrance, a wide, deeply shadowed porch lined with hissing gas lamps. The two-story main house was bracketed by enormous overhanging oaks. Jules got out of the car and stared up at the shimmering beveled-glass windows. "Hey—wouldn't this make a perfect setting for a movie of one of Agatha Longrain's vampire potboilers?"

Doodlebug retrieved his purse from the backseat. "Actually, it already has been. Three or four years ago, this block was crawling with Hollywood types. That's how I first heard of the guest house. After the shoot, it quickly became a favorite of film industry muckety-mucks. The owners specialize in that sort of exclusive California visitor now. Which is wonderful for me, because they've learned to not bat an eyelash at the most bizarre eccentricities under the sun. Or moon, in my case."

Doodlebug checked in, and then the two of them walked through the manicured grounds to the Governor Claiborne Cottage, the largest of the outbuildings, which sat a good hundred feet from any of the other cabins. It even had its own goldfish pond. Jules knelt down and stuck his fingers in the water. Half a dozen plump orange fish darted to their hiding places beneath bright green lily fronds.

"Hey, if you get hungry in the middle of the night, you could always have yourself a fish fry."

Doodlebug smiled and unlocked the door. "Oh, I can do *much* better than *that*. Come inside and see."

Jules followed his visitor into the cottage. In the middle of the bedroom sat a stunning four-poster bed, and in the middle of the bed sat Doodlebug's gleaming mahogany coffin. The smaller vampire gestured for Jules to follow him into the kitchen. He opened the full-sized refrigerator. The bottom two shelves were lined with bottles of rich red blood.

"All the comforts of home, my friend."

Jules's eyes widened. "Whoa-*ho*! And I thought *Maureen's* fridge was well stocked! Where'd all this come from?"

Doodlebug shut the refrigerator door and sat at the breakfast nook's table. "One of the nicest fringe benefits of being the spiritual director of my Institute for Heightened Alpha-Consciousness is that my disciples pay in blood. Literally! That's not all they give to the center, of course; I couldn't afford to keep it running on blood alone. But each member voluntarily contributes a pint every six weeks, which meets my needs quite admirably. It's part of the center's recommended physical cleansing cycle, you see. And during their stays, all my disciples eat a strictly vegetarian, macrobiotic diet, which goes a long way toward helping me maintain my 'girlish figure.' While I'm here, I'll have fresh pints shipped to me every other day. Feel free to imbibe—it's quite good for you."

Jules shook his head, stunned. "Jeezus H. Christ! *Everybody's* got a racket! You, those rich dickheads on Bamboo Road—you've all figured out a perfect scam! Rivers of blood comin' out your peckers like cheap beer, and you don't hafta work for it one bit!" He slumped into the chair across from his friend. "Nothin' in this world is fair anymore. Hard work don't count fer *nothin'*. Tradition don't count fer *shit*. Maybe that jerk Besthoff was onto somethin' . . . maybe the days of us 'free-range vampires' *are* numbered, after all."

There was a knock at the door. A porter identified himself and said he'd brought the pot of coffee Doodlebug had requested. After accepting the platter, Doodlebug selected the biggest mug from the kitchen's charming selection and poured Jules a cup of steaming java. "Now, Jules, you aren't being entirely fair, are you? Don't I remember a certain someone who worked in a coroner's office and happily drank the blood of the recently deceased for years?"

"Don't remind me," Jules grumbled. "That was the best gig I ever had."

"You know, you're more than welcome to join me at my institute in California. I've told you that before."

Jules scowled. "Oh *yeah*—couldn't you just picture me dancin' around with them pajama-wearin' weirdos you got out there? Hah! I'd go so fuckin' crazy, before you know it, *I'd* be dressin' up like a girl." He slurped a swig of coffee. "You and that Doc Landrieu—you both want to get me the hell outta here. How do I know you're not both in cahoots with that goddamn Malice X? Well, let me tell you somethin', and let me tell you somethin' *right now*—ain't *nobody* gonna shove me outta New Orleans! Not *you*, not Maureen, not my ex-boss, and for *sure* not some wet-behind-the-ears Negro vampire *asshole*!" He pounded the table, spilling hot coffee onto the floor.

Doodlebug rubbed the bridge of his nose and sighed. "Look, Jules, I want to help you achieve what *you* want. Okay? Obviously, moving you somewhere else is *not* what you want. So let's spend tonight trying to figure out how to get you what you *do* want, which is living here in New Orleans in some semblance of peace. How about we begin with your telling me everything that's happened to you in the past four weeks."

Jules grunted his assent. Doodlebug threw some paper towels on the spilled coffee, then poured his friend another cup and sat down to listen. Jules told him almost everything, starting with the night he'd picked up Bessie and ended up playing reluctant host to Malice X. Being particularly proud of his infiltration of the Moss Avenue police station, Jules blew that part of the story way out of proportion. He was also very liberal in describing his heroic attempts to rescue his irreplaceable collectibles from the fire. Conversely, he said exceedingly little about his five-day exile in Baton Rouge. About his encounter with the gorgeous (but possibly deadly) plus-sized model, Veronika, Jules said nothing at all.

Doodlebug rubbed his powdered chin for several long moments. "There are some things about your story that don't make any sense to me," he said at last.

"Such as—?"

"If Malice X really wants to kill you, he's failed to take advantage of some ideal opportunities."

"Maybe he's just sloppy. Or maybe I been lucky so far."

"Maybe. But aside from your altercation with the three would-be assassins, he's been content at each encounter to either warn you or try to push you out of what he sees as his territory. And he's certainly known for the last three nights that you're back in New Orleans, but with the exception of that one attack, you've remained unmolested. Wouldn't you think he'd have the entire Quarter crawling with his spies and killers by now, if he truly wanted to do you in?"

Jules fished a few stray coffee grounds out of the bottom of his cup with a sterling-silver spoon. "Well, yeah, I guess. But I been real careful these last few nights. You shoulda seen the outfit I put together last night, fer instance—I mean, I was *really* incognito—"

"I'm sure it was a good disguise, Jules, but I still get the feeling you're being let off lightly. It's almost as if your opponent wants to drag this out. As if he's taking pleasure in humiliating and harassing you."

"Huh." Jules raised an eyebrow. "Well, I sure wouldn't put it past the bum."

Doodlebug sat back down and leaned across the table, staring intently into his friend's face. "And here's another question for you. Why do you suppose this Malice X hates *you* so much?"

Jules grunted. "Ain't no big mystery about *that*. Black guys have been gettin' the short end of the stick for a long time, since way before I was around. You and me both remember the Jim Crow days here in New Orleans, so those days weren't so far back. I'm a white guy. He's a black guy. He resents me for it. That's the Song of the South, pal—oldest story around these parts. Case closed."

"Is it?"

"Why the hell not?"

"You aren't the *only* white vampire in New Orleans. Why hasn't Malice X gone after the others?"

Jules rolled his eyes. "That's easy. Besthoff and Katz and them are holed up in their compound on Bamboo Road, where Malice X can't get at 'em. That place of theirs is like a damn fortress."

"I wasn't talking about Katz and Besthoff."

"Who else is there?"

Doodlebug paused before answering. "Maureen."

Jules winced involuntarily. "Huh? What're you saying?"

"Think about it. Maureen sustains herself on victims she lures from her club. Considering that place's clientele, surely not every one of those victims has been a white man. But she hasn't been singled out for any warnings or attacks by this gang of black vampires. Why is that?"

Jules chewed his lower lip. "Ehh . . . I don't think I like what you're implyin' here. Mo can't be tangled up in this. Not *her*. I mean, she gave me a place to stay after Baton Rouge, no questions asked. With all our history an' all."

"I don't like to think it, either, Jules. But these questions won't go away. I think that, very soon, you and I need to sit down with Maureen and ask them to her face."

♠

Early the next evening, barely forty minutes after sundown, Jules and Doodlebug zoomed onto the Lake Pontchartrain Causeway, heading north for Covington. Jules pushed his reluctant auto to sixty-eight, thirteen miles per hour over the posted speed limit. With its jellied suspension, the Lincoln hit the long bridge's expansion joints like a palsied old woman.

Doodlebug, dressed in a scarlet cocktail dress, gripped his armrest tightly and winced as they flounced over each joint. "May I speak plainly?"

Commanding a steering rack as responsive as an asphyxiated flounder, Jules didn't dare take his eyes off the road or even one hand off the wheel. "I wish you would. I never won no prizes for my big-time vocabulary."

"I think this trip is a bad idea."

"I don't remember askin' for your vote." Jules swerved to avoid a low-flying seagull, causing the Lincoln's bald tires to wail. "Say, weren't you the one who just last night was sayin' stuff like, 'Jules, you're the responsible party here,' and 'Jules, I want to help you get whatever it is *you* want'? Was that bullshit, or what?"

Doodlebug sighed. "I wasn't 'bullshitting' you, Jules. But my definition of *help* includes unbiased feedback regarding your decisions. If I held back, then I *would* be bullshitting you."

Now it was Jules's turn to sigh. "Okay. Shoot. I can see I'm gonna get an earful whether I like it or not."

"I think our time this evening would be spent much more productively if we had a heart-to-heart with Maureen."

Jules scowled. "Jeez, *again* with that! We'll get around to it, okay? First things first. We're on a real tight deadline with this recruitin' trip, remember? I've got a digital timer tickin' the seconds away that's hooked up to three gas canisters, all waitin' for me on the other side of this damn bridge."

Doodlebug smoothed the wrinkles from his dress. "You know, it wouldn't be such a tragedy if that gas goes off and you aren't there. The authorities would pass it off as a politically motivated prank. We can still turn around."

"Why are you so damn set against this mission? Is it just because it wasn't *your* bright idea?"

The smaller vampire frowned. "Jules, I have enough bright ideas of my *own*—I never feel jealous of someone else's. Why is this a bad idea? Two reasons. One: You don't need any followers. Two: Even if you did, these definitely *aren't* the sort of followers you want."

Jules squinted as the high beams from an eighteen-wheeler hit him dead in the face. "So I don't need any followers, huh? Have you bothered tellin' that to the dozens of goons Malice X has sicced on my tail?"

"You don't need to beat dozens of goons, Jules. You just need to beat one man."

Jules snorted. "*Ixnay* on the philosophy, okay? This mission ain't up for no debate. My mind's set in concrete." He glanced at his watch, dimly illuminated by the sickly green dashboard lights. "Shit! Look what time it is already! If we don't pick up the pace, that crowd'll fall asleep and wake back up before we even get there." He mashed the creaky accelerator pedal a bit closer to the rusted-out floorboards, brutalizing the already breathless Lincoln.

Doodlebug reached into his purse and applied some fresh powder to his forehead. "Oh yes, we mustn't keep your neo-Nazis waiting."

"Look, they ain't neo-Nazis, okay? They're white supremacists."

"Oh! Of course. How *could* I have overlooked such an important distinction?"

◆

The dirt parking lot outside the American Veterans Union Hall was about half full when Jules pulled up. He checked the lot for television trucks. If reporters were there when the gas went off, he'd just have to recruit them, too, and hope for the best. To his relief, no marked media trucks or vans were evident.

He checked his watch again by the Lincoln's dome light. "We're in luck," he said. "The gas is timed to go off at nine-fifty. It's only nine-forty. We still got ten minutes."

"Oh joy," Doodlebug said, straightening the straps of his dress.

"Let's go inside. I wanna see what's goin' on."

The hall wasn't especially crowded. Jules pushed aside a sinking sense of disappointment as he estimated the gathering at between twenty and twenty-five persons. It would have to do. At least they were nearly all men. Only two women were in attendance. One of them was wearing a *Times-Picayune* badge and typing notes on a laptop. Jules was pleasantly surprised to find a coffee urn and Styrofoam cups on a table near the back. He stationed himself next to the urn and listened to the proceedings.

"Point of order! Point of order!" a man not far from Jules shouted as he leapt from his chair. The speaker was a short man shaped like a papaya, wearing a faded T-shirt emblazoned with the logo BUCHANAN FOR PRES '96/'00/'04/'08. His face was flushed; he beat the air as he spoke. "The reason we're here tonight is to officially draft Mr. Knight as our candidate for parish councilman! This is not the time or the place to be discussing the creation of ethnic homelands!"

"Now, George, I couldn't disagree with you more!" The tall, thin man at the podium also beat the air as he spoke; the two of them looked like they were playing a game of invisible paddle tennis across the room. "If we're to have any hope of drawing Mr. Knight into this race and then winning it, we've got to have *vision*! The old standbys—our 'Three W's' of Welfare reform, Wasteful government, and Waco—they're not gonna cut the mustard this time. Folks are tired of the same-old, same-old. They want *innovative* thinking! They want leadership that isn't afraid to stand up to the real problems facing America!"

A man wearing a Mighty Ducks cap raised his hand to speak. "What I want to know is, do we hafta give the *whole* island of Manhattan to the Jews?"

"Bill, you have a problem with that? It *is* crowded, disease-ridden, and filthy, after all."

A number of audience members mumbled their agreement with the moderator. Bill shifted uncomfortably from foot to foot. "Well, see, I've got this elderly aunt who lives in Battery Park. Can't we just shove the Jews over into the Bronx with the Puerto Ricans and keep Manhattan for us whites?"

The thin man at the podium wearily rubbed the bridge of his nose. "Look, you need to keep in mind that Mr. Knight has already put a tremendous amount of *careful* thought into the exact geographic division of North America. Now, is there any more discussion on this issue before we move on to the next item on the agenda?"

The lone female participant, a worn-looking woman in the advanced stages of pregnancy, raised her hand. "Yeah. I've got something to say. Not to stir the pot more than it's already been stirred, but I've got a real big problem with handing Mississippi over to the niggers. Them gambling casinos in Gulfport and Biloxi are the best thing to happen to this part of the country in *years*. I'll be *damned* if I'll vote for any man who plans on handing those beautiful casinos over to the niggers!"

The hall erupted into a cacophony of angry shouts and competing calls to order. Jules checked his watch, then nudged Doodlebug. "Time for us to take our 'cigarette break,' pal."

"Thank Varney! Any longer in here and I'd have to scrub myself down with lye."

They waited outside beneath the gloomy shadows of the pine trees. Jules sweated with nervous anticipation; would his setup work as planned? Three minutes later Tiny Idaho proved his worth as a gadget man. The shouting from inside suddenly changed to raucous and deranged laughter. Thirty seconds later the only sounds to be heard were crickets chirping and the rumble of traffic from the highway.

Jules rubbed his hands together with glee. "It worked! Am I a hotshot planner or what?"

They went back inside. Unconscious bodies were grotesquely sprawled across chairs, tables, and the floor, their faces still twisted with the muscle spasms of laughter. To Jules, it looked like the aftermath of one of the Joker's rampages from a 1940s Batman comic. He felt tremendously proud of himself. He quickly counted the bodies: twenty-three. Then he headed for the door.

"What are you up to now?" Doodlebug asked.

"Wait and see, pal. I got this all planned out to a T."

He returned a minute later, his arms full of stacks of disposable aluminum baking pans. He set these aside, then began arranging the slumbering bodies on shoved-together chairs, laying out each victim so that the head and neck dangled below the rest of the body.

Jules glanced archly at his companion. "Are you gonna help me, or are you just gonna stand there and watch?"

"Neither, actually," Doodlebug said as he sat himself down by the door and pulled a folded copy of *The New Yorker* from his purse. "This is *your* show. I'm just along for the ride, remember?"

Jules grumbled darkly, but he continued with his work. After twenty minutes he had all the bodies in proper position, aluminum baking pans on the floor beneath their necks. Now came the tricky part. He had to actually drink enough of their blood to ensure that they'd become vampires, but not so much that he'd succumb to the gas's effects and fall unconscious himself.

One of the women began to stir. It was the reporter from the *Times-Picayune*. He'd hoped she would've left before the gas went off, but now he had no choice but to do her. He knelt by her side and unceremoniously chomped down on her neck. She moaned quietly. Her blood had the same metallic, off-taste he remembered from his kayaker victim in the cab. He allowed himself to swallow two mouthfuls—any more than two would be pushing his luck—and then he sucked hard but spat the blood into the pan below. He sucked and spat and sucked and spat until he got a good, steady flow going. Then he let gravity do the rest of the work.

The job rapidly turned into a race against time. He hustled from one side of the room to the other, biting, sucking, and spitting as grunts or twitches of wakefulness called to him. Several times he had no choice but to stop and sit for a minute. Even in small individual doses, the cumulative effect of it all caught up with him, and he giggled as the room shifted around his spinning head.

Finally, Jules was done. He slumped against the rear wall, a few feet away from where Doodlebug was still sitting with his magazine. He felt dizzy and more than a little nauseated. But he was very satisfied with himself. He'd planned his work and worked his plan. Now there was nothing more to do but wait a couple of hours, the time it would take for his recruits to reawaken as fledgling vampires. The nucleus of his army of vengeance.

♦

The *Times-Picayune* reporter was the first to stir. Outside, a trucker blasted his air horn. The woman slowly rubbed her face and mumbled. "*Honeeee* . . . honey . . . turn off the alarm, will you? It's *irritating*. . . ."

Roughly in the order in which Jules had serviced them, the newly born vampires mumbled and stretched and worked the kinks out of their necks and backs. The ex-moderator was the first to attempt to stand. He clung to the podium and swayed like a drunk on a three-day bender. "What . . . what the hell *happened*?" He stared across the room at the other slowly unclouding faces, who in turn glanced about them and looked at each other with wide, surprised eyes.

"We . . . were we all asleep?"

"I remember laughin' like the dickens about somethin' or other. . . ."

"What's with these *holes* in everybody's neck?"

"Red gravy in pans all over the floor—?"

"Hey, Waldo, you're white as a brand-new bedsheet!"

"Boy, am I *thirsty*—"

Jules stepped smartly to the podium and shoved the ex-moderator aside. He beamed with triumph. "Welcome, everyone! Welcome to the happy and growing ranks of the undead!"

The ex-moderator slumped into a chair and rubbed his sore neck. "And who the fat fuck are you?"

"Me? I'm your new leader. My name is Jules Duchon. And I"—he struck his puffed-out chest like a Roman centurion—"am a *vampire*! Now, thanks to me, all of *you* are vampires, too! I can see from your faces that some of you are havin' a hard time believing me. Well, just look at the fang marks on each other's necks. The mark of *my* fangs! You feel thirsty? It's *blood* that you thirst for! In just a few minutes, you can exchange pans and have your first drink. Feel each other. Go ahead; don't be shy. Your skin is the temperature of this room. Since the air conditioner's been running all night, your hides must be pretty darn cool by now."

"He's *right*!" the pregnant woman shrieked. "I'm *cold*! I ain't *never* been cold in July in south Louisiana before!"

"You'll get used to it," Jules reassured her. "Just drink plenty of hot coffee."

"But—but wait a minute!" The *Times-Picayune* reporter stared at her white arms with horror. "I *can't* be a vampire! I'm a rabbi's wife, for God's sake!"

"Holy mackerel! My skin really *is* white!" The man wearing the Buchanan T-shirt lifted it up and insisted that his neighbors take a look at his alabaster belly. "Look at this! Is this incredibly *excellent* or what? I'm the whitest man on the North Shore!"

Immediately, all members of the audience began comparing each other's skin tones and arguing over who, in fact, was the whitest of them all. This contest went on for a few minutes, rising in volume and vociferousness, until the ex-moderator grabbed the gavel from the podium and banged it against the seat of his chair.

"Now simmer down, people! Just simmer down!" He waited until the last arguments died away, then turned toward Jules. "I think it's high time we asked this man why he came here tonight and did this to all of us."

Jules took a deep breath and expanded his chest to its maximum diameter. "I have recruited all of you to fight in a great crusade! A crusade that all of you will have big-time enthusiasm for. The great city of New

Orleans has become infected with the foul, nasty, horrible, *foul* plague of—*Negro vampirism!* That fair city, so historic, so important to good white folks everywhere, is practically *overrun* by colored, bloodsucking hordes! They pollute the air with their so-called rap music and destroy all that is good and pure about white culture! We MUST put an END to this ABOMINATION! Are you all *with* me?"

The rousing cheers Jules fully expected to hear never came. Instead, the man wearing the Buchanan T-shirt said, "So you want us to go back over the Causeway with you to New Orleans and clean that place out?"

"Well . . . *sure!*" Jules smiled as brightly as he could.

The self-proclaimed Whitest Man on the North Shore laughed so hard that his dentures, already displaced by his new fangs, flew out of his mouth. "You . . . want *us* . . . to go back to that cesspool of miscegenation and niggraism? After we spent half our lives making enough money to get the hell *away* from there?"

"But—"

Others in the audience vigorously nodded their assent. "Let New Orleans *rot!*"

"They can all kill each other off for all I care!"

"Damn rich white folks over there *deserve* it for lettin' those niggers breed out of control!"

"*Fuck* New Orleans!"

Jules waved his arms wildly. "Wait! Just wait a minute! Look over there!" He pointed dramatically at the window on the eastern side of the building. "In just four or five hours from now, the *sun's* gonna rise over the horizon and come through that window, and *none* of you know what to do about it! You know what that sun'll do to you? It ain't nice! *I'm* the only one here with the know-how to teach you how to escape the sun— how to live as *vampires!* And if y'all don't do exactly as I say—I ain't teachin' none of you *doodly-squat!*"

The new vampires stared at each other, their pale faces twitching with uncertainty. But then the ex-moderator stood and strode to the podium. "Listen, folks! We don't need this man! I've read every book Agatha Longrain has ever written, cover to cover, three times! I know everything there is to know about vampires!"

The man in the Buchanan shirt shot to his feet. "More good, Christian white folks are moving to St. Tammany every day! Who's to say we can't form our own colony of white vampires over *here*, where there's an endless and ever-growing supply of pure, unpolluted white blood?"

A man in a black suit, who hadn't said a word previously, was the next to rise. "I own a funeral home in Mandeville, folks! I have, in stock, a full line of magnificent coffins that I will be happy to sell for one penny over invoice to every person in this room!"

It was all slipping away. Jules looked beseechingly at Doodlebug, still sitting in the back of the hall with his *New Yorker* on his lap. Doodlebug slowly shook his head and rolled his eyes to the ceiling. Then he put his magazine aside and stood on his chair.

"What *great* ideas everyone has! I can just *feel* all the positive energy flowing in this room. But I'm sure you're all terribly, *terribly* thirsty. I remember how it was when *I* first became a vampire. Well, I know just the thing! Nothing, but *nothing*, beats the zing of drinking your *own* blood. It's incredibly reviving and refreshing! Everybody, check the floor next to your chairs. There's a baking pan there that's filled with your own blood. Trust me, it's a treat like no other!"

Like a pack of ravenous hyenas, the newborn vampires grabbed the pans of blood off the floor and lifted them to their thirsting lips. The red gore ran freely down their faces and necks, staining blouses and T-shirts and polyester neckties alike. The room was filled with the sounds of slurping, gulping, and sweetly satisfied sighs.

Those satisfied sighs didn't last long, however. They were quickly displaced by surprised yelps of pain, then agonized screams, then the wails of dissolving banshees. Before Jules's horrified eyes, twenty-three newborn vampires were reduced to twenty-three puddles of smoking, bubbling goo.

ELEVEN

"So the conquering heroes have returned."

Maureen didn't even bother looking up from her copy of *Ladies' Home Journal* as Jules and Doodlebug stepped into her dressing room. "Where's your glorious army, Jules? Out in the club watching the floor show? Or did you recruit so many soldiers that you had to leave them outside?"

"Don't ask," Jules said, staring sourly at his companion.

Maureen swiveled around on her stool. "Oh, but I *want* to ask! I want to hear *everything*! Jules, how did your brilliant plan work out? I assume from your happy expression that it was a *smashing* success. And, Doodlebug dear, I just *know* you're feeling a warm glow of satisfaction from backing your friend to the hilt."

"Maybe if he *had* backed me to the hilt," Jules said, "we woulda accomplished somethin' tonight. But thanks to Penelope Pukehead here, all I got to show fer the evening is eight gallons of wasted gas and a sick feelin' in the pit of my stomach."

"Jules is a little peeved at me." Doodlebug reached into his purse and applied a fresh coat of imported French lipstick. "I'm afraid I had to pull the plug on him before things got out of hand."

"Pull the *plug*? Is *that* what you call what you did? That was the most *disgustin'* horror show I ever saw! Those were *vampires* you killed! Prejudiced idiot vampires, sure, but still *vampires!*"

Doodlebug gave Jules an honestly sympathetic look. "It was very unfortunate, yes. But I'm sure once you've had a chance to cool off and think the whole thing through, you'll agree with me that it *was* necessary. The only one I feel sorry about, really, is that rabbi's wife."

"You didn't give me a *chance*! I coulda turned 'em around! Sure, maybe they weren't as gung-ho as I expected. But if I just coulda talked to them some more, I'm *positive* I coulda got maybe half of them to sign on—two-thirds, even! But *noooooo*—you hadda go jump the gun and turn 'em all into piles of goo!"

"My, my! The Grand Alliance is fraying already, is it?" Maureen got off her stool and sashayed toward Jules, aggressively thrusting her stomach before her. "Jules, as uncharacteristically dumb as Doodle has been so far on this visit, you can't blame him for this latest fiasco. If anything, I'm sure it would've turned out *worse* if he hadn't have been there with you. You know who you need to be shoveling the blame onto? I'd say *look in the mirror*, but unfortunately, that isn't possible, is it?"

Something in Maureen's tone of voice got under Jules's skin. "Yeah? It's all my fault, huh? I just *asked* for Malice X and his goons to trash me, that's what you're sayin'?"

Maureen leaned across their twin stomachs, putting her nose an inch from his. "Damn you, Jules Duchon!" Her eyes were afire with anguish and self-loathing, and her voice dripped with bitter resentment. "It *is* all your fault! Every second of misery you've endured these past three weeks you've brought on yourself! Yourself! And you've forced me to suffer every miserable second right along with you!"

Jules frowned with befuddlement, not anger. "What're you talkin' about, Mo?"

"You *made* me make him, damn you! You left me alone! I had *no one*! Do you have any *idea* what that's like for a woman like me? Do you? *Do you?*"

She collapsed onto the couch and buried her face in her hands. As the room filled with the sound of her ragged sobbing, Jules stood still as a gray, weather-beaten statue. Only a twitching in the corner of his mouth betrayed that he still possessed the power of movement.

Doodlebug knelt by Maureen's side. He gently stroked her hair. "It's all right, dear. It's all right . . . try to get hold of yourself. I suspected it might be something like this. You have to tell us the rest. We need to know everything."

"Oh God . . . oh God, please forgive me." She choked back her sobs and raised her head from her hands. Tears and fingers had smeared her mascara into a mask of spiderwebs. Only her stained forehead and her eyes, turned toward the heavens, showed above the arm of the couch. "Lord, I know I haven't any right to call on Your name. No right. But if You have any shred of pity for a damned creature like me, please send Your forgiveness."

"Start at the beginning, Maureen."

"Ten years ago, we . . . I just couldn't live with Jules anymore. He was driving me out of my mind. He wouldn't listen to anything I'd tell him. He'd *say* he was going on a diet, that he'd watch what he was eating. But every month I watched him pile on the pounds, get grosser and grosser. He was destroying himself, destroying the beautiful man I'd wanted to preserve forever. . . . Finally, I just couldn't take it anymore. I told him to get out. If he refused to take care of himself, he had to get out. I never meant for him to leave, not *really*—but he took me at my word. He was too bullheaded, too goddamn *dense* to realize that, yes, I'd reached the end of my rope, but actually I was only *warning* him. . . . I wanted him to shape up, to *reform*, not *leave*. . . ."

"So the man who became Malice X . . . you took him as your lover? He was Jules's replacement?"

"Oh God . . . you have to *understand*. The house was so *empty*. After a few months, the silence was driving me out of my mind. I tried making friends at the club. But there was no one there who could *understand* me. I even thought about going back to the compound, back to Bamboo Road. But it had been too many years. I couldn't bear going back there as an utter failure, a fat girl who couldn't hack it on the outside. I was so lonely . . . and the men I brought home with me from the club only made it worse. Some of them, they'd try making conversation before we'd have sex . . . but it never mattered, because I knew that before sunrise, they'd be stiff as day-old doughnuts, and I'd be stuffing them down the furnace chute. White, colored, Spanish, Chinese . . . after a while, I hardly paid attention anymore. Going down the chute, they all had the same face. Exactly the same dumb, surprised, frozen face.

"One night, I noticed this young man staring at me. Oh, sure, they all *stared*, but this one was looking at me different—like he was appreciating me as a woman, not just as a slab of dancing meat. For weeks he came back, five, six nights a week. A colored kid, but he was young, good look-ing. And he had beautiful eyes. A beautiful smile. I waited for him to ap-proach me like the older men did, the ones I'd end up taking back to the house. But he was shy. Finally one night *I* approached *him*. I took him home with me. The night went like it usually did. But after I drank him dry, I stared at him lying there in my bed, and his face was *different*. . . . Never in a million years did I think I'd do it, but I didn't stuff him down the chute. I let him lie there in peace, lie there until he woke up—"

"I can't listen to no more of this," Jules said.

Maureen, eyes wide with terror, turned toward the dead, listless sound of her ex-lover's voice. "Jules? Jules, you have to *understand*, I had no *idea* what would happen later—"

He slowly shook his head, a rusted automaton who could barely heed the commands of distant, weak radio waves. "I ain't listenin' to one more word. C'mon, Doodlebug. Let's get out of here."

The cross-dressing vampire's face was torn, conflicted. His words, usually so confidently spoken, were hesitant, almost mumbled. "Jules—I think—I really think she needs us, right now, to be here with her. Let's hear her out—"

Jules turned and walked to the door. He opened it. In a low tone, speaking into the hallway, he said, "Either you're with her. Or you're with me. Your choice. I'm going now."

◆

"My whole life is a piece a shit."

"No, it's not."

Jules and Doodlebug were sitting at a small, dirty, back corner table at the St. Charles Tavern. Jules hadn't wanted to go anywhere he might see people he knew. Aside from a few listless neighborhood types sitting at the bar, the dim, sour-smelling tavern was deserted; most of its ex-clientele was just up the street a few blocks, at the Trolley Stop Café.

"Sure it is. Sure it is. One big piece a shit. When I was tellin' you about that time two weeks ago I ran away to Baton Rouge, I didn't tell you the whole story. I did stuff I'm ashamed of. Stuff I'll never forget as long as I'm still walkin' this earth."

Doodlebug slowly stirred his cup of coffee. "I'm sure it doesn't really matter, Jules. We've all done things we're, eh, less than happy with. Even me." He smiled, briefly, perhaps hoping to spark a smile in return. It didn't work.

Jules's face, usually so animated as to appear rubbery, was a mask of petrified wood. "You ever fucked a stray dog?" And then it was all pouring out of him—his befriending the dog on the streets of Baton Rouge, how he stole dog food for her and then, violating all the rules of civilized vampirism, turned to a wolf so he could share her meal. Finally, he came to the worst part.

Jules's face was the color of slate. "I got no idea what came over me. One minute I was lying on the ground, feelin' like my stomach would burst from all the food I wolfed down. Next thing I know is, all I can *think* about is sniffin' that dog's ass. I never experienced anything like it in my life. It was like every part of me got shut off except my dick and my nose. Before I could begin to get a handle on what I was feelin', I'm leanin' on her and doin' the business. One part of me was totally disgusted—I mean, I was rapin' this poor, helpless animal, and besides, I had my dick inside a *dog*. Even if it was a wolf dick at the time. But this other part of me . . . Doodlebug, I ain't admitted this to nobody. Before now, I ain't even admitted it to myself. But part of me was enjoyin' it. Part of me was happy I wasn't alone no more, even if my mattress partner was a flea-ridden mutt. And part of me was totally into it, all the sensations, the smells . . . the feelin' of bein' totally outta control."

Doodlebug was speechless for a minute. Another customer came in, and the whir and clatter of a passing streetcar blew through the open door, along with a paper Burger King cup from up the street. Doodlebug took a sip of his coffee. "I don't really know what to say, Jules." He tried forcing another smile. "Uh . . . if your friend has puppies, will you name one after me?"

Jules seemed not to hear. "And now *this*. How could she've done it? Ruin my life, then lie to me and lie to me and lie even more. Y'know, Mo was *everything* to me. She made me into a vampire, so she was almost my second mother. She taught me practically everything I know about bein' a vampire; just like what I taught you. And when I first laid eyes on her, I knew right then, she was the most gorgeous woman I ever saw, and the most gorgeous woman I ever would see. I could hardly believe it when she picked me—*me!*—to be her number one guy. Her paramour, she called me. More years than not, she was my best friend, too; apart from maybe Erato. I mean, for chrissakes, we was practically *married*. She was as close to a wife as I'll ever have.

"And you wanna know the worst thing of all? I worshiped that woman. I always figured she was better than me. Why else you think I took her shit all those years? Every time she'd get all sarcastic on me, I'd tell myself, 'Jules, just shut up and take it. You must deserve it, so hear her out and maybe you'll learn somethin'. She's a smart woman, and she's a better vampire than you, and she knows what she's doin'.' Even when I couldn't do what she told me, couldn't get it right, I always *tried*. What do ya think kept me goin' this past month, when everythin' I touched was turnin' to shit? The thought that, no matter what happens to me, no matter how bad I screw up, Mo'll still take me back. And if Mo would take me back, then I must be worth somethin'.

"But you know what? She ain't better than me. She's not. Since before you was born, she been tellin' me, over and over, beatin' it into my head like a nail: *Don't make no colored vampires.* Like this was the biggest goddamn sin in the world. And I was tempted, too; lots of times. Both before you came on the scene and after you left, I had a few good pals who was black. Guys who weren't married and didn't have no kids, who woulda enjoyed the undead life. Plenty of times I thought to myself how great it would be to have a good buddy who was a vampire like me. But always, like a big glowin' neon sign, her words were in my head: *Don't be makin' no colored vampires.* And I figured she knew better than me. 'Cause I figured she *was* better than me. But she ain't no better than me. She's nothing more than a liar and a goddamn hypocrite. And I got this lousy feelin' that things ain't gettin' any better for me. I thought maybe they would. I thought maybe I could somehow get back the life I had before all this. But everything's goin' downhill, Doodlebug. Shit rolls downhill. And that's where I'm headin'. Downhill."

The door opened again, and a breeze blew the dirty Burger King cup against Jules's shoe. He didn't bother kicking it away. Doodlebug didn't try cracking a joke this time. He looked at Jules's still-full cup of coffee, gone cold. "Can I go to the bar and get you a fresh cup?"

"No thanks. I don't want none."

"What *do* you want? What can I do for you?"

Jules tried thinking. It was a slow process. He felt like his thoughts were drowning in a pan of congealed brown gravy. "Can I stay with you for a while? All I feel like doin' is sleeping. I can't . . . there ain't no way I'm goin' back where I was stayin' before."

♦

Doodlebug spoke to the concierge at the bed-and-breakfast. The concierge, happy recipient of a generous tip, woke the owner and explained the situation. The owner, very well connected and quite sympathetic to the unique needs of California's creative community, made a series of calls. Following a flurry of negotiations, which resulted in a five-hundred-dollar charge on Doodlebug's American Express corporate card and a sworn promise that he would make a thousand-dollar donation to Associated Catholic Charities the following day, the owner of Werlein's Music Stores had an empty grand-piano case delivered to Doodlebug's cottage that night. The huge wooden box, complete with hinged top, filled all but a few square feet of floor space in the suite's sitting room.

Doodlebug was obviously pleased with what he'd been able to accomplish on such short notice. But Jules barely acknowledged the help. He took a pitcher from the kitchen and slowly walked outside. He returned a few minutes later, the pitcher filled with clumpy dirt dug from the perimeter of the goldfish pond, and tossed the dirt into the open piano case.

"Jules, maybe we should drive back to your old house and collect some earth there? What do you think?"

"Don't wanna bother."

"But are you sure dirt from the yard here will, you know, work for you?"

"Guess I'll find out come morning time, won't I?"

"That's not a very reassuring answer."

"It's good enough for me."

Jules stepped onto the couch, which the delivery men had pushed against the wall, then climbed down into the piano case. With Doodlebug's help, he lowered the top above his head. Then he lay down in the thin sprinkling of dirt. Thanks to the assortment of overstuffed pillows Doodlebug had thoughtfully provided, Jules found the box surprisingly comfortable. The darkness was soothing. He closed his eyes. The blackness and quiet beckoned to him like old, dear friends.

♦

Jules very quickly lost track of time. His periods of dreaming and wakefulness blurred together into an undifferentiated mush of memories, regrets, and dark fantasies. Maureen frequently joined him and his mother in his dreams. Their alliances were constantly shifting. Sometimes Jules and his mother would be heaping abuse on Maureen. Sometimes his mother would be savagely berating Maureen and him together. And other times, the worst times of all, his mother and Maureen would act as a tag team of women wrestlers, leaping off the ropes and pounding him with wooden folding chairs or strangling him in choke holds.

An indefinite time later, Jules was startled by a sharp series of knocks on his box. "Jules? It's Doodlebug. Are you awake in there?"

"I am now."

"Look, I'm going out for a while. Can I get you anything?"

"Where are you goin'?"

"Just out for some air. If you want something, just tell me, and I'll take your car and go get it."

"Can you get me a time machine, maybe? So I can go back to ten years ago?"

"No can do, Jules. Sorry."

Jules thought for a while. "Y'know what I'd really like? Some comics to read. Captain America or The Sub-Mariner—"

"Hang on a second. I'm writing this down." A little while later he said, "Okay, got it. Where are your keys?"

"In the top drawer of the dresser, next to my wallet."

"Before I go, can I get you a pint of blood from the 'fridge?"

"Naww. I ain't hungry."

That was a lie. Jules's stomach was rumbling like an empty garbage truck bouncing over the potholes of Tchoupitoulas Street. But he refused to eat anything. Some time later, Doodlebug returned with a bag full of comics, a stand-up flashlight, and a big package of batteries. Jules loaded the batteries into the flashlight, read a few comics, then drifted back into sleep. He dreamed of better, prouder, happier nights, nights when he'd helped win the Second World War as the mighty Hooded Terror.

He was jarred awake by more knocking. "Jules, I need to discuss something with you."

Jules stretched (as best he could in the confined space) and yawned. "Yeah, what you need?"

"I have a friend over at the *Times-Picayune*. Actually, he's not so much a friend as a cyber-acquaintance; I got to know him through a cross-dressers' chat room on America Online. Anyway, he works nights, so I took what we know about Malice X to him, and he agreed to search the newspaper's computer archives of old articles to see if he could dig up any information for us. But I couldn't tell him enough to get him started. You told me that Malice X was once a teenage felon who called himself Eldo Rado. My friend couldn't find any mention of an 'Eldo Rado' in any crime reports from the last fifteen years. He's probably in there somewhere. Maybe the newspaper lists his legal name, or possibly another alias. We need to ask Maureen some more questions. She might be able to help us get more of a lead on him."

"You want more information? *You* go ask her. I'm stayin' put right where I am."

"I really think we *both* need to go question her."

"Ferget it. Ain't gonna happen."

"Jules, I think it's time you come out of your box for a while."

"It's time when *I say* it's time."

That put an end to *that*. By now, Jules's stomach felt like a rabid iguana was inside, scratching furiously to get out. He did his best to ignore it. He put fresh batteries in the flashlight and reread the last two stories in his Justice Society of America comic. The final page ended on a cliff-hanger: The entire Justice Society was chained to a huge rock, prisoners of the evil Ultra-Humanite in his underground cavern fortress. The leering villain was preparing to turn a death ray on the helpless heroes when the comic came to a sudden end. A final caption teased readers with the excitement . . . to come in another thirty days. Jules could hardly believe the effrontery—when he'd been a young vampire, comic books had been a full sixty-four pages, and stories were *always* complete. What a cheap, underhanded marketing scheme! He might be *dead* in another thirty days, not just undead!

♦

The next knocks were different. *Shave-and-a-haircut-two-bits!* Not Doodlebug's style. Doodlebug wasn't musical or rhythmic in the least. "Who's out there?"

"You gonna stay in that box fo'ever, or what?"

Despite his irritation at being disturbed again, Jules smiled. He knew the voice well. It was Erato. "Maybe. I kinda like it in here."

"You know who this is?"

"Yeah."

"Is that all you got to say—*Yeah*? Man, you had me worried *sick* these past few weeks. Last time I seen you, I drop you off, then the next mornin' my wife tells me she saw yo' house burnin' down on the news. I figures you's gonna call, let me know what's happenin', so I leaves my cell phone on. For the next three days straight, I leaves it on, constantly poppin' in fresh batt'ries. I drops by the Trolley Stop every chance I gets, hopin' I'd bump into you or at least hear some word. *Nothin'*. It's like you fallen off the earth. Finally, I go see yo' friend Maureen at her club, and she say she ain't seen you, neither. What the *hell* been up with you, Jules?"

Great. *More* guilt. Just what he needed to be feeling right now. "Look, I'm really sorry, Erato. I really am. It's a helluva long story, pal. And most of it I can't tell you—"

"Oh, I *know*. If you tells me, you hafta kill me."

"Right."

"Yo' friend Miss Doodlebug—*cute* li'l thing, by the way—she tells me you's in a big-ass funk because of lady troubles."

"That's one way of tellin' it, yeah."

"Well, you listen here. Ain't no woman on this earth worth crawlin' in a box for. Now me, I *love* women. I'm married to one. Got another one for a daughter. But women . . . they's *crazy*, man. Got somethin' to do with their hormones or somethin'. And another thing—women can't help it if they got this giant power to hurt us in the heart. It ain't their fault, see. That's just the way things is. If you's honest, you hafta admit that *we* got the same power over *them*. Maybe not in your *particular* case, but in the big scheme a things, anyhow."

Jules mulled over what his friend was telling him. It made sense, or it seemed to. Unfortunately, nothing Erato had said was motivating Jules to leave his box one bit. "Yeah . . . So how's your family doin', Erato. Everybody okay?"

"Oh, fine, fine. My little girl's none too happy about her score on those SATs. She wants to go to LSU in Baton Rouge, see. I told her she got plenty of time to retake that test. Worse come to worse, she can go to that junior college, Delgado, for a couple of years and get her grades up. Then she can go to Baton Rouge if she still want to."

Jules knew his friend was acting more nonchalant than he really felt. Erato's big dream for years had been that his daughter Lacrecia would go to a top-notch college and start a prestigious career. That was a good part of the reason Erato worked himself the way he did, pulling both day and night shifts with the cab company. His friend the family man had aspirations and worries Jules could only vaguely imagine. "I hope she can pull those test scores up," Jules said. "So both of you can get what you really want. I know you got a buncha stuff weighin' on your mind, Erato. I'm sorry I been addin' to it. I never meant to."

"Yeah. I know. You got a good heart. So are you comin' outta that piano box or not? All the guys over at the Trolley Stop been askin' 'bout you. Even them guys that grumble 'bout you takin' up too much space at the bar. So what I should tell 'em all, huh?"

Jules felt trapped. By the box, by people's expectations of him, by luck that seemed to get worse and worse with each rising of the moon. Staying right where he was seemed to be the least of all possible evils. But even *that* was causing pain to people he cared for. "Aww, shit if I know, Erato . . . just tell 'em all to be patient. I still got a lot to think out. I don't know when I'm comin' out. If ever. Just lemme think, lemme think . . . there's so fuckin' much to think about, y'know?"

"Well, don't be thinkin' *too* much—too much thinkin's what done Elvis in. He stopped singin' and started thinkin' too much, and then he sat down on that toilet and you *know* what happened then."

"I'll keep that in mind, pal."

"You do. And I ain't gonna ferget aboutchu, y'hear? I be back soon. By the way, whose Looney Tune idea was it to put a *piano box* in this itty-bitty room, anyway? You lie in there much longer, I's gonna think you's some kinda *vampire* or somethin'. Ain't never *heard* of such nonsense over a woman before. *Shee-yit!*"

"So long, pal. Take care." Jules felt a tiny but growing urge to jump out of the box and chase after Erato, then follow his friend over to the Trolley Stop. But he wasn't quite ready to leave the comfort of the buffering darkness.

He heard the door open again. "Jules, it's Doodlebug. Since you're still boxed, I take it that Erato's visit was less than fruitful?"

Jules felt tears welling up behind his eyes. A sob caught in his throat. He felt like he was six years old again, nursing a stinging bloody lip from a schoolyard brawl, and for the first time ever, his mother wasn't there to protect him. He was abandoned. Betrayed. Alone.

"Aww, Doodlebug, why'd she hafta go and do what she did?"

His friend sighed. "Oh, Jules . . . I wish I had a good answer for you. I wish people were more perfect than they are, that they'd always be consistent and make wise decisions. I wish I could wave a magic wand and make your hurt go away, and give you back your house and your car, and make all your enemies take up gardening instead of running you ragged. But I can't do any of those things."

"So what are you tellin' me? That life sucks and I just gotta get used to it?"

"No, not exactly. . . . Maybe the best thing I can say is this. Sometimes people find themselves in a situation that makes them do things they never imagined they'd ever do. Sometimes a man is starving and desperate and alone, and he becomes a wolf who pushes aside a hungry mutt for a few mouthfuls of dry dog food. And maybe that wolf-man then finds himself caught in the power of his animal senses, and he climbs on that mutt and mounts her, despite the revulsion his human brain is feeling. If you'd told me a year ago that you would never, *never* eat dog food and have sex with a mutt, and then everything happened the way it did, would that make you a hypocrite?"

"Uh, I dunno. . . ."

"Maureen was alone, Jules. Whether your leaving was her fault or not, she was still alone, for the first time in many years. And Maureen's never been the kind of woman who tolerates aloneness well. She was terribly lonely. And so she did something she'd thought she'd never do. Something she told you *you* should never do, even. She never thought she'd be hurting you, or putting you in danger. All she was thinking of was companionship. If you'd just let yourself, I'll bet you could feel some empathy for her. Some sense of understanding."

Jules didn't *want* to understand. He wanted to stay bitter and hurt and mad as hell at Maureen. He wanted to nurse it for all it was worth. But what Erato and Doodlebug had said made sense, loath as he was to admit it. He thought back to where his head had been during his miserable week in Baton Rouge. If Maureen had experienced even a tenth of that pain and desperation after she'd ordered him to leave, he couldn't rightfully damn her for grasping another companion to her ample bosom. Even if that companion ended up being a nasty shit like Malice X.

From the next room, low music infiltrated his makeshift coffin. Jules strained to hear the notes. He could just make out the tune. Jules smiled a small, hesitant smile. It was Bix Beiderbecke playing "Tin Roof Blues."

"Hey, turn that up, would ya?"

No answer. The bits of melody were followed by a powerful, mouth-watering aroma. Coffee. Freshly ground chicory coffee, strong as armor plate, being brewed tantalizingly close. If he listened hard, he could hear the heavenly liquid slowly coming into existence, transmuted from the ordinary elements of water and grounds . . . *drip, drip, drip.*

Jules grinned. So the little mascara maniac was trying to lure him out of the box. Jules had to give him an A+ for effort. Wouldn't be right to let all that energy go to waste. *What the fuck . . . guess it's time for this ol' caterpillar to leave the cocoon.*

He slowly lifted the lid of the piano box. The lights in the room were off. Doodlebug had lit some candles instead. Good kid; he hadn't wanted Jules to be smacked in the retinas by a hundred-watt bulb.

He tried climbing out of the box. Not having been on his feet in nearly three days, his legs buckled at the same instant he lost his balance. He hit the couch like a falling oak, breaking one of the antique's legs.

Doodlebug ran from the next room. "Jules! You should've asked for help!"

Sprawled over the slanting couch, Jules grimaced and rubbed his knee. "When have you *ever* known me to ask fer help? *You* shoulda been standin' by, waitin' to give it to me!"

Doodlebug helped his friend sit relatively straight on the couch. "Of course. You're absolutely right. How utterly thoughtless and selfish of me." He smiled warmly. "What can I get for you?"

"Your coffee smells like the best thing ever to grace the planet. But I'm hungry as all fuck. And bring me my bottle of Doc Landrieu's pills. I left 'em in that dresser, next to my keys."

"Your wish is my command, *sahib.*"

Doodlebug brought him his pills and two pints of chichi California blood. Jules almost swallowed the mug the blood was served in, he was so hungry. He quickly realized the bullshit behind the old saw that said hunger could make any food taste great. This blood tasted *awful.* It reminded him of the first time he'd ever drunk skim milk. No richness, no tang, hardly any zing to it at all. But blood was blood, and ravenous as he was, he was in no position to be fussy. He took a second long swig, then hastily opened the pill bottle and counted out six tablets in his palm. He had no idea whether taking that many at once might be bad for him. But the thought of reexperiencing his former state of decrepitude scared him even more. And after all, Doc Landrieu hadn't told him *not* to catch up on his dosage when he missed a pill or three. He gulped the pills down his dry throat two at a time.

"Feeling any better?"

Jules felt life seep back into his extremities. "Yeah. I'm startin' to." He pulled his feet out of the piano box. "One thing I been wonderin' about for the past three nights now. That evil shit you pulled with them Knight supporters—how'd you know gettin' them to drink their own blood would make 'em dissolve like that?"

Doodlebug smiled slyly. "Oh, *that* little trick. That was a useful bit of vampiric lore I picked up from my spiritual guides in Tibet. They were all vampires themselves, you know. The cornerstone of their wisdom and spiritual practice is the freeing of oneself from vampiric desires. Particularly the desire for blood. All of them were many centuries old. And not a one of them had ever imbibed a single drop."

"You're shittin' me. Either that, or *they* were shittin' *you*."

"Not at all. They provided me with proof. And the best proof of all was that, during my entire stay of more than three years, I never witnessed any of them drink the blood of men or animals. None of them ever suffered for the lack."

"So what'd you eat for three years? Yak gruel? Don't tell me *you* went three years with no blood."

Doodlebug stared out the window, his delicate features wistful and sad. "Would that it were so. No, they provided me with ample blood to drink during my stay. I'd been a blood-drinking vampire for far too many years by the time I first heard of their teachings. I could never hope to approach the blissful equilibrium enjoyed by those quiet, serene monks. But that was actually part of the reason they welcomed me to study with them—the fact that I was a confirmed blood drinker. In order to add to the ranks of their order, they need a 'fallen' vampire like me on hand. While I was with them, I was the one who turned their human initiates from ordinary seekers to fledgling vampires. When the newborns awoke, they found two objects sitting in front of them . . . a meditation staff of humble, weathered wood, and a silver bowl filled with blood. The monks directed them to choose only one, the object they most desired. Those who chose the meditation staff were admitted as novices into the lowest ranks of the monks. Those who chose the bowl of blood, well . . . let's just say the monks didn't tolerate failure of will gladly."

Jules whistled with grim appreciation. "Wow. That's really hard-ass. If it was *me* being given that choice, I'd end up a puddle of red goo, fer sure. So, like, how many passed the test?"

"During my thirty-nine months in the monastery, sixty-three initiates came to our mountaintop. Two became novices. After a few months, the sight and odors of bubbling puddles of flesh no longer turned my stomach."

"Huh." Jules stared at his diminutive friend with new eyes. The kid had done some major growing up since Jules had broken off relations three decades ago. Maybe he could be a help in the fight against Malice X after all. "Speaking of turned stomachs, mine's doin' a helluva lot better. Howzabout you and me split that pot of coffee you brewed. Then howzabout we go pay a visit to Miss Maureen."

♦

"Jules! You've come back! Thank every angel who ever lived!"

Jules let her embrace him. But he didn't move a muscle to hug her back. Despite understanding her a little more, he was a long way from forgiving her.

If Maureen noticed that Jules didn't return her embrace, she didn't show it. "Baby, I was worried *sick* about you! I thought I might never see you again! I haven't gone into work the past three nights. I've just stayed home, waiting here by the phone, praying that you'd call or come by. Neither of you bothered to tell me where Doodlebug was staying! I was going out of my mind. Simply going out of my mind!"

Jules said nothing. For a few long seconds an electrically charged silence hung like a thunderhead in Maureen's living room. Doodlebug was the one who finally broke it. "I'm staying at the Twelve Oaks Guest House. It's a lovely spot, tucked away on Bayou Road. I have my own goldfish pond. . . ."

Maureen wasn't paying attention. She hadn't taken her eyes off Jules's face. Her own face wavered between fear and cautious hope. She took his hands and pulled him over to the couch. "Come sit next to me. Come. You have no idea how *good* it is to see you." Their two large forms took up every inch of the spacious couch. She kept one of his hands pressed between hers, nervously kneading and caressing it as though it were a pet dove that might suddenly fly away. "What can I do, Jules? Tell me what I need to do to make things right with you."

"Only one thing you can do for me. And that's rat out Number Two Lover-Boy. Tell me everythin' you know about Malice X."

Maureen quickly looked away, but Jules caught the frightened look on her face. "What's—what's there to tell? It's been *years* since I spent any real time with him. And they weren't exactly good times, either. I put as much about him out of my mind as I could."

"That ain't gonna hack it, Maureen. I ain't takin' no excuses. You wanna get back in my good graces? Then you give with the information.

You give us somethin' to go on, somethin' to track him back to his burrow with. Spill—I want his name, rank, and serial number, who tailors his zoot suits, where his grandma makes groceries, his fuckin' *shoe size*, okay?"

Jules's litany had reduced Maureen to the verge of tears. "Don't make me get involved! I'm *afraid*! He's capable of anything! Don't make me tell you things he'll know came from me . . . *please*."

Jules's voice reeked of bitterness. "Baby, you're *already* involved. You was involved in this stinkin' situation way before I ever was. There's no backin' away from it now."

"I have to agree with Jules, Maureen." Doodlebug knelt by Maureen's side and took her hand in his. "It's impossible for you to go backward. Your only hope of regaining your balance is to go forward. The more you're able to help us, the quicker we can find him. And deal with him. The quicker you'll be out of any possible danger."

Maureen's lower lip quivered. She looked at Jules, then Doodlebug, then back to Jules. "He . . . he called himself Eldo Rado. Like the car."

"I *know* that already," Jules said with more irritation than was helpful. "I already got that nugget of info from the goddamn horse's mouth hisself."

Doodlebug waved him off. "Calm down, Jules. She's made a start. Honey, did he ever tell you his real name? His birth name?"

"Nuh-no. No, I don't think he ever did. In fact, I'm sure of it. *Eldo Rado* was his gang name. He was proud of it. Everyone had to call him that. He never told *anyone* his real name. Not that I ever knew of. I think he'd done things . . . things maybe he didn't want his family connected with."

"Did he tell you the street he grew up on? Which schools he attended?"

"How about the name of his best friend?" Jules asked. "Or his favorite uncle?"

"Wait—wait, don't *rush* me! Give me time to *think*. To try to remember. His street . . . no, no, he never told me that. He grew up in Uptown, I think; I can't say which part. Central City? Irish Channel? It could've been either. Or even Broadmoor. Schools . . . oh God, I *wish* I could remember!"

"How about a buddy? A relative? He ever introduce you to anyone?"

"Jules, we weren't exactly *intimate*. He was a very private man. Secretive. I don't think he wanted his friends to meet me. Nearly all the time we spent together was either at Jezebel's or at my house. I never saw where he was living. A few times he took me with him to some other clubs, to hear music—"

"You remember which clubs?"

"Of *course* not! They were all in colored neighborhoods. Little dirty holes in the wall. I didn't pay them any attention."

Jules snorted with disgust. "So basically what you're tellin' me here is that this guy you turned into a vampire and regularly shared your coffin with, you pretty much knew *squat* about. *Real* good, Maureen. My hat's off to ya. Fangs fer the memories, babe."

"I'm *trying*! Can't you see that I'm *trying*?"

"Well, how about answerin' me this, then? How come this guy hates *my* guts so much? How'd *I* get mixed up in this little romance of yours? What'd I ever do to this guy to make me number one on his hit parade?"

"I don't *know*! I used to talk about you, I guess."

"Talk about me? Like what? What'd you say to that guy about me? You weren't comparin', y'know, our *sizes* or nothin'?"

Maureen shot Jules a withering look. "What kind of a tramp do you take me for?"

"Well, what, then?"

"Oh, I don't know. . . . He never talked about *his* family and friends, and we had to talk about *something* while we were together, when we weren't—you-know-what-ing—so I talked about *you*. When he'd turn on the radio to some music that he liked, I'd tell him what kind of stuff you liked listening to. Whenever a cabby that I recognized would come into Jezebel's, it'd remind me of you, and I'd tell some funny little story about you. Sometimes he'd try bringing me a present, some flowers or something. So I'd tell him about all the really darling, funny gifts you used to give me, like that teddy bear with the third eyeball sticking out of its forehead. You remember that? I still have it. Another thing—for years I tried drumming into his head all the rules about living as a vampire, the rules *you'd* never had any problems following, but he never wanted to listen, not even to commonsense stuff like 'the more vampires you make, the fewer victims left for *you*.' If *you*, with your thick head, could follow the rules like a little angel, why couldn't *he*?"

Jules's heart sank lower and lower as he listened to Maureen rattle on. All this time, he'd thought maybe there was some chance Malice X could be forced to listen to reason. Some chance that, if Jules could just show up with a big enough gang of his own, he and his enemy could sit down like rational men at the bargaining table and work some mutually acceptable deal. Fat chance of *that*. Thanks to who-knows-how-many years of Maureen's nagging and invidious comparisons, the only way this war could go down was dirty and personal.

"Holy Christmas, Mo . . . if I were Eldo Rado, *I'd* hate me, too."

"What? What are you saying? That this is somehow all *my* fault? Is that it? Well, a girl's gotta talk about *something*, doesn't she? It can't just be *wham-bam-thank-you-ma'am* every night—he didn't *talk*, Jules! Do you understand? I had to do the talking for *both* of us!"

"Yeah, I understand, baby. Perfectly." He turned to Doodlebug. "Let's get outta here. She ain't gonna tell us anything more useful. Maybe I should just hang out at my usual spots and let him come to us."

Maureen grabbed his hand as he tried extricating himself from the couch. "Jules! Don't go yet. I want to be helpful, Jules. I'm trying so hard. I have papers for you to sign! Insurance papers so you can get some money for your house! I went to the safe deposit box at the Whitney Bank. I still had the key from years and years ago. From when we were like a married couple, and you trusted me with everything. Ever since your mother was still alive, the bank's been sending a check from your account every month to the insurance company—"

Jules headed for the door, or tried to. "What good's money gonna do me if I end up with a stake jabbed through my ticker?"

Maureen dragged him over to the dining room table, where she had the insurance papers laid out. "Just sign them!" She forced a pen into his paw. "What can it hurt? Maybe you can get yourself another Cadillac. Maybe you can replace some of those old jazz records you lost. As co-executor, I've already filled out everything I could. I made X's everyplace you need to sign. See? Right there—"

Jules reluctantly signed everywhere Maureen had made a big purple X. Doodlebug joined them at the table. "Maureen, anything else you remember could be of vital importance to us. Do you recall any distinctive clothing he wore? Maybe a shirt with the logo of a favorite bar? A jacket with a school mascot on it?"

Maureen sat despondently at the table and leaned her head on her fists. "I've tried, I've tried so *hard*, but I just can't remember. . . . Wait. Wait just a minute! There *was* a jacket. A jacket he used to wear lots of times. It was from some school. It had a bird on it!"

Jules scowled as he continued to sign. "Oh, that's real helpful, Mo. A bird. There are only—what? Ten thousand different kinds a birds? Was it a parrot? A chicken hawk? A hummingbird, maybe?"

"I'm not an expert on *birds*!"

"Do you remember what color the bird was?" Doodlebug gently asked.

"Umm . . . blue, I think. No, I'm *sure*. It was blue and white."

"A bluebird? A blue jay?"

"A blue jay, I guess. That sounds right."

"Jesuit," Jules mumbled. "What was that fucker doin' with a jacket from Jesuit High School?"

"That's *it*!" Maureen cried. "I remember now! He told me he went to Jesuit! The priests gave him a special scholarship! He played on one of the sports teams . . . not football or basketball. Maybe the bowling team?"

Doodlebug's face brightened. "If we could get our hands on the right yearbook—"

Jules completed the thought. "We could learn his real name."

"Just one problem. It's summer. All the schools are out of session."

"But they open up on Monday nights," Maureen interjected. "All the Catholic schools. During the summer they do open houses on Monday nights, so parents who are looking for a school for their kids can check them out."

"How do you know?" Jules asked suspiciously. "When was the last time *you* sent a kid to Catholic school?"

"It just so happens that one of my regulars at Jezebel's has a thing for Catholic schoolgirls. Summer is his favorite time of year. He pretends to have a daughter and he goes to all the girls' schools' open houses on Mondays and ogles the students. I can't tell you how many times he's begged me to use a school uniform in my act. It's simply impossible to find those plaid skirts in my size."

"Monday nights, huh? That's tomorrow." A broad grin spread slowly across Jules's face. "Doodlebug, ol' pal, I think it's high time we look into gettin' you that high school education I made ya miss fifty years ago."

"But Jesuit's a boys' school, isn't it?"

"Heh. That's right, slugger."

TWELVE

"I feel perfectly *hideous*," Doodlebug muttered.

Jules pulled alongside the curb in front of the Banks Street Bar and Grill, two blocks west of Jesuit High School. The tremendous crush of parents and potential enrollees who'd come out for the school's open house prevented him from parking any closer. "Shaddup already. You got no reason to be whinin'. I let you pick out your own outfit at Wal-Mart, didn't I?"

"And a fat lot of good that freedom of choice did me. Ye gods . . . even their Women's Department was filled with the most awful grotesqueries imaginable. But the Boys' Department—that shapeless denim, those threadbare sports logo T-shirts—all I can say is, I pray it'll be *another* forty-eight years before I shop for boys' clothing again. And must I wear this ridiculous baseball cap?"

Jules climbed out of the car onto pavement so broken and tilted it looked like the floor of a fun house. "It's either that or chop off your hair, pal."

"But plenty of boys wear their hair long nowadays."

"Not at Jesuit they don't."

They walked toward the imposing three-story brick edifices that overwhelmed Banks Street. In contrast to the Catholic grandeur of the school buildings, the surrounding houses were tired and dingy, leaning wearily shoulder to shoulder like a police roundup of overworked hookers crowded into a freight elevator.

They walked into the main academic building and were immediately immersed in a sea of anxious parents, overfriendly faculty, and too-bored-for-words pubescents. Doodlebug stared coldly at the current Jesuit students, standing around nonchalantly in their light brown, paramilitary-looking uniforms.

"What a perfect bunch of Fascists-in-training," he whispered harshly to Jules. "Cannon fodder for the next Nathan Knight campaign. And the Jesuits are supposedly the *intellectuals* of the Catholic Church? This descent into the inferno makes me even *more* grateful to you for making me miss high school."

Jules spotted a nun in the crowd. He grabbed Doodlebug's sleeve and pulled him over to her. " 'Scuse me, Sister. My boy and me wanna take a look at your library. Can you maybe point us in the right direction?"

"Oh, you must mean our Resource Center!"

"Yeah, I guess so. That where you got yer books and stuff?"

"Oh, sir, our Resource Center has much more than just *books*! It's also our computer hub, audiovisual lab, and creative graphics shop. It's one of the finest knowledge facilities of any high school in the South. We're very, *very* proud of our Resource Center."

"Yeah, I can see that. So where is it?"

"Just take those stairs at the end of the hall to the second floor, then turn right. Or we have an elevator just around that corner there."

"We'll take the stairs. Thanks, Sister. Have a swell summer."

The short nun sniffed the air like a groundhog emerging from its hole on the first day of spring. "Say, do you smell something *burning*?"

Jules was already pulling his companion down the crowded hall. He grimaced, then cuffed the side of Doodlebug's head. "D.B.! Put out that damn cigarette!"

They ducked into the stairwell. Both vampires sighed with relief. Jules headed straight for a water fountain tucked in the corner and splashed cold liquid down the neck of his shirt, dousing his smoldering skin.

"You just *had* to chat up a nun, didn't you?" Doodlebug said, fanning his burning arms. "I didn't appreciate that whack to the head, by the way."

Jules tossed handfuls of water in his friend's direction. "Look, I found out where the library is, didn't I?"

"Resource Center."

"Whatever. Sorry about the wallop. I had to think fast."

"Next time, let your brain do the thinking, not your hands."

They climbed the stairs to the second floor. The Resource Center wouldn't have looked out of place at a medium-sized university. The facility seemed to have more computers than books. After a few minutes of searching, they found the yearbook collection in a dimly lit, musty-smelling annex room.

The dusty wooden shelves were lined with thick, hardbound editions of *The Jayson* dating back to the 1920s. Jules scooped up ten of the big volumes, starting with the 1976–77 edition and ending with the one dated 1985–86. He set the stack of yearbooks on a nearby table with a heavy thud.

"According to what Mo told us, he coulda been here at Jesuit any of these years."

"Let's get cracking, then," Doodlebug said. He looked around him, clearly uncomfortable, and hugged his arms to his sides. "The sooner we're out of here and away from all these crucifixes, the happier I'll be."

"Amen to that, brother."

"Are you sure you'll be able to recognize him?"

"Oh, yeah," Jules said, laying the first volume flat and skipping over the sections on Student Life and Athletics to the pages with portraits of freshman students. "I got his ugly puss memorized. Maybe he's a little younger and a little browner in these yearbooks than he was when I saw him, but there's no way I'd mistake him for anybody else."

♦

Ninety minutes later the multitude of crucifixes on the walls and in the pages of the yearbooks had begun taking their toll. Both vampires were sweating profusely. Jules was able to skim the first three or four yearbooks fairly quickly; the number of black students during those years was small, only four to six a page. As the years became more recent, the numbers of black students increased. He found himself having to concentrate more closely, matching the sharp chin and cold, cruel eyes of recent memory against a larger number of possible matches. Many of the faces were soft and relatively innocent; these he was able to discount pretty quickly. Others seemed warier, already cynical and hardened . . . even kids lucky enough to go to Jesuit weren't immune to the tough influence of the streets, Jules had to remind himself.

He wiped his clammy forehead with his sleeve, then cracked open the 1981–82 *Jayson* and flipped to the freshman photos and descriptions. In no time one portrait leapt off the page and drop-kicked him square on the nose.

"Holy shit . . . I found him."

"Are you sure?"

"Sure I'm sure!" He quickly read the description beneath the photo. "Look at this—the little fucker was a member of the *debate* team! No wonder he talked such a blue streak before pissin' on my coffin."

"Let me see." Doodlebug pulled the yearbook to his side of the table. Jules prodded the portrait with a thick forefinger. "Malik Raddeaux? *That's* his name? I'm surprised. I wouldn't have expected his real name to be so close to his *nom de guerre*."

"Talk English, would ya?"

"To his gang name. It *is* pretty clever, though—substituting *Rado* for *Raddeaux*."

Jules pulled the book back to his side and read the capsule description again. "Be sure and compliment him when you meet him."

"That won't be long in coming. Now that we have a name to feed to my contact at the *Picayune*, we should be able to land some solid leads."

"Maybe we won't even hafta bother with your pansy pal at the newspaper."

Doodlebug frowned. "Why not? You have a better idea?"

Jules smiled triumphantly. "You didn't read the whole description, did you? These *Jayson*s, they're pretty thorough. Didya notice how they list the names of siblings who attend other Catholic schools? Our boy Malik's got himself a sister."

♠

The first Elisha Raddeaux listed in the phone book turned out to be a fifty-eight-year-old great-grandmother raising two generations of children in a three-room New Orleans East apartment. The second Elisha Raddeaux had left town, leaving no forwarding address with her former landlord or neighbors. The third and final Elisha Raddeaux lived in a modest but well-kept camelback shotgun on Laurel Street, a couple of blocks from Tipitina's Uptown Music Club.

The neighborhood was on the dicey side. Several houses hadn't been occupied in months, maybe years, and were well tattooed with the tags of various neighborhood gangs. Piles of dirty gravel filled the street's larger potholes, poverty-row Band-Aids for a road in dire need of major surgery. Abandoned shopping carts lay on their sides in the high grass that fronted most of the lots.

In contrast, the house they'd come to visit was recently painted, with a tall, straight fence surrounding it, a neatly trimmed lawn, and a large tin-roofed utility shed out back. Jules tried opening the gate, then noticed it was locked with a neon-green Kryptonite U-lock. Luckily, the gate had a buzzer attached. He rang it.

A moment later a young black woman cautiously pushed aside the drapes from her front window. She looked to be about the right age— late twenties or early thirties, which would fit with the information Jules had gleaned from the yearbook. She opened her window a few inches, just enough to make a shouted conversation feasible.

"What do you want? It's late."

"You Elisha Raddeaux?" Jules asked.

"Maybe. Maybe not. Depends what you need to see Elisha Raddeaux about."

"We're here to talk about your brother Malik."

Her expression remained coldly impenetrable. "I don't got no brother Malik. You got the wrong address. Go bother somebody else."

She started to close her window. The humidity made it stick. She cursed. Doodlebug took advantage of the brief opening. Dressed in a flattering silk blouse and high-slit skirt, he was the model of confidence again. "Ms. Raddeaux? We have a very important reason to speak with your brother. We know all about his special condition. We need to warn him about a new bloodborne disease that's been ravaging the blood-drinking community. It's vital that we reach him."

She stopped struggling with the window. "You on the level with this? You sayin' he might be in some kinda health trouble?"

"My name is Debbie Richelieu, Ms. Raddeaux. I'm a physician and researcher from California. My staff and I have been tracking the transmission of this new disease across the country. I've made it my business to get word of a few simple precautions to every known blood drinker. My associates and I overlooked the initial outbreak of AIDS, and we're determined not to repeat that mistake with this new syndrome. Will you talk with us?"

She stared suspiciously at Jules. "Who's the fat dude?"

"That's Julius. My assistant. Don't worry, he's quite harmless."

The drapes fell shut. A few seconds later the front door opened and Elisha Raddeaux walked across her well-tended front lawn to the gate. Jules was surprised to see that she was wearing a black catsuit and a matching, rhinestone-trimmed jacket; given the late hour, he'd expected her to walk out in a rumpled bathrobe. Her tiny waist flared into an impressive set of hips, wide enough to carry a week's worth of groceries and half a Little League team. The fullness of her hips wasn't mirrored in the contours of her face, however. As she unlocked the gate, Jules could see some of the same angular harshness in her features that he'd noted in her brother's.

She warily hefted the U-lock in her fist and swung open the gate. "C'mon in. I guess we *do* have somethin' to talk about, after all."

"You two go on ahead," Doodlebug said. "I'll be right in. I left something in the car."

Jules followed her into the house. He'd been inside dozens of camelbacks just like this one, enough that he had a pretty complete mental picture of what the interior would probably look like. This one didn't fit the bill at all. The furniture was surprisingly modern and high rent. The walls of the long, narrow living room were lined with European-looking leather sofas, German stereo components, and a flat-panel TV big as a casino billboard. A freestanding waterfall burbled in one corner. The dining room was decorated with real oil paintings, not prints. Several of them featured jazz combos, Jules noted with appreciation.

"Nice place you've got here," he mumbled.

"Thanks," she answered, barely looking at him. "So what's the story with this disease? And how did you know Malik is a bloodsucker?"

Jules smiled weakly and shrugged his shoulders. "I'm just the assistant. We gotta wait for Dr. Richelieu. He, uh, *she's* the expert."

"Fine." She looked at him with more interest. Did her eyes flare with a glimmer of recognition, or was this just his jumpy imagination acting up again?

Whatever the look was, it made him uncomfortable. He took a few steps toward one of the couches. The leather-swathed cushions looked soft and inviting. "Mind if I sit down?"

She pulled one of the hard-backed oak chairs away from the dining table for him. "Not at all."

Doodlebug came through the front door. "Sorry to keep everyone waiting. Did I miss anything?"

"I'm not sure I can be of much help, Doctor," the woman said. "Me and Malik . . . we ain't what you'd call close. I ain't seen him in a long time. Maybe five, six years."

"Do you have any idea where we might find him?"

"Oh, I hear he still be around town somewhere. Here and there. He never did stay in one place very long. Time comes to dust the apartment, he just moves on to a fresh one."

"Do you have friends in common? Any relations who might know how we could get in touch?"

"Before I put you in touch with other folks to bug in the middle of the night, how about tellin' me some more about this disease?"

Doodlebug sat down at the table and folded his hands together thoughtfully. "It's a degenerative bone disease. Very painful. It leads to weak, easily fractured bones and can't be reversed once it passes a certain stage. During the early, reversible stages, no symptoms are apparent; the disease can only be detected through a special blood test of my own devising."

Elisha Raddeaux looked less than fully convinced. "And how does one catch this nasty bone disease?"

"By ingesting the blood of an HIV-positive individual or a carrier of the hepatitis C virus."

"I see." She stared long and hard, first at Jules, then at Doodlebug. "Look, I'll do my best to help you. There's no love lost between me and my brother. I sure don't approve of what he is and some of the things he done. But I figure nobody deserves to be sufferin' with no disease. Give me some time to think, and maybe I can come up with somethin' for you two to go on. In the meantime, can I get you anything? I got some crumb cake, and I can make a pot of coffee."

Jules's face lit up. "Hey, thanks! Some coffee'd be *great*. I'll pass on that crumb cake, though."

"Anything for you, Doctor?"

Doodlebug smiled and shook his head. "Oh, no, thank you. I ate just before we came over."

She stood from the table and headed for the kitchen. "It'll be a few minutes. I got one of them old-fashioned percolators that takes a while to get goin'." She closed the kitchen door behind her.

Jules gave Doodlebug the thumbs-up sign. "Hey, pal," he whispered, "that's some great bullshit story you came up with. Bone disease . . .

yeeuuch! So, whadda ya think? She on the level? You think she's gonna help us out?"

Doodlebug eyed the kitchen door pensively. "I'm not sure. Something seems off. Her body language didn't match her conversation—"

From the far side of the door Jules heard the distinctive tones of a push-button phone's keys being pressed. "Shit! She's makin' a call! She's rattin' us out!"

He started to get up from the table, but Doodlebug caught his arm. "Don't worry about that." The slender vampire grinned. "While I was outside, I took a little precaution. She won't be getting through to anyone until after South Central Bell makes a service call."

Jules overheard a soft expletive in the kitchen, followed by more button pushing, followed by still more, and stronger, profanity.

"Guess this means I won't be gettin' my coffee," Jules said wistfully.

He jumped as there was a loud crash in the kitchen. Now he *did* get up from the table. "Hey! You, uh, you okay in there?"

"I'm fine," the woman's voice answered, a little too strongly. "Just had a little accident. No problem."

"You need a hand with somethin'?"

"*No!* I'm just *fine!* Don't you concern yourself none."

Jules looked uncertainly at his companion. His resolve hardened. He went to the door and opened it.

"Die-ie, you fat fuckah!"

She charged him like an enraged lioness, slashing wildly with jagged wooden pieces from a broken bar stool. He dodged as best he could. But one of her improvised stakes connected with an ample love handle, shredding his new safari suit and taking a decent-sized chunk of him with it.

"*Ahhh!* You fuckin' *bitch!*"

The other stake gouged his cheek, leaving a bloody trail. He tried grabbing her, but she was astoundingly fast and strong. She shrugged off his bear hug as if he were made of tinfoil, bouncing him into the dining room wall and spilling him heavily to the floor.

Then she whirled on Doodlebug. What happened next occurred almost too quickly for Jules's pain-clouded eyes to follow. Doodlebug moved like a ninja from a Bruce Lee flick. First his foot crashed into her wrist, sending a stake flying. She thrust her other dagger at his chest. He ducked low and bent her weapon arm sharply over his shoulder. Jules heard a sharp break and an even sharper scream. Then Doodlebug became a blur of motion. His whirling kick exploded against the side of her head and sent her flying against the dining room wall.

She still wasn't down for the count. Jules struggled to clear his vision. His side burned like hell. He looked down—his left side, from mid–rib cage down, was drenched with blood. Weirdly, the front of his safari suit was stained with brown smudges. He rubbed one of the smudges. Some of the brown came off on his finger; oily, like wet paint. Makeup. It was makeup.

"Jules! I need some help here! I can't hold her much longer!"

"You *fucks!*" she screamed. "You won't get away with *nothin'*! I'll kill you! Fuck you *both* up!"

Jules stared at Malice X's sister. Most of the makeup on her arms had rubbed off during their brief struggle. Her exposed skin was deathly gray.

She was a vampire.

"Jules! Snap out of it! Or do you want to have to fight her all over again?"

She was a vampire, just like he was. He struggled to get up from the floor. She writhed and thrashed in Doodlebug's tight grasp, trapped in his arms like a live electrical wire. A vampire.

"Jules! Grab one of those stakes she dropped! Run her through before she breaks away!"

He felt like he was moving in slow motion. Like he was swimming through cream of mushroom soup. He leaned down and picked one of the stakes off the floor. She spat at him. He could see her fangs very clearly as she pulled her lips back to curse and hiss.

"Jules! Come *on*! Get with the program!"

He stared at the stake in his hand. "I—I just can't do it."

His friend looked incredulous. "*What?* What's the problem? You've killed *hundreds* of people before!"

"Yeah, but . . . but they was *food*." An inner voice screamed at him that he was being ridiculous—he and his friend were in danger. Any squeamishness didn't count for a bag of beans. But voice or no voice, he couldn't make his hand move. "This here—this is *different*—I mean, she, y'know, she's one of *us*."

"This is one *hell* of a time to develop moral qualms!"

The struggling woman kicked viciously at Jules. She barely missed knocking the stake from his loosening fist. "I *know*—I'm *sorry*—but I just can't do it."

Doodlebug's sigh sounded like steam boiling from a braking locomotive. "Ohh-*kay*—any *other* bright ideas about what to do with our charming hostess here would be *greatly* appreciated!"

Jules gulped hard. He felt horrible. He was useless. Worse than useless. "We could stuff her in her coffin. It's gotta be around here someplace."

"Well, *find* it, then! And hurry!"

He ran through her kitchen, stepping quickly over the broken remains of the bar stool, and peered into what looked to be a bedroom. "D.B.! It's here! A big mahogany coffin!"

He ran back to the dining room to help his friend half drag, half carry the shrieking, thrashing woman to the room behind the kitchen. Jules was suddenly grateful she'd chosen to live in this crappy neighborhood; none of the neighbors would pay a bout of crazed screaming any mind. He shoved the coffin's lid open with his foot, then he and Doodlebug forcibly stuffed her inside. As soon as Jules was able to slam the lid shut, he lay on top of it and hung on for dear life.

"Guess I'm the heaviest thing in the house. Look, I'm really sorry about before—"

"We'll talk about it later," Doodlebug said, breathing heavily. "Right now we've got to find some way of keeping that coffin shut tight. You can't lie on top of it ad infinitum."

Jules's stomach bounced as the coffin rocked. Elisha actually managed to lift the lid and its massive passenger an inch or two, but the coffin's tight confinement left her no real leverage. "See if you can find some rope or wire," Jules said. "Maybe a hammer and nails. She's got some kinda utility shed out back."

Doodlebug smoothed stray strands of lustrous auburn hair away from his face. "You'll be all right?"

Jules smiled ruefully. "Sure. First time my weight's ever done me any good."

He watched Doodlebug unlock the rear entrance and step into the backyard. After a minute or two, the coffin stopped rocking beneath him. Jules cautiously sat up straight, still keeping his full weight centered on the lid. Then he heard his captive begin to sob. Softly at first, then louder and with greater abandon. It was one of the saddest, most pathetic sounds he'd ever heard.

"Oh Malice, *Malice*—I done *failed* you! I done *failed* you, honey dearest. . . ."

What kind of a brother would turn his own sister into a vampire? Jules's already abysmal opinion of his enemy plunged even lower, if that were possible. He tried not to listen to Elisha's agonized cries and moanings. The things she was saying . . . things no sister should ever say or even *think* about a brother. Did Maureen have even the slightest notion of the depraved creature she'd granted vampiric powers and immortality to? The kind of creature she'd shared her bed with?

Doodlebug returned with rope, hammer, and nails. Jules continued sitting on the coffin while his companion drove a score of three-inch nails through the lid and into the coffin's walls. Then Jules lifted the coffin, one end at a time, while Doodlebug wrapped it tightly with thick nylon rope.

"There . . . we shouldn't have to worry about *her* for a while," Doodlebug said, patting his forehead and neck with a handkerchief from his purse. He glanced at Jules's blood-soaked side, his eyes brimming with concern. "Let's take a look at that. Is the wound deep?"

Jules gingerly pulled the shreds of his safari jacket and shirt away from his wounded left side. He winced as the fabric, glued to his wound by drying blood, tore open newly formed scabs. Jules kept his eyes tightly shut, afraid to look at his own blood.

"It's not too awful," he heard Doodlebug say. "She didn't tag you that badly. It's already healing."

Jules opened his eyes. Now that the scraps of clothing were out of the wound, it was free to close properly. He watched, fascinated and a little nauseated, as his violated skin almost magically reknit itself.

"I saw some interesting things out back," his relieved friend said. "You need to come take a look yourself."

He followed Doodlebug out to the storage shed, a large corrugated metal structure that took up most of the backyard. His friend had torn off the door lock. Jules had no idea what to expect when Doodlebug yanked the light string. What was revealed was way, *way* down the list of what he might've imagined.

It was a lab of some kind. Bunsen burners and beakers and glass tubing, the sort of stuff Doc Landrieu might play with. Plus a bank of filing cabinets and three humming refrigerators.

Jules was mystified. "What kinda place is this?"

"It's a drug lab. A heroin processing lab, to be exact."

"*Heroin?* What the heck do a buncha vampires need to fuck around with *heroin* for?"

"Good question. Let's try to find out, shall we?"

They spent the next twenty minutes rummaging through the contents of filing cabinets, ledgers, and hand-scrawled notes scattered around the lab. Most of the paperwork dealt with the supply trail and distribution network of a hot new commodity called Horse-X.

Jules broke open the locked bottom drawer of the last of the filing cabinets. He pulled a thick black three-ring binder from the back of the drawer. Almost immediately he knew he'd struck pay dirt. It was a manual describing the care and feeding of a long list of priority clients.

He flipped through the pages. Some of the names slapped him in the face like a bucketful of ice water. "Holy shit! I *know* these people! Know *of* 'em, anyway. . . . Some of these guys are high up in the police department. You got lawyers here who made millions workin' all them casino deals. Whoa-*ho!* You got names here that belong to hizzoner the mayor's top politicos."

He handed the binder to Doodlebug. The younger vampire spent a few minutes reading intently. "This is bigger than we ever imagined. It seems your friend Malice has his tentacles in nearly every corner of the city."

"Yeah . . . Horse-X: It's not just fer the ghetto anymore."

Doodlebug closed the binder. "It's not safe for us to stay here much longer. I'm sure this is a very active little lab. Ms. Raddeaux's partners could show at any moment. Let's gather up what we can and beat a prudent retreat."

They searched for any document that might list a physical address for Malice X, but their hurried survey only turned up the names of lower-level operatives and a series of post office boxes. Jules retrieved a pair of old D. H. Holmes shopping bags from the house, and they stuffed a generous sampling of binders and folders into the bags, including the revelatory black binder.

Back in the house, Jules grabbed utility bills, photo albums, a shoe box full of canceled checks—anything that could potentially provide them with Malice's connections or current whereabouts. A set of matching coasters next to the drying rack in the kitchen caught his eye. He'd seen them all around the house, but he hadn't paid them any mind until now. They were all from the same Central City neighborhood bar. Club Hit 'N' Run.

He stuffed one of the coasters into his pocket. When Doodlebug came into the kitchen carrying a very full D. H. Holmes bag, Jules tossed him one of the drink holders. "Here's where we need to head next, pal. Seems like this joint is a popular hangout with Sistah Souljah in the coffin there. Maybe it's a popular hangout with Brotha Bas-turd, too."

Doodlebug read the name of the club. He looked up at his partner, and his fire-engine-red lips puckered into a half frown. "Not so fast, Mr. Hooded Terror. Your performance tonight wasn't exactly what I'd call confidence-inspiring. I think we have a little work to do before we attempt to beard this lion in his lair."

Jules thought about arguing. Then he looked down at his blood-splattered clothes, scowled, and clamped his jaw tightly shut.

Doodlebug scooted him toward the front door. "Earlier tonight you sent me back to high school. I had such a *fabulous* time. Well, my friend, now it's *your* turn to go back to school. Vampire University, in fact. And I just happen to be dean."

THIRTEEN

"Are you ready for a major surprise?"

Jules rolled his eyes to the ceiling. "Right now, the only thing that's surprisin' me is that we're sittin' on our asses in your cottage instead of stakin' out the Hit 'N' Run Club. What's all this bullshit about you teachin' me to be a better vampire? Kid, I was an A-One vampire when your *mama* was in diapers, much less *you*."

Doodlebug smiled. "The only ignorant man is he who refuses to learn, grasshopper. Now change into a wolf. I have something very important to show you."

Jules grumbled. Then he reminded himself that his embarrassing failure of nerve at Elisha Raddeaux's had nearly gotten Doodlebug's arms wrenched from their sockets. Maybe he owed his friend a little indulgence. He started unbuttoning his jacket, then stopped. "Hey, this isn't some kinda trick you're pullin' to get me naked, is it?"

Doodlebug snorted. "Don't flatter yourself. I dress like a woman, but that doesn't mean you're my type."

Reassured, Jules stripped off his safari suit, shoes, and underwear. He concentrated on the full moon, Lon Chaney Jr., and lots and lots of hair. At least his transformations were coming more easily now. They still made his bones and joints ache, but that was nothing new; five decades of ever-increasing obesity had left him achingly familiar with aching bones and joints.

The universe shifted around him. The visual world turned black and white, like the picture on an old Philco TV, whereas the sensitivity of his ears and nose jumped a hundredfold. His long gray nose twitched; Doodlebug was wearing a pungently vile perfume, a witches' brew of citrus extracts and boar musk. Jules sneezed violently, three times in quick succession.

"Jules? Can you understand what I'm saying? If you can understand me, scratch the floor twice with your right paw."

He really wished Doodlebug would stop screaming. But he complied, thumping the polished floor twice with the thick black pads of his right front paw.

"Good. Now come with me into the living room. It's a tight squeeze with your coffin in there, but we'll manage."

His furry gut dragged as he followed his friend from the kitchen. Doodlebug opened the lid of the piano case that served as Jules's coffin.

"Take a peek inside. You should find this very interesting."

Whatever was inside smelled weirdly familiar. He trotted up to the big wooden box, placed his front paws on the edge, and peered in. The thing that had invaded his coffin certainly didn't *look* familiar. It was like a huge, pulsating slug, but a slug that couldn't hold a steady shape for more than a second or two. It filled most of the floor of the box; Jules guessed it was between six inches and a foot deep. He couldn't tell what color it was, of course, but the shadings and the blotchy patterns on its surface shifted as frequently as its shape did.

Why the hell did the thing smell so damn *familiar*? . . . With a start of recognition, Jules realized what the peculiar odor reminded him of. The big, amorphous slug smelled exactly like *he* did, himself, after a few lazy nights of skipping showers, drinking coffee, and lying around in his undershirt reading old comic books.

"Change back to your normal shape now. But keep your eyes on that thing in your coffin."

Jules did as Doodlebug requested. As his hind legs unbent and his arms lengthened and his nose shortened, he watched the grayish blob. While he was changing, it gradually grew smaller, like a tubful of dirty, soapy bathwater disappearing down the drain. But the piano box didn't *have* a drain. By the time he was on hands and knees instead of hind paws and forepaws, the slug-thingie was entirely gone. He reached in and touched the soil. The dirt was dry and crumbly, just as it had been the last time he'd slept. Whatever the thing had been, it had left no trace of itself.

"Holy mackerel," Jules muttered. "What the hell *was* that? And where the hell did it go?"

Doodlebug crouched down beside his friend and placed his arm on Jules's shoulder. "That was the part of you that you weren't using at the time. As for where it went, when you needed it again, it vanished from your coffin to rejoin the rest of you."

Still naked, Jules leaned against the side of the couch and covered his privates by squeezing together his trunklike thighs. What Doodlebug was implying made him dizzy. "Come again?"

"You heard me. It's *you*. And I think you suspected it yourself while you were a wolf. I watched your nose twitch very sharply while you were leaning over into the box."

Jules rubbed his forehead wearily. His life was taking yet another turn toward the bizarre, and he wasn't sure he liked it. "Yeah, I heard you. I'm just not sure I *believe* you." The whole notion made him nauseated, as if he'd just watched himself having open-heart surgery. "How come no vampire I ever met knew about this—this slug-thingie?"

"There's a very simple reason. How many vampires bother to peek back inside their coffins after they've transformed into another shape? Not many. And vampires tend to be solitary. Most large predators tend to keep to themselves, with the notable exceptions of lions and killer whales. So it's not as if many vampires would have a companion who might notice this unusual phenomenon. My Tibetan teachers, however, have lived in very close quarters with one another for untold centuries. On a wintery night in the very distant past, one among them made the shocking discovery of where all that extra mass goes when vampire-man becomes vampire-other."

Jules was more perplexed than ever. "'Extra mass'? Whoa! Don't forget, you're talkin' to a guy with a ninth-grade education here. And half of *that* was in catechism. Keep it simple, will ya?"

Doodlebug smiled gently and helped Jules to his feet. "Come back into the kitchen and I'll make a pot of coffee."

Jules pulled his pants and shirt back on, then sat at the kitchen table. Soon the air was alive with the blessed odor of chicory.

"Have you ever read anything about Einstein's theories regarding mass and energy?" Doodlebug asked.

Jules scowled. "Does the pope bless abortions in a whorehouse?"

"Ohh-kay. I'll do my best to keep this, uh, basic, then." He poured two mugs of coffee and joined his friend at the table. "One of Professor Einstein's most famous theories regarding how the universe works is called the Conservation of Mass. All of the 'stuff' in the universe can be classified as either matter—like you or me—or energy, like sunlight. All things that are made of matter have mass."

"You mean weight, right?"

"Well, that's a limited way of looking at it. But if it's easier for you to think about it that way, yes, mass can be thought of as weight. Getting back to our friend Einstein, the good professor said that mass can neither be created nor destroyed. Under certain very unusual circumstances, such as a nuclear chain reaction, mass can be converted to energy, but mass can never simply disappear. Now, when you just changed to a wolf, not only your shape changed. Your mass, or weight, changed, too. You went from a man of approximately four hundred and fifty pounds to a wolf of, oh, I'd guesstimate about two hundred. That extra two hundred and fifty pounds or so didn't disappear. And it wasn't converted into energy, either. Or else the entire state of Louisiana and a good part of Mississippi would be a smoldering crater now. The mass had to *go* somewhere."

Jules took a long, deep gulp of coffee. "So you're sayin' it went into my coffin."

"Yes. You saw it and smelled it yourself. It didn't *look* anything like you because it was undifferentiated proto-matter, temporarily separated from the conscious and subconscious organizing power of your brain. But I could tell that your supersensitive wolf nose found the proto-matter's odor intimately familiar."

Jules winced. "Jeezus . . . I really *stink*, then." He took another swallow and was lost in thought for a minute. "So you're tellin' me this *always* happens, every time I change into somethin' else? My extra mass, or whatever, goes back to my coffin, like a batter runnin' to home base?"

"Yes. Actually, to be more exact, your extra mass goes back to the last place you slept. If you'd slept last night in the trunk of your Lincoln, that's where we would've found that slug-thingie. This behavior is most likely what originated the custom of vampires putting soil on the floors of their coffins. Maybe some prehistoric vampire discovered that the isolated proto-matter needs soil's nourishment to remain viable."

Jules waved his hands in front of his face as if he were swatting pesky mosquitoes. "Whoa! Just when I think I'm startin' to follow what you're sayin', you zoom up into the clouds again. Look, this is real interesting and all; it's like watchin' an episode of *The Outer Limits* and discoverin' that I'm the special guest star. But why the heck does this matter right now? You said you was gonna teach me to be a better vampire, somethin' that could help me fight Malice X better."

Doodlebug smiled again, but his eyes betrayed glimmers of irritation. "Jules, you're not letting me finish. There's more. A *lot* more. You're capable of feats you've never even imagined. Let me show you an example."

Doodlebug's face hardened with concentration. His slender form began wavering, and a thick mist escaped from his blouse and skirt. A moment later he stood in front of Jules as a little girl—complete with pigtails—who looked about eight years old. With his clothes all billowy, Doodlebug might have been a cross-dressing tyke who'd snuck into his mother's closet and tried on her fancy party outfit.

"Oh, I see how this could be *real* useful in a dustup with Malice X," Jules said.

Doodlebug didn't smile. "Just go to the bedroom and look inside my coffin."

Jules got up from the table, edged around the piano case in the living room, and walked to the four-poster bed in the next room back. He opened the lid of Doodlebug's coffin. Inside was another pulsating slug-thingie. Only this slug-thingie was much smaller than his own had been; if his proto-matter had weighed 250 pounds, this blob had to be about a tenth that size, maybe 25, 35 pounds.

Suddenly the proto-matter began to vanish from the coffin, disappearing down a nonexistent drain just as the other one had. When it was entirely gone, Doodlebug called to Jules in a high, childlike voice, "All right, now come back into the kitchen."

The mini version of Doodlebug was sitting on one of the kitchen chairs with a large black cat purring contentedly on his lap. Two other cats, a big orange tabby and a white Siamese, rubbed against the loose folds of hosiery bunched around his skinny legs.

The tabby trotted over to Jules and began rubbing aggressively against his leg. The big vampire's nose twitched. His sneeze made the windows rattle.

"Ohh maannn . . . get these damn cats *outta* here! I got pet allergies like you wouldn't believe." He rubbed his nose and tweaked it from side to side. "Where the hell'd they come from, anyway? They the owner's?"

Doodlebug called to the tabby with a nod of his head. The big orange cat left Jules's leg and hopped up on Doodlebug's lap. "No. They're mine. More precisely, they're *me*."

"Huh?"

"You watched the proto-matter in my coffin disappear, didn't you?"

"Yeah, sure, but . . . since when could a vampire change into a *cat*? Much less *three* cats?"

"Didn't you tell me that Malice X changed into a black panther?"

"Well, yeah. But I figured that was just 'cause he was a black guy. I figured, y'know, maybe black vampires follow different rules or some-thin' from us white vampires. Like I can change to a couple of animals from Europe, where my people come from, so I guess he could change to a couple of animals from Africa."

Doodlebug's hands kept the two cats on his lap satiated with plea-sure. The third cat, the Siamese, sniffed and scratched at the cottage's back door, perhaps sensing the pondful of fat goldfish waiting outside. "That's not a bad supposition, Jules. Actually, there's a germ of truth in what you said, although not in the way you'd think. Let me ask you this: After you became a vampire, how did you first learn that you could transform into a bat, a wolf, or mist?"

Jules pulled one of the kitchen chairs as far away from the three cats as he could and sat down. "I dunno. I guess Mo taught me." He rubbed the stubble on his chin and thought some more. "Come to think of it, I guess I already knew I'd be able to do those things, even before Mo told me anything at all."

"How so?"

"Oh, y'know, readin' vampire stories in *Argosy* as a kid. And there were even some movies I saw. Silent movies at the big theaters on Canal Street."

"So when you first became a vampire, you already knew what vam-pires could do."

"Sure."

"And how do you suppose Maureen learned about it before she gave you lessons?"

"Heck, same way I did, I guess. Some older vampire taught her. And she probably already knew about vampires even before that, from readin' novels or penny dreadfuls. How about you? How'd you learn? When I first approached you outside that candy store, you knew exactly what I was offerin'."

Doodlebug smiled. "Oh, I used to *swim* in vampire lore. *Weird Tales,* comic books, movies—*Dracula's Daughter, Son of Dracula, Mark of the Vampire*—I saw them all. By the time I met you, I knew perfectly well what to expect. And that's my point."

Jules looked mystified. "I lost ya somewhere."

"When it came to vampires, I knew what to expect: Vampires sleep in coffins. They need to drink blood every couple of nights or so. They can change into three other forms—bat, wolf, and mist. So when I became one myself, I only tried doing those things I already believed vampires were capable of. I was limited by what I *thought* I knew."

"Are you sayin' vampires can change into *anything*?"

"Not *anything*, no. But my Tibetan teachers showed me that the range of possible transformations is far, *far* more varied than the three options that became part of the petrified forest of European legends. One could spend a hundred lifetimes attempting to master all the possible permutations. Some of my teachers have devoted centuries to that very quest."

"Hold on a minute. Malice X never went to Tibet to study with them monks. How come *he* could change himself to a panther?"

"I can only assume he wasn't exposed to media portrayals of black vampires that would've affected his mind-set when he became one himself. Even if he was familiar with the same movies and stories that you and I grew up with, they didn't mold him and limit him in quite the same way. There may be African folk legends he was exposed to that center on men transforming into panthers."

"Let's see if I got this down. What you're basically sayin' is, what we can do as vampires is all a mind-over-matter kinda thing, right? Like them Indian guys who can walk across fire barefoot, just 'cause they *think* it ain't gonna hurt them none."

"Exactly."

"So the next time I run into Malice X, I can change myself to King Kong and stomp the creep into a smear on the sidewalk?"

"I'm afraid *that* particular transformation is out of the question. Remember what I said about mass? Mass can't be created or destroyed. But there *is* something you can do that Malice X cannot. And the wonderful thing is, you can do it thanks to a personal attribute you've always considered a handicap."

"Oh yeah? What would that be?"

"Jules, unlike me or Malice X, you are *blessed* with mass. Four hundred and fifty pounds of it. Forget about trying to recruit a platoon of followers. You don't need them. With some guidance and practice, you could will yourself to become a trio of hundred-and-fifty-pound vampires."

Jules walked along a twisting, looping path of yellow chalk his friend had drawn on the concrete floor of Maureen's basement. Doodlebug, now six inches tall, sat on his shoulder.

"Faster," the Barbie-doll-sized Doodlebug said. He struck Jules's shoulder repeatedly with an iced tea spoon. The tiny blows didn't sting, but they were irritating.

"Hey, is that really necessary?" Jules said as he resentfully plodded around the maze.

"I'm the bird that taps against the window."

"The *what?*"

"The distraction that will inevitably present itself at your most crucial and vulnerable moment of concentration. Remember, you're learning to form and control multiple bodies, which requires the clear mind and keen mental vision of the finest archer. You'll need to maintain this pure mental state in deadly combat, surrounded by perhaps dozens of enemy vampires, explosions, and flying projectiles. Even the tiniest distraction while you are manipulating multiple bodies could prove fatal, if you let it. Now walk the path *faster.*"

Doodlebug whacked his earlobe with the spoon, which really hacked Jules off. He'd show that pint-sized pest. Aping Jackie Gleason's nimble *Honeymooners* dance steps, he pirouetted and dipped along the path, careful to keep his toes precisely on the chalk line. He felt Doodlebug grab hold of his collar, and he smiled as he heard the spoon clatter to the floor.

"That was the easy part," Doodlebug said. "Nursery school. I don't think you'll be able to take this next exercise so lightly."

Jules stared at the electric train set. Doodlebug had instructed him to assemble it so that the tracks crisscrossed the yellow chalk line. The train was a souvenir from Jules's and Maureen's happier days together, a hobby they'd shared on those long nights when there was nothing good on TV and one or both of them weren't in the mood for sex. He was surprised Maureen had hung on to it. He finished assembling the looping track, complete with tunnel, bridge, flashing crossing lights, and New England–style town center. Then he placed the locomotive and its ten connecting cars on the track and hooked the electric control box into a wall socket.

While Jules was on his hands and knees, Doodlebug shimmied up his sleeve to his shoulder. "Very good. Turn on the train to its maximum speed. You are to walk the chalk path, counterclockwise. Here's the complicated part: You must time your movement so that wherever the chalk path and the train tracks cross, you and the train reach that intersection simultaneously. You are not permitted to stop and wait for the train to arrive—you may slow or quicken your steps, but you must keep moving at all times."

Jules eyed the layout carefully. The chalk path and the train tracks intersected at six points, arrayed at nearly even intervals around the basement. It didn't look too hard.

It was harder than it looked.

Six attempts later—make that three crushed model autos, five flattened pedestrians, and one crumpled church steeple later—Jules made it around the entire course successfully, meeting the train at each intersection. He sat heavily on a bench by the wall, toweling off his dripping forehead and neck as if he'd just run the Crescent City Classic.

He grinned a Cheshire cat smile, despite his exhaustion. "How about *that*, Tinkerbell? I think I earned myself a coffee break."

"Actually, Jules, I was just about to suggest that you brew a pot of coffee. . . ."

♠

Ten minutes later Jules stood at the starting line again. This time, however, he held a china cup and saucer in each hand. Both cups were filled with steaming-hot coffee. Doodlebug had returned to his normal size and shed his Barbie clothes for a black leather skirt, neon-pink tank top, and black vinyl thigh-high boots. He sat on a stool with the train set's control box in his lap.

"I'd like to see *you* do this, hotshot," Jules grumbled.

"Oh, those monks had me doing much more unpleasant things than this," Doodlebug answered brightly.

"Yeah? Well, I still think this is a dumb-ass idea. This is Mo's best china you got me messin' with here. I bust any of it up, there'll be hell to pay."

"That'll give you all the more incentive to concentrate, won't it? On your mark, get set—"

Doodlebug switched on the train's juice. The coffee cups clattered jarringly as Jules headed down his increasingly hateful path. He made the first intersection. Despite much clattering of cups and saucers, he timed the train's journey through the tunnel perfectly and made the second intersection with nary a spill. At the third intersection, however, his right toe clipped the corner of a trestle bridge as the train passed over it.

"Shit—*aoww-aoww-aoww-aoww!*"

Jules spent the next fifteen minutes soaking his throbbing hands in a bucket of ice water. Doodlebug was good enough to mop up the spilled coffee and sweep the broken china into a wastebasket.

"Do you want to call it a night?" Doodlebug asked.

Jules wiped his hands on his pants. "Naww. I'm sure Malice X ain't restin' on *his* laurels. Lemme try it a few more times."

Doodlebug poured fresh coffee into two unbroken cup-and-saucer sets and handed them to his friend. Jules lined up back at the starting point. The big vampire took a deep breath and closed his eyes, trying to clear his mind of all distractions. His hands still throbbed. What if he spilled steaming coffee on them again—? No; that didn't matter. What mattered was what Doodlebug had promised him. What mattered was the fact that if he worked hard enough, his enormous bulk, the target of endless insults and humiliations over the years, could become an asset instead of a liability. Then Jules Duchon would *really* throw his weight around.

Jules opened his eyes. "Are you ready?" Doodlebug asked.

"Ready as I'll ever be."

The train lurched into motion. But Jules didn't lurch. He flowed along the path like a blob of mercury guided by electromagnets. *No need to rush,* he told himself. *I know exactly how fast that train moves—I got plenty of time to make the intersection.* Doodlebug's words bathed his mind like a refreshing warm shower: *Flow. Peacefulness. Connectedness.* The cups and saucers he held in his hands weren't heavy at all. There was no clatter, no nervous sloshing. They were part of his limbs, connected to him. Like the path was connected to him. And he knew the train like he knew the beating of his own heart.

He successfully passed the first intersection five full seconds before he was cognizant of having done so. The trestle bridge didn't trip him up in the slightest. He passed over it without causing even a stirring in the coffee cups.

But then something changed. The train hit an invisible wall of rubber. Some evil outside force took control of his calm mastery and twisted it, slowing everything down.

"You—you're changing the train's speed! You can't do that!"

"I most assuredly *can*," Doodlebug answered.

"No, you can't! Not *now*!"

"The bird that taps against the window, Jules. It always pops up at the worst possible time."

"*Fuck* the fuckin' bird!" He was losing it. The cups and saucers were cups and saucers again, not part of his hands. Their clattering sounded like the approach of an onrushing streetcar. The train sped up again. Then it slowed to a crawl.

Sweat fell into Jules's eyes. "Take that bird and shove it up your— *aoww-aoww-aoww-aoww!*"

The passing train was caught in a deluge of falling coffee. The tracks sparked. The electrical discharge traveled almost instantaneously around the track to the control box, which shorted out with a sharp *pop-pop-pop!*

Doodlebug sat stunned for a moment. He stared at the smoking control box in his lap, then stared at Jules, who was fuming even more than the blackened, ruined wall socket.

"Well . . ." the somewhat embarrassed taskmaster said. "I guess we'll be breaking for the night. No wonder my teachers had me juggling live rats instead of racing electric trains."

◆

"Wolf *and* bat. You can do it, Jules."

Jules had hardly slept at all the previous day. He'd tossed and turned in his piano box, his mind crammed full with thoughts of Maureen *(what does she know that she hasn't told me?)*, Elisha Raddeaux *(has Malice X found her? does he want to kill me even* more *now?)*, the mysterious Veronika *(what's the deal with that screwy dame, anyway?)*, and his upcoming training session *(what if I can't hack it?)*. But now he was back in Maureen's basement, naked as a jaybird, warily putting himself in Doodlebug's manicured hands again.

"Shouldn't we be trying this closer to where my coffin is?" Jules asked, rubbing the side of his nose. The more questions he asked, the longer he could put off having to make his first attempt. "I mean, we're clear across town from where my slug-thingie's gonna end up."

Doodlebug didn't appear to be swayed. "Think about this logically. In all your years of changing to a bat or a wolf, has it *ever* made a difference how far you were from your coffin? Stop stalling. Let's just give it a try, shall we?"

The little martinet was onto him. Jules sighed. Wolf and bat. Bat and wolf. He closed his eyes and concentrated. Full moon. Wings. Long nose, long fangs. Long, skinny fingers. Bushy tail. Tiny legs and itty-bitty talons. Powerful jaws. Hair. Ears like a rabbit's, only not as fuzzy and cute. . . .

The basement began to fill with smoke. Jules sensed his body waver and shimmer, going in and out of focus like the picture on an old vacuum-tube TV. For the briefest of instants Jules's form was replaced by a creature from a Hieronymus Bosch phantasmagoria—a wolf's head with a tiny rodent body, black wings sprouting from the tip of its long nose frantically flapping in a vain attempt to keep from falling over. It half yelped and half hissed before it lost its shape. Then it melted into an amorphous gray mass that splattered against the concrete floor with a re-sounding *shhglorp!*

The floor was hidden by fleshy smoke again. When it cleared, Jules was lying on his back, gasping for breath and bathed in sweat.

"Jules!" Doodlebug rushed to his friend's side and helped him sit up. "Are you all right?"

Jules coughed heavily, then shook his head to clear away the cobwebs. "I been—*ahchem!*—better. I been a whole *helluva* lot better."

"What happened? Why did you try transforming into both animals at once?"

"Ain't that what you've been yammering at me to do these past two nights?"

"I'm afraid you misunderstood. You should only attempt one transformation at a time—when you have one form fully under control, *then* you create the other."

Jules grabbed his shirt and mopped off his forehead. "You sayin' you want me to change into a wolf or a bat first, and *then* pull a second animal outta that gray glop five miles away?"

Doodlebug appeared mystified. "Well . . . *sure*. I thought I was very clear on that."

Jules dabbed off his glistening chest, then tossed the soaked shirt into a corner. "Lemme tell you somethin'. There's no way in *hell* I'm gonna be able to muster the concentration to pull a second animal outta my hat once I'm a bat or a wolf. With all those super senses rushing in on me, I got too much jumpin' around my wolf-mind or bat-mind to pull together a second body. It just ain't gonna happen."

Doodlebug crouched in front of his friend, put his hand on his shoulder, and looked him directly in the eye. "I beg to disagree. Last night you achieved a special state of mind. Until I was able to distract you and shatter your concentration, you had succeeded in dividing your consciousness. You were paying equal attention to three factors at once."

Jules's stonewalling thawed into a wary hopefulness. "Huh. You really think so? I was doin' that good?"

Doodlebug smiled and patted his friend's well-padded shoulder. "You were doing *much* better than 'good.' You'll be able to reach that level again; I have no doubt. All it takes is work. Practice, practice, practice. Plus a little faith in yourself. Shall we try it again?"

◆

Which animal was the easiest? It made sense to do the harder one first and then, when his concentration and mental faculties weren't at their sharpest, attempt the simpler one. The wolf was a heck of a lot more similar to his normal form than the bat was. Transforming into a bat was downright alien, and more than a little creepy. Growing those long, long fingers, and then stretching his skin paper-thin between them . . . *yuck*. The bat was definitely the more difficult of the two.

Jules thought bat-thoughts. His old familiar body, with which he'd shared a decades-long love–hate relationship, melted away. Jules looked around the room, emitting his ultrasonic shriek more by instinct than by rational choice. He could sense Doodlebug's lithe, graceful presence by the shape of the echoes that bounced off him. He tested his wings, beating them tentatively against the stubborn pull of gravity. No dice. Even with the extra vitality granted him by Doc Landrieu's wonder pills, his bat-form was still too obese to become airborne under its own power. Why? Why couldn't he become a *thin* bat?

Too many questions—his rodent brain ached from them all. Right now, he had other irons in the fire. Like pulling a wolf out of his trick bag. He shut down his echolocation, clenched his weak eyes shut, and thought the most cogent wolf-thoughts he could manage. Something started to happen—

"No, Jules! Not *that* way!"

What was the matter? He was doing it, wasn't he?

He could sense the long wolf snout emerging, complete with its wet nose and fearsome incisors. Unfortunately, he also sensed something else going on—his left wing was disintegrating even as his wolf snout took shape!

"Use the mass in your coffin, Jules! The *extra* mass! Don't reshape what you've already got with you! Pull *more* in—"

But it was too late. Jules's grotesque little homunculus was missing its left wing and much of its ears, but a wolf's levitating jaws were attached to its chest by tenuous floating strands of protoplasm; he splattered into a grayish puddle with a sickening *shhglorp!*

Jules needed nearly forty minutes of recuperation before he had the strength, not to mention the intestinal fortitude, to try again. This time he managed to hold his bat-form steady while pulling about a quarter of a wolf from the proto-matter stored in his distant coffin. However, he would've done better to build the canine's hindquarters first. Starting with the head meant that the wolf's potent senses shattered his concentration before he even reached the neck. Both his bodies imploded, ending up as sluglike puddles on the floor, then a very disoriented and disgruntled Jules.

Three *shhglorps!* later, the door at the top of the basement steps opened. Maureen, dressed in one of her Velcro-laden dancing costumes, inserted herself through the doorway.

"How's the training coming? I'm on my one o'clock break at the club, so I thought I'd walk over and see how you guys were making out."

Jules said nothing as Maureen descended the steps. Whether this was because of exhaustion or a reluctance to have anything to do with her, he wasn't quite sure. Doodlebug rushed to fill the dead silence. "Jules has made some pretty impressive progress. The last couple of hours, though, he's hit a wall. Not unexpected, really. We all do. So we'll be taking a break."

"You have him punching sides of beef yet?" She hummed a few bars from the *Rocky* theme and performed some girlish shadowboxing. She stopped when she saw she wasn't getting even the faintest shadow of a smile from Jules, who was still lying on the floor. "Jeezus . . . he *looks* like a side of beef." She walked over to where he lay flat on his back, breathing in labored, phlegmy gasps. "Hey, you been rummaging through my costume jewelry lately?"

This out-of-left-field question yanked a response from him. "What the . . . hell . . . kinda reason . . . would I have . . . to dig through your *jewelry*?"

"I have no idea. But tonight I was looking for some pieces I haven't worn in a while, and I noticed that your vampire baby teeth were missing."

Jules dragged himself to a sitting position and set his shirt over his lap. "My baby teeth? What're you talkin' about?"

"Your *vampire* baby teeth. Don't you remember? I saved them and kept them in a pill bottle. They were so *adorable*. I still remember the night you lost them. Twelve months to the day after you first became a vampire. Remember? You were so *scared*. I mean *terrified*. You thought you'd never have fangs again. You were running around this house hollering like your pecker had just fallen off. It was funnier than the Keystone Kops and Fatty Arbuckle put together."

"Yeah, I remember. You were a regular Saint Theresa that night. Real supportive. So what's all this about my vampire baby teeth?"

"They're *gone*. Like I said, I kept them in this pill bottle, and I kept the pill bottle at the bottom of this box of old costume jewelry. Nobody ever dug through that box except me."

"Well, *I* didn't take them."

"But you were the only one who would've known they were there."

"What do I need my fuckin' *baby* teeth for? I need another pair of fangs like I need a pack of *Hispanic* vampires on my case. You lost 'em, that's all."

"Yeah. I guess you're right. What does it matter, anyway?" She picked up a folding chair that was leaning against the wall, opened it, and sat down. It groaned like a packhorse on its last legs. "So let's see your stuff, hotshot. Let's see what Doodlebug's taught you so far. Put on a show for ol' Mo."

Jules mopped his forehead with his shirt. "Forget it. I'm whipped."

"Oh, come on, Jules. I walked all the way back here from Jezebel's—"

Jules's voice had more steel in it this time. "I said forget it. I been beatin' my head against the concrete floor all night. The only thing I'm good for right now is watchin' an old John Carradine flick on video."

Maureen crossed her arms stiffly. "Well, that's a *fine* attitude to have. I suppose John Carradine will show you in ten easy steps how to get out of the mess you're in?"

Doodlebug, sensing trouble brewing, stepped between the two of them. "Uh, Maureen, Jules really *has* been working awfully hard tonight. This isn't the best time—"

Jules lit into Maureen as if Doodlebug weren't even there. "Y'know, you got a *helluva* lotta nerve, waltzing in here now and givin' me shit when you ain't even been here to see how I've been knockin' myself out. You got no *idea* what you're talkin' about."

Maureen didn't back down a millimeter. "Oh, don't I? I think I know enough to recognize a *quitter* when I hear one. Winners don't crawl away to lie on a couch and watch old horror movies when they're beat. Winners keep plugging away until they've got the *game* beat."

"Well, *thank* you, Knute Rockne. I'm all inspired now. 'Scuse me—I gotta go jam a stake up your old boyfriend's ass for the Gipper, okay?"

Maureen flinched, but her voice remained steady. "I see you've got *plenty* of vim and vigor left when it comes to blaming me. How about applying some of that energy where it'll make a difference, like learning how to be a better and *smarter* vampire?"

"Aww, hell, why don't *you* try it, Maureen? You think it's so goddamn easy? Go ahead. Change to a bat and a wolf at the same time. Or change into three ballerinas. No—*four* ballerinas! I ain't the only one around here 'blessed' with excess mass."

"That's right. You just happen to be the one with a bright red bull's-eye painted on your mass."

"Painted there courtesy of *your* out-of-control sex drive—!"

The upstairs phone rang, the bell that ended this round of the super-heavyweight championship bout. Maureen rose from her seat, her cheeks flushed. "Excuse me, Jules. Maybe we'll continue this—discussion—once you're decent." She tossed his trousers at him before heading back up the stairs.

Two minutes later she stuck her head through the door again. "It's for *you*, buster," she said. Her voice was a barely contained froth of scorn, anger, and hurt.

Jules, flabbergasted, stared at Doodlebug. "But—but nobody knows I'm here. Right?" Doodlebug shrugged his shoulders. Jules turned back to Maureen. "Who is it?"

"I didn't care to ask." Her nose twitched, as if she'd just caught the scent of something unmentionably vile. "It's some *woman*."

Jules finished wiggling into his trousers. Then he hurriedly climbed the steps, wincing as his bare foot snagged a splinter, his mind seething with equal parts curiosity and trepidation. Maureen had left the receiver lying on her kitchen table. Jules picked it up, his heart beating both with excitement and the exertion of hustling up the stairs.

"Hello?"

"Hello, Jules?" He recognized the voice before she said another word. "It's Veronika."

Her husky, Memphis-tinged but New York–inflected voice set off a grenade in his brain. A hundred questions whizzed past each other like shrapnel. Unfortunately, his mouth could process only one question at a time, and the resulting traffic pileup resembled the Lake Pontchartrain Causeway during a hurricane evacuation.

"What—how—you tried to—you, *you*—"

"It's extremely important that I see you again."

One question finally tore loose of the pack. "How did you know I'd be here?"

"I know all sorts of things about you."

"What the hell's this all about? Who *are* you?"

"I know I owe you an explanation—much more than an explanation. I want to come clean, Jules. But I can't do it over the phone."

Jules saw Maureen staring through the doorway with the intensity of a hawk eyeing a plump field mouse. Doodlebug was standing next to her. Jules tried to keep his voice low. It wasn't easy. "What the hell do you want?"

"I need to see you again."

All thoughts of stealthiness were blown out the window by the fury of a male ego scorned. "You must be outta yer fuckin' *mind*! Do I look retarded? Am I some drooling *idiot*? You tried to *kill* me! You invited me up to your room with, y'know, with false pretensions—I thought you were *into* me!"

"Honey, I can explain—"

"*Explain?* Explain *what*? That you're some kinda vampire-huntin' wacko—oh yeah, I *saw* your little arsenal in the bathroom under the sink. But idiot me, I clambered into that hot tub with you anyway. And boy, did I pay—you tried to *boil* me like some fuckin' four-hundred-and-fifty-pound *crawfish*!"

Even with the bad connection (she was on either a cheap cell phone or one of the battered-and-abused pay phones in the Quarter), he could hear the anguish in her voice. "Jules, please believe me—I *had* to do it! I had no choice! They're watching me all the time. My loyalty was *already* in question. So I had to do *something* to you—but I picked the *least* lethal weapon they gave me. Don't you think I *hated* doing it? I've been crying my eyes out ever since you ran out of my hotel room. I hate myself for letting them force me to hurt you."

Jules's head was swimming. "Wait a minute—who's this 'they' you keep talkin' about? Your loyalty to *who* was bein' questioned? And what'd you stick in the tub water, anyway?"

Her voice lightened a bit. "Oh, *that*—that was holy water. A little vial of it. That's why you felt the burning and I didn't."

He waited for her to continue. She didn't. For all her tearful apologies, she was still yanking his chain. "Again, lady—who's this 'they' that's makin' you do all these bad things?"

Her voice turned serious again. "I told you—I can't explain that over the phone. It's too dangerous. They could be listening in on our conversation right now."

Maureen was standing with hands on her shelflike hips. "Jules, who the *hell* is that on the line with you? This is *my* house—I don't appreciate you giving out my number to your goddamn floozies!"

Jules put his paw over the phone and glared at Maureen. "Shut your face and gimme some peace! I'm tryin' to figure things out here—"

"Not on *my* phone, you aren't! And never, *ever* tell me to 'shut my face,' you womanizing *freeloader!*"

Trapped between two obstinate women was no place to be. "Look," he said huffily into the receiver. "If you ain't spillin', then I'm ending this conversation right now. You got two seconds before I slam this phone down. One-one-thousand—"

"Wait!" The phone was silent for a few long seconds. "I—I can't reveal their identities over the phone. But I can tell you this—they know you were the one who killed those twenty-three people in Covington."

Jules's heart plummeted. He'd almost forgotten about that little misadventure. "You mean the Knight supporters?"

"Yes. My handler headed up a special crisis intervention team following the massacre. They tagged you as the culprit within forty-eight hours."

"How . . . ?" He was sinking again. Sinking into the grasping mud that underlay every street and sidewalk in New Orleans, just when he thought he'd been starting to climb toward the light.

"I can help you, Jules. We can help each other. I know this operation. I've been near the center of it for the past eighteen months. I know I hurt you, but I'm not your enemy. I want to be your *ally*, if only you'll let me."

Her words clutched him like silk tentacles. Jules realized he had no choice but to find out what she knew. "All right . . . where do I meet you?"

"Would the Palm Court be okay? In half an hour?"

"Sure." He hung up the phone with the weariness of a death-row inmate who'd just been denied his final reprieve.

Maureen's fists were still planted on her hips. Only now they were trembling. "So now you're going to meet this whore of yours?"

Jules shuffled toward the basement to retrieve the rest of his clothes. "Ain't none of your business, Maureen."

Doodlebug grabbed his arm. "What's this I overheard about the Nathan Knight rally?"

Jules shook him off and headed down the steps. "I got some investigating I gotta do. And I gotta do it alone."

Maureen followed him down the steps. "*Investigating!* I know what you'll be 'investigating'! You'll be 'investigating' that whore's *pussy*!"

Jules pulled on his shirt. "I should be so lucky," he mumbled to himself under his breath.

Doodlebug descended the steps. "I don't like the sound of this. If you're going somewhere tonight, I'm going with you."

Jules turned a steely gaze on his partner while he tied his shoes. "Like hell you are. Sometimes a man's gotta do what a man's gotta do. And this here man's gonna do it."

"But—"

"'But' *nothin'*. You're off the case tonight, Doodlebug. You try to tag along, I'll send you packin' back to California. This is a solo job. The Lone Ranger rides the prairie. And Tonto hightails it back to the wigwam."

Maureen tailed him back up the stairs. "Jules—listen to me, Jules! If you walk out that door . . . if you *walk* out that *door*—I'll never *speak* to you again!"

Jules put his hand on the front doorknob. The words *Frankly, my dear* . . . flittered briefly through his mind, but he decided he could be more original than that (if not quite as pithy). He turned to face her. "Y'know, Maureen, I just realized somethin'. You're a helluva lot more worried that I might get laid than you been scared I might get killed. Well, you can rest your pretty little head, babe. 'Cause before the night's over, I might do *both*."

♦

Jules arrived at the Palm Court half an hour later. He'd darted from doorway to darkened doorway through half the Quarter. When he squeezed himself through the entrance to the club, the wait staff were beginning to put chairs on top of the tables. Nearly all the late-night crowd had cleared out. Half a dozen young musicians, plus a couple of middle-aged veterans Jules recognized from traditional jazz sessions around town, were packing up their instruments. Porkchop Chambonne, standing near the end of the bar, was engaged in a heated discussion with a younger man whom Jules recognized as Roddy Braithwhite, the club's owner.

The elderly musician's eyes lit up when he noticed Jules enter the room. He stopped arguing in midsentence to call his friend over. "Jules! Hey, Jules! C'mon over here!" He turned back to the owner. "Now *here's* a man who remembers how good the music useta be. Jules, tell him about my big bands back in the forties and fifties."

"Uh, Chop, that was my dad, Jules *Senior*, remember?"

The trumpet player huffily smoothed his stringy comb-over back into place atop his head. "Oh, *stop!* I ain't got time for that foolishness right now. Rod here is tellin' me I can't have my big band no more. He wants me to cut back to a quartet, or even a *trio!*"

The club owner looked acutely embarrassed. "Uh, Mr. Chambonne's a little upset—"

"*Upset!* You want me to lay off half my frickin' band! Rod, I ain't gonna be around this earth forever. How is them teenagers gonna learn enough to become the Porkchops of tomorrow if I can't have them in my band *today?*"

The owner stared at the floor. "In a perfect world, I'd employ you and your big band—hell, a *twenty*-piece band—from now until the end of time. I'm a music fan. You know that. But I'm also a businessman. And right now I'm a businessman who's facing four new competitors in the Quarter. I just can't afford to hire the whole band anymore. Maybe you could get some of the youngsters to sit in on weekends—"

"Them boys can't afford to be doin' no *volunteer* work! They's savin' up for college. Tell him, Jules! You's a regular customer around here. *Tell* him what a big attraction my big band is—"

Just then Jules saw Veronika waving him over from the far corner. "Uh, Chop, I'm really sorry, but I gotta go. Look, another night, maybe we can do us some brainstormin' on this situation—"

The bandleader angrily waved him off. "Oh, the *hell* with you, then!" He immediately redirected his pique at the owner, reiterating the hardships his laid-off band members would face, beating his leather cap against the bar for emphasis.

Jules felt perfectly awful as he shuffled toward the table in the back. He slumped into a chair across from Veronika, glancing back over his shoulder at the diminutive bandleader, silently praying the old man wouldn't suffer a coronary.

"Thank God you came!"

Jules reluctantly turned his attention toward his companion. "Yeah, I'm here. Now make like a Hurricane glass and spill."

Veronika looked cautiously around the rapidly emptying room. She nervously laced her fingers on the table and leaned closer to him.

"Have you ever heard of the Strategic Helium Reserve?"

"No."

"Virtually no one has. Do you know what an airship is?"

"That's like a blimp, right?"

"Very good. During World War One, the U.S. government established a crash program to develop a lighter-than-air scout fleet for the navy. Helium is a much more stable gas than hydrogen, which is what the Germans used for their airships—the *Hindenburg* exploded, remember? America built the only large-scale plants in the world for the production of helium. After the war, the federal government established the Strategic Helium Reserve, to ensure that the navy would always have an adequate supply for its scouting fleet."

Jules squirmed in his chair. "That's a real interestin' history lesson. But what the hell has any of it got to do with me?"

"I'm coming to that. Now when was the last time the navy flew any airships?"

"I dunno. World War Two, maybe?"

"That's right. The navy had already retired its last airship, the *Akron*, before World War Two. During the war, all they used were a few blimps for antiaircraft coverage. By the late forties the navy had no airships or blimps at all. But year in and year out, Congress kept funding the Strategic Helium Reserve. It's still being funded, even though the navy hasn't used a cubic foot of helium in more than fifty years."

Jules rubbed the end of his nose. "I guess now is when I'm supposed to ask, How come?"

Veronika's voice fell to a whisper. "Certain elements in the armed forces and federal law enforcement found the Strategic Helium Reserve to be a useful front for activities they didn't want Congress or the public to be aware of. Things like possible alien incursions into our biosphere. Unexplained, widespread cattle mutilations. Strange atmospheric phenomena that would black out America's radar defense network for days at a time."

Jules grunted with the beginnings of understanding. "Things that go bump in the night. Like me."

"Like you, yes. I'm an employee of the Strategic Helium Reserve. A year and a half ago, I was specially recruited to work on your case."

A red-skirted waitress approached their table. "Last call, folks. What'll it be?"

"I'll have another one of these," Veronika said, pushing her half-empty goblet toward the waitress. "A strawberry margarita. Tell the bartender to make it a little sweeter this time."

"Sure thing. Anything for you, sir?"

Jules nodded without taking his eyes off Veronika. "Coffee." He waited for the waitress to walk out of earshot. "Now I guess the next question I'm supposed to ask is, How come you're tellin' me all this? It's not that hard to guess from the stuff you were packin' beneath your bathroom sink that your job is to get ridda me. I figure I can trust you about as far as I can toss you. Which ain't that far. How do I know you ain't got the block surrounded by feds with wooden stakes and crosses, waitin' for me to walk outta here with you?"

"Let me show you something." She retrieved her purse from beneath her seat. When she unzipped it, Jules scooted back from the table, a look of alarm on his face. She laughed. "Oh, don't worry. I'm not reaching for garlic spray."

"*Garlic spray?* You've got *garlic spray*?"

"Of course. The agency wouldn't send me out into the field less than completely equipped. Here." She handed him a photograph. It was of a shapely young woman in an evening gown, clutching a trophy to her ample chest.

"Who's this?"

"That's me. It was taken a little less than two years ago, after I'd just won a statewide Miss Plus-Sized beauty contest."

Jules looked at the picture again, this time more closely. It was Veronika's face, all right. There was no mistaking that tiny cleft in her chin. But it was pushing the boundaries of the believable that the plump-but-pretty girl in the photo and the supersized goddess sitting across from him could be one and the same person. This picture was two years old? Nobody could gain that much weight that fast. Not even Jules himself.

The waitress returned with their drinks. After she left, Jules felt Veronika's hand on his thigh. "It seems unbelievable, doesn't it? That the ordinary girl in that photograph could have been transformed into the . . . freak . . . that I am today."

Jules was stunned by the depth of self-loathing in her voice. "Baby, you're no freak—"

She clenched her eyes shut. Her hand tensed on his thigh. "You have no *idea* what they did to me. All I wanted was to go to a good university. To start an exciting career. Maybe serve my country in the bargain. The agency recruited me right after I won that beauty pageant. I had no way of knowing at the time that they'd sponsored the entire thing. In return for five years of service, they promised me the moon. All I had to do was agree to certain . . . *experimental* procedures."

She ran her hands down her figure, tracing the massive globes of her breasts and the majestic roundness of her hips. Despite his wariness, Jules sensed his little soldier responding, waking up for morning reveille. "This body," she said mournfully, "it's not . . . normal. Not *natural*." She took a long sip of her margarita. "My handlers, they knew all about your preference for supersized women. So they designed this body I'm wearing as the ultimate honey trap. Most of what you see isn't really me. It's implants. Sixty percent or more of my, uh, curves are thanks to special lightweight saline-gel implants. The implants weigh much less than an equivalent volume of real flesh would. Otherwise, I'd probably be immobile at this size."

She brushed a tear away from her cheek with a perfectly manicured fingertip. "They . . . they *promised* they'd reverse it all. When my five years were up. But I found out that was a pack of lies. A woman contacted me. An ex-employee of the agency's. Another one of their 'projects.' They'd turned her into a freak, too. When they didn't need her anymore, they strung her along for years, buying her silence with constantly broken promises of turning her back to normal. She just got older and older. Her body grew less able to tolerate the horrible things they'd done to it. She stays in hiding and just waits to die. I don't want to end up like that, Jules. I *can't* end up like that."

Jules almost forgot to breathe. Her story hit him like a wrecking ball made of silicone. "So, uh, how do I fit into all this? What can I do?"

She gazed into his eyes. She was Venus and Rita Hayworth and

Jayne Mansfield all rolled into one. "I don't want to grow old. I don't want to decay into a pathetic heap like she did. I want to stay young forever, Jules. I want you to make me your vampire queen."

♠

They checked into a different hotel from the one Veronika was registered in, a precaution that Jules, even in his state of enthralled horniness, insisted upon. As soon as they closed the room door behind them, Veronika wrapped her silky arms around Jules's neck and planted a luscious kiss on his waiting lips.

"Darling," she said as she slowly pulled away, "I'm *starving*! Let's celebrate and order room service! I simply *adore* early-morning breakfasts! I know you can't join me, of course, but you'll be having *your* breakfast soon enough. We'll stick it all on the government's tab, okay?"

Jules sat on the edge of the soft mattress and unbuttoned his collar. "Sure . . . my tax dollars at work," he murmured dazedly.

She phoned the front desk and ordered virtually every item on the room service breakfast menu, then she sat next to him on the bed. "Oh, Jules, this is so *exciting*! What does it feel like, to be a vampire?"

"What does it feel like?" Jules didn't know what to say. But it didn't matter, really. "It feels good. You'll like it."

"Will I be able to change into a bat, like in the movies?"

"Sure!"

She kissed him again. "What is it like, to fly over a city on your own wings? Is it beautiful?"

Jules tried to remember the last time he'd actually flown. Who had been president then? Kennedy? But he remembered how New Orleans had looked from the air, the lights of the river-embraced city twinkling like an enormous crescent-shaped Christmas display. "Yeah, it was beautiful, baby."

A knock on the door interrupted Jules's reverie. Veronika got up and opened the door. "Oh, isn't this *wonderful* looking!" She ushered in the waiter, who carefully steered his cart heaped with steaming platters of fruit-covered pancakes, eggs over easy, hash brown potatoes, and strawberries drowned in cream.

She tipped the waiter lavishly, then attacked the strawberries and cream, balancing two of the plump berries on her spoon at a time. "Dessert should come *first*, I always say!" She turned those liquid eyes on him again. "Oh, Jules, can you imagine how *sweet* all this will make me taste? All those months they had me studying you, learning your habits, they had no idea I was developing the biggest *crush* on you." She ate the last of the strawberries, then lifted the bowl to her lips and drank the remaining cream. "*Mmmm . . .* simply *delicious.* I used to lie in my bed at the compound and fantasize about you all night long."

It was all Jules could do to keep himself from ravishing her right then, drinking in her sex and then gulping down her blood. But through an extraordinary exertion of will, he reminded himself that the whole point of tonight's adventure was to gather information.

"You, uh, you said earlier that your handlers found out it was me who did in those twenty-three boobs across the river. You got any idea how they was able to pin it on me?"

"Oh, do we *have* to talk about this *now?*" She pouted briefly, then dug into the tall stack of blueberry- and baked-apple-covered pancakes. "Oh, *all* right. If it'll make you happy. They did some kind of tests on that goop you left on the floor. They were able to separate out your saliva, then genetically match it against some kind of tissue sample of yours."

Tissue sample? What kind of sample could the government have? He hadn't been in a hospital since before World War I. He certainly hadn't donated any blood for the past eighty years or so. Doc Landrieu? Sure, the doc had poked and prodded him to satisfy his medical curiosity, but Jules couldn't believe his ex-boss would've betrayed him.

A more recent recollection hit him. *The baby teeth. The missing vampire baby teeth.* Sure. It made sense. Who knew how long they'd been missing? If it was the teeth, that meant they'd been ferried to the feds either by Maureen or by her ex-lover-boy. Had Maureen asked him about the missing teeth to throw suspicion off herself? He didn't want to think it. But it was possible.

"Babe, you said those guys in your agency were teachin' you all about my habits and my likes and dislikes. You got any idea where they came by that kinda information? It's not like I ever put it on a Web site or nothin'."

"Oh, don't worry about all *that!*" she said brightly. "Once you turn me into a vampire, we'll move down to Mexico together. The agency won't bother with you once you're out of the country."

Mexico? Everyone and their brother wanted him to move south of the border! "Just humor me and answer my question, huh?"

"Ohh-*kay.* I was never privy to what all the higher-ups had their noses into. But I think I remember somebody telling me once that your case came to the agency's attention when somebody from local government called in some favors from the FBI. The FBI realized this was out of their depth, so they referred it to my agency."

"'Local government'? You mean from New Orleans City Hall?"

"I guess. I think it was somebody pretty high up. An alderman or somebody."

Who had connections at City Hall? Not Maureen; although with all the Mardi Gras balls she used to attend, it was conceivable that she might have some political connections. Doc Landrieu was well connected throughout the local political community—local politics had been his life. But Jules still refused to believe that his old patron had turned against him.

That left Malice X. What kind of connections could a drug-dealing, ex-gang-member vampire have at City Hall? Wait—that big black binder he'd grabbed from Elisha Raddeaux's heroin lab had listed some of the mayor's top aides as clients!

"Oh, here's something else I remember," Veronika said. "My handler mentioned that he had a local contact regarding your case. Some guy he'd meet up with at this bar on Wednesday nights."

Jules could barely contain his eagerness. "You remember the name of this bar?"

She forked another load of sugar-coated pancakes into her pretty mouth. "Umm . . . it had a funny name. Hit-Me-Up. No, that wasn't it. Hit-and-Go, maybe?"

"The Hit 'N' Run Club?"

"That sounds right. Yeah, I think that was it."

Bingo! Wednesday night was tomorrow night. Now he and Doodlebug would take the fight to Malice X instead of waiting for him to catch up to Jules. The element of surprise would be in Jules's pocket, for once, instead of pressing against his throat.

"That's fuckin' *great*, baby!" He reached his arms around her ample form and kissed her lustily on the side of her neck.

She grinned at him and wiped a blob of syrup from the corner of her mouth. "Let me give you something *better* to get you all hot and bothered. Tell you what. For every bite of breakfast I eat, I'll take off one article of clothing. And when I'm all out of articles of clothing, it'll be time for *your* breakfast."

How fortune could turn on a dime! Only hours ago he was covered in sweat, sitting on a cold concrete floor, enduring a browbeating from Maureen. "Baby, that's a better deal than the Pilgrims gettin' Manhattan for a handful of beads!"

As the eggs disappeared into her mouth, the shoes and socks came off her feet. A croissant accounted for her blouse and linen jacket. The last bites of pancake were traded for her skirt and the colorful silk scarf adorning her neck.

Finally, all that was left on her body were her bra and panties. All that was left on her plate was half a grapefruit. Smiling wickedly, she plunged her spoon into the moist, pink fruit.

"Wait!" Jules cried, bestirring himself from his erotic haze. "Don't eat that!"

"Why not?"

"It's too sour. It might sour up your blood."

"But I *love* grapefruit! And I still have my underwear to take off."

"Let me worry about your underwear. Just forget about that grapefruit, huh?"

"You big meanie!" She giggled as she fell into his waiting arms, then engulfed his mouth with a kiss.

A minute later, he almost wished he *had* let her eat the damn grapefruit, just so she would've taken off the damn bra herself. Why the hell did lingerie manufacturers make their products so incredibly complicated? The clasps on this thing would've bedeviled a tag team of Edison, Einstein, and Joe DiMaggio. Finally, he got it loose. The resulting plunge into infinite softness immediately made him forget about his momentary frustration.

So *this* was the payoff. Ever since he'd been a little boy, Jules had suspected that the bad things in the universe were balanced out by good things, or vice versa. Just not necessarily of equal magnitude. Most of his life he'd spent dreading the coming deluge of shit that would follow some tiny, insignificant good thing like finding a quarter on the street. But this time, *this time,* the deluge of shit had come *first.* And if the universe played by its own rules, that meant the balancing payback had to be even bigger and better. Tonight, he was making love to a gorgeous young woman whose fondest wish was to become his vampire queen. Tomorrow night, he and Doodlebug would squish his mortal enemy like the sewer-crawling cockroach he was.

Veronika moaned lustily. While his mind had been wandering, she'd managed to remove his shoes, socks, and shirt, but his trousers and underpants were prompting squeals of frustration. Once he lifted his behind off the bed, the trousers came off easily enough. His underpants were more problematic, being tightly clasped between his manly belly and his overexcited soldier. Veronika solved the conundrum by ripping them off. Soon thereafter her own panties went flying across the room like a pink bat.

She pushed him down onto the bed, signaling that she wanted to be on top. *Fine,* Jules thought; since she was the lighter of the two of them, it was only fair that she do most of the work. Besides, the view was bound to be spectacular.

She climbed on top of him, and the room temporarily disappeared behind an engulfing curtain of flesh. Then she straddled him, and her soft hand found his eager-to-serve soldier. She wiggled her posterior a little. There was an instant of erotic limbo while the biologic geometries adjusted themselves. Then he felt it.

Mission Control, we have ignition. . . .

Wow! Being inside her was the most intensely wonderful sensation he'd ever experienced. It was right up there with that first big gulp of blood after days of going without. His body was a Saturn V rocket, flames bursting from its base as it trembled with the mighty effort of breaking free of earth.

Gantries are clear, all systems are go—

He was going too fast. *Way* too fast. If he wanted to make this last more than five seconds, he'd better concentrate on something other than the rocket. He watched her thigh muscles bulge majestically as she pumped him for all he was worth.

Ten, nine, eight—

Aww, hell; there was no stopping liftoff now. The best he could do was squeeze as much sensual experience into the next few seconds as he could. He reached for her breasts

seven, six, five—

and they were fabulously soft, so ample (he wished his hands were bigger), maybe they were phony but he didn't care, they sure as hell felt *great*, he squeezed and squeezed

four, three, two—

and squeezed and squeezed, she was loving it, "Yes! Yes!" she said, and then there was a funny noise that sounded something like *shplittt!*

And then there were two terribly sharp-looking wooden stakes sticking out where her nipples had been.

Abort mission! Abort mission!

"Oh no!" she cried. "Not *now*! NOT NOW!"

He looked up into her eyes, and paradise was lost. He saw her awful moment of indecision—to be or not to be—and then he saw the room begin to disappear as she fell forward, her right breast-stake aimed directly at his heart.

His rocket, suddenly just a frightened little soldier again, retracted into the dubious shelter of its sheath. Jules rolled to the left as quickly as his blubber-hindered muscles would allow.

"AAOWW—*shit!*"

The stakes missed his heart. But his right shoulder suffered a gouging, and her weight and momentum actually drove her right stake through the loose fold of skin on his upper left arm and buried it deep in the mattress. Pain supercharged his strength. He pushed her off him, bloodily dislodging the stake from his arm in the process. Veronika landed on the floor with a loud thud.

Dazed, Jules watched the blood from his torn left arm stain the white sheets crimson. He heard Veronika stirring. *Fortune turns on a dime, turns on a fuckin' dime. . . .* He forced himself to move. His injuries were messy, but they weren't deep—despite the pain, he still had full use of his stabbed arm.

"Jules! It was a *mistake*! An accident! Please believe me!"

She was on her feet, her face beseeching him, her arms outstretched, begging for a forgiving embrace. But those twin stakes still pointed at his heart like the warheads on a pair of torpedoes.

"I want to be your queen! We can still make it work, darling! Let me prove my loyalty—I can help you with the black vampires!"

She came at him. He scanned the room for a defense, a weapon— anything. All there was was the uneaten half of a grapefruit.

Jimmy Cagney had the kiss-off thing down pat: a gesture was worth a thousand words. He picked up the grapefruit and mashed it in her face.

"*Ahhhgh!* My *eyes!*"

She blindly ran to the bathroom. Jules watched with no small satisfaction as she rammed into a wall on her way. Then he retrieved his clothes. He found himself wishing he were one of those superheroes who could simply say a magic word and have their uniform appear on them, perfectly pressed. This retrieving of a wadded-up mass of clothing was getting to be an aggravating habit.

He left the room door open. Slamming it wasn't worth the energy.

He had to husband all of his energy for tomorrow, when he would finally get the Malice X monkey off his back.

Tomorrow would be better.

Tomorrow *had* to be better.

Women!

FOURTEEN

The damp wind blowing off Bayou St. John felt good against Jules's skin. It was a proud wind, a strong wind. A wind for heroes.

He placed his footlocker on the long, low hood of his Lincoln, and then he unlatched it. The cloak and hood smelled a little musty as he lifted them out of the box and unfolded them. But the breeze quickly freshened them. He wrapped the cloak around his beefy shoulders and fastened the stiff, cracked leather clasps. Then he pulled the hood over his head, gently adjusting its frayed mouth- and eyeholes. The aged fabric was more snug than he remembered it being. It felt like a second skin. A new face. A reborn face.

The wind lifted his cloak behind him and made it snap smartly, like Old Glory whipping from the topmast of a speeding destroyer chasing after deadly U-boats in the Gulf. A light rain began falling from the gray sky. It beat against his chest like a second baptism, scouring the accumulated years away. He felt like a young vampire of sixty-five again—no, *fifty*. There was nothing he couldn't do. All the Veronikas and Malice X's of the world were merely obstacles, just cases to be solved. The Dark Fright had returned.

Jules pointed to the grassy banks of the bayou, now lined by luxury condominiums and the campus of the LSU Dental School. "I can still see it, Doodlebug. It's like it's still there."

"The Higgins Boat Plant?"

"Yeah. The Higgins Boat Plant. Three-quarters of a mile long. Spitting out new landing craft into the bayou as fast as you could snap yer fingers. Eisenhower said the Higgins boats won the war. And we kept the plant safe, didn't we? For three years, we kept it safe."

"We sure did, partner."

Jules took a step back to appraise Doodlebug's new costume. It consisted of a sunburst yellow leotard, metallic purple tights, a matching purple domino mask, and shiny black vinyl go-go boots. The white calfskin gloves were a nice touch. "I'm almost embarrassed to admit it," Jules said, "but this new outfit of yours looks a helluva lot better than the old one ever did. Thanks for remembering the old color scheme, though."

"Sure thing." Doodlebug smiled. "You *know* I'd never pass up a perfect opportunity to dress up."

Jules took a last look along the bayou, imagining the long-gone landing craft factory he'd invested so many long nights protecting. Then he turned toward the car. "Let's hit the road. We got us a stakeout ahead, and I don't want my hood gettin' soggy."

Doodlebug placed himself between Jules and the door. "Costume or no costume, I'm not at all comfortable with your confronting your X before we've finished your training. As your adviser, I'm duty-bound to tell you that."

Jules gently but firmly pushed him aside and opened the door. "You done your duty, then. Look—I know where that bum's gonna be tonight. This shit has gone on long enough. I don't wanna stall no more. Besides, I got me an equalizer. Here. Lemme show you."

He lifted a large box out of the backseat, set it on the Lincoln's roof, and opened it. Then he removed a large black object that looked like a cross between a pistol-grip crossbow and a child's Special Forces action toy.

"Tiny Idaho made this for me. After last night, I came up with the idea of it firin' pellets loaded with garlic powder, in addition to the wooden darts I originally wanted. What a whiz that guy is. He was able to add the extra features while we were hangin' out by his work table talkin'. See this little button here? It lets me switch between the two types of ammo."

"Very clever." Doodlebug took the weapon and examined it from all angles, then handed it back to Jules. "I don't recall the Hooded Terror ever using a gun before."

"Yeah?" Jules carefully put the gun back in the box, then put the box back in the car. "Well, that's because the Hooded Terror was facin' dumb-ass fifth columnists his last time up at bat. That sorry buncha losers could hardly hit the side of the Higgins Boat Plant with a mortar shell from thirty yards. I figure Malice X and his bunch should be a little more bat-tleworthy, them being vampires and all."

"I expect you're right," Doodlebug said. He got into the car. The rain began to beat a little harder against the Lincoln's windows, and the thin reeds by the bayou's edge were splayed flat against the black water by sudden gusts of wind.

♦

Jules drove down Esplanade to North Broad Avenue, a once thriving, middle-class commercial corridor now split evenly between rent-to-own rip-off joints and sagging, boarded-up storefronts. He fiddled with the radio tuner while steering around abandoned cars and rusty muffler husks, trying to get WWOZ to come in strongly. The Lincoln's radio was acting up; the Wild Magnolias' "Iko Iko" faded in and out of clouds of static.

"Fuckin' Ford Motor Company piece of shit . . ." Jules muttered to himself.

"You promised me earlier you were working out a plan," Doodlebug said, tying back his long hair into a sensible braid. "I'd like to hear it. I assume you *have* a plan, don't you?"

"Well, sure. Sure I do. I went and got the gun, didn't I?"

"So you plan to shoot him with the gun?"

"No."

"*No?*"

"No," Jules repeated. "Vampires don't kill other vampires. Maybe I didn't teach you that too good, but that's one of them commandments I live by. The gun? I plan to *threaten* him with the gun. After, y'know, we rough him up a little. To show him we mean business and he can't rail-road me no more. Then I'll talk to him, man to man."

"Uh-*huh*. Do you plan to have this little heart-to-heart before or after he sics his vampire goons on you and rams a stake through your chest?"

Jules snorted. "I've got that worked out, okay? He won't be expectin' us. We can stake out his car, hide in the shadows. I figure he'll have at most one or two bodyguards with him. And between your kung-fu tricks and my Tiny Idaho special, we should be able to knock them out easy. Then big, bad Malice X is all ours."

Jules stopped for the light at the corner of South Broad and Tulane Avenue. The busy intersection was dominated by the gray stone hulk of the Criminal Court Building, a failed, boarded-up Goodfeller's Fried Catfish Shack, and an immaculate, golden-arched McDonald's.

"Y'know, that McDonald's there," Jules said as the light changed, "it appeared overnight. Like magic. I was passin' this corner for weeks while workmen leveled the old building on that corner and prepared the concrete slab. Then one night, they brought the restaurant in on the back of a flatbed. They plunked it down in the concrete, and by the next night it was open for business. Magic."

Doodlebug glanced briefly at this miracle of modern commerce. "Maybe you're expecting a little too much magic tonight? Let's say that everything goes exactly as you described. We take care of his bodyguards and pull him into some dark, empty alleyway. What makes you think you can convince him to leave you alone—short of killing him?"

"*Again* with the killing! You wanted to kill his sister, too, didn't ya? Look, this Malice X, whatever else he may be, he's a businessman. Sellin' drugs is a *business*, just like sellin' toothpaste is. And if he's a businessman, that means he can be bargained with. If I can show him that I can't be pushed around, that screwin' with me is bad for his business, I can get him to cut a deal. Some kinda quota deal on black victims—maybe two a month for me, and the rest of the time I'll get by on white tourists and blood you ship me from California. I got his black binder of customers, don't I? I can always use that as a bargaining chip. Besides, we got somethin' in common . . . we've *both* had to put up with Maureen's shit. *That* should count for something."

"I see. And what's your fallback plan?"

"Fallback plan?"

"What are you going to do if your calculations of Malice X's character are wrong?"

"I dunno—didn't them Tibetan monks of yours teach you some superduper hypnotic whammy you can lay on him?"

"No."

"Bummer." Jules's spirits sagged momentarily, but they quickly reinflated as he experienced a brainstorm. "Hey! I *got* it! Here's what we can do to really put the quakes in him. You tell him about all these nasty extra powers you got. Then you give him a demonstration. Wave your arms around like Mandrake the Magician, then stare at me real hard and mean. And what *I'll* do, see, is I'll do like I did in Maureen's basement and try to turn into two animals at once. I'll change into some horrible two-headed mess, then collapse into a pool of goo. Then you'll wave your arms around again, and I'll reappear as me, moanin' like you just cut my balls off. After that, he'll be thinkin', *Shit—if he'd do that to his buddy, just to prove a point, what'll he do to me?* He'll be crappin' his pants big time!"

Jules waited for some sign of enthusiasm from his companion. But Doodlebug just stared out the window. "Huh-uh," he said finally, shaking his head. "Interesting plan, very creative. But it won't work."

"Why the hell not? It'd sure scare the shit outta *me!*"

"That's the problem. It would scare the shit out of *you.* Malice X isn't another you. He doesn't think like you. The two of you *are* brothers, in a way, just not identical twins. You're more like Cain and Abel. The farmer and the hunter."

"Now wait a minute—Malice X and me are *both* hunters!"

"Technically, maybe. But you've always been content to gather whatever resources are conveniently at hand. That's a big part of why you're so reluctant to give up black victims—you're accustomed to them, they're abundant, and they're convenient. Malice X, on the other hand, appears to be working very hard to change the city's status quo, to remake his environment in his own image—"

"I'm no damn loafer, if that's what you're tryin' to say!"

"No, that's *not* what I'm trying to say. Just let me finish. Cain and Abel both wanted to impress their Creator with their offerings and bask in His approval. Both you and Malice X, over the years, have tried to impress Maureen. According to what Maureen has told us, *your* offerings met with greater favor. In the Bible story, Abel's inadvertent one-upmanship of his brother had fatal consequences. Your position is even worse than Abel's was. Imagine if Adam weren't around, and both Abel and Cain desperately, fervently wanted to marry their mother. Take that ancient stew of jealousy and hurt feelings, stir in some Oedipal yearnings, sprinkle in a generous pinch of racial animosity, and you have a perfect recipe for murder. Very bloody murder."

Jules slowly circled halfway around the brick pile of the Broad Street Pumping Station, part of a massive drainage system designed to suck accumulated rainwater off the streets and flush it into Lake Pontchartrain.

From the look of the clouds overhead, the system would have its work cut out for it tonight. He had to admit Doodlebug's analogy made a certain amount of sense. "So me and Malice X, we're Cain and Abel. What the hell do you want me to do about it?"

"There's only one thing you *can* do. Kill him before he kills you."

Jules pulled over into a bottle-strewn empty lot that, until a few years earlier, had been the Bohn Ford Used Car Lot. He shoved the transmission into park. "Before we go another block, I wanna ask you something. For somebody who lived in a monastery and wears a dress, you come off as one *helluva* bloodthirsty sonofabitch. What's the deal, Doodlebug? Who's the real you?"

Jules turned off the radio. The Lincoln's roughly idling motor made the dashboard rattle as he waited for his friend to answer. Doodlebug sighed. "Do you remember what I told you about the monks' initiation test for new vampires? The choice between the meditation staff and the blood?"

"Yeah. The ones who picked the blood ended up as puddles of red goop."

"That's right." The rain began falling again. It hit the windshield in fat splatty droplets, bursting against the glass like watery kamikazes. "They barely tolerated me. The monks. They let me stay and learn because I was useful to them. My fangs and blood thirst gave them the potential for fresh initiates. They were never rude or unkind. But they let me know, in very subtle ways, that I was among the fallen. That in this life, debased by my surrender to the blood lust, I have no chance of redemption. They taught me to hope that, if I diligently study the paths of discipline, I might make the right choice during my next incarnation as a vampire."

Next incarnation? In all his long decades as a vampire, Jules had never once thought about what might come after. "Jeez . . . that sounds even more hard-assed than Catholicism."

Doodlebug managed a grim smile. "Perhaps. So, my friend, maybe you see why I don't share your view that ending a vampire's existence is wrong. With the exception of that small group of monks on their mountaintop, all of us vampires are tainted by having drunk the blood of our fellow creatures. All of us are fallen. By ending a vampire's endless life of blood drinking, I may free a fallen soul for a second chance to achieve true and pure immortality."

"Whoa whoa *whoa*!" Jules whacked his steering wheel in frustration.

Again Doodlebug was twisting the rules of vampirism into crazy knots! "Just before, you was tellin' me I have to kill Malice X before he kills *me*, right? And now you're sayin' it would be a *good thing* if I got killed? Ain't that a contradiction of terms?"

Doodlebug smiled. "You're swifter on the uptake than I sometimes give you credit for. But don't worry—this isn't some plot on my part to get you killed. I want you to have the best shot possible at doing 'the vampire thing' right on your next go-around, and we haven't finished your training." He patted Jules's shoulder reassuringly. "Besides, there's no telling what sort of person you might be reborn as . . . and I have to admit to a certain fondness for the imperfect-but-charming vampire you are now."

Jules's head stopped swimming. As convoluted as his friend's reasoning was, it made a bit more sense to him now. "Well . . . okay, then." He shifted the transmission lever back into drive. "But one more thing— we're at least gonna *try* my original plan, right? Before we do anything more drastic?"

"Your problem demands your solution. I only advise. You're the boss, Jules."

He didn't detect any sarcasm or ambiguity in his partner's voice. Jules pulled out of the empty lot and turned onto Washington Avenue, heading for Central City and Club Hit 'N' Run.

He passed a large white-columned building that he remembered as the Broadmoor Cinema. Now it was the Rhodes Funeral Home. Jules glanced at the long black Cadillac hearses lined up in front, and a frightening thought occurred to him.

Doodlebug had said he didn't want Jules to die, not yet. But would his friend, ashamed of his own fallenness, thirsting for a second chance, welcome his *own* death in the coming battle?

♦

Jules performed a slow drive-by past Club Hit 'N' Run. He circled the block, searching for some sign that their quarry was inside. The club occupied both halves of a shotgun double house on Melpomene Street, half a block off Oretha Castle Haley Boulevard. As he scanned the trash-strewn streets for Malice X's Cadillac limousine, Jules's mind wandered to the days when Oretha Castle Haley Boulevard had been called Dryades Street. Back then, before World War II, it had been home to numerous Jewish businesses. Jules recalled the bearded men, wearing their funny little black skullcaps, who had run the bakeries, shoe stores, and tailor shops, all open on Sunday but closed on Saturday. By the early 1970s, when the street was renamed for a local civil rights activist, the bearded men in their skullcaps were long gone. Now the area was an economic fringe zone, an incubator for gangsters and petty criminals, avoided by tourists and middle-class locals like a radioactive crater. Jules had actually done a good business there over the past couple decades; most Central City residents didn't own cars, at least not reliable ones, and he was one of the few cabdrivers willing to respond to calls from the neighborhood.

The sight of a familiar long, black, custom-built Seville jarred Jules back to the present. "There she blows," he said, pointing to an alleyway off Melpomene Street, across the street from the club, four storefronts closer to the river. The brightly polished limousine had been backed into the alleyway, mostly out of sight of the street. A pair of orange barricades had been placed at the mouth of the alley, presumably to prevent any other cars from parking in front of the limousine and blocking it in.

"It's a good setup for us," Jules said. "He's gotta go back in that alleyway sometime tonight to get his car. I didn't see any rear exit; the back of the alley is blocked by that gardening supplies warehouse on Baronne. Once he's in there, we can trap him and any bodyguards real easy."

"Maybe it's *too* good a setup," Doodlebug replied. "Didn't you see that guard lounging by the side of the car? The car's windows are tinted—there could be half a dozen more guards waiting inside."

"Then we'll just have to take care of them, won't we? Remember 'The Case of the Skull-Faced Nazis'? How many crummy guards did we have to polish off *that* time? Compared to that, this'll be a cakewalk."

"Whatever you say, Jules." Doodlebug didn't sound convinced.

Jules turned the corner onto Baronne. "Hey—while we're in uniform, it's 'Hooded Terror,' 'Terror,' or 'H.T.' "

"Oh, yes . . . it's *vital* that we protect our secret identities. How could I forget?"

A pair of large, grayish brown German shepherds chased each other across the street, forcing Jules to slam on the Lincoln's brakes. "Shit! Fuckin' dogs got a death wish! Damn mutts ain't got no collars, neither." Muttering to himself about the dearth of dogcatchers in New Orleans, he parked along the curb while he still had a few shreds of asbestos left on his brake drums.

"Well, H.T., how do you propose getting that guard out of the way?"

"Simplicity itself, my dear D.B.," Jules said, regaining his composure as he cut the motor. "Once you take off that mask, you can pass for a civilian real easily, considerin' the kooky way women dress nowadays. So here's what you'll do, see? All you gotta do is waltz up to that guard like some ditzy, airhead tourist who's lost her way; boy, I *wish* we had a Hurricane glass! Anyway, you distract the guard—show a little leg, and bounce those little titties of yours around. Use your imagination; I don't wanna think about it much. Get him to turn away from the mouth of the alleyway. Then I'll come in with a plank or a pipe and whack him over the head."

Doodlebug rolled his eyes. "You've been reading *way* too many pulp mystery stories, Jules—"

" 'H.T.' "

"Whatever! What stereotypical thinking! Do you really think *every* man drops a hundred IQ points whenever he sees a woman sashaying his way? What if he doesn't like white women? What if he's a happily married deacon in his church? For that matter, what if he's gay?"

Huh. Creepy, but maybe Doodlebug had a point there. "So you don't like that plan?"

"No—I definitely do not."

"Well, okay, don't get your panties in a bunch. Here's another plan. If he's human and he's eaten anything at all in the last twelve hours, I can get him runnin' outta that alley like a rat with its tail on fire. Then *you* can whack him over the head."

"How do you plan to manage that?"

Jules grinned beneath his hood. "Hey, you ain't the *only* one who's developed new powers since that last time we met."

"If this would only work on a human, what do you think the chances are that he's a vampire?"

"I dunno—why wouldn't Malice X have human flunkies, as well as vampires?"

"Good point. He could only afford to create a small number of vampire followers; he needs to supply them all with blood, and if he makes too many of them, there's no way he could remain inconspicuous for long. Maybe only his top lieutenants are vampires. Keeping an eye on his limo is a fairly low-level chore. Still, if the guard *is* a vampire, what then?"

Jules grabbed his unwieldy black dart gun from the backseat. "Then there's *this*."

Doodlebug raised an eyebrow. "So you'll kill him with a dart through the heart?"

"Who said anything about killin'? I'll *wound* him. And then you can whack him over the head."

There was no shortage of scrap lumber lying in the derelict lots along this stretch of Baronne Avenue. Doodlebug quickly selected a solid, hefty plank for himself. They turned the corner onto Melpomene Street and instinctively ducked within the shadows. Darkness covered the street and broken sidewalks like a muddy, threadbare blanket. Jules and Doodlebug wrapped themselves in this blanket as they approached the alleyway that held Malice X's black limousine.

Jules flattened himself against the brick wall adjoining the entrance to the alley. Why was he hesitating? Was he nervous about going into action as the Hooded Terror again? Afraid he couldn't live up to the heroic tradition he'd established for that identity? Going into action was like jumping off a high dive, he told himself; the worst part was taking that first step, but then gravity took over. He peeled himself off the wall and lurched into the alleyway, his hooded bulk blocking nearly two-thirds of its width.

"Hey, Jeeves, how about a spin in that car a yours?"

The guard gaped at the tremendous apparition in front of him. "Who or *what* the fuck are you supposed to be?"

Jules steeled himself for a full-strength application of his Diarrhea Stare. Luckily, the guard was looking him right in the eyes. "You can call me the Hooded Terror," he said, forcing himself to recall his last few solid meals and their terrible aftermaths. "The 'Hooded' part is a no-brainer. The 'Terror' part will become obvious real soon."

The guard reached for his holstered gun, but then he clutched his stomach and doubled over. "Oh *Mama*—!" Horrifying rumbles and squealings emitted from the man's gut as he stumbled past Jules toward the street. Jules barely had time to turn around before a resounding *thunk!* announced that Doodlebug had performed his half of the operation.

Together they dragged the unconscious man to the back of the alley. Jules sucked in his belly as best he could but still scraped his love handles against the rough brick wall and the polished flanks of the car. It was a tight squeeze, but he made it.

Doodlebug placed his nose close to the tinted windows and stared inside the car. "I can't see anyone. If no one came piling out while we were shanghaiing that guard, I don't suppose we have any hiders in there."

"Then let's go find us a good stakeout spot."

They crouched behind an abandoned Mercury Grand Marquis sitting on Melpomene two houses down from the alleyway, situated so that Malice X wouldn't walk past it on his way back to his limousine. The massive Mercury made an excellent vantage point; all four wheels and tires had been removed, so the vehicle sat flush on the ground, and weeds had begun colonizing the rusting shell. With the way weeds grow in New Orleans, Jules figured, in a few more years it wouldn't be recognizable as a car at all. It would be a big green lump.

The two large stray dogs that Jules had nearly run down trotted over to their hiding place. They sniffed Doodlebug's legs and wagged their tails. "Geddoutta here!" Jules whispered fiercely, shooing them away with a piece of loose weatherstripping from the car. "We ain't got nothing for you to eat! Keep buggin' me and I swear I won't *touch* the brakes next time. *Scat!*" The dogs scampered off in the direction of the club.

They watched the club for the next half hour. The left side of the building, labeled HIT, was larger and better maintained, benefiting from a fresh coat of paint and deeply tinted, double-paned windows. The right side, wearing a sign that read RUN, was hardly more than a take-out liquor shack, marred by a sagging porch, dangerously leaning steps, and flaking paint. The only discernible activity came from the few customers who entered the RUN portion and exited a few minutes later carrying quarts of beer. Snatches of rap and R&B music escaped into the hot night each time they opened the leaflet-plastered door. No one entered or left the HIT side, at least not by the front door. The windows, tinted like those on the limousine, revealed nothing. The only sound to escape that side of the building was the steady hum of a powerful air-conditioning condenser.

"Not much action here," Jules said, more to break the silence than anything else.

"No," Doodlebug replied. "If Malice X conducts his drug and business transactions in that building, we can safely assume he's doing it in the nicer side. It's likely his customers have a less conspicuous entrance than the front door. Maybe a rear entrance that connects with one of those abandoned houses on the other side of the block."

"But no matter which door he uses, he's gotta come back this way, to get his car."

"Unless he contacts his driver by cell phone, and his driver pulls the car around to the back entrance."

"Yeah. But tonight his driver's takin' an unscheduled nap. So he's gotta come. Sometime before sunrise, he's gotta come."

◆

After another twenty minutes, Jules's adrenaline rush had completely subsided. It was replaced by the kind of dull torpor he remembered from thousands of nights of waiting for customers in his cab. The broken sidewalk was beginning to make his rear end and lower back ache, despite the thin cushioning provided by his wadded-up cloak. He kept having to shoo scurrying palmetto bugs away from the two of them, although Doodlebug didn't seem bothered by the big cockroaches. To top things off, their observation post didn't exactly smell wintergreen fresh. The pungent, chemical odor of dripping motor oil mingled with the scents of human and dog piss and week-old garbage, a combination Jules doubted even a roach could love.

Jules tapped his friend on the shoulder. "Hey, D.B., don't you wish we were out by the bayou again, stakin' out the Higgins Boat Plant? Boy, were those nights sweet. Nothing around but us and the moon and the trees and the water. Everything smelled clean, like the ocean. Shit, I even miss them ol' Nazis."

Doodlebug smiled, but his eyes were serious. "Watch yourself, Jules. Too much nostalgia can be like a cancer. It'll eat you up from the inside."

Jules waved off the remark. "Oh, c'mon . . . tell me you don't miss plenty of stuff about the old days. What's so bad about nostalgia? What's wrong with wantin' the same things I've always wanted, with missin' the way things used to be?"

Doodlebug ran his forefinger along the leaves of a vine that had twisted itself luxuriously around the Mercury's rear axle. "Nothing's wrong with wanting the same things you've always wanted. We're all entitled to want whatever it is we do. But you need to be flexible enough to seek those same old goals in new ways. The world around us is constantly changing. Sometimes even *we* change. Take a deep look at yourself. Maybe the Jules of today actually wants different things than the Jules of fifty years ago did."

"Yeah, whatever," Jules mumbled. A flying roach landed on the toe of his boot. He flicked it off, giving it a nice spiral trajectory. It splatted against the broken shell of the Mercury's side-view mirror.

Doodlebug reached over and yanked the corner of his hood; Jules's eyeholes ended up over his nose. "So, Man of Mystery, are you going to tell me anything more about what happened to you last night? Maureen and I were privy to an ugly phone conversation. And you came home pretty torn up. But the only thing I could get out of you was that you'd learned where Malice X would be tonight."

Jules couldn't decide whether to share with Doodlebug what he'd learned—about the vast governmental apparatus that sought to crush him by any underhanded, sneaky, disreputable means available. The thought of it made his blood boil—his own government, the very government he'd fought to protect back in World War II! He squeezed the Mercury's front wheel rim until the rusted sheet metal crumpled in his fist. Should he tell Doodlebug? A distraction like that could only hurt right now. One threat at a time. Besides, if he went into the whole story, he'd probably end up having to tell the sexy parts, too. And he definitely didn't want to rehash all *that*.

"Not now, kid. Maybe when you're older. Us old bulls, we gotta keep *some* secrets."

His friend let the matter drop. Jules was about to lose himself again in memories of his golden war years when the door of the RUN club burst open. Jules leapt from Memory Lane back to Melpomene Street—every muscle in his massive frame tensed as he waited to see who would exit the building.

Two pear-shaped, middle-aged women stepped out onto the rickety porch, beers in hand. They lingered to talk a few seconds longer with someone still inside the bar, then laughed and walked down the uneven steps to the sidewalk. Jules's stomach growled. He found himself licking his lips; in happier times, these ladies could've meant an evening's amusement, followed by a good, hearty meal.

Both were wearing T-shirts with a photo of a woman's face on them. As they walked down the opposite sidewalk in his direction, Jules was able to get a better look at their shirts. Beneath the photo of the woman's face were the words: HAVE YOU SEEN ME? Jules's blood ran cold as he remembered the posters he'd seen taped to shop windows in the French Quarter. He was almost afraid to look at the silk-screened image of the woman's face, but he forced himself to. Sure enough . . . it was Bessie. Bessie's plump brown face was plastered on a pair of massive chests bobbling toward him up the sidewalk. A ghost in the shape of a steel bear trap, she had clamped hold of his leg and wouldn't let him go.

"Sonofa*bitch* . . . I can't believe it . . . she was a nobody, a nothing, *why*—"

"Jules, what are you talking about?"

Just then, the door on the HIT side of the club swung open for the first time since they'd arrived on Melpomene Street. A broad-shouldered, tall black man exited. He was made even taller by six-inch platform shoes and a wide-brimmed hat crowned with massive white feathers. Jules recognized him immediately. It was Malice X. And he was alone.

"Forget about it," Jules said breathlessly. "That's *him*. It's showtime."

"That's him? Where are his bodyguards? This doesn't feel right—"

Jules clamped a paw over Doodlebug's mouth. "Shaddup, kid. I'll never get another chance like this. Just follow my lead."

They watched as the black vampire crossed the street without bothering to check for oncoming traffic. *Confident bastard,* Jules thought. *Boy, am I lookin' forward to wipin' that cocky smirk off his face.* He pulled himself into a crouch, ready to spring toward the alley's entrance. His heart raced. His knees were shaking—whether from excitement, fear, or the strain of holding up his 450 pounds, he couldn't tell.

He picked up his gun from the sidewalk. Malice X walked into the alleyway. It was now or never—in seconds, the black vampire would discover his unconscious sentry and race back out onto the street. About twenty yards of broken sidewalk separated Jules's hiding place from the alley's mouth. As a young man, he could've run that distance in little more than five seconds. Now? Who knew?

He pushed off from the car and launched himself into a run. Holding the unwieldy gun in his right hand threw his stride off. The soles of his boots sounded like small bomb bursts as they slapped the sidewalk. He felt his cloak billow out behind him like a battle flag.

Jules reached the entrance to the alleyway. He nearly panicked—he couldn't see Malice X anywhere. But then he spotted his rival behind the limousine, hunched over the man Doodlebug had knocked unconscious.

Breathing hard, Jules spread his legs wide and aimed the gun at Malice X with both hands, a pose he remembered Harry Callahan striking in the *Dirty Harry* movies. "Freeze, dickhead!" he shouted with the most aggressive growl he could muster. "We got you covered!"

Malice X stood. "Who's *this*?" He took two steps forward, halting next to the Cadillac's rear tire. "Lemme see . . . Orson Welles is dead an' buried, so I guess it must be my ol' buddy Jules Duchon. Who're you two dressed up as? Fat Man and Robin?"

Jules fingered the gun menacingly. "An' who are *you* supposed to be—Chuckles the Pimp?"

Malice X clutched his heart. "You *wound* me! Actually, Wednesday night is Classic Blaxploitation Night in my household; last week, I dressed as Truck Turner. Helps keep those Hump-Nights lively, seein' as I plan on being around for an eternity of them."

"Maybe you won't be around for as many as you think," Jules said. "Unless you agree to play ball with me, that pimp suit'll be the blax- ploitation outfit they bury you in."

"You think?" The black vampire walked steadily up the narrow cor- ridor between the car and the wall. His eyes flashed darkly. "That wasn't very nice, what you did to my sister."

Jules kept the gun pointed at his rival's chest. "We coulda done a lot worse. But we didn't. 'Cause we're reasonable men. But not so reasonable that I won't fire half a dozen mini stakes through what passes for your heart if you keep comin' at me."

"Oh, you won't," Malice X said. But he stopped nonetheless. "Y'know why not? 'Cause if you *were* gonna do it, you woulda done it al- ready. You wanna *talk*, is what you want. You wanna say your piece, get all them heavy frustrations off your fat chest. Then you wanna hear what I got to say back. You know the rules of the game as well as I do—the nasty ol' villain *always* gets to spill his nasty ol' plans before the hero does him in. Break the rules, an' you'll never work in this town again."

Jules's face went hard as weathered marble. "You don't think I'll use this gun?"

Malice X scowled. "Fuck *no*, man."

Jules angled the gun's nose up five degrees and pulled the trigger. The mechanized crossbow-type mechanism fired its wooden dart at a ve- locity of five hundred feet per second. The projectile struck Malice X in the concavity just below his left collarbone. On its journey into his gray- ish flesh, it broke the links of a gaudy gold chain. The vampire's medal- lion clattered to the cobblestone alley.

"Oww." Malice X looked down at the dart protruding from his shoulder, a disbelieving look on his face. He clutched the tail of the dart and yanked it loose, offering no more than a brief grimace, although blood ran freely down his partly bare chest, staining his white silk shirt. He crushed the dart to splinters in his fist. Then he leaned down to the cobblestones and scooped up his medallion, dropping it into a pocket beneath one of his jacket's winglike lapels.

"Huh. You actually managed to *surprise* me. Didn't think you could do that. Tell you what. Since you managed to exceed my expectations, you get to say your piece."

Jules didn't relax his aim. "That's mighty cocky, fer a guy who's got a gun pointed at his heart."

"Hey—either you can waste my patience on stale macho banter, or you can say your piece. Your choice, fat man."

Jules took a deep breath. Although his heart still beat double time, he felt calm. Amazingly calm. "Okay. This shit between you and me, it ends here. Tonight. Look, I can understand you bein' pissed off at me and all. I know how Maureen can be. I know how that woman can get under your skin, believe me. But you've had your pound a flesh. You burned down my house. You destroyed a century's worth of good stuff. You made my life hell for a month. Enough is enough already."

Jules gathered his thoughts. He'd start the bargaining a little high; it was always smart to ask for more than you really wanted. "Now me, I'm a reasonable man. I got you in my crosshairs. I could kill you right now. But I'm not gonna. I'm not gonna, 'cause we're gonna make us a deal. Bottom line: There's no way in hell I'm leavin' New Orleans. I was born here back when William McKinley was president. This town's in my blood. That's Number One. Two: A vampire in this town can't expect to make any kinda decent livin' preying on white victims only. The way *I* see things, vampires is vampires and victims is victims, no matter what color they are. A fair share is a fair share, period. And that's all I want— *my fair share*. Here's my deal. I can make do with, oh, let's say one black victim every two weeks. Twenty-six a year. No, tell you what, we'll make that twenty-*five* a year, 'cause I'll skip one black victim in honor of Black History Month."

Malice X looked at Jules with the same disbelief as when he'd stared down at the dart protruding from his body. Only this time, the disbelieving look dissolved into laughter so hard he doubled over and clutched his knees. "*Man,* that's the *funniest* fuckin' shit I heard all month!" He wiped his eyes with a monogrammed silk handkerchief snatched from his pocket. "I'm tempted to keep you around just for yucks. You want a deal? *Here's* the deal. I play around with you 'til it ain't no fun anymore. Then I kill you. Deal?"

Jules didn't see any reason for laughter. "I'm still the one holding the gun, asshole. Maybe after your return trip from Fantasy Island you'll be willin' to talk turkey—" He was distracted by cold, wet noses burrowing beneath his pant legs. He glanced down to see two pairs of gray canine eyes staring into his. "*Again?* Fuckin' mutts been doggin' me all night long! Shoo! Geddoutta here!" Keeping the gun pointed at his adversary, Jules kicked furiously at the two large dogs, whose muzzles and tails flashed within the folds of his black cloak. "Doodlebug! How about makin' yourself useful here?"

"Uh, Jules, I don't think these animals are *dogs*—"

Malice X's sharp, high-pitched laughter echoed through the alley-way again. "And you think *I'm* the one on a trip to Fantasy Island? I knew you'd be comin' after me here. Didn't take no big detective work; I knew it from what you stole from my sister's house. It was just a matter of waitin' for you to show. And since you read my business binders, you know I'm the source for a new, improved type of street drug, a derivative of heroin I call Horse-X, patent pending. What you *don't* know is what it is that makes my Horse-X so special. Oh, sure, it's three times as potent as run-of-the-mill heroin; that's what makes it attractive to the user. What makes it attractive to *me*, apart from the fact that it buys me things like this fine-ass Cadillac car here, is a very *interesting* property of my blood when it's combined with an opiate. See, anybody who snorts or shoots up the stuff becomes *exquisitely* sensitive to my hypnotic powers. I don't even hafta be lookin' at 'em, Jules—if they're within a quarter mile of me, all I hafta do is *think* real hard about what I want 'em to do, and I play the suckers like dime-store kazoos."

The black vampire smiled. "Now, how many users and abusers of Horse-X do you figure are hangin' within a quarter mile of this here *lovely* alleyway?"

"Kill him, Jules," Doodlebug said, his voice hard as tempered steel. "Kill him while you still can."

Jules's thoughts were as scattered as the blobs of color in a Jackson Pollock painting. It had been so perfect. He'd been doing it all *his* way. But now everything was spinning out of control again—

"*Jules!*"

"What—?"

"Oh *shit*, just give it here—"

Doodlebug grabbed the gun from Jules's hands. With a fluid and in-tuitive motion, he fired a pair of wooden shafts directly at Malice X's heart.

"Too slow, little mama!" The darts struck and pierced Malice X's velvet jacket, but the wily vampire had already transformed his upper torso to mist. The projectiles clattered harmlessly against the far wall.

Other sounds jolted Jules from his stasis. From somewhere above him, hurried footsteps scuffled, dislodging roof tiles that exploded to dust on the cobblestones below. Heavy fabric unfurled, disturbing the stagnant air in the alleyway. Jules looked up. The storm clouds and faint stars were partially blocked by the tight mesh of a heavy-gauge net, no doubt put there by some of Malice's faceless minions. This batproof barrier covered the entire top of the alleyway.

But not the entrance. Malice X stood at the back of the alley. They could make a break for it—

Jules swiveled away from his nemesis. Behind him, Doodlebug had already trained Tiny Idaho's gun on a new set of targets. The dogs—no, *wolves*—were shimmering like oil slicks on water, their forms elongating, growing more muscular and less hirsute. Their faces foreshortened, taking on features that Jules knew all too well—the feral leers of the vampires who had hunted him through the streets of the Quarter.

That wasn't the worst of it. Far from it. Jules's balls shriveled when he heard the staccato impacts coming from the street, like the approach of a rapidly moving hailstorm. But it wasn't hail. It was the sound of dozens of footfalls. Dozens of mind-controlled zombies converging on the alleyway.

The Hooded Terror closed his eyes and wished he were back at the bayou again.

FIFTEEN

Too fast—everything was happening too *fast*!

Jules rushed Malice X, trying to pin him against the wall with his superior bulk. But his antagonist avoided Jules's clumsy lunge easily, leaping over him onto the roof of the Cadillac.

An inhuman scream made Jules turn back to the alley's entrance. Doodlebug had fired two darts into the face of the shorter of Malice X's two vampire lieutenants, catching him midway through his transformation from wolf to man. Almost simultaneously, Doodlebug hurled a vicious side kick through the taller vampire's midsection. Jules recognized this vampire as Cowboy Hat, the leader of the toughs who'd attacked him near Maureen's. The kick dislodged wet hunks of gray proto-matter, splattering them against the brick wall, disrupting Cowboy Hat's change back to human.

"Jules! Catch!"

Doodlebug pitched the crossbow back toward Jules. It missed the net covering the top of the alleyway by inches. The big vampire reached up and—*yes! Caught* it! The catch felt like the climax of a recurring dream. He was back on the St. Ignatius football field, running long for a decisive touchdown. Usually he dropped the ball, but tonight—well, tonight he caught the gun, all right, but his thick fingers got wedged in the magazine, spilling darts and garlic pellets onto the ground.

Shit! Tiny Idaho had only given him a single lesson on how to load the thing! He'd never collect the spilled ammo and reload it in time!

The vampire with two darts protruding from his face lunged wildly at Jules. His agonized curses were eloquent testimony that having his cheekbone and nose re-form around those two missiles must've hurt like hell. Not sure the gun would fire, Jules flung his free hand forward to hold off his attacker. His palm collided with the blunt end of the dart protruding from the attacking vampire's nose. The unintended impact drove the missile deeper into his skull. Spasming violently, the black vampire plunged to the ground, letting loose a howl that must've shaken the stained-glass windows of Garden District mansions a mile away.

Jules stared, horrified, as his erstwhile opponent writhed in agony on the cobblestones at his feet. He'd never done *anything* like that to a fellow vampire before.

The smack of leather against bone, coming from the alley's entrance, distracted Jules from his ethical predicament. All flying feet and speed-blurred fists, Doodlebug was holding off a horde of mind-controlled neighborhood folk who surged, blank-faced and silent, toward the alley-way. He was trying desperately to slash an escape route through the seemingly endless bodies, tossing attackers aside like a garbage collector heaving trash sacks. But by sheer weight of numbers and insensitivity to pain, the zombies were slowly forcing him back into the alley.

Before Jules could take a step to help his friend, viselike talons dug into the flesh of his calves. "Muthahfuckah," a pain-racked voice croaked. "Gonna make you pay for what you done to Sonny and me . . . gonna make you pay in *spades*, soon as I get myself togethah—"

Cowboy Hat hung on to Jules's legs with unholy strength, even though his lower body was only tenuously connected with his torso. Jules watched, both fascinated and sickened, as Cowboy Hat's body completed its transformation, rebuilding itself in the process. His bones fused and veins reknotted as the torn shreds of his skin surged together like a colony of mating slugs.

Dazed, nauseated, Jules pointed the gun at his assailant's forehead. "Leggo, or I'll . . . I'll shoot. I swear I will—"

Cowboy Hat's face was twisted by pain and hate. "Do yo' *worst*, you fat fuck. You *still* be a dead man—"

Not knowing whether any ammunition remained in the magazine, Jules closed his eyes and pulled the gun's trigger. He heard a click as a cartridge slid into firing position, a *phffutt* as it raced out the barrel, and a rotten-egg *blatt* as it struck home.

The odor of something unbearably pungent burned the hairs inside his nose and forced Jules's eyes open—the stench of concentrated garlic.

Cowboy Hat immediately released his grip on Jules's legs. He bellowed like a branded mule and rubbed frantically at his eyes. Jules was close enough to feel the garlic fumes bite at the patches of skin exposed by gaps in his costume. As he was backing away toward the car, powerful arms reached from behind him and yanked the weapon from his hands.

"That's a *nasty*-ass toy you got there, Jules," Malice X said. "Lemme take that off yo' hands, boy—that's *definitely* for children over the age of three."

He squinched one eye shut and sighted along the barrel, aiming at Jules's crotch. "Shee-*oot!* You could *hurt* somebody with this! There oughta be a *recall* on these!" He grinned and wadded up the crossbow gun's metal and plastic armature like a soggy paper plate. Then he tossed it over his shoulder into a trash heap at the back of the alley.

Jules braced himself for an attack. But Malice X merely crossed his arms and smiled. He made no movement in Jules's direction at all.

Why isn't he comin' at me?

As if to answer Jules's unspoken question, Malice X leaned languidly against the wall and said, "Man, this is more fun than front-row seats at cage-match wrassling." But the sweat on his forehead betrayed the strain caused by mind-controlling his dozens of drug-addicted slaves.

Jules took the risk of turning his back on his nemesis—no matter how good Doodlebug was, his friend couldn't hold out alone against an onrushing tide of zombies forever. He waded into the fray, a buffalo charging into a tightly bunched flock of sheep. Only these sheep had knives, tire irons, and busted planks with bent nails protruding from the ends. One woman in a pink dressing gown pounded his flabby side with a can of baby formula.

Jules found himself experiencing a savage, angry exhilaration. His assaults didn't have anywhere near the fluidity and grace of Doodlebug's twirling kicks, but he had mass in his favor. He used his elbows like a lesser man would use a two-by-four. His fists were the size of whole frozen chickens. All the frustration, hurt, and humiliation of the past month powered those fists like rocket fuel. He hadn't cut loose like this since his glory days in the early 1940s. But for every wino or saggy-shorts teenager he flattened, three more surged forward.

The sidewalk outside the alley began to resemble a set from a Sam Peckinpah war movie—bleeding bodies stacked like sandbags. But each "sandbag" still writhed with baleful life, and, short of a broken neck, eventually surged back into the attacking horde. Individually, none of the assailants was much of a threat. But cumulatively, their clumsy blows, knife thrusts, and attempts to stake him were wearing Jules down.

"D.B.!" Jules shouted as he body-slammed the baby-formula-wielding woman against the brick wall for the third time. "Any bright ideas?"

"Maneuver Double-Eagle!" Doodlebug shouted back in the midst of breaking a man's arm. "Cover me while I change, and then I'll cover you!"

Maneuver Double-Eagle? What the fuck is that pantyhose-wearin' fruitcake talkin' about? Jules watched, dumbfounded, as his friend launched into a gold-medal-winning backflip, landed on the roof of the limousine, and immediately stripped off his top and bra. Jules's view of his friend's augmented pulchritude was a brief one, for Doodlebug quickly transformed into the largest bat Jules had ever seen.

Double-Eagle, huh? Jules glanced at the narrow gap between the hanging net and the heads of his attackers. *Oh, I get it—!*

Taking advantage of Jules's distraction, three zombies dashed into the alleyway, seeking to grab Doodlebug before he could take to the air. But Jules grabbed the biggest one by the legs and swung him like a club, bouncing one zombie off the Cadillac's chrome grille and knocking the other into a woman who was trying to brain Jules with pieces of a baby stroller. Doodle-Bat vigorously flapped his six-foot wingspan, launching himself from the top of the limo.

Now it was Jules's turn. There was no way *he* was going to do a backflip onto the Cadillac's roof—instead, he picked up a rusted car bumper, slung it across his shoulders like a yoke, put his head down low, and charged. Four hundred and fifty pounds of vampire plus fifty pounds of steel made for a formidable battering ram. Jules knocked down six attackers and threw a dozen more off-balance. Then he retreated to the front of the Cadillac.

Jules didn't bother stripping off his hood, cloak, or clothing; he wouldn't be flying under his own power, and the bunched-up fabric would give Doodlebug something to grab hold of. Instead, he concentrated on transforming, double time, to the smallest bat he could. The painful melting/shrinking/stretching sensations were almost old hat *Little, littler, littlest—!*

Seconds later he was swimming in a sea of clothing. Strong talons gripped his hood, and Jules felt himself leaving the cobblestones. His boots and pants remained behind as the two bats struggled into the air, levitated by a single set of wings.

Fingers grasped at his hanging cloak, pulling the two of them back down. Suddenly, Jules heard broken, staticky words in his head—*shirt, grab hold of shirt*—so he disentangled himself from his black cloak and sank his talons into his white shirt, just before Doodlebug let go of the cloak. Then he climbed up the shirt to Doodlebug's tiny red-haired legs and grabbed hold of them with his own feet. His friend flapped toward the narrow window of open sky between the net's edge and a sea of grasping hands.

The world was upside down. Zombies clung to a ceiling of cobblestones and jumped down at him, only to snap back as though held fast by bungee cords. Those words in his head—they were *Doodlebug's*? He could read Doodlebug's mind because they were both bats—? No time for puzzles—open sky was coming up fast. There'd be plenty of time later to ask Doodlebug about his latest trick—

At the last possible second, figures skulking on the rooftops along the alley unfurled a second net. Its mesh web tauntingly closed the gap just as Doodlebug reached it. His wing tips caught momentarily in the thick nylon strands. Jules thought he'd be dropped for sure. But with powerful wing beats and amazing control, Doodlebug was able to extricate himself without dropping his passenger. Even so, the tiny door on their cage had just been flung shut in their faces. Jules's heart sank. They were trapped. And Cowboy Hat had shaken off his garlic poisoning; he looked ready to eat stainless steel and shit Ginsu knives.

Jules heard the staticky voice in his head again. *Malice X . . . key*— This time, pictures accompanied the barely distinct words. He saw what Doodlebug wanted him to do. But it seemed impossible—*no one* could transform as fast as he was being asked to. Then another image invaded his brain. The image of a miniature train racing steadily around its track. It calmed him, centered him. As they approached Malice X, Jules knew he could do what he had to.

He concentrated on an empty bathtub. He pictured his hands turning on the spigots. Liquid Jules flowed out the faucet. He grabbed the spigots and twisted them to full blast.

Mass flowed back to him in an overwhelming rush. Once again, he was 450 pounds of fighting-mad vampire. A Jules-bomb, dropped from fifteen feet up. Plunging toward his nemesis, empowered by gravity and velocity to squash him with thousands of pounds of crushing force. Malice X stared upward, frozen by the apparition of a falling, naked Jules. They locked eyes. Jules, dead on target, smiled ruthlessly.

And then Malice X, lizard-quick, stepped out of the way.

(Cripes, is this gonna hurt—!)

Jules belly flopped onto the cobblestones. The impact was equivalent to a Chevy Suburban and a city bus, both cruising at twenty miles per hour, smacking head-on. Unfortunately for Jules, he was the Chevy Suburban. Every puff of air was expelled from his lungs. Three ribs cracked on impact.

He lay stunned for a few seconds. Then he sucked precious air into his chest, which felt full of broken glass, and struggled to get to his feet. *Hurtin' in places I didn't know existed—gotta get up or I'll be dead for real.* . . . He made it to his hands and knees before incredibly powerful hands dug into his fat shoulders and, amazingly, lifted him into the air.

"Man, I owe you—*uh!*—a whole *world* of hurt for what you done to Sonny and me," Cowboy Hat said, grunting with exertion. "I'm gonna—*uh!*—stash you somewheres you won't weasel away from, while I gets my *tools* ready."

His vision clouding with pain, Jules saw brown wings dive toward his assailant, but Malice X knocked Doodlebug's bat-form aside before he could claw Cowboy Hat's face. He heard the shadowy vampires on the roofs above him laughing. Warm drops of liquid struck his face; were they spitting at him? No—it had started raining again. Then his center of gravity shifted radically, grinding his broken ribs together. Cowboy Hat body-slammed him into the narrow gap between the limousine and the brick wall. The pain Jules experienced in transit was nothing compared to the pain of his landing.

Blackness . . .

When he opened his eyes again, he wasn't sure whether he was awake or in the midst of a nightmare. His eardrums were stabbed with shrieks of approaching sirens. The hot-rodded V-8 in the limousine's engine bay thrummed into life, vibrating the car's flank roughly against his wounded side. The dozen zombies in the alleyway looked like they were emerging from comas. Some immediately fell to the ground and screamed as they experienced the extent of their injuries. Others ran or limped off into the night, scattered by the sirens like a pack of foraging rats startled by the sudden brightness of a flashlight.

Jules felt a pair of hands grasp his shoulders and massage them in a friendly, almost brotherly way. "Hey, Jules?" Malice X's breath blew hot and damp against the side of Jules's face. "It's been real, and it's been fun. Heck, I hate to take a powder when things're just gettin', y'know, *intense* an' all. But it just ain't *smart* for a vampire to get hisself thrown in Central Lockup. And you an' me, we're *smart* bloodsuckahs, huh? Assuming you don't get sun-fried in some jail cell, this'll let us stretch out our fun 'til the next boogie-down. The big one. Me, I can hardly wait."

The hands left his shoulders. A few seconds later Jules heard a door on the opposite side of the limousine open. "Oh, Jules? One last word to the wise. Or the not-so-wise. Get some pussy while you still can."

The door slammed. Jules felt the limousine lurch into gear. Spinning tires shot broken cobblestones into his face. The Cadillac's black flank dragged him a dozen feet along the broken brick wall before finally releasing him. His legs folded under him like wet paper. Jules felt himself plunging into jagged darkness again. The limousine rocketed onto the street, jumping a curb and showering the fleeing ex-zombies with a hail of undercarriage sparks.

But before he could retreat to comforting oblivion, Doodlebug was pulling him to his feet. "We need to get back to your car," Doodlebug said, draping Jules's arm over his shoulder. "How badly are you hurt?"

Jules winced as he took his first stumbling step. "Ribs—busted, I think—"

Doodlebug stared at him with wide, sorrowful eyes. "Jules, I am *so* sorry for dropping you and getting you hurt—"

"No—was a good idea—" The sirens grew louder. The falling rain caught strobed reflections of flashing red lights from a few blocks downtown. "Help me—grab my hood and cloak, would ya? And the car keys—"

Doodlebug scooped up the faded black garments and draped them around Jules. His own colorful ensemble had been scattered across two city blocks by the fleeing limousine. "The police are very close—can you walk any faster?"

"I'll, *uh,* do my damnedest, pal."

Melpomene Street looked like the end of the world. Or maybe the aftermath of the Zulu and Rex Carnival parades. The street was strewn with refuse of every kind, as half the neighborhood dropped their makeshift weapons and scattered for the refuge of apartments, bars, or the unlit depths of abandoned buildings. From the sound of the approaching sirens, at least half a dozen police cruisers were speeding up Oretha Castle Haley Boulevard from downtown. A police car had already screeched to a halt at the corner of Melpomene and Oretha Castle Haley, cutting off the escape route of a crowd of ex-zombies.

Doodlebug dragged Jules toward Baronne Street. They stepped around the sprawled bodies of combatants too badly hurt to run any farther. Mothers, still dazed, looked frantically for their children. Teenagers pushed the wounded into the gutters in their rush to escape.

"All this confusion should help us get away," Doodlebug said hopefully.

Jules grimaced as his ribs pinched organs never meant to be pinched. "Yeah—two naked white guys—*ahh jeez*—we'll blend into this crowd real good."

They rounded the corner onto Baronne. Jules's Lincoln was parked in the middle of the block. The battered gold car had never looked so beautiful to Jules before. "Guess you're gonna hafta drive, buddy," he groaned. "Lemme lie down on the backseat. . . ."

His friend tried to be gentle as he assisted Jules onto the back bench, but the process of squeezing his bulk through the narrow aperture was nearly as wrenching as getting smeared by the limousine along the alley wall. At least the engine started on the first try. *Thank Ford for small favors,* Jules thought as he stared at the car's sagging head liner, fighting off unconsciousness.

"How do I get out of here?" Doodlebug asked, his voice tight with tension. "Should I head for Claiborne Avenue?"

"Not—Claiborne," Jules gasped. The sirens were now so loud, they sounded like they were inside his skull. "Cops'll be all over Claiborne. Go down to—St. Charles Avenue. Drive slow, normal-like. Wrap my cloak around you. Cops won't think to stop a—white woman—drivin' on St. Charles—"

"Left at the corner?"

"Yeah—*left* . . ."

Oblivion grabbed Jules tightly this time.

♦

The next time he opened his eyes, the car wasn't moving anymore. He wasn't in the car. Every part of him throbbed with pain; it was even worse than when he'd been boiled in holy water. Jules tried to figure out where he was. The light was dim. He seemed to be inside a building with a very high ceiling, close to a huge, shiny wall. Doodlebug's shadow looked immense and grotesque against the pearly surface.

"Where—where are we?" Jules croaked.

He saw his friend's worried face hover above him. "You're awake? Good. We're in a theater. I parked in a delivery alley behind Canal Street. After that battle we were in, the streets were swarming with police patrols; I thought we'd better lie low awhile before going back to the bed-and-breakfast."

"A theater . . . that'd be either the Joy or the Loews' State Palace. Maybe the Saenger . . . cripes, I feel like hell. . . ."

"I tried being gentle when I pulled you out of the car and carried you in here. I hope I didn't make your injuries worse—"

"We're right by Charity Hospital, aren't we?"

"I think so. That's the big filthy art-deco building behind the government complex, isn't it?"

"Yeah. That's the one." Jules took a quick inventory of his probable injuries. Broken or cracked ribs—three or four of them, for sure. Maybe a dislocated left shoulder. And if any of the ribs were busted clear off and were hopping around, possibly a perforated lung or kidney or something. "Wish I could check myself in there. I'm all busted up inside. Way more than a day or two of lying in my coffin can cure." Jules felt his limbs begin to quiver. Then he was shaking all over. He sensed sweat rolling down his neck and sides. Was this what going into shock felt like? "Take me to Doc Landrieu. He's a friend. My ex-boss. He's helped me before. He could probably tape up my ribs, keep 'em from grindin'. And maybe he could dope me up, too."

"Actually, I've got a better idea." Doodlebug knelt down and stared directly into Jules's eyes. "I'm going to hypnotize you. And then you're going to heal yourself."

"You're off yer rocker. You know as well as me that one vampire can't hypnotize another."

"Normally, you're right. But you're on the edge of going into shock. Your natural, subconscious mental defenses against hypnotism have to be greatly weakened. You've already proven that whenever you're able to achieve the proper level of concentration, you're capable of higher-level vampiric metamorphoses and body control. What I'd like to try is to implant a posthypnotic trigger. One you can 'pull' whenever you need to achieve that heightened state of concentration."

The waves of nausea, sweating, and chills were becoming worse.

"Whatever! Give it your best shot, and do it fast. 'Cause if it doesn't work, you're gonna hafta drag my ass over to Doc Landrieu's lickety-split."

"All right. Just hold still, and keep your gaze focused on mine."

"You got a pocket watch you gonna twirl?"

"No. Just start counting backward from one hundred."

Jules fought to make the shaking in his limbs stop. "Hokay. Here goes. One hundred, ninety-nine, ninety-eight, ninety-seven, ninety-six, eh, ninety-six . . . ninety-uhh . . . ninety . . ."

He was back in Maureen's basement. He felt strong, as though he'd just swallowed an entire bottle of Doc Landrieu's miracle pills. He sensed Doodlebug, invisible, floating above him, strengthening him even more. His mind was wonderfully, perfectly clear. The train set appeared around his feet, growing organically like a stop-motion fantasia from a kiddie movie. The twisting chalk line materialized, too, a luminous, beckoning pathway. He held his arms straight out from his shoulders, and two sets of coffee cups and saucers landed in his hands. The tiny locomotive puffed into life. Without his commanding them to, Jules's feet set out along the path, moving with the speed and smoothness of ball bearings rolling along an oiled metal track. He hit all of his marks without altering his pace one iota, without even trying. It was *easy*. It was easier than anything he'd ever done.

Jules blinked. Once, then three times in quick succession. He was back on the theater's floor, still lying down. Was he all healed up? He still felt sweaty and nauseated. Hesitantly, he raised his arm and set his hand down on his ribs. He applied a tiny bit of pressure. The resulting shock wave of pain nearly made him double over.

"*Owww!* You lousy rat-bastard liar! It didn't work! I'm still as busted up as before!"

"Well, of course you are. You haven't *done* anything yet. All we've accomplished so far is to implant the posthypnotic trigger. That part of it worked fine. My theory concerning your mental state was right on the mark."

Jules scowled. "Well, goody for you. I'll be sure to have the monks mail you a gold star to stick on your forehead. What now, smarty?"

"Do you remember how I was able to change my breast size and alter my waist–hips ratio? You should have the same type of control over your body's composition. A good visual metaphor is helpful. Umm, did your mother knit?"

"She didn't make woolen booties, if that's what you mean. But let's see . . . when the war rationing was on, and you could hardly buy nothin', she used to hafta mend my socks pretty often."

Doodlebug smiled. "Very good. Here's what I want you to picture in your mind, after I have you say your trigger words. Imagine your mother mending your socks, threading the new thread through her needle and sewing the holes in the fabric up good and tight. Then imagine that your hands replace hers and continue with the sewing, only what you're sewing together is *bone*, not cloth. Finally, imagine a skeleton like the one that used to hang in your high school science lab, but it's *your* skeleton, and it's whole and undamaged and perfect. Do you have all that?"

"Yeah." Jules blinked again as sweat from his forehead stung his eyes. "So what's my magic word, Merlin?"

"*Train set.*"

"Do I hafta picture it, or do I just say it?"

"Doing both wouldn't hurt."

Jules started to take a deep breath, but the expansion of his rib cage hurt so much that he quickly expelled it. He took a much smaller breath, then closed his eyes and said, *"Train set!"*

Pain and fear were instantly swept from his mind. His thoughts were distilled water, perfectly clear and sharp. He saw his mother sitting in her scallop-backed Victorian parlor chair, knitting basket on her lap, squinting hard as she threaded her needle through the frayed edges of the toe rip in his coarse black woolen sock. Then he saw himself in the same chair, with the same needle and thread in his hands, only his knitting basket was filled with broken pieces of his ribs. One at a time he was fitting his ribs together, then pushing the needle through the broken parts (it slid through as easily as it would through foam rubber) and suturing them together. As he imagined all this, he felt the burning in his sides begin to lessen. *(It's working! It's really working!)* He knit eagerly but methodically, making sure not to miss even a single tiny piece of rib in his basket, test-fitting various segments of bone together like jigsaw pieces to ensure he was creating the proper matches. With each stitch, he felt himself grow stronger.

When all the pieces of rib were gone from his knitting basket, Jules imagined the pièce de résistance—his own gleaming skeleton, perfect and unbroken, hanging from a harness at the center of a freshly scrubbed science lab, admired by dozens of nubile schoolgirls in short plaid skirts.

Jules opened his eyes. He took a deep, deep breath, expanding his chest to its fullest, most impressive dimensions. The pain was nothing more than an awful memory.

He grabbed his friend's shoulders before Doodlebug could say a word. "I *did* it! I *actually* did it! Just like you said, I imagined the knitting and the mending and the whole time I was thinking it, it was actually *happening*! You're a *genius*! A vampire Einstein!"

The usually imperturbable Doodlebug surprised Jules by blushing a deep red. "I'm just happy it worked so well. You, uh, you really had me worried there for a while." He reached out, tentatively, and placed his hand on Jules's cheek for the briefest of instants. The younger vampire's eyes may have revealed more warmth than he wanted to show. Jules found himself suddenly feeling acutely uncomfortable.

"We should probably lay low for a while yet," Doodlebug continued, a little too quickly. "Before we go very far, I'm going to need clothes. That cloak of yours will cover you up in a pinch. But if we get pulled over on the way back to the bed-and-breakfast, I'd rather not answer the officers' questions while naked."

"If this is a theater, maybe there're some costumes lyin' around in a dressing room. Worse comes to worst, there might be an apron down behind the concession stand we could swipe."

"Any port in a storm," Doodlebug said. "I have your flashlight from the glove compartment. Shall we go exploring?"

Doodlebug helped him off the floor. The flashlight's beam revealed that the tremendous shiny wall Jules had been staring at was the back of a movie screen. The two of them walked around the screen to the front of the stage, and Jules immediately recognized one of the landmarks of his youth. Staring out at the hundreds of seats, he felt like a teenager again.

The Loews' State Palace, in its prime, had been one of the top two movie theaters in downtown New Orleans. In the nearly eighty years since it had been built, the world of moviegoing had changed radically. Going downtown was anathema to modern-day audiences; they watched their movies in multiplex theaters built on old cotton fields. The State Palace had somehow hung on, though. For the last few years, the grand old theater had played host to dance raves and revivals of classic movies.

Jules shone his light onto the tremendous balcony and side wings that, by themselves, could probably seat nearly eight hundred people. His beam reflected off the dusty but still-glittering crystal segments of three enormous chandeliers; the dazzling reflections momentarily turned the huge theater into a disco. Jules recalled coming here as a young vampire and sitting nervously beneath one of those chandeliers, while on-screen Lon Chaney's Phantom of the Opera dropped a similar chandelier onto the heads of an audience of opera patrons.

"Hey, Jules! Shine the light down at the floor. I think we may've found something for me better than just an apron."

Jules played the flashlight beam into the empty floor space in front of the first row of seats, the area once reserved for a live orchestra. Off to both sides were portable clothing racks, holding what looked like musical theater costumes. He noticed that a banner had been hung from the front of the stage. He descended the stairs to the floor so he could read it.

"Hey, get a load of this: CELEBRATING AMERICA'S FAVORITE MUSICAL— SINGIN' IN THE RAIN—45TH ANNIVERSARY. Looks like they've got a live stage show to go along with the movie."

Doodlebug was already rifling through the costumes hanging from the racks. "These costumes are *gorgeous*! I recognize a lot of them from the musical numbers. Let's see . . . here are outfits from 'Be a Clown,' 'Good Mornin',' of course 'Singin' in the Rain' . . . oh, how *wonderful*! This has to be one of my favorite movies of all time. Debbie Reynolds was simply *precious*!"

Jules took in Doodlebug's enthusiasm with a jaundiced eye. If he didn't put the brakes on, his friend could be trying on outfits until after sunrise. "Hurry up and pick one out, okay?"

"Ohhh . . . just *look* at this beautiful dress," Doodlebug said, running his hands across smooth white chiffon, apparently not hearing a word Jules had said. "I think Cyd Charisse wore one like it in the 'Broadway Ballet' number—"

Jules sighed in resignation. "Aww, go ahead, then. Have your fun. You've earned it after tonight, I guess. Actually, though you probably won't believe it, *Singin' in the Rain* is one of my all-time favorites, too."

"Really? I thought your taste runs more toward Jimmy Cagney gangster pictures."

"Well, it *does*. But when *Singin' in the Rain* came out, me and Maureen were havin' one of our periodic fallin'-out times. I'd always liked Gene Kelly—back then the girls used to tell me I looked like a taller Gene Kelly, see, only I didn't know how to dance none—and anyway, I figured maybe seein' a lighthearted musical might cheer me up some. So I went to see it; right here in this theater, in fact. And I *loved* it. The whole time I was watchin' it, see, I was imagining that Gene Kelly was me, and that Debbie Reynolds was Maureen. Shit, I musta watched that picture fifteen times before it left town. Some nights I'd imagine that Cyd Charisse was Maureen, instead of Debbie Reynolds, if I wanted a, y'know, a more *spicy* viewing experience."

Doodlebug finished buttoning up a replica of one of Debbie Reynolds's yellow-and-green summer dresses and then smoothed the cotton over his thighs. "Ahh, now I feel *human* again." He cocked his head and squinted hard at his friend. "Say . . . I wouldn't be at all surprised if that posthypnotic trigger I gave you helps tremendously with your multiple transformations. Care to see whether I'm right?"

Jules looked around him. "What? Here?"

"Why not? There's plenty of room. It's only 2:45 A.M.; we wanted to wait a bit before heading back to the B-and-B, in any case. And I'm dying of curiosity—healing your own injuries may have speeded up your mastery of multiple forms by weeks, maybe months."

"Eh, I dunno," Jules said, staring at his feet and shuffling them some. "This has been a real ball-buster of a night. I mean, I'm exhausted as hell. Besides, the floor in here, it's that sticky floor like what they got in all the old movie theaters. I might get all that floor stickiness mixed in with my slug-thingie, and then I could end up with monster acne, or somethin'—"

Doodlebug, looking about as unconvinced as a vampire could be, planted his fists on his hips and slowly shook his head. "Excuses, excuses . . . it's *so* important that you make the attempt right now, while that posthypnotic suggestion is still strong."

"Well . . ."

"Look. We might never get another chance to put you over the top. I can't stick around forever, Jules. I have responsibilities back home. And even if I *could* stick around and help you forever, it wouldn't be good for you. You need to fly solo."

♦

"No rest for the wicked," Jules mumbled to himself from the floor in front of the movie screen. Before he had time for second thoughts, he repeated his trigger. Immediately, his mind was washed sparkling clean. Biology, physics—it was all instinctive to him now. His transformation into bat-form was the easiest he'd ever experienced. Disappointingly, his bat-shape was still as rotund and flightless as it had been for the last twenty or so years. As soon as he felt fully settled in his batness, he mentally probed the ether for the remainder of his mass. He gently pulled at it. Creating his wolf-form was as easy as filling a bucket from a hose.

The theater echoed with the sound of applause. Even though it was just Doodlebug clapping, to Jules's four extraordinarily sensitive ears, it sounded like the Rockettes doing a tap number just above his heads. "Oh, Jules! You've done it! I knew you could! I *knew* you could!"

It had been so easy, so painless and effortless, that it took the two Juleses a few seconds to recognize what he'd accomplished. Bat-Jules and Wolf-Jules stared at one another, almost disbelievingly. He saw himself, and he saw himself seeing himself, and he saw himself seeing himself see himself. It was dizzying, like being in a fun house hall of mirrors.

His wolf-self had an overwhelming desire to sniff his bat-self up close and personal. This was so exciting! Wolf-Jules gazed deep into Bat-Jules's black, beady little eyes and admired the lively, curious intelligence there. *Sure, maybe the little winged guy's a bit rounder than he should be, but just look at that terrific wingspan!*

Bat-Jules was hardly less admiring of his fellow. *He's so noble looking! And lovable! No wonder that bitch in Baton Rouge found me irresistible!*

Wolf-Jules nudged Bat-Jules with his nose as he was sniffing him. The resulting sensory feedback loop—his touching himself touch himself touching himself, ad infinitum—overloaded both of Jules's brains. His concentration shattered. Both of Jules's bodies devolved into pools of proto-matter before vanishing in clouds of fleshy mist.

"Ohhhh mannn . . ." he sputtered after he'd re-formed, sprawled facedown on the floor. To his disgust, his left cheek was stuck to the tacky surface. "What happened? I was doin' so great. . . ."

"Don't worry about it. You did fabulously well. The shock of direct physical contact between two bodies sharing a single, generalized consciousness is enough to overwhelm any vampire at first."

On his second attempt, Jules was able to maintain separate wolf- and bat-forms for six minutes before losing his concentration. Next up, he was able to flop around the floor as three individual bats for nine and a half minutes—before exhaustion, more than lack of concentration, forced his collapse.

While Jules was toweling himself off, he decided to ask the question that had been bugging him virtually since the first night Doodlebug started training him. "Hey, D.B., even tonight, even with my usin' that posthypnotic trigger-thingie you gave me, how come all my other bodies are still so *fat*? I mean, I still can't get even an inch off the floor when I'm a bat, 'cause my damn bat-belly's like an anchor holding me down. What's up with that? Multiple bodies is a kick and all, don't get me wrong. But it's about as useful in combat as bein' able to juggle eight heads of lettuce, if all my bodies end up as fat and slow as my regular body."

Doodlebug pursed his lips thoughtfully. "I've done some thinking about that very subject. I don't believe your other bodies *have* to be fat and slow at all. I think you create them that way out of habit. I think that, somewhere along the road, you got used to the notion of Jules Duchon as obese and clumsy, and you got comfortable with that. I think your wolf-belly drags the ground because you *believe* it should, and that your bat can't fly because you *believe* it shouldn't."

Jules was quiet for a long moment. "That can't be right," he said finally. "I've *wanted* to be a skinny bat. I've *tried*. Don't you think all them times my life's been in danger—that time by the lake with the Levee Board cops, or tonight in the alley—don't you think I tried with all my might to become a bat that could *fly*? Why would I hold myself back like that, when my *life* depended on it? It's gotta be that I just . . . *can't* . . . do it."

Doodlebug walked over and sat in the chair next to him. He started to reach for Jules's hand, then hesitated and pulled back. "Jules, I'm not a trained psychologist. But it's pretty obvious to me that someone, a very long time ago, convinced you that you weren't worth much. Whoever that was, they inserted a little facsimile of themselves into your head, just like I inserted your posthypnotic trigger earlier tonight. And that little mental facsimile whispers to you not to try, because if you try you might fail. And only someone who is worth something can afford to fail, so you'd better not take the risk."

Halfway through Doodlebug's soliloquy, Jules had clamped his hands over his ears. "I know what you're doing," he said. "I read about it in *Newsweek*. You're psychobabbling me. *Blah-blah* toilet training *blah-blah* self-esteem *blah-blah* inner child. . . . Well, it's not gonna work, Dr. Ruth. I'm not gonna let you get away with blamin' all my problems on my mother."

"Who said anything about your mother?"

"*You* did."

"I did not. I never mentioned your mother. *You* mentioned your mother."

Jules got red in the face. "I did *not*!"

"Yes, you did," Doodlebug responded coolly.

They sat in silence for three long minutes. Doodlebug was the first to break the uneasy quiet. "Tell you what. Let's try something new. One last thing. We'll do it together this time."

Jules didn't respond in any way. Not even a grunt.

"You said that *Singin' in the Rain* is one of your all-time favorite movies, right?" Doodlebug continued. "That people used to tell you that you looked like Gene Kelly, and that when you watched this film, you imagined you *were* Gene Kelly? Well, go ahead. *Be* Gene Kelly. I'll be Cyd Charisse. We've got all the costumes we need right here. We can do one of the dances from the movie. I've shown you how you can turn your imaginings into solid reality. Don't just imagine yourself as a slender, graceful Gene Kelly—*be* him."

Jules tried not to respond as Doodlebug nudged him. But he realized that the younger vampire would just keep talking until Jules said *something*. "That, hands-down, is the single most *idiotic* idea you've come up with since you've been back in New Orleans."

"What's so idiotic about it?"

"I told you before. I don't dance."

"No problem. We'll do the fantasy duet from the 'Broadway Ballet' sequence. Cyd Charisse does all the moving in that number. Gene Kelly just stands there and looks awestruck."

Jules sighed. He felt like he was speaking with a retarded child. "Even you can't dance without music, right?"

"No problem. I'll run the film. We'll wait until that part comes, and then we'll dance along with it."

Again Jules sighed. "No matter what I say, you're gonna do it anyway, aren't you?" he said flatly. "So go ahead. Get it over with. Put on your costume and play your games. Only the joke's on you, pal, 'cause there ain't any outfit on either of them racks that comes anywhere *close* to fittin' *me*."

"We'll just see about that," Doodlebug said, and smiled.

◆

After twenty minutes of trial and error, loading and unloading various reels of film, Doodlebug found the reel that contained the "Broadway Ballet" sequence. As the film stuttered into life, Jules found himself sucked into the images on-screen. Despite his resistance to the whole idea, hearing Gene Kelly sing "Gotta Dance!" and watching him stride around those Broadway sets in that athletic, manly, yet compellingly graceful way of his brought back memories both good and surprisingly bitter-sweet. Jules was shocked by how much Gene Kelly resembled what he remembered of the young, human Jules Duchon. Not so much the physique (even in his best shape ever, Jules had to admit, he'd been nowhere near as buff as Gene Kelly)—more the smile, warm and cocky and reassuring all at once, and the friendly cast of the eyes.

When Gene Kelly saw Cyd Charisse stride through the doors of the Broadway casino, and the scene melted into a fantasy tableau of the two of them dancing together in an ethereal paradise, Jules didn't see Cyd Charisse; he saw Maureen. It was Maureen in the flowing white gown, her fifteen-foot train soaring behind her in the wind, her beautiful long hair spilling over her bare shoulders. It was Maureen who danced around him, wrapping his torso and arms with her gauzy cape, who dazzled him with her angelic footwork, exciting a brilliant smile from his lips. It was Maureen who danced away, her arms futilely beckoning, as the fantasy dissolved into the harshly lit reality of the casino, and she turned away from him to accept her gangster boyfriend's cold embrace.

Jules sensed Doodlebug standing next to him. His friend was dressed in a duplicate of Cyd Charisse's fantasy gown. "They were beautiful together, weren't they?" Doodlebug said.

"Yeah. They were."

The younger vampire sorted through the costumes on one of the racks, looking for one in particular. "I'm going back up to the projectionist's booth to rewind the film and run it again. While I'm up there, put these on."

He handed Jules a white three-button shirt and a pair of black dancer's pants. Jules checked the waist size listed on a tag inside the pants. *Heh.* They were a size thirty. Jules hadn't been able to button a pair of size thirty pants around his waist since Calvin Coolidge was president.

He looked back at the screen. Gene Kelly, devastated by Cyd Charisse's rejection, exited the casino with sagging shoulders. But outside, he ran into a green, young dancer, an overeager kid who reminded him of how he himself had been when he'd first hit the Great White Way. The kid's spirit proved contagious. Before he even knew what he was doing, Gene Kelly was dancing across the screen again, just for the sheer, crazy joy of it. The spirit was contagious to those off the screen, too.

"Train set," Jules said.

His flesh was clay, and Jules was Michelangelo. In less than a second, he had his thirty-inch waist. His well-muscled chest descended in a sharp V to his trim midsection. His legs were slender and sinewy. He slipped the shirt over his head, then slid into the size thirty pants. When he buttoned them, he still had half an inch to spare—he actually needed the belt that was hanging on the rack.

The film had stopped while he was getting dressed. Now it started up again. Doodlebug descended the stairs from the balcony, a fifteen-foot gauze cape trailing behind him. He gestured toward the large barrel-fan sitting in the wings of the floor area. Jules walked over and turned it on. The powerful wind ruffled his hair just as the opening bars of "Broadway Ballet" sounded from the speakers on either side of the screen.

Doodlebug joined Jules on the floor. The wind from the fan made his feathery cape soar into the air, reaching almost to the height of the balcony. They waited for the on-screen ballet to reach the fantasy sequence between Gene Kelly and Cyd Charisse.

Then they danced.

Or, rather, Doodlebug did all the dancing, and Jules looked handsome and upright and a little awestruck.

As soon as the fantasy sequence was over, Jules attempted to extricate himself from the yards of white gauze his partner had wrapped around him. Doodlebug took advantage of Jules's temporary captivity to rush over and hug him. The unexpected embrace completely shattered Jules's concentration, and he burst out of his dancer's clothing, swelling like a balloon attached to a fire hose. But it didn't matter. He'd always remember that he'd been able to fit in a pair of size thirty pants. And he'd remember that his dreams, if given half a chance, could be stronger than his doubts.

When Doodlebug released him and stepped back, the younger vampire had tears in his eyes. "Oh, Jules, *congratulations*. You've *graduated*— you've achieved the rank of summa cum laude from Vampire U. My work here is finished."

"What do you mean, 'finished'?" Jules grabbed his cloak and wrapped it around his suddenly exposed flesh. "You still gotta teach me all that fancy kung-fu stuff you know. Finished? We've barely started. Besides, you're my partner. We've gotta see this thing through *together*."

"Really, there's nothing more you need to learn from me," Doodlebug said, a hint of wistfulness in his voice. "Come on." He gave Jules a comradely pat on the back, then unsnapped the beautiful but utterly impractical cape from the neck of his dress. "Let's go back to the B-and-B and get some sleep."

♦

The next evening Jules awoke feeling completely refreshed. He checked his watch before opening the lid of his coffin. Eleven forty-two P.M.? No wonder he felt refreshed—he'd overslept by a good three and a half hours. Why hadn't his friend woken him up? No matter, though. He and Doodlebug could make this a strategy night. He'd perk up a big pot of coffee, and they could spend a relaxing evening brainstorming. It'd be fun.

He opened the lid of his coffin and sprang up like a robin eager for the first worm of the morning. The room was dark. In fact, the entire cottage was dark. "D.B.? You up yet?"

He climbed out of his coffin and flicked on the light switch. "Doodlebug?"

No answer. He stuck his head into the dark bedroom. "Hey, pal? Rise and shine, buddy!" He turned on the light. Doodlebug's coffin wasn't sitting on the four-poster bed. It wasn't anywhere in the bedroom. "What the *hell*—?"

He went into the kitchen. There was a handwritten note sitting on the table. He picked it up and read it.

> *Dear Jules,*
>
> *By the time you read this, I'll be on my way back to California. I know this is a strange way for us to part, but I felt it would be for the best. This is your time to shine, Jules. I feared that if I stayed any longer, I would get in the way of your full maturation. I have taught you everything that you need to know, and I trust completely in your ability to do what needs to be done. Even though I am not there with you, my thoughts and best wishes will be with you always. Just remember that you can have the things you've always wanted, but in order to acquire them, you might have to look at them in a new way.*
>
> *I've left you an open line of credit so you can continue to stay in the cottage as long as you need to. Please don't hesitate to call on me again if there is ever any other way I can be of some help, or if you just want some company. Consider coming out my way one of*

*these Halloweens—my town's Halloween parade is even wilder
than the French Quarter's. Great seeing you!*
Love,
Rory

He read the note a second time, just to make sure he hadn't misread.
Nothing changed. It wasn't a gag.

Jules turned a paler shade of white.

Like a dormant virus reactivated by a cold wind, the fear was back in
the pit of his belly. All too suddenly, he was on his own again.

SIXTEEN

Erato.

Jules thought the name over and over as he drove toward the Trolley Stop Café. Erato was the last friend left whom Jules trusted. Erato could advise him, guide him through shark-strewn waters. He had a solid head on his shoulders—not much in the way of book learning, maybe, but reams of diplomas from the school of the streets. On top of that, Erato was a black man; he'd *have* to have insights into Jules's predicament that were beyond Jules's reach. Jules had no choice but to finally play it straight with him—he'd have to take the risk of revealing to his friend the vampiric side of his nature that he'd kept secret for years. *Erato can handle it,* Jules told himself. He'd have to.

The notion of turning to Erato had come to him the previous night, after reading Doodlebug's note had driven Jules into an almost mindless panic. He'd called Erato's cell phone incessantly for three hours. But the frantic vampire had been continuously stymied by busy signals. Finally, exhausted by fear and frustration, he'd crawled back into his coffin and fallen into a sleep haunted by nightmares. Most of his evil dreams had Jules trapped on a sinking barge in the middle of the Mississippi, chained to the deck as hundreds of rats scurried across him to flee the sinking vessel.

Tonight Jules wouldn't bother monkeying around with the telephone. He'd see Erato face-to-face. Jules turned onto the vestigial rump of Basin Street, a thoroughfare made famous by early jazz tunes, but nearly erased from existence by the creation of Armstrong Park thirty years ago. He passed the ugly concrete pile of Municipal Auditorium, site of wrestling matches, Mardi Gras balls, and Disney on Ice; recently it had been home to a minor-league hockey team and a failed casino. Just past the auditorium, a roadblock outside the First District police station blocked his progress.

Jules braked to a halt in front of a pair of police cruisers and stuck his head out his window. "What's goin' on, Officers?"

A weary-looking cop motioned for him to turn around at the intersection. "Basin's blocked off from here to Iberville. No through traffic allowed. Some kinda Night Out Against Crime demonstration. Cut over to Rampart Street if you've gotta make Canal."

"Thanks, Officer."

Jules started to make a left turn across Basin when he spotted what looked like Erato's cab, parked in a closed gas station. He pulled into the lot, which was crowded with other parked cars. Sure enough, it *was* Erato's cab—there was that dumb-looking pair of sun-faded, pink fuzzy dice hanging from his rearview mirror.

Jules backed out of the jam-packed parking lot and rounded the corner onto Rampart. He found an open space beneath a live oak next to Armstrong Park; not the safest stretch of asphalt in New Orleans by any means, but considering the terrors he'd recently lived through, Jules didn't give the neighborhood's dicey reputation a second thought.

He walked past the police station and crossed the line of barricades. At least the presence of so many cops would ensure that he'd be relatively safe from ambush until after he'd had a chance to find Erato and talk with him. Finding him might not be so easy, however. The street and the grassy neutral ground in its middle were occupied by several hundred tightly bunched demonstrators. Most of them were waving their hand-painted signs at the police station and the cordon of cops; smaller groups were giving interviews for the benefit of a large contingent of reporters and cameramen. Other attendees were purchasing hot dogs and soft drinks from vendors who'd set up carts on the sidewalk outside the St. Louis Cemetery.

Now that he was closer, Jules was able to read the protesters' signs. EQUAL JUSTICE FOR ALL, several read. Others read, MURDER IS MURDER,

RICH OR POOR, or JUSTICE FOR HOMELESS VICTIMS. One elderly black lady had loquaciously painted her sign in tiny, carefully formed capital letters, A PINT OF POOR BLACK WOMAN'S BLOOD IS WORTH THE SAME AS A PINT OF RICH WHITE MAN'S BLOOD. Actually, Jules could quibble with this last sentiment; in his experience, a pint of a poor black woman's blood was *much* tastier and more filling than a pint of a rich white man's blood.

Any lighthearted quips immediately evaporated from his mind as soon as he saw the T-shirts the demonstrators were all wearing. They featured the same grainy, laser-copied photo of Bessie that he'd seen on posters in the French Quarter and on shirts in Central City. Only this time they were emblazoned with the caption BESSIE AGAR, GONE BUT NOT FORGOTTEN.

Suddenly Jules heard a familiar voice calling him from the far side of the crowd. "Jules! Hey, *Jules*! Whatchu doin' round here?"

Erato pushed his slightly pear-shaped form aggressively through the press of bodies, ducking beneath signs and barely avoiding collisions with sauerkraut-and-mustard-laden Lucky Dogs on his way to Jules's side. "Man-oh-man, you are about the *last* body I'd expect to see here," he said, breathing a little hard after his dash across Basin Street. He grabbed Jules's paw with both his hands. "You want a T-shirt to wear? Some of the ladies in the group are pretty big, y'know, so maybe I can find one in yo' size—"

Jules had the dizzying, unreal feeling that he was a contestant on a new TV game show, a mean-spirited amalgamation of *Candid Camera*, *This Is Your Life*, and *The Twilight Zone*. "Forget the T-shirt, Erato. I'm only here 'cause I been lookin' for you the last twenty-four hours. I was headin' over to the Trolley Stop when I saw your cab. What's goin' on here with all these people? And how come you're involved?"

"It's National Night Out Against Crime—you knew that, right? All over town, neighborhood associations, homeowners, are gettin' together and havin' barbecues. Makin' it clear to the criminal element that the lights are *on* and somebody's watchin' the streets, y'know? But it's not just people with homes that are the victims of crime, see. An awful lot of the victims of robbery and murder are those folks what don't *have* a home—"

"Yeah, yeah, yeah," Jules said in a rush, "but what does this have to do with *you*?"

"You know what it says in Scripture—'There but for the grace of the Lord goes me'? Well, for a few years now I been a volunteer for this program sponsored by the cab companies and the Social Service Department. It's called C.A.H.R.T., like *go cart*. Stands for 'Cabbies Assisting Homeless Residents with Transportation.' I pick up homeless folks from the shelters and give 'em rides to jobs or services or the hospital, all for fifty cents a ride. So over the months I got to know a buncha them pretty well—you're a cabbie yo'self, you know how folks talk when they're in your backseat. Some of these folks, I'll be pickin' 'em up for weeks and weeks, and then they'll up and disappear without a trace. Happened often enough to start worryin' me. So I decided to help organize this demonstration here, to make the cops pay attention to crime against the homeless."

Jules felt himself reddening. How many of those "disappearances" had he been responsible for over the past few years? Dozens? He didn't even want to venture a count. Hearing his buddy talk this way hurt worse than falling on his face from two stories up. He grabbed Erato by the shoulders. "But why *Bessie*? Why the T-shirts? Why the posters? Why have I been seeing that woman's face all over town?"

Erato's thick eyebrows lifted in surprise. "What? You knowed Bessie?"

Jules tried applying the brakes to his emotions. He hoped Erato hadn't noticed him blushing. "Uh, a little. I gave her a few rides."

"Oh yeah? Well, Bessie was—*is,* gotta remember to say *is*—a very special lady. That woman had nothing, y'know? But every time I gave her a ride, all she could talk about was what she needed to be doin' for other folks. Walking donated groceries to old folks too sick to leave their homes. Watchin' the kids of moms tryin' to work and get off the welfare." His face darkened. "It just pisses me the fuck *off* that the cops pay more attention to statues gettin' stolen from cemeteries than when some homeless woman like Bessie Agar goes missin'—like her life ain't worth *shit*—"

Jules felt as small and repulsive as a booger smeared on a dinner plate. Erato must've noticed the profoundly distressed look on his friend's face, because he gripped Jules's shoulder and said, "Aww, I'm sorry to bring you down like that, man. I shouldn't have gone off on a tear. Hell, Bessie could still turn up, y'know. There's still hope."

"Yeah, she could still turn up," Jules parroted in a flat, mechanical voice. In his mind's eye, he saw Bessie's rich red blood pooling on the plastic sheet covering the floor of his Cadillac, and her skin fading from a rich chocolate brown to a dull, lifeless gray. He saw the gun in his hand, and the neat little hole the small-caliber bullet made in the base of her skull, and how her body floated like a big pool toy before sinking into the murk of Manchac swamp.

A TV reporter standing on neutral ground motioned for Erato to come do an interview. Erato shouted that he'd be over in a minute, then turned back to Jules. "Say, buddy, you said before that you been tryin' to track me down. Sorry for bein' hard to get a hold of—I been real busy makin' sure we'd have a good turnout tonight. What can I do for you? I gotta say, it's *great* to see you up and around. You had me kinda worried with your lyin'-in-the-piano-box shtick. Glad *that* nonsense is over and done with. So whatchu need?"

"Nothin', Erato. You're a real busy man tonight." Turning back in the direction of his car, he couldn't even meet his friend's eyes. "Forget about it. It was nothin' at all. Have a good rally, huh?"

"Uh, sure thing!" Erato yelled after him, sounding more than a little confused. "Let's get together next week at the Trolley Stop and talk about that C.A.H.R.T. program, okay? Maybe I can get you to volunteer with me?"

Jules didn't even attempt a reply. He pretended not to have heard his friend, and concentrated on pushing through the crowd. Just six weeks ago, learning about the C.A.H.R.T. program, with its convenient supply of unsuspecting homeless victims, would've seemed like manna from heaven. Now the thought of what he would've done with that knowledge made his stomach churn.

Jules trudged toward Rampart Street, his feet heavy as concrete slabs. Although he was surrounded by hundreds of people, he felt achingly alone.

◆

The big vampire drove aimlessly for a while, barely noticing things like stop signs, traffic lights, and pedestrians. Driving in the shadow of the elevated expressway grew uncomfortable—the massive steel buttresses looming above him reminded Jules of the relentless fate hanging over his head—so he turned off onto Tulane Avenue.

Too late, he realized where he was. "Jeezus, my life's runnin' in a big fuckin' circle," he whispered harshly to himself. To his left, silhouetted in moonlight, loomed the Romanesque towers of St. Joseph's Church. His childhood church, and the same house of worship he'd found himself drawn to the night he'd submerged Bessie's body in the muddy waters of Manchac swamp.

The massive front doors were open, beckoning him inside. He parked on the other side of the street and walked across Tulane Avenue's six lanes. A sign posted on the church's front lawn announced that the church was conducting special evening Masses during the Night Out Against Crime.

Jules felt a desperate, burning need for—what? Forgiveness? Absolution? Redemption, maybe? Whatever this nebulous but powerful need was, he knew that he felt scared, abandoned, sick of being who he was, and terribly, terribly alone. More than anytime since he'd been a little boy, he wanted someone stronger and wiser than he was to tell him everything would be all right. Even if it wasn't true. He just wanted to hear it.

He squinted to avoid seeing the crucifixes outside and walked into St. Joseph's. Almost immediately, he felt his skin begin broiling; it felt like the sunburns he used to suffer at Lake Pontchartrain at the start of summer, right after school had let out. He avoided the baptismal font like another man would avoid a pool of boiling lava. The big church was empty. *Must be between Masses,* Jules told himself. More surprising to him was the dull drabness of the tall stained-glass windows. After thinking about it a minute, he realized that in nearly all his memories of this church, the windows had been made radiant and beautiful by the sunlight streaming through them.

He wanted to go somewhere he hadn't been since he was twenty years old. He wanted to sit in the confessional booth. The green light above the booth's door was lit. He grabbed the handle, then let go as if a cobra had bitten him. The handle felt as hot as a glazed pot fresh out of the kiln. His attempt at entry had left the door slightly ajar, however, so Jules gingerly pushed it open with the toe of his shoe.

The booth was much smaller and tighter than he remembered it being. He barely fit on the kneeler, and his knees were jammed into his overhanging stomach. The church was air-conditioned; still, Jules felt like a king cake baking inside a McKenzie's Pastry Shoppe oven. Sweat coursed down every square inch of his body, but it failed to cool his burning skin. The stale air inside the booth was soon clouded with white, oily smoke.

After a moment, Jules heard the wooden door on the other side of the screen slide open. He waited for the priest to say something, but then he remembered that the parishioner always speaks first. Embarrassed, he tried to recall the proper opening words.

"Uh, forgive me, Father, for I have sinned. It's been . . . let's see . . . eighty years since my last confession; maybe eighty-five years. Lemme think here . . . uh, I have purchased pornography—"

"Excuse me, my son. Surely you realize that smoking is not permitted in the confessional booth."

Jules was slightly stunned at having been interrupted midconfession by the priest. "But I'm not smoking, Father."

"I smell smoke."

Jules waved his arms around, trying to disperse the smoke, but his exertions only made his skin burn faster. "Uh, yeah—I came from a bar, see, a real smoky bar—not that I was *drinkin'* or nothin' . . . me and my pals, we were havin', uh, a Bible study session in the back. . . ."

"Please, my son, do not add to your sins. Just stub your cigar out. I realize the terrible power of nicotine addiction, but surely you can wait until after you've completed confession."

"Uh, okay." Jules made a noise with his foot like he was stubbing out a cigar on the floor. "Back to what I was sayin' before . . . my sins . . . I have purchased pornography on, uh, numerous occasions. I used the pornography to commit, y'know, onanism. On, uh, numerous occasions. I have fornicated—although the last time I did it, I didn't go all the way. I have thought disrespectful thoughts regarding my mother. Oohh, this is a bad one—I had sexual intercourse with a dog."

"A *dog?*"

"Yeah, but there were extenuating circumstances. Getting away from the whole sex thing, Father, what I really came to talk to you about is this—is it a sin to kill for food?"

The priest paused before responding. "Are you telling me that you killed someone and stole their food?"

"Uh, no. Not exactly. What I'm talkin' about is killing some—, uh, some*thing* and eating, uh, part of it. That's what I done."

"I see. Before Adam and Eve were expelled from the Garden, they ate only the fruits and plants that were permitted them; they were vegetarians. However, once they committed Original Sin, carnivorousness became part of the natural order of things, and since then man has been permitted to eat of the lower animals. However, if you have stolen an animal that belonged to another and slaughtered it for food, this could be considered sinful. Not for the act of eating meat, but for the act of theft."

Jules coughed. His throat was parched, and the oily smoke from his own skin was irritating it even more. "That's not it, either. See, I'm sort of a hunter. I hunt to eat. Only . . . well . . . I don't hunt lower animals. Not exactly."

"What *do* you hunt?"

Jules sighed heavily. "People. Human beings."

"You hunt *people* and you *eat* them? You're telling me you're a cannibal?"

"No, Father," Jules said hastily. "I don't wanna give you the wrong idea. I don't *eat* people, not really. How can I explain this, in some way that'll make sense to you—? Okay. Here goes. I drink people's blood. I'm a vampire."

The priest was silent for a moment. When he spoke again, his voice was angry and dismissive. "The confessional is no place for pranks or jokes. Please take your warped 'sense of humor' somewhere else and leave this booth for those who truly wish to use it."

The door behind the screen partition began to slide shut. "Father, wait! I'm not bullsh—, I mean I'm not feedin' you any baloney here! I really *am* a vampire! That smoke you smell—that's not from a cigar, it's my *skin* that's burning! I'm burning because I'm inside a church! I swear to the Big Guy in Heaven I'm tellin' you the truth!"

The door stopped sliding shut. Jules pressed his advantage. "Father, I could *show* you stuff. I can change into a bat. Or a wolf. I know it sounds ridiculous, but it's true. Or you can take a crucifix and press it against my skin. It'll brand me like an iron right outta the fire, honest truth so help me—"

"Stop. I'm willing to take you at your word. Whatever else, I believe that *you* honestly believe what you are telling me."

Jules sucked in a deep breath, then slowly exhaled. "Thanks, Father. That's really white of you. I mean that."

"Hrrmm . . ." The priest cleared his throat. Jules had the sudden realization that he might not be speaking with a white clergyman. "How about telling me why you decided to enter the confession booth tonight? That's not usual behavior for a vampire, is it?"

"No . . . it's not." Jules wiped his forehead with his sleeve. Flecks of parched skin, gray as ash, drifted down through the smoky air. "It's just that . . . Father, I don't think I'm gonna be on this earth much longer. I think I'm gonna get killed, and this time it's gonna be permanent. I've drained a lotta folks over the years . . . to live, to survive. I always explained it away by tellin' myself I'm no worse than the hunter who loads up his deer rifle, then goes out into the woods to bring home some venison. But lately—well, just tonight, this friend of mine, a good friend, he told me some things—and I can't look at it in the same way no more. All them killings, they're eatin' me up inside. I don't wanna go down to the grave with all that on my conscience."

"How many people have you killed, my son?"

"In the last eighty, eighty-five years . . . I've gotta figure about two fangings a month, sometimes three . . . minus the thirty-odd years I worked for the coroner's office . . . I'd hafta estimate a thousand to twelve hundred."

Jules heard a soft choking sound from the far side of the screen. "Have you—have you ever tried subsisting on the blood of lower animals?"

Jules sighed. "I been there, Father. Believe me. Been there and tried that. Way back in World War One, right after I became a vampire, I tried doin' the patriotic thing and not munch on my fellow Americans. Instead, I put the bite on anything I could get my hands on—stray dogs and cats, mules, even a dairy cow once. I found out it's like tryin' to live on water and crackers—boy, did I feel like shit after a while. Later on, after Pearl Harbor, I tried the same thing again. Thought maybe I'd tolerate it better, since I'd been a vampire longer. No such luck. But I found a better way to be a good American—the docks and factories were teemin' with fifth columnists, filthy spies and saboteurs. . . . I ate good during the war."

"Help me to understand—is human blood absolutely *necessary* for you to survive? Or is it a substance like heroin, a drug you've become addicted to? If you had to, could you subsist on the same foods ordinary humans eat?"

Jules didn't care for the direction their discussion was taking. All he'd wanted to do was confess, get his assignment of penitent prayers, receive absolution, and leave as fast as possible. "No, Father. I can't eat no normal foods. Not for the last twenty-five years or so. They won't stay down. They shoot out both ends—it's a *mess*, believe me." His conscience stung him like a nestful of aroused wasps; he wasn't telling the Father a big, fat *lie*, not exactly, but he was withholding a good part of the truth. "Eh, I guess, y'know, I suppose I need to qualify that a little. I can't eat no normal foods while I'm in my *regular shape*. There've been a few times—really rotten, low times, times so lousy I don't even wanna think about them—when I been forced to change into a wolf and scrounge around for some scraps or dog food to eat. I guess I been able to tolerate solid foods good enough those few times—"

"So then, conceivably, you would be able to survive by—*ahem*—changing into a *wolf* whenever you feel the need to eat?"

Jules sensed himself sliding down a slippery slope. "Well, eh, it's possible, maybe, just not real *probable*—"

"Indulge me a moment—you could subsist on solid foods, and drinking human blood would no longer be necessary?"

"Look, Father, you're takin' me into real uncharted territory here. What you're suggestin' has never been tried for any long period of time—and besides, it's *way* beneath my dignity as a vampire. If you'll excuse me sayin' so, you askin' me to do *that* is like me askin' *you* to screw a nun. It just ain't *done*. No vampire in America would even look me in the eye if they knew I'd done *that* kinda eatin'. Well, *practically* no vampire. Anyway, I don't know why we're even discussin' this, seein' as how I probably won't be eatin' or drinkin' anything much longer."

When the priest spoke again, Jules could tell he was on the verge of slamming the partition door shut. "I've been very patient. Exactly *what* do you want from me?"

Jules tried to make his tone as respectful as possible (considering that his lips were beginning to blister). "Father, I thought that was *obvious*. My mother, bless her soul, raised me in the Church. I'll admit I ain't been the greatest Catholic the last eighty years or so, but it hasn't been my fault. I just want the same thing any parishioner wants when he walks outta the confession booth—a list of 'Hail Marys' and rosaries to say, so I can get this awful weight off my shoulders. I've done what I'm supposed to—I've come in here and told you all the crummy stuff I've done. I've confessed, and I'm not even on my deathbed yet. I want you to 'poof' me, Father, so that I'm sin-free when I sail off into the Last Roundup."

Jules felt satisfied with himself. His plea had been heartfelt, spiritual, and well worded. But suddenly the Father's voice took on that hair-raising, Satan-slamming resonance that Jules recognized from the *Omen* movies. "There is no penance unless the sinner intends to sin no more. Will you foreswear the drinking of human blood and dedicate the rest of your unholy existence to the service of Christ?"

"Aww, c'mon, Father, we just been through this. I said I'm sorry. I just want to clear my slate, that's all. Look, I never had no choice over whether I became a vampire or not —"

"Insincere penitence is like unto blasphemy in the eyes of our Lord. Vampire or not, you defile this holy church with your lies and deceptions. Get out. Do not return here until you are ready to sin no more."

The priest closed the sliding door with a resounding smack. "Father, just a few 'Hail Marys,' that's all I'm askin' here—"

"*Out!* Get *out*! Leave at once, or I'll have the police *throw* you out!"

♦

When he found himself back out on the trash-strewn sidewalk, Tulane Avenue looked even more desolate and abandoned than before. Jules kicked an empty can of Dixie Beer into the street, then brushed flakes of dead skin from his arms and neck.

"Boy, he sure was in a snit," Jules muttered to himself. "Maybe the altar boy had a headache last night."

He was immediately sorry that he'd said it. His head involuntarily jerked sideways as he pictured his mother hauling off and slapping his face, every one of her ninety-eight pounds behind the blow.

It was a fortuitous hallucination. While his head was cockeyed from the imaginary blow, Jules's gaze fell upon the billboard mounted on the roof of the furniture store across the street. A mariachi band played in front of an outdoor café, the musicians grinning ludicrously big grins, as if they were all hooked up to IVs brimming with tequila. Continental Airlines was advertising new direct flights to Mexico City and Cancún. FLY TO MEXICO CITY FASTER THAN YOU CAN DRIVE TO MORGAN CITY, the billboard commanded.

Like a bursting grenade, the name hit him. *Doc Landrieu!* Hadn't Doc Landrieu practically begged him to move to Argentina and become an assistant in the doctor's liposuction practice? Hadn't his old boss enticed him with visions of grateful Latin women and endless supplies of delicious fat-laden blood?

Sure, he'd put the doc off at the time. Having just escaped from five nights of hell in Baton Rouge, Jules had been in no frame of mind to even consider leaving New Orleans again. But that was then, and this was most definitely now. Going off with Doc Landrieu was the perfect solution. Even if Argentina had its own indigenous vampires, Jules wouldn't have to worry about turf battles, because he and Doc Landrieu would be harvesting their own supply of blood in a nonintrusive, completely private fashion. They wouldn't be stealing resources from anybody.

He stood on the desolate sidewalk and thought about it some more. Hooking up with the doctor would ensure Jules a constant supply of those miraculous antidiabetes pills; a good thing, especially since he was down to his last two or three. After a year or two of their working together, the doctor could probably come up with a cure for him, making the pills unnecessary. Argentina wasn't New Orleans, but it would be all right.

Jules crossed the street to his car with a renewed sense of purpose. Maybe he'd bombed in St. Joseph's, but salvation was only a ten-minute drive away.

♠

The Mid-City side street next to the Jewish cemetery was silent and empty of people when Jules pulled up in front of Doc Landrieu's house. No Night Out Against Crime block parties were going on in the neighborhood. The street lamp on the corner was out, leaving the otherwise well-tended block in uncustomary gloom.

In contrast, Jules's mood was bright as the midday sun in Buenos Aires. He'd decided on the drive over that he would invite Maureen to fly south with him. Relief and happiness had swelled his heart with a sense of forgiveness; he was sure they could work out their differences in the big open spaces of Argentina, freed from the pressure-cooker atmosphere of New Orleans. And wouldn't Doc Landrieu be thrilled to remove not one but *two* vampires from his home city!

Brimming with eager anticipation, Jules rang the doorbell. While waiting for Doc Landrieu to come to the door, he continued grinning like a kid who'd just won a shiny ten-speed bicycle. But Doc Landrieu didn't come. Jules rang the bell again. The house remained dark.

He checked the driveway. Doc Landrieu's car was there. Maybe he was down in his workshop and hadn't heard the bell? Jules squeezed past the doctor's car and circled to the back of the house. No lights shone through the narrow windows of the basement workshop.

Maybe the doctor had gone to bed early. That had to be it. He was a heavy sleeper, perhaps, and the bell wasn't loud enough to wake him. Or maybe the bell was busted. Sure. It could be any of those things.

Whatever the deal was, Jules sure couldn't wait for morning to talk with his ex-boss. It was kind of rude to wake the old man up if he was sleeping, but considering how eager Doc Landrieu had been to take Jules away from New Orleans, surely the doctor wouldn't get too miffed over missing a few hours of shut-eye.

With his vampiric strength, Jules was certain he could knock a heck of a lot louder than any doorbell. Hoping he wouldn't crack the door's fresh coat of forest-green paint, he rapped the stout wood panels. Yielding to his assault, the door swung open.

Jules was frozen with surprise. He hadn't hit it *that* hard. Not hard enough to bust the lock. Not even hard enough to dislodge the latch. Someone had left the door only partially shut.

Jules pushed the door the rest of the way open. "Doc Landrieu? Hey, Doc? It's Jules Duchon."

The house was quiet. Jules's fingers fumbled along the wall until they located the light switch. The front parlor was unoccupied, but seemingly undisturbed. The big-screen television and stereo set were still where he remembered them. So the house hadn't been burglarized. Maybe the doc was getting forgetful in his advanced age?

"Doc?" he called, louder than before. "It's Jules. Hate to wake you, pal. But I decided to take you up on your offer."

Still no response. Jules walked deeper into the parlor. Behind the sofa, between the edge of an expensive Persian rug and the hallway leading to the study and the kitchen, he found a brass floor lamp. It had tipped over and fallen onto the hardwood floor. Shattered pieces of colorful Tiffany glass were scattered across the polished teak.

Jules felt his heart sink. His boots crunched bits of broken glass. Dreading what he might find, he checked the kitchen, then the study, turning on lights as he went. He climbed the stairs, fear making his heart pound more unbearably than exertion ever had. The three upstairs bedrooms were empty and mute, betraying no traces of violence.

There was only one place left for him to check. He descended the stairs to the first-floor basement, where Doc Landrieu had his workshop and lab. Halfway down the stairs, the odor hit him. Jules's last, brittle hopes disintegrated. After eighty-plus years in the vampire business, he knew the stench of decaying flesh all too well.

He found Doc Landrieu stretched out on his main worktable. His clothing and loose folds of his skin had been pinned to the table with long, skinny nails, as though he were a beetle on a high school biology dissecting tray. Broken lengths of glass tubing, tubing that the doctor had used for distilling his compounds, projected from his corpse like the quills of a porcupine.

Transfixed by this desecration of a man who had been his friend and mentor, Jules stumbled closer to the table. The unfrozen part of his mind noted that the fragments of glass tubing had not been driven into the doctor's body haphazardly. The entry points had been chosen very carefully, sited to intersect with major veins and arteries. Dried residue of blood marked the inside of each hollow piece of glass.

Straws. That's what the glass tubes had been. His killers had sucked Doc Landrieu dry, like a shared ice cream soda.

Something had been forced into the doctor's mouth. Something dark brown and roughly egg shaped. Half of it still protruded from his dead, blue lips. Jules stared at it. It was a coconut. A small, painted coconut. It didn't make sense. Not until Jules pulled it from his friend's mouth and saw what was painted on it.

It was a Zulu coconut. Not a true Zulu coconut, but a close facsimile of that most prized throw from New Orleans's oldest black Mardi Gras krewe. It was painted just like a real Zulu coconut, a dark smiling face with white rings around its eyes and mouth. The only difference from the authentic article was that this Zulu coconut had fangs.

Jules had seen many dead bodies during his long sojourn on earth. Hundreds of them. But apart from his brief viewing of his mother's lifeless body before he had consigned her plain pine coffin to the damp earth of the paupers' cemetery, Jules had never seen a friend's corpse before.

Doc Landrieu's grotesquely disrespected body expanded until it filled Jules's entire field of vision. Staring into this horrible abyss, he saw his own future. He had three antidiabetes pills left; they were jangling in a little plastic pill bottle in his pocket. When they were gone, he would degenerate back into the arthritic, breathless, almost immobile hulk he'd been five weeks before. He would be a sitting duck. They would catch him without even breaking a sweat. They wouldn't be satisfied with simply killing him. He would be humiliated. He would be disgraced. He would be put on display.

His fleshless skull would be mounted on a spear, a painted coconut jammed between its jaws.

♦

Jules hadn't been back to his old place of employment in years. He pushed open the heavy, art-deco doors that led into the morgue's examination rooms, and the overwhelming odor of formaldehyde sent thirty years of memories cascading through his weary brain. He'd never had any reason to come back here after he'd retired; with all the changeovers in city administrations, none of the staff working there now would even remember him. With one important exception. One employee would still remember Jules, and after Doc Landrieu's demise, only he could prevent Jules from becoming a helpless, crippled target.

Marvin Oday owed Jules a big favor. As the first black employee above the level of janitor hired by the coroner's office, and then only at Doc Landrieu's insistence, Oday hadn't had any friends among the otherwise all-white technical staff. With the exception of Jules, that is. Jules knew what it felt like to be the odd man out, so he'd befriended Oday and shown him the ropes.

Since Jules's retirement, Oday had gone on for several advanced degrees, and he was now the office's highest-level civil servant, second only to the publicly elected coroner. During the few years they'd worked together, Oday had always shown a marked preference for working the graveyard shift. Jules hoped this trait had remained constant.

For once, Jules was in luck. He found Oday in the gunmetal-gray office behind the examination rooms.

Jules knocked on the large window that separated the office from the closest examination room. The short, gray-haired chemist-physician looked up from his paperwork, and his eyes immediately widened with surprise when he saw his old coworker.

"Jules Duchon! Is that you?"

Jules walked through the door into the office. Despite renewing a friendly acquaintance, a circumstance he'd normally have treasured, his voice was leaden. "Hey, Marvin. Yeah, it's me. How ya been?"

Oday stared at him with disbelief in his eyes. "Jules, you must be blessed with some of the most *youthful* genes on earth! I swear, you haven't aged a *day* since the night you retired. You've, uh, well, you've put on a little weight since I saw you last, but then haven't we all?" He shook Jules's hand vigorously. "What brings you back here? You aren't looking for your old job back, are you? Heh. I'm only a few years away from retirement myself, you know. Amazing as it seems. I was just getting started when you were still here, and now I'm gray-headed and ready to be put out to pasture."

Jules removed the pill bottle from his pocket. "Yeah, it's good to see you again, Marvin. But this isn't a social call. I need to ask you a favor."

"Sure. If it's within my power, and it's not unreasonable, I'll do whatever I can for you. You have a dead body you need to get autopsied?" He smiled.

Jules didn't return the smile. He placed the pill bottle on Oday's desk. "You're a chemist. I need you to analyze these pills. They're a special kind of medication, and they're real important to me. I can't get any more from where I got them the first time. I need you to find out what they're made of. If it's possible, I want you to make more for me, or at least tell me where I could get it done."

Oday raised an eyebrow. He frowned. "We aren't talking about an *illegal* medication, are we? If not, I don't see why you can't take these to a pharmacist and get your prescription refilled—"

Jules cut him off. "They're an experimental medication. Doc Landrieu came up with them for me. But he can't make any more."

"Doc *Landrieu* came up with these for you?" Oday's face relaxed into a grin. "How's that old rascal doing? I'd heard that he was still fooling around with a chemistry set between rounds of golf. So now he's in the medicine business? Let's see . . . the last time I saw him was a couple of years back, at a charity fund-raiser. You've seen him recently, I take it?"

"Yeah. I've seen him."

"So how come he can't give you more of these pills he invented?"

Jules involuntarily grimaced. He felt lost in a poisonous fog. "It's a long story. I can't go into it. Look, Marvin, just analyze these for me, okay? I won't ask you to make more for me. Just tell me what's in them."

Oday picked up the pill bottle and eyed it thoughtfully. "Well . . . I suppose there's no harm in that. I can set aside some time later tonight, in fact. You'll leave these with me?"

Jules took the bottle back from Oday. He popped the top off, shook out two of the white tablets marked with an *A*, and placed them on Oday's desk. That left only one pill for him to take. One pill for tomorrow night. After that, he'd be at the mercy of some chemist somewhere. Or at the mercy of Malice X.

"Thanks, Marvin. You're a good friend."

"Yes. Well, *you* were a good friend, back when I needed one." Oday sighed. "How can I reach you once I have your results?"

"You got a White Pages I can use?"

"Of course." Oday opened up a desk drawer and handed him a phone book.

Jules looked up the number of the Twelve Oaks Guest House. "Try me at this number. I'm in cabin number four." Then he thought to give him Maureen's number, as well. There was always a chance he might have to seek refuge in her house. "If you can't reach me at this bed-and breakfast, try me at this friend's number, okay?"

While he was writing Maureen's phone number on a pad, Jules's thoughts were tugged to Malice X's final, mocking words of advice. *Get some pussy while you still can.* He'd taken the taunt as just another install- ment in a long series of threats. But after the obscenity that had been committed against Doc Landrieu, those words took on a different and awful significance.

The pen burst in Jules's fist, splattering ink across the desk. A surge of terror-propelled adrenaline nearly exploded his heart from his chest.

"Maureen!"

SEVENTEEN

Maureen hadn't answered her phone. *That doesn't mean anything,* Jules told himself over and over. He pushed the Lincoln hard, overextending its flaccid suspension and denting its axles in the pits of unseen chuck-holes on Canal Street. *That doesn't mean anything, 'cause she's probably workin' at Jezebel's.* No one had picked up the phone at the club, either. But *that* didn't mean anything, because no one ever picked up the phone at that damn dive. So he'd had no choice but to drive like a bat out of hell to the French Quarter.

Even this late, parking was tight in the upper Quarter. Jules had to park three blocks west of the club, just a block from Maureen's house. He walked as fast as he could, brushing past bunches of wild-eyed frat boys and sport-jacketed conventioneers crowding the sidewalk. He nearly tripped over the legs of an unconscious drunk, half hidden in the shadows at the intersection of Iberville and Bourbon, but he recovered his balance and hurried onward.

The caricature of Maureen posted in the glass display case in front of Jezebel's was even more faded than Jules remembered. He propelled himself up the foyer's steep steps two at a time, vaguely recalling the nights when he'd had to rest after every third step. Tonight his muscles answered his desperate commands without complaint, but he wondered how long it would be before his drug-fueled vitality evaporated.

The club was surprisingly empty. The greeter, a balding retiree in a plaid jacket, looked half asleep. He perked up slightly when Jules approached. "No cover charge tonight, buddy. Buy three drinks, get the second one free—"

"Is Maureen here?"

"Who?"

"*Maureen.* One of the dancers. I've gotta see her right away."

The greeter's tall forehead wrinkled with thought. "Maureen? One of *our* dancers? Can't say I know of any 'Maureen' around here, mister. 'Course, I'm kinda new, just doin' this to supplement my Social Security—"

Jules grabbed the old man's shoulders. "You've *gotta* know her! She's only the biggest fuckin' star this dump's got! She's blond, got hips out to here—she's as big as *me*, practically—"

The greeter's eyes sparkled with sudden understanding. "*Oh! That* one! You mean Round Robin, mister. Ain't got no 'Maureen' around here—"

Jules nearly screamed with frustration, but he managed to control himself. "Yeah. *That's* who I mean. She here tonight?"

The old man sighed disgustedly. "Boy, that girl's sure got a following! You're the tenth customer been askin' after her tonight. Well, she ain't doin' her regular show. I don't know why, no sir. But don't walk out on me—we got one hell of a terrific drink special tonight—"

Jules spotted a bartender he recognized. "*Yo!* Winchell!" Jules called out when he was still five paces from the bar. "You seen Maureen around anytime tonight?"

The bartender looked up from the glasses he was scrubbing with a dirty wipe rag. "Not tonight, pal. She was in last night, but she left after her first set, and she didn't make it back for her second. The boss was pretty pissed. Dinah might know something. She filled in for Maureen last night."

"Thanks, Winchell," Jules said. He stalked past the stage, where a slender, buxom dancer wriggled in front of mostly empty tables, and headed for the door marked PRIVATE—EMPLOYEES ONLY. He shoved the door open and went down the hall to Maureen's private dressing room, which Dinah sometimes shared with her. The room was dark and empty.

He tried the other dressing room next. Thankfully, Dinah was there. She was carefully applying a ponderous set of false eyelashes in front of an illuminated mirror when Jules burst in. The eyelashes fluttered to the floor as she spun around. "Jules! Honey, am I ever glad to see *you*! What's going on with Maureen?"

"I was about to ask you the same thing," Jules answered, barely remembering to step to the side so Dinah wouldn't spot his unreflection in the mirror. "I'm tryin' to find her. The bartender said she skipped outta here last night."

"What? You haven't been with her? But that call last night—I thought she ran out of here to be with *you*!"

Jules felt a tremor in his chest. "You know who called her?"

"No. I've got no idea. She wouldn't say, but she looked awful worried—"

"You were with her when she took the call?"

"Yeah. We were in her dressing room. She's got a private line installed, since nobody ever picks up the phone out front. It hardly ever rings, so I was pretty surprised when it rang last night. After she said hello she got this terrible look on her face, like she'd just heard somebody had died or something. I asked her what was up, but she wouldn't tell me nothing. She just said she had to leave right away, and asked could I cover her second dance shift. Then she ran out of here. She was so worried, Jules, I figured the call was either *from* you or *about* you."

"And you haven't heard from her since?"

Dinah's eyes grew wide. "No! And that's what worries me so. I mean, it's not like Maureen to miss work. She's *devoted* to this job. She's never out sick. The few times she's had stuff come up, she's always gotten hold of the boss the night before and arranged for someone to cover for her. Her running out of here was strange enough. But then when she didn't come in tonight for her first shift, and nobody had heard from her—"

Jules spun toward the door. "Thanks, Dinah. You're a peach."

"Where're you going now?"

Jules was already out in the hall when he answered. "To her house," he called out hoarsely, not looking back.

"But, Jules, I already been there! I rang and rang, but nobody answered—"

Dinah's words faded in his ears as Jules charged through the club. He didn't even notice the consternation he caused the embattled dancer onstage, or the exaggerated haste with which the greeter abandoned his stool and got out of Jules's way. His mind had room for only two thoughts. The dreadful tableau he'd left behind at Doc Landrieu's house. And the even more terrible vision he feared was ahead of him.

Back on the sidewalk, he began to run. He pushed himself as hard as he could, cursing his body for its inability to move faster. He couldn't breathe the thick summer air fast enough. Were his heart an engine, it would've burned oil and thrown a rod. A skinny wolf would be faster, he thought. A cheetah, faster still. Not worth it, he told himself—he'd have to waste time squirming out of his clothing, and he only had a couple of blocks to go.

A calming notion sprang to mind, a counterweight to the wave of panic that was threatening to give him a coronary. Maybe he was imagining a horror show that didn't exist? Doc Landrieu had meant nothing to Malice X; all the good doctor had been to him was a tool with which to jam splinters under Jules's fingernails. Killing Doc Landrieu had been like spitting out a wad of gum.

But Maureen . . . Maureen was another story entirely. In the world of vampires Jules had been raised in, one's blood parent was every bit as dear and precious as one's birth parents were. Malice X had been willing to smash the rules in other ways—particularly in his blithe willingness to abandon the mutual nonaggression pacts that had stabilized vampire societies for untold centuries. But Maureen . . . hadn't she told Jules that Malice X had loved her? Hadn't this whole rotten feud been at least partly fired by *jealousy*? If the thought of Malice X's romance with Maureen had been a dagger in Jules's heart before, now he clung to that very same thought like a life raft in a storm surge.

He finally came to Maureen's stoop. Her front door was locked. This was a good sign—if Malice X or his goons had been there, why would they have bothered to lock the door when they left? Some of the murderous tension unknotted in his shoulders as he fumbled through his pockets for the key. But as he unlocked the door, he couldn't help thinking, *What if he'd wanted to make sure no strangers walked in and disturbed things? What if he'd wanted to make sure only folks with a key could get in? And who else would have a key to Maureen's house but me?*

His heart pounding hard, he opened the door. The house was dark. All was silent, except for a steady, rhythmic swishing sound. After a second, Jules recognized the noise as the ceiling fans in Maureen's front parlor, turned up to their highest setting. Maureen, like most vampires, enjoyed the heat. She wouldn't have the fans on unless she was entertaining company. But the darkness ruled that out.

"Maureen?"

No one answered.

Jules stepped into the pitch-black entrance foyer. He held his hands extended in front of him, fumbling along the wall for the light switch. Something hard and blunt struck him in the face. He swung his fists wildly, blindly. His left forearm connected. Whatever his assailant was, it was surprisingly light. It clattered on impact. A second later, completely silent, it hit him in the face again.

Jules batted it away a second time. This time, he ducked before it could hit him. His fingers found the light switch.

His antagonist was an oblong black object hanging by a piece of twine from the light fixture. It was about the size of a large paperback book. Jules grabbed the rope to stop the thing from swinging. It was a videotape. It had a note taped to it. The words were written with a black marker, in large capital letters:

WATCH THIS—DON'T EAT IT

Jules yanked the plastic cassette from the rope and wadded up the note. He walked into the parlor, steeling himself for the worst. The heavy purple draperies that lined the windows billowed inward, outside breezes battling the countervailing wind power of the ceiling fans. Maureen never left her windows open. She hated the drunken chatter from tourists passing on the street. With her windows closed, the thick walls of her two-century-old house cocooned her in silence. But now the draperies fluttered inward. Not just in the parlor; the windows were open in every room that Jules could see.

"Maureen?"

It was a forlorn, useless holler. Jules knew that. But he repeated it twice more, as though her name were an incantation to drive away evil spirits—or turn back the clock. He turned on more lights. A thick coat of fine, white dust covered all the exposed surfaces in the parlor and dining room—end tables, seat cushions, Victorian red velvet sofas, the hardcover biography of "full-figured gal" Jane Russell that Maureen had been reading when he'd stayed with her last. He'd never seen dust in this house before. Maureen was an impeccable housekeeper; one more reason why it had been virtually impossible for them to live in the same home together. Jules touched the dust on the dining room table with his forefinger. He felt sick.

Listless, empty, Jules shuffled back into the parlor and shoved the videotape into Maureen's combination TV-VCR. While the set was warming up, he gently cleared the dust away from one of the sofa cushions and sat down. He didn't bother to check if the tape was rewound. He knew it would be.

What came on-screen looked at first like a modern, color remake of the old Claude Rains thriller *The Invisible Man*. A seemingly empty man's suit—black jacket and trousers, white shirt, narrow black gangster's tie—strutted around behind what looked like a gray-and-red mummy. Ribbons of gray duct tape partially encased a billowy-huge red satin mini dress and queen-sized fishnet stockings, which were both bound to a tall-backed kitchen chair. Unlike the men's suit, the satin mini dress had an attached "face" of sorts. An oval of flesh-colored powder floated a few inches above the dress's plunging neckline, highlighted with lips formed of fire-engine-red lipstick, almond-shaped ovals of black mascara surrounding empty eye sockets, and thick black false eyelashes that fluttered quickly, nervously, like dragonfly wings.

Jules recognized the room they were in. It was Maureen's kitchen, only thirty feet from where he now sat. The red satin dress whimpered. Jules knew it was Maureen's whimper; but it was easier to think of it as the red satin dress's.

The black suit clapped its invisible hands together. "Welcome to *Chiller Theater*, kiddies," it said with Malice X's mocking voice. "Tonight's thrilling episode is called *The Fuckin' Traitor Ho 'Fesses Up*. Sponsored by those fine folks at Big Shot Beverage Company, the makers of cold drinks that turn black men sterile."

"Malice, please," Maureen begged. Her voice sounded choked with mucus and tears. "Please let me go. You said you just wanted to talk. What's with all this crazy nonsense, baby? I've been good, honey. I *swear*. I never said anything to anybody that could get you in trouble. Let me loose. You said you'd tell me what had happened to Jules if I came here and met you without telling anybody. And I did exactly what you asked—"

"Lyin' *bitch*!" The black suit backhanded the oval of flesh-colored powder, smearing its lipstick into a red scar. "You can't speak two fuckin' sentences in a row without sayin' his name! *Bitch!* Who the fuck *else* told fat boy and his queer sidekick where my sister lives? Who the fuck even told them I *had* a fuckin' sister? Huh?"

Maureen was weeping. Jules saw that the battered side of the powder oval was swelling like rotten fruit. "It—it wasn't me, Malice. You gotta *believe* me, baby. I never knew where your sister lived. I *swear* it! I can't even remember if you ever told me you *had* a sister. I didn't knife you in the back, baby. I'd never do anything to hurt you, I *swear.* . . ."

The black suit moved behind the red satin dress. Maureen's face jerked backward, as though her hair had been roughly yanked. "Yeah, that's right, baby," Malice X said, his voice lower, almost inaudible. "You'll never do anything to hurt me. That's 'cause you *can't* hurt me. I'm way beyond gettin' hurt by the likes of you. But I can hurt *you*, baby. I can hurt you *real* good."

He stepped off-camera for a few seconds. When he returned, he was holding a five-foot-long wooden spear. Carved of an exotic dark hardwood, it was a cross between harpoon and phallus. "This is a Yoruba ceremonial spear, baby," Malice X said. "I got a whole collection of these. Bought it at auction. I was biddin' against three different museums. Thing cost me half as much as my Caddy. Nice, huh?"

Maureen nodded her head weakly.

"Now where you think I oughtta stick this fine thing, huh?"

"Nowhere, Malice—"

"Shut the *fuck* up!" Maureen's head snapped back again. "I didn't ask you to say nothin'! That was a fuckin' rhetorical question. You wanna say somethin'? Say your last sweet honey-words to your fat fuck of a boyfriend."

Tears turned the mascara around Maureen's eyes to black rivers that scoured the powder from her face and stained the red satin of her dress. What emerged from her mouth wasn't words; it was a preverbal cry of despair, torn between a futile plea of innocence and a moan of bottomless regret.

The first word she managed to utter was his name. "Jules . . . if you can hear this . . . Jules, I'm so sorry. I'm so sorry for everything, darling. I can't—I'm just so very, very *sorry*, baby." On the left of the screen, partially off-camera, Malice X raised his spear to strike. Maureen's empty eye sockets stared directly into the camera. "*Jules!* I *love* y—"

The spear plunged through the patch of red satin covering her heart. What Jules heard then was only a faint aural shadow of the scream that had rocked the kitchen hours before. No recording instrument on earth could begin to capture the death-shriek of a vampire. Even so, the sound that assaulted him from the TV's small speakers was enough to make his ears bleed.

He watched, transfixed, as layer after layer of Maureen appeared on camera, only to progressively flake away like crumbs of burned pastry. First her plump white skin shimmered into view; then the thick layer of yellowish fat beneath; then a highway map of veins and arteries and organs; and then her bones. Jules tried to look away from the TV screen. But he couldn't. Finally, the camera's cold eye showed just a crumpled red dress and a sagging, empty pair of stockings, held partially erect by yards of drooping duct tape. On the chair's cushion and on the floor were mounds of sugary white dust.

Malice X returned to the center of the picture. "Now, wasn't that *fun*, kiddies? Special visual effects courtesy of Industrial Light and Tragic Magic. And dig that Dolby Surround Sound! Feel free to rewind the tape and watch that part over again. I'll wait." The suit stood unmoving.

Jules felt numb inside. He could name a list of emotions long as his arm he should be feeling right now. Horror. Grief. Anger. Hate. He pictured himself shoving his fist through Malice X's waiting image. Rending what remained of the set into tiny particles of plastic and metal. But he didn't do it. He couldn't move. He asked himself, *Didn't TVs used to have vacuum tubes inside?* That's what was inside him. A big vacuum tube, empty even of air.

Finally the suit on-screen began moving and talking again. "Okay. Now you've had enough time to take that bathroom break and get yo'self another beer. Back to business. Way I see things, you don't have too many friends left to lose, Jules. Who's left? Lessee . . . there's that cabdriver buddy of yours, right? And then there's that old-timey jazz musician. But I'm not totally unreasonable. Tell you what. I won't off your two buddies if you agree to do one little thing for me. Meet me in personal combat. One-on-one. *Mano a mano.* I'll even be a sport about it. You get to name your spot. Just call the toll-free number at the end of this tape to let me know your preferred place and time. Phone's in the kitchen, in case you don't remember. I'll expect to hear from you no later than midnight, Friday. Otherwise, this town's gonna be short one cabby and one horn-playin' geezer. Remember, that call's toll-free. So don't delay! Call now!"

Midnight, Friday. Tonight was Thursday. The screen turned blue, and a local telephone number strobed against the bright background. The large white numerals flashed across the screen like the tag end of a late-night infomercial. Jules didn't move to write the phone number down. He watched it dance across the glass tube until it was burned into his brain. Then the tape ended. The screen dissolved into static.

A strong breeze blew the coating of dust from the top of the television onto the floor. The sight of Maureen's last remnants being scattered into the corners of her home, and perhaps lost forever, propelled Jules off the sofa. He focused his battered consciousness solely on the chore of collecting as much of the dust as he could. Like a sleepwalker, he stumbled into the kitchen to search for a whisk broom and dustpan. He found them in a slender broom closet by the refrigerator. He needed something to collect the dust. Something more substantial and respectful than a cardboard box or garbage bag. He spotted a large glass vase filled with silk flowers on the dining room table. Jules emptied the silk flowers into the kitchen sink.

The chair that Maureen had been taped to was still in the center of the kitchen. The crumpled duct tape and empty dress and stockings offered mute testimony to Maureen's final, agonized seconds. But Jules wouldn't let himself think about that.

♦

Almost two hours later, he was nearly done. He had scoured the entrance foyer, the front parlor, the music room, the dining room, and the kitchen. He had moved sofas, tilted an upright piano, and whisked out the corners of long-disused closets. He had beaten the dust out of cushions and rugs, gently blown it from between the ruffled pages of beauty magazines, and even whisked it from the narrow grooves in the soles of his boots.

The vase was filled nearly to its top. He had probably mixed Maureen's remains with a goodly proportion of ordinary household dust; it simply couldn't be helped. Now the final part of his chore was before him. The most difficult part—the part that would force him to think about Maureen, the woman, instead of Maureen, the sugar trail. The last thing he had to do was to dislodge those particles of his lover that had remained stuck to the duct tape, and collect whatever dust was still hidden within the folds of Maureen's undergarments.

Brushing the tape with the whisk broom accomplished nothing. The bent straw only got stuck to the glue itself. Jules had better luck using one of Maureen's nail files to scrape the dust off, but it was still hard going. Fitting, in a way. Maureen had always been a stubborn woman.

He was almost afraid to touch her panties. Afraid her avenging spirit might incinerate the first male to touch her underwear—too many men;

that's what had led her to this. He lifted them gingerly, like he was handling the Shroud of Turin. A thimbleful of dust was cupped in the cotton panel in the crotch. Jules carefully raised the panties over the vase, then tipped the dust in. He felt self-conscious about what he did next, but he did it anyway. He held the red silk against his nostrils and breathed in deeply. Nothing. Even that was gone. Even her scent had crumpled into dust.

Jules opened several of the drawers beneath her kitchen counter, looking for some aluminum foil to seal up the vase. A small pile of bills and letters was sitting on the countertop. The letter on top of the pile was addressed to him, care of Ms. Maureen Remoulade, cobeneficiary. The letter was from the Claims Department of the First Union Firemen's Casualty and Insurance Company.

Inside was a check for twenty-one thousand dollars.

The phone rang. Jules yanked the receiver off the wall. "You fuckin' sonofabitch," he said before the caller could utter a sound. "Got impatient, huh? Thought I wasn't gonna call your fuckin' chat line? Well, you jumped the gun, asshole—"

"Hello? Jules, is that *you*?"

The voice wasn't the sneering, somewhat high-pitched voice Jules had been expecting to hear. "Uh . . . yeah, this is Jules," he answered, a little embarrassed. "Who's this?"

"It's Dr. Marvin Oday. You know, your old morgue buddy? Well, I've gotta hand it to you, Jules. You and Dr. Landrieu are quite the kidders. If nothing else, you livened up a slow night by giving me a good laugh."

Jules tried to decipher this comment, but drew a complete blank. "What are you talkin' about?" His mind felt like curdled pudding. "This about those pills I asked you to look at?"

"Those little white *A* pills you gave me? Oh, I've looked at 'em, all right. You really got my curiosity going with all that talk about secret, non-FDA-approved research. I thought maybe my analysis would take a couple of nights, at least. Only took me about ten minutes, though."

Events were shifting back and forth too fast for Jules to follow. He knew he should feel grateful, but he'd forgotten how. "You know what's in them pills? That's great, Marvin; that's really, yeah, that's really great. You've done me a big favor. So you'll be able to make more of them for me?"

"The first rule of comedy is never try to squeeze more humor out of a used-up joke. You want more pills? Cough up two bucks and get your butt over to a drugstore. 'Til next time, Jules—"

"Wait! Marvin, don't hang up yet! You've gotta tell me what's in those pills!"

The receiver was silent for a couple of seconds. "Hold on—you mean Dr. Landrieu didn't let you in on the joke?"

"*What* joke?" Jules cried, totally exasperated. "What the hell is in the damn pills?"

"Aspirin, man. Ordinary, generic table aspirin."

Jules mumbled good-bye to his old coworker and hung up the phone. He went into the dining room and sat down, resting his elbows on the table and leaning his forehead against his hands. *Aspirin. Ordinary table aspirin.* That's what had stripped the years off his weary, weight-burdened body? *That's* what had canceled the shooting pains in his knees, restored wind to his lungs and strength to his biceps?

It didn't seem possible. Ordinary, common aspirin. But it had worked. It had worked just like Doc Landrieu had told him it would. Jules had no doubt about that. Maybe there was more to aspirin than just headache and hangover relief. Studies had recently shown it could prevent heart attack victims from suffering a second attack. Maybe his ex-boss had discovered more about aspirin than was commonly known?

Another notion occurred to Jules. Maybe Doc Landrieu had discovered more about *Jules* than Jules had known. Maybe the pills hadn't done the work at all. Maybe what had really done the work had been his own trust, his own *belief* that the pills would help him.

A placebo. Doc Landrieu had slipped him a placebo. That rotten bastard. Here Jules had trusted him, believed in him, and his old boss had abused that trust, twisted him around his pinkie finger just so he could get Jules to reconsider moving with him down to Argentina—

Jules barely had time to work a good mad up before the delayed-action epiphany kicked him in the head like the business end of a French Quarter mule:

It wasn't the pills at all. It was me. *It's* always *been* me.

Everything Doodlebug had tried to convince him of was true. Jules had been transforming into a wolf with a barrel-belly because that was the only kind of wolf he'd believed he could become. He hadn't flown in years because he'd lost faith in his ability to leave the ground. He'd suffered from aches and pains and shortness of breath for decades, all because an unending stream of newspaper articles and TV shows had told him a person of his size *had* to suffer these things.

None of it had been necessary. Maybe it had been safe and comforting . . . he'd always had a ready excuse at hand whenever he screwed up. But those excuses were a part of his old, familiar self that should've burned up when his house did.

His form and his fate were in his own hands.

He was 450 pounds of Grade-A, USDA-choice vampire. It was time he started acting it.

He picked up the phone and dialed the number from the tape. An unfamiliar voice answered.

"Get me your boss," Jules said. "Tell him it's the fat man."

Two minutes later, Malice X came on the line. "I guess you figured out which end of the tape to stick in the machine, huh?"

Jules briefly considered five or six snappy comebacks. But he was in no mood for banter, clever or otherwise. "You and me, Malice. Let's do it. Let's get this shit over with."

"*Whoa-ho-ho!* You sound *serious*, man. But I guess losin' a friend and a lover in one night can do that to a guy. Just name your time and place, Julio."

"Tomorrow night. Ten o'clock. Your place."

"You mean where I live?"

"Whatever hole in the ground you crawl into at the end of the night."

Malice X laughed. "You hit closer to the truth than you know, man. How come my house? Not that I mind, but you've got me curious."

"I don't want you worryin' about me settin' an ambush for you. I want you to feel nice and comfortable."

The black vampire laughed again. "Why, that's downright *ballsy* of you, Jules! Stupid, but ballsy. I like that. Fine. My boys'll watch, but they won't interfere; I promise. 'No ambushes' . . . *heh*. You *kill* me, man!"

He gave Jules directions. The instructions were nothing Jules needed to write down. Malice X lived in the heart of the city, barely a mile from Maureen's house. At the center of everything—but hidden, invisible— deep down. Jules was surprised when he learned the location of his enemy's home, but after a few seconds of thought, it made perfect sense.

So in nineteen hours and twenty-three minutes, Jules would battle his nemesis deep beneath Canal Street. That suited Jules just fine. It meant he'd have less distance to travel when he dragged Malice X down to hell.

EIGHTEEN

Jules stared at the insurance check in his hand. Twenty-one thousand dollars. More money than he'd ever held in his hands in his whole, long, often impoverished existence.

A bus rumbled past, spewing a cloud of diesel smoke over the Hibernia Bank automated teller kiosk at the corner of Royal and Bienville Streets. Jules signed the back of the check, then sealed it in a deposit envelope. The envelope glue tasted like peppermint motor oil. He stuck his rarely used banking card into the machine's slot, then realized with a sinking feeling that he couldn't remember his numeric password. After a second of gastric upset, he smiled ruefully when he recalled that he hadn't picked a numeric password at all. He punched in M-A-U-R-E-E-N. The machine flashed its electronic version of "A-OK."

Twenty-one thousand dollars. He could do a lot of good with that kind of money. Maybe he couldn't make amends for all the rotten things he'd done over the past eighty years. But he could make life better for the few friends he had left.

◆

Half an hour after the Palm Court Jazz Café had closed, the stretch of Decatur Street in front of the club was deserted. Deserted except for a tired musician loading equipment into his creaky Coupe DeVille.

"Hey, Chop. How're they hangin'?"

The elderly bandleader finished placing his trumpet case in his trunk and turned around. "Jules? Seems like I'm seein' you all the time nowadays. How's that new lady friend of yours? The big curvy blonde I seen you with?"

Porkchop Chambonne made an exaggerated hourglass shape with his hands that described Veronika pretty accurately. Jules grimaced. "Don't ask. That one's poison."

"Oh. Sorry to hear that. She looked . . . interesting, that one did." He shrugged his stooped shoulders. " 'Fraid you got here too late to catch the band. You'll have one more chance, though. Me and the big band play one more gig, night after next. Then I've got to let most of the boys go. Cuttin' back to a trio."

"That's what I came to see you about. Here. I got something for you."

Jules handed a check to his friend. The bandleader's eyes popped big as soup bowls when he read the amount. "Five thousand dollars? Where'd you get this kind of money? And why are you givin' it to *me*?"

"My ticket hit big on the Pick-Four Lotto," Jules said. "I already got most of everything I need. So I wanna help you keep the band together. Five thou won't keep you goin' forever, but maybe it'll help you hang in there until better gigs come calling."

Porkchop Chambonne leaned against the trunk of his car, still staring at the check. "I, well, I don't rightly know what to say, Jules. Nobody's ever given me this kinda dough for nuthin' before. I'm not sure I can accept this kinda gift from you."

"Don't think of it as a gift. There's somethin' I want you and the band to do for me."

"Oh?" The bandleader raised an eyebrow and glanced slyly at his benefactor. "Now the other shoe drops. What's the pitch?"

"It's nothin' bad, Chop," Jules said quickly. "You and the band have done jazz funerals before, haven't you?"

"Well, sure. Practically every traditional jazz group in the city has, at one time or another. Sure."

"I've got this friend, see . . . I *had* this friend. A real special friend. She, uh, she died last night."

"Oh. I'm real sorry, Jules," Porkchop Chambonne said quietly.

Jules waited a second before continuing, waiting for his friend to ask how it had happened. But the bandleader maintained a respectful silence, and Jules was profoundly grateful that he didn't have to make up any stories about how Maureen had died.

"Maureen, my, uh, my friend, she lived her whole life in the Quarter. Worked here, too. All her pals are French Quarter people. I think she'd really appreciate a New Orleans jazz send-off. She always liked music. She was a dancer."

"When's the funeral? Will the holy service be at St. Louis Cathedral or up at St. Patrick's?"

"She, umm, she wanted to be cremated. There won't be a funeral; not really. And she wasn't much of a churchgoer, so she didn't want no holy service. To tell the truth, she worked at Jezebel's Joy Room most of the last twenty years. And that's where most of her buddies work. So what I'd like—what I think *she'd* like—is if you and the band could parade past the club, and then go past her house on Bienville, between Dauphine and Rampart. Tomorrow night, around midnight or so, after any gigs you guys might have. It's kinda weird, I know. But she was always a night person. Like me. Do it in the daytime, I'm not sure she'd hear it."

"She have any favorite songs or spirituals we oughtta play?"

"She liked show tunes. The old ones, from forty or fifty years back."

"I'm sure we can whip somethin' up. And if it's all right, there's an original number I'd like to play, too. Somethin' I been foolin' around with for a little whiles now. Actually, you were kinda my inspiration for it."

"Sure. I trust your judgment, Chop. Whatever you think's appropriate. You think we should be worrying about permits for that late at night?"

The bandleader made a dismissive gesture. "Naww. Maybe if we was paradin' in front of the Pontalba Apartments. But those blocks you want us to circle, them's mostly music clubs, bars, strip joints, or warehouses. Nobody's gonna mind us none."

"So you'll take the check?"

Porkchop Chambonne glanced at the check again, shaking his head with disbelief as he read the amount one more time. "Sure, Jules. I'll take this check. If that's how you wanna spread your money around, who am *I* to argue?"

"Great. Hey, just one more favor. I've gotta make a call, and I don't have any change on me. Can I maybe borrow thirty-five cents?"

The old man made a mock-stern face. "I don't know! Are you good for it?" He dug into his pocket and retrieved two quarters and a pair of dimes. "Here. Make yourself *two* phone calls."

Jules shook his friend's hand and took the change. "Thanks. That jazz funeral tomorrow night, I know it'll be somethin' to hear. Chop . . . you may have a hard time believing this, but ever since you started playin' music, well . . . I've been your biggest fan."

Porkchop Chambonne rubbed his mocha-colored chin, speckled with white stubble. Then he smiled slyly and gave Jules a deeply knowing look. "Yeah. I believe you. You and your 'daddy,' you *both* been my biggest fans. I'm mighty sorry for your loss, man. I surely am. But me and my students, we'll make a heavenly noise to guide your friend to her final reward."

Jules hadn't thought seeing the little diner again would affect him this much. The place had only been in business for the past four years, a tiny blip in his life. And Jules had groused heartily when his nightly coffee crew of cabbies and cops had decided to pull up stakes and move from the St. Charles Tavern to its new rival up the street. But the Trolley Stop Café really had become a home away from home for him. Anyway, it wasn't the physical particulars of a place that made it a home. It was the people inside that did.

People like Erato.

"Hey, pal. Thanks for coming out," Jules said.

"No problem," Erato said. He leaned across the table and pushed a chair out for Jules to sit in. "Slow night, anyway. And I been a little concerned about you, ever since you ran off from that rally earlier. You doin' all right?"

Jules sat down heavily and placed his vase on the table. "I've had better nights."

"What's with the vase? Somebody send you flowers?"

"It's . . ." Jules considered the wide range of possible lies he could tell his friend. He decided now wasn't the time for lies. "It's Maureen, Erato. It's—it's her *ashes.*"

Erato didn't say anything for a minute. His eyes turned harshly on his friend. "That's *evil*, man. That ain't no kinda joke to be makin'. It ain't funny."

Jules's expression didn't change one iota. "It's not a joke. I'd give anything in the world for it to *be* a joke. Look at me, Erato. Tell me if I'm pullin' a gag."

His friend looked at him long and hard. Slowly, reluctantly, Erato's expression shifted from indignant anger to shock. "Jesus . . . You ain't shittin' me. How—when—how the fuck did this *happen*, man?"

"I . . . *shit*. I can't give you no details. You're the best friend I got in this world, and if there's anybody I'd wanna tell, it's you. But Maureen wouldn't want me to tell you. And I've gotta honor what I figure her wishes would be."

Erato stared at his hands. Jules watched the man's face turn a deeper shade of brown and his large, callused hands clench into fists. "Why the hell are you layin' this on me if you won't trust me—if you don't think enough of me to tell me what happened? Maureen was *my* friend, too. Don't you think I got a right to know?"

Jules swallowed. Hard. "Yeah. You got a right to know. I just don't got a right to tell you. And if you don't think that's tearing my guts to pieces right now, then you don't know me."

Erato's fists slowly unclenched. Jules saw grief, hurt, anger, and resignation carve themselves into his friend's face in turn. "Okay," Erato said at last. "What can I do?"

"Take this vase, Erato. Take Maureen for me. Take her home with you, and put her on a windowsill that has a pretty view. Where she'll get lots of sun and be warm all the time. That would mean a helluva lot to me."

"Jules, I—I mean, I said I'd do anything I can, but . . . but that's not for *me* to do. She belongs with *you*."

"She belongs with someone who can take care of her. Someone who's gonna be around for a while. And I don't think that someone is me."

"What do you mean? Where are you going?"

"I can't tell you."

Erato's eyes blazed. "Aww *fuck*!" He slammed his palm down on the table. "What the hell *is* this? You yank me in here, stir me up like a hamster in a Mixmaster, and then you won't tell me *shit*! What's with all this bullshit, man?"

Jules took another check out of his pocket and pushed it across the table. "Here. Maybe this'll make the bullshit go down easier."

Erato took a few seconds to read the check. "Twelve thousand dollars. Made out to me. 'To send Lacrecia to LSU.'" He pushed the check back across the table. "You are just *full* of surprises tonight, aren't you? Where'd you get this kinda money?"

Jules pushed the check back toward Erato. "Take it. I want you to have it. It'd make me real happy, knowin' that I helped send her to college in Baton Rouge. Since I know that's what you really want for her."

Erato didn't touch the check. "I ask you *again*. Where'd you get this kinda money?"

Jules sighed. Withholding information from his best friend was one thing. Telling him an out-and-out lie was another. "It's part of the insurance payout from my house."

"So what are you givin' it to *me* for? Don't you need a place to live?"

Jules stared down at the table. Without his wanting it to, his gaze drifted to the green glass vase and the white dust inside. "That's what I was hinting around at before, see. I won't be needing no place to live. I won't need a car or a record player or a set of dishes or nothin'. After tomorrow night . . . well, lemme put it this way. We won't be drinkin' coffee together in here no more, pal."

Erato grabbed his arm. "You aren't—you aren't plannin' on killing yo'self, are you?"

Jules smiled ruefully. "Naww. Nothin' like that. I figure another guy'll do it for me. But not before I get in some licks of my own."

"If you're in bad trouble . . . let me help."

"Forget it. These guys I'm tusslin' with, they're way outta your league. They're outta the cops' league. I've gotta handle this in my own way, on my own."

"Oh? And what sorta league are *you* in? That's *bullshit*, man. If you're in the kinda trouble you think you won't walk away from, you need *help*. And who's gonna help you if your friends don't?"

Jules stood up. He squared his shoulders and stared Erato down, using a tone of voice he'd never thought he'd ever use with his friend. "Now you listen up. You are *not* gettin' tangled up in *my* business. Ever since this whole mess got started, I've been scramblin' for ways to get other people to do my dirty work for me. All that ducking and running, you know what that's ended up gettin' for me? Two of my best friends killed. That's what. And here you are, volunteerin' to become the third. Jeezus, Erato, do you realize what you've *got*? You've got all the good stuff in your life that I'll *never have*. A wife. A family. Things you done for other people that you can be proud of. Now listen. You go back to your house tonight, and you crawl in bed next to your wife, and tomorrow morning you deposit that check in your bank account. You hear me?"

The black cabdriver didn't say a word in response. He picked up the check from the table, folded it in half, and stuck it in his shirt pocket.

Jules watched him and smiled with satisfaction. "Thanks for being my friend, Erato," he said. And then he walked out the door of the Trolley Stop Café, for what he figured would be the last time.

The Lincoln was parked out back, on the shadowy fringes of the Central City neighborhood where Jules last encountered Malice X. Jules felt a spear of anguish in his chest when he thought back to that night. If he hadn't been so squeamish about killing a fellow vampire . . . if he'd fired his wooden darts through Malice X's heart when he'd had the chance . . . both Maureen and Doc Landrieu would still be among the living.

Jules heard footsteps behind him. Numerous footsteps, none heavy enough to be a man's. He whirled around to face them, enraged that anything would intrude on his mournful thoughts.

Dogs. Or wolves; he couldn't tell. Five of them, standing at the edge of the parking lot, all staring up at him.

Jules realized he wasn't afraid. He wasn't even particularly surprised. "Couldn't wait 'til tomorrow night, huh?" he scowled. "I thought Malice wanted to polish me off all by himself. Doesn't matter." He picked up a broken piece of plywood from near his feet. "Come on, then! Let's get this goddamn business over with!"

But the wolf-dogs didn't come any closer. Not one of them growled. Their muscles weren't tensed; they were clearly interested in him, but they weren't angry or fearful. The beasts' tails moved slowly from side to side. It might've been a trick of the light, but Jules thought he could almost see friendliness in their eyes. And their scent—he *knew* that scent from somewhere. The sense memory was as strong as his recollection of Maureen's perfume, even if he couldn't for the life of him place it.

The largest of the pack, the leader, separated itself from the others and slowly ambled toward Jules. Wondering whether he'd end up with five fewer fingers, Jules nervously extended his hand for the animal to sniff. But it didn't pause at the preliminaries—it immediately licked his fingers, as enthusiastically as a boyhood pet. The lead wolf-dog rested its muzzle on his hand, staring up at Jules with big blue-gray eyes, eyes that were both weirdly intelligent and piercingly familiar, as mysteriously known to him as the other wolf-dogs' scents had been. It pressed its cold, damp nose against his hand for several seconds, as if maybe trying to comfort him somehow, trying to tell him that in this big harsh universe perhaps Jules wasn't as alone as he thought. Then the big wolf-dog licked him a second time, wagged its tail, and returned to its fellow pack members.

Jules cautiously unlocked his car, still grasping the plywood fragment. He started the engine and backed out of the lot. The wolf-dogs continued watching him as he drove past. He tried looking at them a final time in his rearview mirror, but they were already gone.

◆

Jules awoke the next night at eight forty-three. He felt surprisingly well rested. *So now I know the trick to a good day's sleep,* he told himself. *Help your pals, and have your mind made up. Easy. Shame I learned that lesson with only one day's sleep left to me.*

He opened the cottage's refrigerator and removed two of the three remaining pints of California blood that Doodlebug had left behind. Jules downed them both, straight out of the plastic bottles. It was a definite bummer that his last blood meal was this weak, watery, almost tasteless plasma. But it was also good, in a way. Drinking California blood was like downing a vitamin shake; New Orleans blood was like a Christmas ham feast, the kind of repast that makes you dopey and sleepy enough to enjoy the Vienna Boys Choir on TV. He would need his strength tonight, so skipping a meal wasn't an option, but he couldn't afford to be weighed down.

He wrote two checks for the remainder of the money in his checking account, one to Billy Mac for what Jules still owed on the Lincoln, the other to Tiny Idaho for the weapons he'd made. Jules recounted that when his father had passed on, he'd also passed on a bunch of bad debts to Jules's mother. The memory left a bad taste in his mouth, bad as spoiled blood. If Jules was to leave this earth, he'd do so debt-free.

He had two stops to make before he faced his destiny at the foot of Canal Street. His first stop was the E-Z Mart at the corner of South Claiborne and Tulane Avenues, in the dusty shadow of the Pontchartrain Expressway overpass. The proliferation of these little all-night convenience stores had been one aspect of progress that'd made a vampire's existence easier. He located his two items quickly. The total for the tin of Qwik-Start lighter fluid and the book of matches came to three dollars and forty-three cents. Jules handed the clerk a five-dollar bill and told him to keep the change. The two items fit easily in one of his safari jacket's huge Velcro-flap pockets.

Jules clambered into his despised Lincoln for what he hoped would be the last time. He had to turn the ignition key and give the accelerator five pumps before the big, gutless motor finally turned over. It didn't matter. Real soon now—just another few blocks—and this shit bucket would be somebody else's problem.

He turned onto Claiborne Avenue, driving beneath the vibrating canopy of the elevated expressway until he reached the New Orleans Police Department's impoundment lot, an open-air jail for dozens of vehicles. They ranged from jalopies held together with Bondo and duct tape, hauled in for unpaid parking tickets, on up to Porsche Speedsters confiscated from drug dealers. The impounded cars were protected from the elements by the thick ceiling of the expressway, and protected from vandals and thieves by a twelve-foot fence topped with razor wire.

Jules briefly reviewed his options. As he idled the Lincoln, he observed two cops in the guard shack, watching TV. Option One: He could park the Lincoln, go over to the gate, and call the guards over. Then, once they were within eye contact, he could hypnotize them to open the gate for him. That would be the prudent way. Option Two: He could throw prudence to the winds and do it the fun way.

Option Two was it.

He drove past the lot, then swung the Lincoln around with an ear-splitting shriek of cheap tire tread. He gunned the engine, heading toward the gate with all the momentum he could muster. His speed when he hit the gate wasn't very impressive, barely twenty miles an hour. But the Lincoln's sturdy frame and two-and-a-half-ton bulk were more than adequate for the job. The big coupe lost its grille and front bumper, but the fence got the worst of it—both sides of the gate were hurled toward the guard shack in a shower of sparks and broken metal.

He swung the Lincoln into an empty patch of weeds in a corner of the lot and cut the engine. He didn't bother removing the key before he flung the door open and got out. Hell, he was donating the car to the NOPD, so he might as well leave them the keys. The guard shack's door burst open. The two cops came running out, one of them sporting just-spilled gravy from a half-eaten roast beef po' boy all over his blue shirt. *Definitely not two of New Orleans's finest,* Jules thought.

"*Shit!* Lookit my *shirt!*" the gravy-splattered cop hollered. "Mister, you'd better *pray* you can convince us that was an accident—"

"He ain't stoppin', Carl," his partner said. "I don't think that was any accident." The cop unholstered his revolver. "Freeze right where you are, mister—"

Jules concentrated on an image of a train set, chugging steadily along its toy tracks. "No, *you* freeze," he said.

And they did.

"Now here's the deal," Jules said, barely pausing long enough to register surprise at his mental feat. "I was never here, okay? You never saw me crash through your gate. Another thing—that white Cadillac Fleetwood over there? It was never on this lot. What you guys had *instead* was this pile-a-shit Lincoln here. In three minutes, you two dream-birds are gonna wake up. Gravy Boy is gonna feel all mortified about joyriding in the Lincoln and mashing down the gate when the brakes went out on him. By the time the next shift arrives, you two will've pieced together some phony-baloney story to feed your bosses."

Jules walked over to his Cadillac. It was parked between a racing-green Jaguar XJS convertible and a gleaming BMW 8-Series coupe, but to Jules it was the finest car on the lot. He lovingly caressed one of its long, white tailfins. Boy, had he missed this automobile.

He dug the spare key out of his pocket and opened the door. The scent of aged leather was almost intoxicating. The Caddy's faithful old big-block V-8 turned over on the first turn of the key, without a hiccup of complaint.

If Fate insisted he go where final death waited, he'd go there in his own damn car.

NINETEEN

So this is how it feels to be inside a pinball machine, Jules thought as he walked inside the casino. He strode past row after row of slot machines, all busily flashing, pinging, and jingling for row after row of empty chairs. On the outside the gambling hall at the foot of Canal Street resembled a gigantic suburban bank building, festooned with tons of neon in a vain attempt to disguise its pedestrian origins. On the inside Jules thought it looked more like Vegas . . . in the aftermath of an army germ-warfare experiment gone wrong. Apart from costumed employees, the place was practically deserted. Many of his fellow cabbies had been enthusiastic when the casino had first been approved by the legislature. They'd all figured it would attract more big-spending tourists. But rather than pulling in tourists, the casino had mostly attracted locals. And when they exited for home, empty-pocketed, they left in city buses, not cabs.

He walked to the side of the main room closest to Convention Center Boulevard. Just as he'd been told, there was the private elevator, flanked by two tuxedoed guards. Guards, not doormen; doormen didn't sport holsters and squared-off bulges beneath their suit jackets.

Jules approached the guard on the left. Both of the men were white; Jules wondered whether Malice X got a little charge out of lording it over white employees. "I'm Jules Duchon. I got business with your boss downstairs."

"Ah, yes. The fat man. We were told to expect you." The guard pressed the elevator's call button. A few seconds later, the door swished open. "Don't forget to press the DOWN button once you're inside. It's the one with the little red arrow that points to the floor."

"Thanks, wise guy." Jules flipped him a nickel before entering the elevator. "Here's a tip for your trouble."

The elevator was trimmed in tufted red velvet. "Looks like the coffin I could never afford," Jules muttered to himself. The doors opened onto a shockingly large space, a high-ceilinged cavern where no cavern had any right to be. Jules felt like Arthur Conan Doyle's Professor Challenger, who'd descended to the South Pole and discovered dinosaurs instead of glaciers.

"So this is where they dug it," Jules said softly, wonderingly. "The tunnel to nowhere." He thought back to the time, decades ago, when Canal Street had been snarled with earthmoving machines. More than thirty years had passed since the demise of the ill-conceived Riverfront Expressway project, a spur of highway that would've cut the French Quarter off from the Mississippi and permanently shadowed Café Du Monde with six lanes of elevated traffic. While a group of dedicated preservationists had fought the project in court and in Congress, the road builders had pressed forward, digging a massive tunnel beneath the International Trade Mart, a twenty-story riverfront monolith that stood in the path of the planned highway.

Then, against all expectations, the preservationists won their fight. The highway was canceled. But the tunnel endured. Its entrances were closed off; it didn't make sense to fill in the hole that remained, but no one could come up with a use for it. Over the years, everyone forgot it was there.

Almost everyone. The man who became Malice X hadn't even been born when the tunnel was first dug, but someone older than he had remembered the big hole by the river. Someone who realized that, with enough money invested, the hole would make an ideal sunproof lair for vampires.

The black vampire had certainly invested his wages of sin impressively. In the center of the tunnel was a Greek Revival mansion that wouldn't have appeared out of place on St. Charles Avenue. A glassed-in garden and courtyard, a third as big as a football field, filled the space between the mansion's two rear wings. A small fleet of tricked-out luxury cars and sport-utility vehicles was parked next to a gated access tunnel at the cavern's far end. Most unusual of all, however, was what covered the cavern's ceiling—a canopy of glittering stars and bright planets. Jules hadn't seen such a glorious night sky within the city limits since before the widespread adoption of electric lights.

Jules stared upward, slack-jawed, as a meteor shower highlighted the faux sky. "Impressed?" Malice X's wry, scornful voice boomed from hidden loudspeakers. "It's a shame you won't be around to see our beautiful sunrise," the electronic voice continued while Jules searched futilely for its owner. "But it's the sun*sets*, man—that's when my light dude really earns his keep."

"I didn't come for no IMAX show," Jules grumbled in the direction of the house. "You gonna show your face, mother-killer, or do I have to tear your place apart lookin' for you?"

" 'Muthah-*killer*'? For a sec there, I thought you might shock me and cuss me somethin' more colorful. You sound like a man in a hurry. Relax. I'll make things as simple as possible. To find me, just follow yo' heart's desire."

A series of pencil-thin beams of light illuminated dozens of beignets lying on the cobblestones. The sugar-laden squares of fried dough formed a winding pathway that led around the side of the mansion. *He'd better enjoy his little jokes about my weight,* Jules thought. *Bastard won't be making them much longer.* As he followed the path of beignets, the spotlights stayed a few yards ahead of him. The path ended at the doorway to the glassed-in courtyard.

Jules opened the door, made of crimson stained glass, and stepped into the spacious garden. They were all there, standing behind the flowers and neatly trimmed hedges that enclosed a central square of immaculate lawn. He recognized about half the dark gray faces that stared him down. The toughs who'd surrounded him and Doodlebug in the alley outside Club Hit 'N' Run, who'd nearly killed him outside Maureen's house. Cowboy Hat was there, still sporting his distinctive western wear and the chip on his shoulder. Even Malice X's sister was there, glaring at Jules evilly. She spat sharply into a hedge as he closed the door behind him.

Jules didn't look at her for long. He quickly locked eyes with the man he'd come to close accounts with. Malice X sat in an ornate wicker porch swing, squeezed comfortably between a pair of adoring, buxom women vampires. In contrast to the rest of Malice's entourage, they paid Jules no attention at all, contenting themselves with running their long-nailed fingers across their master's broad biceps and nearly bare chest.

"Welcome to my 'humble abode,' Jules," Malice X said, smiling a Cheshire cat grin. "Welcome to Palace X." He kept his arms snugly around his companions, leaving himself insouciantly vulnerable to any sort of projectile weapon Jules might've sneaked in under his coat. "All those priests at Jesuit High, man, they kept tellin' me I hadda go to college to make somethin' of myself, to *be* somebody. What the *fuck* did they know, huh? You know where all this comes from? Smarts, man. I came up with a good product, I marketed it right, and then I stashed my profits away in tech stocks. The joint upstairs? It wouldn't *exist* without me. Those yo-yos who wanted to build the world's biggest casino, they couldn't get their ducks in a row. Couldn't line up the financing, didn't have the pull with the local politicos. I could, and I did. I was their—what'd they call it? Oh, yeah. Their 'white knight.' *Heh.*

"And you know what? I accomplished all this in less than a decade as a vampire. Less than *ten years*. How long've you been a bloodsuckah, Jules? Eighty years? A hundred? And what's been the peak of your success? Tempting fat-ass old bag ladies into a cab even more broken down than they were?"

"You done bragging?" Jules asked flatly.

"No." Malice X smiled again. "I'm not. Had yourself a good time with that chippie from the Strategic Helium Reserve?"

Jules was careful not to let any emotion play across his face. "So you were behind that, too. You ain't tellin' me anything I haven't already figured."

"But you *gotta* admit it was slick—one vampire siccin' the vampire hunters on another. You know why I did it? Not because I thought I couldn't do the job on you myself. I pulled the feds' strings because I *could*. Because it was *easy*. I had all these bigwigs at City Hall eatin' outta my hand, beggin' me for their next dose of Horse-X. They had connections, and their connections had connections. I wanted to see what the feds had. What kinda antivampire doohickies they could come up with. And if I could find that out and make your life miserable at the same time—hey, I *never* pass up a two-fer."

"Yeah? Well here's a two-fer for you. I left your fed dame lookin' like a sap, and I'll do the same to you."

Malice X laughed. "Hey, I got no *doubt* you left her lookin' like a sap. You walk around lookin' like a sap *all* the time." He laughed again, and then his smile faded. "But you ain't gonna be walkin' outta *here*, sappy lookin' or not."

Jules had no more patience for banter. It was time to call his rival out. "You gonna back those words up? Or are you just gonna sit there and threaten me to death?"

Malice X pushed his lady companions aside and rose from the swing. His silver Lycra athletic pants glistened like polished chrome, and his ribbed undershirt did little to conceal his chiseled abdomen and oiled, bulging pectorals.

"Preston, fetch us the stakes," he said.

Cowboy Hat picked up what looked like an antique rifle case and laid it at Malice X's feet. The lieutenant unlatched the case and opened it. Inside were two identical shafts of maple wood, about four feet long, each with both ends sharpened to a deadly point.

"This is an idea I copped from a boss *Tomb of Dracula* comic," Malice X said proudly. "In this one issue, see, ol' Drac was challenged by this other bloodsuckah as to who should be king of all the vampires. So Drac proposed a 'Duel by Stake'—two vampires, two stakes, and only one vampire walks away. Wicked, huh?"

Jules eyed the twin stakes warily. The introduction of such weapons didn't come as a complete surprise to him. Before the days of gentlemen's agreements and arbitration in the vampire world, duels like this had been distressingly common. Anyway, if he played his cards right, he could twist the introduction of stakes to his own advantage. "Okay. I'll accept your terms. On one condition," he added.

Malice X raised an eyebrow. "Who said anything 'bout any 'conditions'?"

"*I* did," Jules said. "I'm on your turf, ain't I? Surrounded by your friends and flunkies? If you're so cocksure you're better than me, and you've got home-field advantage on top of that, what's the harm in throwin' me one little bone?"

"That tub-a-lard ain't got no right to demand *nothin'*!" Malice X's sister shrieked, her face contorted with contempt. But many other on-lookers murmured that they wanted to hear Jules's demand. The mur-murs were subdued and nearly anonymous, but they were insistent.

Jules watched Malice X's face carefully. Clearly, the black vampire agreed wholeheartedly with his sister's admonition; but just as clearly, he couldn't risk losing even a fraction of the respect granted him by his underlings. Jules enjoyed seeing flickers of indecision play across his rival's mouth. "All right . . . name it, fat man. One condition."

"I win this duel, I get your coffin. You burned up mine when you torched my house. I need a new one."

"That's *it?*" Malice X's momentary indecision morphed into incredulity. "*That's* your one condition? I thought maybe you'd want me to fight with both hands tied behind my back or somethin'—"

"That's my condition. And I want it down here *now*. Where I can see it. Before we start our duel."

"Why the hell d'you want that for?"

"So you can't welsh on me after I win."

Malice X started to protest, but his objections melted into rich laughter. "Fuck yeah, man. Sure! I gave you a chance to make this dustup halfway fair, and if that's what you want, that's what you get, man. It's your fuckin' funeral, and you got a right to screw it up any way you wanna." He turned to his chief lieutenant. "Preston, take a coupla dudes and fetch my coffin from the master bedroom. Make it snappy, huh? I wanna get in a coupla rounds of blackjack upstairs before the sun rises."

Cowboy Hat grunted his assent, then nodded to a pair of toughs, and the three of them disappeared into the mansion. Malice X turned back toward Jules. "So what do *I* get when *I* win? And don't be tryin' to pawn off that lame-ass car of yours on me."

Jules thought about this for a minute. "If you win, you get to scatter my ashes in the parking lot of the Esplanade Mall, so my sufferin' soul is stuck in the goddamn suburbs forever."

Malice X laughed sharply. "Shit, man, fuck the parkin' lot. You goin' in the mall's *urinals*."

"Whatever," Jules muttered. And he managed a tight little grin of his own as he watched Cowboy Hat and the others maneuver Malice X's polished teak coffin through the double doors into the courtyard.

"Okay, it's here," Malice X said. "Satisfied?"

"Yeah," Jules said. He took off his safari jacket, then knelt down to untie his boots and pull them and his socks off. Next to come off were his shirt and undershirt. He had unbuckled his belt and was unzipping his trousers when Malice X interrupted.

"What th' hell you tryin' to do now—nullify my knockout by nauseatin' me with your nudity?"

"I'm strippin' down for action," Jules said, sitting on a stone bench while he peeled off his trousers and began the arduous task of extricating his underpants from between his massive thighs. "You got a problem with that?"

"No problem. Just a silly li'l question: How the hell do you plan on holdin' a four-foot stake when you got wolf's paws or bat's claws?"

"You let *me* worry about that," Jules said, smiling inwardly. He scooped up his pile of clothing and walked boldly across the open square to where Malice X stood. He made no attempt at all to cover his privates (mostly hidden by his stomach, anyway) or to hide his tremendous, quivering white ass from the onlooking crowd. For the first time he could remember, he wasn't ashamed, either of his naked body or having strangers see it. His overwhelming mass was an asset, not a handicap—his secret ace in the hole, secret even though it was in plain sight of everyone. He'd show them all, before the night was done. He'd show them what a fat vampire could do.

He dumped his clothes next to the coffin. "So they'll be handy when it's time to cart this thing away," he said. He glanced at the two long stakes in the leather case near Malice X's feet. "How about lettin' me have one of them pig stickers now?"

"Give him one, Preston," Malice X said. Cowboy Hat grunted wearily, selected one of the stakes, and held it out to Jules.

"Gimme the other one," Jules said.

The lieutenant looked quickly to Malice X, who shrugged irritably and said, "Let 'im have it." Cowboy Hat handed his boss the first stake, then gave Jules the second one.

Jules backed away to the far edge of the open square of grass. He broke the stake twice over his knee, snapping it into three stubby weapons. Before his rival could do more than grunt with surprise, Jules whispered two words to himself.

"Train set," he said.

It was the most difficult transformation he'd ever attempted. He concentrated on thoughts of all the little tough guys he'd admired in the movies—Alan Ladd, Jimmy Cagney, Edward G. Robinson. Little tough guys who didn't put up with shit from anybody; fighters worth twice their weight in a scrap. He was going to do something even Doodlebug couldn't do—he was going to carve three middleweight vampires from one heavyweight.

He felt his bones melting. He sensed the familiar pull of his far-off coffin on a portion of his great mass, but he resisted, concentrating on keeping it all present, splitting himself like an amoeba. His nerve endings were afire, but he refused to settle for the familiar, the easy. Images flashed through his splintering mind—Jake La Motta; Sugar Ray Robinson; the mayor of Munchkinland in his little purple suit . . .

The fleshy mist began to clear and coalesce. For a moment Jules felt like he was on the wildest caffeine jag of his life. But then the static in his brain *(brains?)* died down to a tolerable buzz. He'd done it. Again he experienced the vertigo of looking at himself watching himself stare at himself. Where there had been one 450-pound Jules, there now stood three 150-pound Juleses.

Unfortunately, he'd concentrated too much on the Munchkins and not enough on Jake La Motta.

Three identically obese nude dwarfs stared at each other and murmured in unison: "Oh, shit."

Malice X's jaw nearly bounced off the turf. "This—*this* is your big parlor trick? *Midgets?*"

There was no time to try again. Even if there had been, the triplicate vampire couldn't muster a fraction of the necessary energy. He *(they)* were stuck. The three Juleses had no choice but to make the best of it. They bent their barrel-like bodies and snatched up the pieces of stake with their stubby little hands.

Malice X clapped his hands together and raised his face to the artificial heavens above. "Ladies and gentlemen, this proves what our preachers been sayin' for years—God is a black man. Wait, lemme rephrase that. Since the Good Lord don't answer vampires' prayers, I guess the Devil be a black man, too!"

Jules sensed his three consciousnesses splitting away from each other, like pieces of stuck-together saltwater taffy being pulled apart. He was becoming three separate people—Jules 1, Jules 2, and Jules 3—none of whom exerted direct control over the other two.

Three consciousnesses: Jules 1 prayed that they'd all remember the plan. Jules 2 tried contacting the other two telepathically but only got a shooting pain in his sinuses. Jules 3 didn't place his trust in either prayer or telepathy. "Snap out of it, guys!" he shouted. "Let's surround him!"

Malice X grinned and hummed a few bars of Randy Newman's "Short People." Then, without bothering to slip out of his clothing, he transformed smoothly and slickly into a panther. The big, muscular cat immediately lunged at Jules 2, knocking the rotund dwarf flat on his back. The panther's three-inch-long incisors tore at its prey's fat throat.

"Aaaahhhhhhh!" all three Juleses screamed.

The pain traveled from one to the other like a power surge through a live wire. Jules 1 nearly dropped his stake to clutch his own throat, but he stifled the reflex and ran toward the enemy with all the speed his stumpy legs could muster. *I might be a dwarf,* he told himself, *but I'm a* vampire *dwarf!* He pictured his legs as stubby but powerful springs, and he leapt onto the crouching panther's back. Before the creature could shake him off, Jules 1 plunged his stake into the cat's side.

The panther shrieked with pain and rage, immediately releasing its choke grip from around Jules 2's throat. Jules 3, unengaged in the struggle, found himself caught between equally powerful and desperate urges. *The plan—he's distracted—now's the time to hit his coffin—* But one of his other selves lay bleeding on the grass, while the other was menaced by a snapping set of jaws reaching back to bite him in half. *Fuck the plan! Improvise!* Jules 3 grasped his stake tightly in both fists and ran toward the melee, howling a wordless battle cry and aiming the point at the panther's heart.

Unfortunately, Jules had never studied veterinary science or even basic biology. He buried his stake in the animal's liver. Instead of crumbling to dust, the panther erupted with an earsplitting bellow. It bucked like a snakebit bronco, hurling Jules 1 from its back and knocking Jules 3 violently to the ground. Jules 1 tumbled twenty feet through the air before striking his head on a planter and landing in a heap. He didn't move or make a sound.

The panther tried dislodging the two stakes with its teeth. It managed to pull out the weapon hanging from its side, but it was unable to reach the one perforating its liver. It shrieked and spat with frustration. Its form wavered, then melted as it transformed back into Malice X.

The black vampire grasped the stubbornly lodged stake with both hands, took a deep breath, and yanked it from his body. *"Fuck!"* He sucked air through his clenched teeth. Tears ran freely from his red-veined eyes, and specks of blood flew from his mouth as he exhaled again. *"Fuck-fuck-*FUUUCK! That hurt like a *muthah,* you little cocksuckers!"

Jules 2, still gushing blood from fang wounds in his neck, tried desperately to rally his strength. He began weakly crawling away. He didn't get far. Malice X kicked his retreating foe onto his back, then pinned him by planting his right foot deep in the dwarf's soft stomach. He reached for his long stake, temporarily discarded when he'd transformed into the panther.

Jules 3 shook off the cobwebs just in time to see Malice X raise his weapon above the prone, helpless form of Jules 2. But instead of immediately plunging it into the trapped dwarf's heart, the black vampire grinned sadistically and started to sing.

"Short people got / No reason—"

He brought the stake down hard, burying it in Jules 2's plump left shoulder. The already wounded dwarf screamed with fresh agony. Jules 3 screamed with him, envying Jules 1 his unconsciousness. Malice X yanked the stake out and raised it above his head again.

"Short people got / No reason—"

This time he drove the weapon through Jules 2's rib cage. The vampire's inhumanly powerful thrust completely impaled the dwarf and embedded the sharp point deep in the ground. Jules 3 sensed his other self slipping into shock. Fighting a wave of encroaching darkness, he charged the black vampire on wobbly legs. But his feeble counterattack was stopped dead by a contemptuous backhanded blow, which both broke his nose and sent him flying into a shrubbery.

Dazed, bleeding, sprawled upside down in an azalea bush, Jules 3 could only watch as Malice X finished his deadly song.

"Short people got / No reason—to LI-IIIVE!"

This time was the deathblow. The thrust through the heart. Jules 3 had no idea what would happen—would all three of them crumple to dust simultaneously? No time for any whispered good-byes—no time for anything as he felt maple wood savage his heart, as he smelled blood and tasted salty iron and choked on his own effluvia as he felt his body coming apart. . . .

But he didn't come apart. He didn't dissolve or crumple or blow away. Jules 3 pawed himself to make sure he was still all there. All his important parts seemed intact, still hanging upside down in the azalea bush. His other self wasn't so fortunate, though. On the patch of grass where Jules 2 had struggled so valiantly just seconds before, there was now a faintly pulsating pool of gray proto-matter, the two-edged stake projecting from its center.

"What the hell is *this* now?" Malice X grimaced disgustedly as he wiped proto-matter residue off his bare foot onto the grass.

Jules 3 didn't have time to puzzle through the vampiric metaphysics behind what was happening. Their only chance now was to somehow force Malice X to transform again, to make him unwittingly send part of his mass to his coffin. He rolled out of the azalea bush and ran to Jules 1's side. The other dwarf was still stone-cold unconscious.

Jules 3 grabbed his duplicate's shoulders. "Wake up, kid! Wake up! It's the bottom of the ninth and we're five runs behind—"

Out of the corner of his eye, Jules 3 saw Malice X tentatively jiggle the long stake still protruding from the pool of proto-matter. "Guess maybe I best leave that in there for now," the black vampire muttered. "No prob—Jell-O Puddin' Man here done dropped *his* stake, and I seriously doubt he'll be havin' any need for it. . . ."

Jules 3 whirled around to protect his prone twin. But all he saw was a flash of foot, then a shower of stars as a bomb exploded in his midsection. He was vaguely aware of being airborne again before he landed bone-jarringly at the edge of the onlooking crowd. Seconds later, he sensed the agonizing decomposition of another third of himself.

"And then there was one," Malice X said, brushing his hands together briskly. "I really gotta *thank* you, Jules. Who woulda thought I'd get the chance to kill you three times? Shit, I wish you coulda split into *ten* little dudes."

Jules 3 picked himself painfully up from the turf. Near as he could tell, that last kick had broken two or three of his ribs; yet he refused to face death lying down. It was over. His plan was impossible now. But he'd done the best he could. He'd put his life on the line to protect Erato and Chop, to avenge Maureen and Doc Landrieu. He had nothing to be ashamed of.

Malice X picked up a discarded piece of stake from the ground. "Ready or not, loser, here I come. . . ."

The last remaining bit of Jules tightened his feeble grip on his own chunk of wood. He struggled to avoid blacking out as his smiling nemesis approached. He felt his body sway as he fell into micro sleeps. He was hallucinating, dreaming. He had to be. Otherwise, the clouds of mist condensing above the glass panes of the greenhouse and seeping in beneath the garden's doors made no sense at all—

One crash, then another, and suddenly it was raining glass. Jules saw, in the midst of the descending shards, a pair of large, wedge-shaped gray forms. The creatures landed on four powerful legs and immediately moved to cut Malice X off from Jules. The three clouds of mist that had drifted in beneath the doors were taking on a similar aspect, snarling menacingly as their low, muscular bodies congealed. Canines as big and nasty as the Hound of the Baskervilles—the same animals he'd encountered the night before outside the Trolley Stop! Jules blinked once, then twice, but the beasts didn't fade away like some drunk's pink elephants.

They barked viciously at Malice X, lunging and snapping at his legs as they moved in a pack to surround him.

These weren't just dogs, Jules realized. And despite their distinctive wolflike features, they weren't wolves, either. They were something new, both familiar and unfamiliar—these five creatures were *vampire wolf-dogs*!

"You lousy *cheater*!" Malice X screamed as he kicked at the wolf-dogs' heads. "All bets are off! See how you like fightin' a dozen brothers at once, you fat *freak*!"

Two of the wolf-dogs leapt for Malice X's throat, their fangs flashing in the multicolored garden lights. But by the time their jaws slashed the space where his throat had been, Malice X was no longer himself. Jules heard the flapping of desperately beating wings as the black vampire beat a hasty tactical retreat. The wolf-dogs snapped furiously at empty air as they leapt after the fleeing bat, which flittered toward the broken glass dome high above.

Jules turned his attention to the crowd behind him. All eyes were locked on the bizarre spectacle in the center of the garden. Now was his chance—

He ran to Malice X's coffin and snatched his safari jacket off the ground. He retrieved the tin of lighter fluid and the box of matches from the right-hip Velcro pocket. Jules opened the coffin. Inside, a three-inch-deep layer of gray proto-matter glistened and pulsated—nine-tenths of Malice X's bodily mass. Limbless, voiceless, sightless. Helpless. As helpless as Maureen had been when Malice X plunged a stake through her heart.

Jules bit the cap off the tin of lighter fluid. He squirted the combustible liquid all over the proto-matter and the coffin's velvet lining.

"Look! Over there!" Malice's sister shouted. "What's he doin' to Malik's coffin?"

Jules struck his match against the side of the coffin. It lit on the first try. Remembering the inferno that consumed his home, he tossed it inside. The proto-matter ignited like a whiskey-soaked slab of Brennan's Restaurant's bread pudding.

The effect on the bat high overhead was immediate. It shrieked, and the unnaturally piercing cry shattered several more of the glass panels overhead. Its wings crumpled, crushed by an invisible fist. Then it plummeted toward the ground. Into the nails and jaws of five vengeful creatures eager for a taste of blood.

"Malik! Brother!"

Jules almost felt bad for her. Almost. Malice's sister would've thrown herself into the feral pack, would've tried to pry the pieces of her brother's blood-spattered body from the wolf-dogs' teeth, had Cowboy Hat not wrapped her in a powerful restraining embrace.

"*Malik!* They're *killing* him! Preston, let me *go*! Damn you, they're *killing him*!"

The smoke from the burning coffin made Jules's eyes water. It smelled greasy and evil, like rancid andouille sausage that had been left on the grill too long. Malice's sister stopped twisting in Cowboy Hat's grasp, and her curses collapsed into sobs. The wolf-dogs finished their bloody work and trotted over to Jules's side. Several wagged their tails as they sniffed him. One licked his hand, leaving behind flecks of reddish foam.

Malice's sister stopped sobbing as abruptly as she had started. She stared at Jules with a hatred that made his balls seek the safety of his belly overhang. "He *cheated*. You heard my brother. He *broke* the *rules*. Kill him, Preston . . . kill him for me. . . ." Her voice shifted from a whiny, almost childlike tone to shrill invective as she whirled to face the others. "*All of you!* What are you standing there for? Kill him! *Kill him for me!*"

The wolf-dogs moved into a protective phalanx around their master. They growled at the dozen vampires standing at the edge of the garden. Jules stared into Cowboy Hat's shadowed face. "You an animal lover, Preston? *I* am."

The former chief lieutenant didn't make a move in Jules's direction. Neither did any of the others.

Still surrounded by his wary, protective pack, Jules pulled the stakes from the centers of the two pools of proto-matter pulsating weakly on the grass. Strength and mass flowed into him almost instantly, tributaries rejoining a river that had nearly run dry. In seconds he was his old self again, all 450 very welcome pounds.

Malice's sister sank slowly to the ground. Looking in the blankness of her eyes, Jules could see that her spirit was broken. At least for now. But the face of the tall man in the buckskin jacket and ten-gallon hat was still hidden by shadow.

"So what's it gonna be, Preston? I got no real beef with you. You gonna let me walk outta here, take over the Horse-X trade yourself, become the new big man? Or are you gonna play 'avenging flunky' and maybe end up like your ex-boss there?" He pointed to the lumpy red smear at the center of the garden.

All eyes turned to the man in the cowboy hat. He pushed its wide brim up with a flick of his forefinger and scratched his forehead. For the first time, Jules could see his eyes. They were tired. "You walk, fat man. Pick up your shit and get the hell outta here." He pressed a large red button on a console next to the mansion's back doors. Jules heard a distant rumbling echo from the far end of the vehicle tunnel, a rumbling that must've been the door to the outside opening. "But this ain't over. Don't expect things to just go back the way they was for you. This town ain't friendly territory, and it'll never be again. You're goin' down. Maybe not tonight. But some night, when you least expect it. . . ."

Jules gathered his soot-covered safari jacket, pants, and shoes from next to the smoldering coffin. "Just remember to bring some doggie treats when you come visitin'," he said, patting a wet nose. "They prefer bat wings to Milk-Bones."

Surrounded by his canine saviors, he walked to the door of the garden and opened it. Then he left the underground lair he hadn't expected to walk out of, his head held high, and no vampire dared block his way.

But despite experiencing a triumph bigger than he'd ever hoped for, Jules's victory was made hollow by three little words:

This ain't over.

TWENTY

"Top a the world, Ma! Top a the world!"

Jules's shouts echoed off the brick walls of the Warehouse District behind the casino. Even as echoes, his shouts sounded forced and phony.

He should be ecstatic. Or glad. Or at least relieved.

But Jules was none of those things. Malice X was gone. Yet that fact hadn't brought back Maureen. It hadn't even brought back a single King Oliver platter from his melted record collection.

One of the wolf-dogs—the leader—seemed to sense his melancholy. It nuzzled his hand gently; its cold nose on his fingers felt good in the humid night air. Another of the pack tried to cheer him by example, prancing around Jules and leaping boisterously, bouncing its paws off his stomach and chest.

Now Jules was able to take a closer look at his rescuers. Were these really his . . . pups? Was *that* why they'd seemed so familiar to him outside the Trolley Stop? All of the wolf-dogs had light brown spots on their chests and upper forelegs. His canine companion in Baton Rouge had similar markings, hadn't she? It was hard for Jules to remember; he hadn't been in his most lucid frame of mind during that night of *amour*. But the wolf-dogs' scent was so viscerally familiar, and he was sure he'd gotten more than a noseful of the friendly bitch's scent in that alleyway. His human-self might not remember that particular odor, but his buried wolf-self certainly would.

If they *were* his pups, how did they get born and grow up so fast? It was barely a month since Jules's trip to Baton Rouge. Dogs didn't gestate *that* fast, did they? On the other hand, it wouldn't exactly have been any normal pregnancy. He'd never knocked up anybody before, human, vampire, or otherwise. Who knew *what* the rules were when a vampire was involved?

Jules sat on the front steps of a shoe repair store and let the wolf-dogs lick his face while he patted their noses and scratched behind their ears. There was another possibility, he realized suddenly; the wolf-dogs didn't *have* to be his pups, not necessarily. Maybe Doodlebug hadn't left town when he said he had. Maybe his old friend had stuck around, watching him from the shadows, waiting for a time when Jules would really need him.

But Doodlebug wouldn't want to help him as Doodlebug. No— doing so would toss all that self-esteem/self-reliance psychobabble he'd regaled Jules with out the window. Doodlebug would figure out a way to be sneaky. He'd try to help in a way that would make it seem salvation had been the universe's reward for Jules's own actions. Hadn't Jules taken pity on a poor, stray animal, gotten her food, and kept her warm for a night? His karma had come full circle, Doodlebug might say; the universe had saved his big, fat behind a month later.

Maybe. Or maybe not. Jules gave each of the wolf-dogs a final scratch behind the ears, then stood up. They sure *seemed* like real wolf-dogs. But then again, Doodlebug was a very talented vampire.

It didn't really matter, he supposed. Either way, Doodlebug or pups, beings he'd had a hand in creating had stood by him in his time of need. After all, in a world where some men could turn into bats and preferred the taste of blood to andouille gumbo, what was one more mystery? Maybe he'd discover the truth someday. Or maybe he wouldn't. He'd lived this long not knowing where the first vampire had come from, or why the Saints had never made it to the Super Bowl.

The pack voiced friendly, parting barks as they loped up the deserted downtown street. One by one, they transformed into clouds of mist and began drifting west. Toward Baton Rouge. Or California.

"So long, guys," Jules called after them, waving. "If you're Doodle-bug, thanks. If you *aren't* Doodlebug, thanks. Next time we meet, the biscuits are on me."

Jules continued walking up Tchoupitoulas Street to where he'd parked his Cadillac. Now that he was alone he felt the weight of loneliness bearing down on him again. *This ain't over.* The three words mocked him, haunted him. He didn't want to spend an eternity fighting for turf. All he wanted was for things to go back to the way they had been. To be able to drink a cup of coffee in peace. To be able to listen to the soaring clarinets of a New Orleans jazz band without constantly looking over his shoulder. To chow down on a plate of red beans, smoked sausage, and trout almondine—well, that was pushing it, but he could dream, couldn't he?

A large, round shape stepped onto the sidewalk from the shadowy entrance foyer of Vic's Kangaroo Café. It wasn't a kangaroo. It was a woman. A very familiar woman.

"Hail the conquering hero," she said.

It was Veronika. "You were *magnificent*, darling," she said. "I heard the whole fight sitting in our operations center. It came through loud and clear on the bugs we had the construction crews plant when Malice X built his underground compound. If only you hadn't run away the last time we were together! I *told* you I could've helped you beat those black vampires! But you had to be a big silly and do it all on your own."

Jules winced and shut his eyes tightly. Was it true? If he hadn't run out on Veronika, could he have confronted Malice X nights earlier? "I could've maybe polished him off before Doc Landrieu bought it," he murmured. "Before—before Maureen . . ."

He felt Veronika grab his hand and squeeze it playfully. "Oh, but it doesn't really matter. You did *great*! I *knew* you were the horse we needed to bet on. But those pansy superiors of mine wouldn't commit to one side or the other until they'd seen 'decisive action' of some kind. So I helped you."

Jules opened his eyes. " 'Helped' me? Helped me *how?*"

He saw what might've been the tiniest of blushes light up her cheeks. "I hope you don't mind, dearest—I gave you a little push. You were waffling so—I wasn't sure if you were going to fight or run away to Argentina—so I decided to give you a reason to do the right thing."

"What—what are you talkin' about?"

"Well—*lllllll* . . ." Her dimpled face took on a Shirley Temple expression of mischief mixed with innocence. "You see, what happened was, I went to Malice X and I sort of *implied* that your friend Maureen had ratted him out to you. I thought maybe he'd rough her up some, just a little, enough to make you really angry and give you that enraged-macho-testosterone edge you needed. And it worked—I mean, Malice went a little *overboard*, the big doofus, but the *important* thing is that you finally stood up for yourself. You *kicked his sorry behind*, sweetie! You're my champion!"

Jules felt his hand go cold and clammy in Veronika's tight grip. He pulled loose. He'd rather have his hand up a squid's butt hole than be touching this woman's hand. "Gee. Thanks."

Her beautifully sculpted mouth arched into a frown. "Oh, now don't go all sulky on me! It was you or them, don't you see? I only did what I had to to make sure it would be *you*! And now that you've proved to the agency what a good fighter you are, they'll back you to the hilt. You can make me your vampire queen, just like we talked about before, and *together* we'll clean out these nests of vampires here in New Orleans. Then the agency will relocate us down to Mexico or Colombia. They won't give a hoot how many necks we bite down there. In fact, we'll get bonus payments if we help the Drug Interdiction Force kill off some drug traffickers before they sell their poison to American children. It's a win–win situation all around, see? Vampire paradise for two!"

Jules felt the beginnings of nausea in his gut. He didn't want to look at her. He stared at the worn stoop and broken sidewalk behind her. Something stirred in the shadows. Something small and furry. Jules wished they could trade places. "And what if I don't wanna have nothin' to do with your 'vampire paradise'?"

Veronika laughed sweetly and grabbed both of his hands. "Oh Jules! Silly boy! Whoever said you'd have any choice in the matter? I have a very capable team backing me up who can track you wherever you go. And where would you run to? Back to Baton Rouge?" She laughed. "But really, darling—why would you want to turn me down? Isn't 'vampire paradise for two' way, *way* more tempting than a nasty old stake through the heart?"

The small, furry thing behind Veronika was a rat. A white rat. It climbed to the top of a pile of broken pavement, stood on its hind legs, and sniffed the air. Then, as if it smelled something distasteful, it dropped back down on all four legs and scurried back into a hole in the wall. Jules found himself wishing it'd been one of those see-through rats

Chop had told him about, the kind whose skin was translucent because it never felt the touch of the sun. Then he could tell the old bandleader that he'd seen one, too.

Somewhere in the dim back corners of Jules's mind, a door opened just a smidgen, allowing a tiny crack of light to break through.

"Jules, honey? Are you with me here? What are you staring at?"

"Huh?" Jules blinked his way back to the real world. "Uh, nothin'. So what's Step One of this big plan of yours? I turn you into a vampire?"

Veronika smiled. "That would be a *marvelous* way to start."

Jules glanced around him. "So where d'ya wanna do it? Behind the restaurant here? In my car?"

She laughed. "Oh, I don't think so . . . it's not that I don't *trust* you, Jules my dear. But we really should do it back in the Quarter, where my associates will know to keep an eye on us while I'm between life and un-death. I wouldn't want you to think you might be able to get away with, you know, draining me dry and then destroying my *brain stem* or some such foolishness. And besides, the Quarter is so much more *romantic*. Let's do it back at my hotel. I've spent the last few nights at the Chateau Le Moyne Hotel on Dauphine Street."

"That's not far from Arnaud's Restaurant, right?"

"That's right. Arnaud's is just a block or two away. Why?"

"Well, after I turn you, how about we start eternity together with a nightcap at Arnaud's? I'll have me a joe, and I'll treat you to a mint julep. Sound good? I'll meet you at your hotel room in forty-five minutes."

Veronika raised an eyebrow. "How about we go back to my hotel room *now*. What do you need forty-five minutes for?"

Jules ruefully brushed black soot from his jacket. "Babe, if we're gonna celebrate at Arnaud's, I can't walk in there lookin' like *this*, can I? The maître d' wouldn't let me walk through the front door. Just lemme run and get myself a change of clothes."

"You wouldn't be thinking about *bolting*, would you?"

Jules put on his best poker face. "*Bolting?* Heck, the thought never even crossed my mind. Tell you what. I swear, on my honor as a vampire, that I won't leave the French Quarter. If that's not good enough for you—well, your backup can track me anywhere, right?"

"That's right." Veronika pursed her full lips. "I suppose it'll be impossible to keep you under my thumb every second of every night for the rest of eternity. I'll have to give you a *little* rope . . . All right. You've got forty-five minutes. One *second* longer than that and I'll send the team out after you. And trust me—their methods are a lot less soft than mine."

"I can believe that." Jules took another look at her abundant curves, so reminiscent of Maureen's. "See ya in forty-five, babe—to not show for what we got planned, I'd hafta be a real rat."

◆

Jules parked his Caddy in front of the motley collection of Spanish Colonial buildings that made up Arnaud's Restaurant. Usually it was impossible to find a space there, but at this late hour most of the diners had finished their meals, and only a few patrons lingered in the bar.

He walked around to the back of the famous Creole institution, to where the kitchen's rear door opened onto a narrow alleyway that held the restaurant's Dumpster. Even Arnaud's *garbage* smelled sumptuous. Jules's food-sensitive nose detected the odors of soft-shell crab saturated in butter sauce, crawfish Monica, chicken and andouille gumbo, and bread pudding in whiskey sauce. A traditional jazz combo of banjo, trumpet, clarinet, trombone, drums, and piano played a final chorus of "Tin Roof Blues" in a nearby Bourbon Street jazz club, granting the garbage alley the ambience of an outdoor supper club.

A busboy exited the kitchen with a huge plastic sack in his arms. With a well-practiced windup, he tossed the sack high into the air, landing it perfectly in the Dumpster's waiting maw.

Jules caught his attention before he could disappear back into the kitchen. "Hey, kid? How much food would you say this place throws out every night?"

The busboy rubbed his shoulders, strained from tossing the heavy sack. "I dunno . . . enough to feed an army, it feels like. Why d'you ask? You want some?"

Something about his insolent tone was familiar. "Say," Jules asked, "don't I know you from someplace?"

The busboy took a step back and looked Jules over. His eyes widened with recognition. "Yeah . . . I *do* know you! You're that creep who almost ran me and my girlfriend over on Decatur a month back!"

The vampire wanna-be. So this is where he made his money. He looked different without his white body makeup, mascara, and skintight black jeans. A busboy. *Not so high and haughty now,* Jules thought.

"You remember my car?" Jules asked.

"Yeah," the busboy replied suspiciously. "Lessee . . . it was a Cadillac, right? A big old white Cadillac?"

"That's right. You like it?"

"What? Your car?"

"Yeah, my car."

"I guess. I mean, it was kind of a phat ride, with those fins on the back."

Jules took his car keys from his pocket and jiggled them in front of the young man. "Well, I'm givin' it to ya."

The busboy was surprised for half a second. Then his face turned dismissive, and he waved Jules off. "You're wacko, man. Get outta here. I've got work to do."

Jules didn't budge. "I'm serious. The car is yours. The title's in the glove compartment. I'll sign it over to ya. All you gotta do is one thing in return."

The busboy crossed his arms, still looking dubious. "Yeah? And what would that be? If you're lookin' for a suck-off, I don't swing that way."

Jules cocked his thumb at the Dumpster. "All you gotta do is, every night before you leave work, make sure the lid to that Dumpster stays open."

"Huh?"

"You heard me."

"That's nuts."

"Do we have a deal?"

"Why do you want the Dumpster to stay open?"

"My business. Don't worry—you'll never have a mess in the alleyway to clean up in the morning."

The busboy eyed the keys warily. "Well . . . how do I know this deal is on the up-and-up? Maybe the car's stolen, or maybe there's a body in the trunk—"

Jules tossed him the keys. "Here. It's parked around front. Check it out. Read the title, the registration papers, my driver's license. They're all there."

The busboy returned three minutes later. He had a cautious smile on his face.

"So?" Jules asked.

"Like I said, it's a phat ride."

"We got us a deal then?"

"Your driver's license didn't have no photo on it."

"My business. Deal or no deal?"

The busboy looked at the Dumpster. Then he looked at the keys in his hand. "Deal," he said.

He turned back to the kitchen, but Jules grabbed his elbow before he could escape. "One more thing. You wax the Caddy every month and change her oil every three thousand miles. I'll be watching. You let her get run-down, I'll *haunt* your skinny ass."

♠

Jules knocked on the door. Even up here, on the third floor of the Chateau Le Moyne Hotel, he could still hear that jazz combo playing on Bourbon Street.

"It's *open*," Veronika's singsong voice answered from inside. "But only if you're a big strong hunk of all-American male vampire."

Jules pushed the door open. As he'd expected, Veronika had arrayed herself on the big bed like a double-page spread from the Victoria's Secret catalog.

"You're nine minutes early, darling," she said. But her smile quickly collapsed as he entered. "You didn't change your clothes."

Jules self-consciously dusted some more soot off his jacket. "Yeah, well, y'see, I got halfway there, to Maureen's house, and then I was so, y'know, *overcome* with *lust* for you that I just hadda come right over here."

Veronika's eyes sparkled, and she held out her plush arms for Jules to dive into. "Oh, *goodie*. I like that. A lot."

But instead of joining her on the bed, Jules walked quickly to the sliding door facing the balcony, unlatched it, and opened it a couple of feet. A front of warm, humid air immediately entered the room.

"Jules? Why did you open the window? It's summertime, sweetie— we've got the *air* on. You're going to make my hair go all frizzy with that outside air—"

"It's too cold in here," Jules said. "I'm doin' this for your benefit— you'll see. When you wake up as a vampire, you'll crave warmth the way a politician craves kickbacks. Why d'you think all them vampires in stories are always climbin' into women's beds? It's not *always* for the blood."

"Oh, all *right*, I suppose *you're* the expert on all this vampire stuff. But how about you make like one of those fictional vampires and climb into *this* woman's bed?"

Jules kicked off his shoes. The fly on his trousers got stuck, so he ripped the stubborn zipper open. Heck, he wouldn't be wearing the damn things again, anyway. Likewise, he didn't bother unbuttoning the buttons on his shirt—he ripped it off. Veronika giggled and beamed with approval at his apparent enthusiasm. Unencumbered by his battle-soiled clothing, Jules clambered on top of her. His lips quickly found her plump neck.

"*Ooohh!*" she squealed. "Darling, didn't you want to start with, y'know, the *other*? Some foreplay, at least?"

"Naww," Jules mumbled, his fangs already probing her neck. "Let's get down to business. Time enough for the lovey-dovey stuff later."

Jules was in no mood to be coy. No tender nibbles or little love bites tonight. As soon as he found her jugular, he bit down with the passionless force and precision of a punch-press machine.

"*OOOOHHH!*"

The salty liquid sprayed into his mouth like a gusher. Blood. The stuff of life. The stern words of the priest at St. Joseph's echoed through his head:

There is no penance unless the sinner sins no more. Will you foreswear the drinking of human blood?

Yeah, yeah, yeah, Father, Jules thought as he gulped it down. *This is the last time. After this last little blood snack, I'll be harmless and peaceful as a little lamb. Even Jesus would approve.*

Could he *really* make this the last time, though? As much as Veronika repelled him, he had to admit her blood tasted *fantastic*. After weeks of Maureen's diet mixture and Doodlebug's thin-as-water California blood, Jules had forgotten what the real thing tasted like. He hadn't experienced anything this orgasmic since the night he'd drained Bessie out by Manchac swamp. Whatever Veronika's other sins might be, self-denial wasn't among them—her blood was chock-full of the fatty lipids that sent him to the moon.

She raked his back with her nails and moaned passionately as he sucked harder and harder. "Yes, darling, oh *yes yes yes . . .*"

Boy oh boy, did she have a lot of blood in her! He tried desperately to focus on his original intent. What he was planning to do—there might be no way back. Even Doodlebug had never tried splitting into more than five bodies at one time. He might subdivide himself so far that his personality, his will, his essence would disappear. Could he live with that?

"Drink me in, baby, drink me all up—I made my blood all sweet and luscious, just for you, Jules baby. . . ."

You can have *the things you've always wanted, but to get them, you might have to look at them in a new way* . . . that's what Doodlebug had written him, and he believed it now. And what were the things he really wanted? Mouthwatering New Orleans food. Soul-warming New Orleans jazz. The sounds and tastes and smells of his city, and the peace to enjoy them.

And Maureen. But he couldn't have Maureen.

"Oh baby, make me your queen—make me your *queen*, baby—we're almost there—king and queen of the vampires forever . . ."

Maureen. She was his queen. No one else.

He forced himself to stop drinking. Jules pulled his lips away from her neck and crouched above her weakly twitching body. He wiped the sweat from his forehead. He'd almost lost control, almost gone all the way.

". . . babe . . . baby, why're you stopping? Don't stop . . . don't stop now . . . I'm almost *there*, I can feel it . . . almost a vampire . . . finish . . . finish me off, Jules—"

Jules concentrated on tiny trains racing over tiny tracks for perhaps the final time. His great naked bulk began to shimmer.

"Jules! *Finish* me *off!*"

Just before his lips melted, he said, "Fuck you and the bureaucrat you rode in on—"

The king-sized bed vanished beneath a cloud of oily mist. Veronika began to scream as multitudes of tiny, clawed feet materialized and ran across her prone body. She screamed louder and louder as the mist cleared and she saw who the feet belonged to.

Rats. White rats. Dozens and dozens of them; 187 in all. Seven hundred and forty-eight clawed feet scurried across her tummy, breasts, and legs on their way across the bed to the open window. Nearly two hundred pink, hairless tails twittered across her fingers, kneecaps, and nose before sliding from sight over the balcony.

Her screams were frenzied, but they couldn't drown out the sweet music coming from Bourbon Street. The rats ran toward the sounds of the music. Toward the sanctuary of thousands and thousands of hidden, sunless crawl spaces within the walls and foundations of the ancient buildings of the Vieux Carré. They skittered toward the music and darkness, and disappeared into obscurity.

And if the rats perked up their ears just right, they'd hear the mournful yet eternally optimistic notes of a jazz funeral circling the Quarter. And they'd hear Porkchop Chambonne's trumpet lead the band into the opening bars of a new song of his own composition:

"The Fat White Vampire Blues."

ACKNOWLEDGMENTS

This book, had it come into existence at all, would've been a far poorer project without the inspiration and support of two departed friends, both of whom left New Orleans and the world far too soon. George Alec Effinger, master science-fiction writer, founded the city's longest continuously running writing workshop in 1988 and gave this beginner much to aspire to. Jules Theobold was coworker and friend; his humor and infectious joy in living not only made early mornings at the office more bearable but provided me a perfect example of why New Orleans and her inhabitants have charmed and delighted writers for generations.

Members of the writing workshop George founded have been there for me, month after month, ever since I joined in 1995. They are my ace in the hole, catching my dumb mistakes and awkward phrases before I suffer from them. Big, fat thanks are due to Lena Andersson, Michael Brossette, Maury Feinsilber, Larry Gegenheimer Jr., Teresa Harms, Joan Heausler, Michael Keane, Mark McCandless, Janet McConnaughey, Gwen Moore, Marian Moore, Laura Joh Rowland, Dr. Jack Stocker, Roslyn Taylor, John Webre, and Fritz Ziegler.

I'd also like to thank Anne McCaffrey, who provided generous encouragement to a starry-eyed thirteen-year-old; Dara Levinson, who has uncommon insight into the people who live inside my head; Lila Taylor, who shared a key anecdote; my agent, Dan Hooker; Ashley and Carolyn Grayson; my editor, Chris Schluep; my family; and, of course, John Kennedy Toole.

ANDREW JAY FOX was born in 1964 and grew up in North Miami Beach, Florida. The first movie he remembers seeing is Japanese monster fest *Destroy All Monsters*, viewed from the backseat of his stepdad's Caprice convertible. Early passions included Universal horror movies, 1950s giant monster flicks, WWII navy dramas, *Planet of the Apes*, and horror comics, particularly Marv Wolfman's and Gene Colan's "Tomb of Dracula." His earliest exposure to literary science fiction came by way of H. G. Welles, Ray Bradbury, and Anne McCaffrey's Pern series; other favorites through the years have included Robert Silverberg, J. G. Ballard, Richard Matheson, and Ursula K. Le Guin.

He attended Loyola University in New Orleans, where he studied social work and wrote a fantasy play for visually handicapped children that involved the audience rubbing their hands on a vaseline-coated foam rubber mermaid's tail and sniffing spoiled sardines. He studied public administration at Syracuse University, then worked at a public children's psychiatric center on Long Island while continuing to write plays (none of which involved sardines). Since returning to New Orleans in 1990, he has worked as manager of the Louisiana Commodity Supplemental Food Program, a federally funded monthly nutrition program for low-income senior citizens. In 1995, following the death of his cousin in the French Quarter on New Year's Eve due to a falling bullet, he helped found the New Year Coalition, an advocacy group that helps educate the public about the dangers of celebratory gunfire. Also in 1995, he joined a monthly writing workshop founded by award-winning SF author George Alec Effinger. *Fat White Vampire Blues* is his first novel to see print.